Are the Kids All Right?

The Representation of LGBTQ Characters in Children's and Young Adult Literature

B.J. Epstein

HammerOn Press

Are the Kids All Right? Representations of LGBTQ Characters in Children's and Young Adult Literature

ISBN 978-0-9564507-3-9

Are the Kids All Right? Representations of LGBTQ Characters in Children's and Young Adult Literature / B.J. Epstein
1. Literary Criticism. 2. Lesbian, Gay, Bisexual, Transgender and Queer. 3. Children's and Young Adult Literature. 4. Cultural Studies.

First published in 2013 by
HammerOn Press, Bristol, UK
www.hammeronpress.net

Cover design and typesetting by Eva Megias www.laneutral.com
Cover font Depalo Sans by Alex Camacho www.alexcamacho.es

Set in Adobe Caslon Pro and Franklin Gothic Medium

This book is dedicated with much love and gratitude to the two most important people in my life: my mother, Paula Epstein, and my wife, Fi Woodley. Their support and encouragement have meant so much to me, and I wouldn't be where I am today without them. I love you both very much. Thank you for being who you are.

Acknowledgements

I would like to gratefully acknowledge the help and support of a number of people. Without them, this book would not have been possible.

First of all, the undergraduate students in my courses in children's literature and queer literature at the University of East Anglia have inspired me with their passion, enthusiasm, and curiosity. I have really enjoyed all our seminars and have found that they have given me new ideas to think about. These students, along with many other people – especially those who are LGBTQ and/or readers of books for children and young adults – have been willing to tell me what literature means to them, what role it plays in their lives, and, in particular, why LGBTQ lit matters. In many cases, such discussions took place at lectures, workshops, conferences, or reading groups, or during informal chats, and sometimes I did not even have a chance to get people's names. So I am very grateful to everyone who has been disposed to discuss this with me, whatever the setting.

Several of the authors whose work I discuss here were gracious enough to answer questions and to tell me about their experiences as writers of LGBTQ literature for young people. Many, many thanks to Marcus Ewert, Elizabeth Kushner, and Lesléa Newman for their books and for their help.

At HammerOn, Debi Withers has been very encouraging and helpful. Her editorial suggestions have strengthened the book and I appreciate the way she believed in me and the subject matter. I would also like to thank Eva Megias for her vibrant cover design.

Finally, I offer huge thanks and much love to my family, especially my mother, Paula Epstein, and my wife, Fi Woodley. It is in large part due to my family that this particular kid turned out all right.

Thank you all.

Contents

INTRODUCTION 1

Motivation 1
A Brief Discussion of Sexuality and Gender 3
Terminology 6
Children's Literature 8
Sexuality, Children and Children's Literature 15
Corpus of Texts 20
Methodologies 22
Structure of This Book 24
Conclusion 25

ISSUE BOOKS 26

Publishing and Practical Considerations 29
Paratexts 32
Confirmation of Normality 39
HIV and AIDS 45
Teaching Through Characters 49
Controversy 56
Conclusion 60

PORTRAYAL AND STEREOTYPES 63

Prejudice and Stereotypes 64
A Brief History of Stereotypes in LGBTQ Literature 73
Queerness as a Problem 74
Causes of Queerness 93

Looking Queer 98
Acting Queer 105
Sex and Marriage 118
The Gay Boyfriend 120
Positive Stereotypes and Challenging Stereotypes 124
Reducing Prejudice and Literature's Role 126
Conclusion 129

DIVERSITY 132

Missing Pieces 133
Bisexuality 134
Transgender 142
Other Shades of the Rainbow 155
Multiple Identities 158
Race/Ethnicity 161
Religion and Spirituality 165
Dis/Ability 181
Age 183
Class 184
Weight/Size and Body Image 187
Conclusion 188

SEX AND MARRIAGE 191

Masturbation 194
Protection 199
Sex 204
BTQ Sex 217
Summary of Sex 218
Marriage 220
Background on LGBTQ Parenting 221
Background on LGBTQ Marriage 223

U.S. Books 227
U.K. Books 232
Northern European Books 233
Summary of Marriage 236
Singletons 239
Conclusion 240

CONCLUSION 241

A Brief Summary 241
A Call to Arms (or Pens): Not a Conclusion, But a Proposal 245

NOTES 249

REFERENCES 263

ANNOTATED BIBLIOGRAPHY 287

INDEX 300

Introduction

In this book, I explore how lesbian, gay, bisexual, transgender, and otherwise queer (LGBTQ[1]) people are depicted in books for children and young adults. I approach this topic from several angles, as will be discussed below, with the overarching aim being to understand what messages about and views of LGBTQ people are offered to young readers and why this matters. I believe that writing – both creative writing and critical writing – can be powerful and activist and that it can contest people's ideas and potentially even change their lives. My question is whether creative writing that features LGBTQ characters challenges or confirms ideas about gender and sexuality, and my hope is to use my own critical writing in a challenging, helpful, and potentially subversive way.

In this chapter, then, I give background on children's literature and on sexuality in books for younger readers, and I set out what I plan to do in this book and why.

Motivation

First, it is important to understand what is at stake in a book such as this one, as writing is not only or even primarily an academic act but also a political one. There are a number of reasons why I have chosen to write a book on this topic. A basic one, of course, is that I wonder what children are being told about the

LGBTQ community, non-heterosexualities, and non-cisgendered identities through the books they read and whether and how this might reflect the greater society in which they live. Literature says something about the society it is about and in which it is written, edited, published, sold, taught, translated, and read, so what children read is a topic of vital importance because the ideas they get from books – and, of course, from other media – will shape them and their larger culture in the future.

Another reason why this book is needed now is that though recent years have seen an increase in research into both children's literature and queer studies, there has been little overlap of this research. While some of the newest research in the field of children's literature looks at the issue of diversity in children's books (see, for example, Gopalakrishnan, 2011, or chapter 6 in Travers and Travers, 2008), often this is in terms of race and religion and sometimes ability, but not sexuality. Barbara E. Travers and John F. Travers cover the topic of sexuality in only one page (2008:287). Gender is mentioned more often (such as Seth Lerer's analysis of books for boys versus books for girls, 2008), but sexuality still seems to be somewhat taboo. If sexuality is not studied much, then diverse forms of sexuality have certainly been rarely discussed (one of the few earlier examples is Weisbard, 2001), although this is starting to change, with new works that are wide-ranging collections of essays on gender and/or sexuality, such as Michael Cart and Christine A. Jenkins' s *The Heart Has Its Reasons* (2006) or *Over the Rainbow*, edited by Michelle Ann Abate and Kenneth Kidd (2011). I have not found a monograph that is an in-depth analysis of non-norm[2] sexuality and gender in children's books. As in any field, it is important to keep up with the latest developments, and for children's literature, publishers are now producing more diverse books; critics and academics therefore ought to explore these texts.

I personally believe that what the next generation learns is an extremely important and essential topic. I also am concerned about the increased numbers of LGBTQ young people who are being bullied and who, in response to such pressure, self-harm or even commit suicide. Thus, I feel that we need to understand what children and young adults are taught about queer topics or about being queer and how this might impact upon their lives and their routes to adulthood. This means, then, that this book is needed in order to explore how non-norm sexualities and gender identities seem to be understood in contemporary, English-speaking cultures today (see the section below on the corpus of texts for the reasons behind this focus), and what children and young adults are told about queer issues through the medium of fiction.

A Brief Discussion of Sexuality and Gender

In order to explore sexuality and gender, it is important to define what these terms mean. "Sexuality as a social construction is considered to be a fluid, non-linear, multifaceted, complex, contradictory, and unstable relationship that can vary across cultures and over historical periods of time, according to the discourses available" (Robinson, 2002:419), and one could perhaps say that this applies to gender as well. Joane Nagel writes, "By *sexuality* I refer to 'men' and 'women' as socially, mainly genitally defined individuals with culturally defined appropriate sexual tastes, partners, and activities." (2003:8, italics original) Of course this definition depends on an idea of gender, and Robert E. Nye writes, "In a sense, gender makes a social virtue out of the necessity of biological sex, policing the boundaries of the sexually permissible, nourishing ideals of sexual love, and dictating norms of sexual aim and object." (2004:12) This is to say that much of our understanding of sexuality stems from a gendered perspective, and Nye writes that it was in the eighteenth century that there was the creation of a "'two-sex' system" (2004:16) and a view towards biological determinism. Obviously, much of this comes from issues of marriage, kinship, and procreation (cf. Nye, 2004:13). What Nagel and Nye both are getting at is the idea of "appropriate" "norms", i.e. that there are right and wrong ways to be sexual, and thus right and wrong sexualities, and right and wrong ways to be gendered.

In general, western cultures believe there to be two genders, and it is heterosexuality (opposite-sex relationships and sexual practices) that has been considered right, appropriate, and the norm. Still, it is worth remembering that homosexual (same-sex) practices do not always mean homosexuality, and that practices and identities can be understood in many different ways in different cultures (cf. Nye, 2004:14), and have been more or less accepted at different times in different places. Nagel writes that it was in the late nineteenth century that homosexuality became an understood identity (2003:50), although Nye says that "[b]y 1900 or so the entire range of what we still take to be "perversions" were integrated into clinical practice and came gradually into discursive use in the broader culture. The word "heterosexual" was also introduced at about this time as a deceivingly neutral description of "normal" sexual aim." (2004:19) In addition, since this time, some cultures have made certain, often homosexual, sexual practices illegal or have forced homosexuals to be sterilised (cf. Nye, 2004:21), or even murdered. Besides the technicalities of law, there are also societal norms about who can do what with whom, who can wear what, who can do which jobs, and so on, and this too affects those who do not have norm gender or sexual identities. While this is not the place for a history of homosexuality or other types of sexuality, this brief discussion highlights how controversial and challenging non-heterosexualities can be, and also how a culture's understanding of sexuality can change drastically over time. I would also like to argue that as Judith Butler has written about ways in which gender can be and is performed (1990/2006), I think that sexuality, too, can be and is performed, and these depictions can be portrayed in literature. There are hence power issues related to how both gender and sexuality are performed and portrayed, in society in general and also within literature. When it comes to children in particular, as Kerry H. Robinson puts it, "[a]dults have defined what children should/should not be, or should/should not know. Children who have an understanding of sex and sexuality are often 'othered' as 'unnatural children', with 'unnatural knowledge." (2002:419)

In terms of why it is worth studying sexuality or gender at all, as Lois Tyson points out, both are important parts of identity (2011:172). Andrew Solomon discusses the difference between what he terms horizontal and vertical identities:

> Because of the transmission of identity from one generation to the next, most children share at least some traits with their parents...Attributes and values are passed down from parent to child across the generations not only through strands of DNA, but also through shared cultural norms.
>
> Often, however, someone has an inherent or acquired trait that is foreign to his or her parents and must therefore acquire identify from a peer group...Such horizontal identities may reflect recessive genes, random mutations, prenatal influences, or values and preferences that a child does not share with his progenitors. (2012:2)

According to Solomon, being queer, or deaf, or autistic are examples of horizontal identities. People with horizontal identities must create or find their own cultures and communities. If we are interested in understanding identities and their formation, then sexuality must be studied as well, even if it sometimes seems taboo or awkward or uncomfortable, as Tyson, among others, acknowledges (2011:172). She writes that "human sexuality is a dynamic, fluid force: it's always changing and growing, and its boundaries are not permanently rooted in any one rigid definition or in any single category" (2011:178), and I would therefore like to know if literature – especially children's literature – reflects this idea of sexuality and also gender. What are we telling or showing young people about their current or potential lives as gendered and sexual beings? And how in particular are we doing this when it comes to non-norm identities? Since sexuality is often considered a rather adult topic, one that may be inappropriate or even taboo for younger people, it may be that featuring it in children's literature is seen as sensitive, or even dangerous. However, sexuality has huge implications for behaviours, values, and identities, and it is something that all people must come to terms with at some point.

Terminology

So far, in explaining and defending my choice of topic, I have used words and phrases such as "gay", "queer", "non-heterosexualities", and "LGBTQ", and I think it is important to pause to consider these terms at this stage. I recognise that terminology is a slippery area, with terms seeming acceptable one day and offensive the next. With that in mind, I apologise in advance for any terms that might offend; I have done my best to use the generally accepted terms of today and I certainly have only the best intentions in using these words or phrases, but I realise that a month, a year, or a decade from now, the terms might already be outdated and considered to be in bad taste. With this being said, in some cases I use different terms simply for variety. For example, I use terms such as "female homosexual", "lesbian", "gay female", or even just "gay" interchangeably. Also, I often use the abbreviation LGBTQ to stand for lesbian, gay, bisexual, transgender, and otherwise queer. Where others may use the "Q" to mean "questioning", I prefer "queer", because it includes questioning, along with intersex, asexuality, sadist, masochist, fetishist, polyamorous, and anyone else who would like to be under this alphabet soup umbrella. I have not added extra letters for each of those orientations/identities/terms because that seems excessive. Using "Q" to cover all these terms is not to say that all these people are or must be labelled as queer; I believe everyone is free to choose the label/s they[3] prefer, or none at all. Still, "queer" is a useful label, one that I myself like, so I use it and its derivatives, such as "queerness", throughout this book.

Despite acknowledging that people should choose their own labels, in order to explore queer texts, I have had to make some choices, which in some instances means that I have had to choose labels for books and/or characters. So texts that feature characters who label themselves and/or are labelled by others as queer in some way, or who act in ways that can be understood as queer (by which I mean non-norm), are discussed in this book. I am aware that not everyone would agree that I should analyse these texts – for example, a person who identified as transgender once told me that since I am what she considered to be cisgender, I have no right to discuss transgender issues – but as I label myself as queer and consider myself an ally to all in the queer community regardless of my own identities and circumstances, I have chosen to take on this very queer project and to try to explore topics that so far are much ignored, even maligned. In short, then, I here have decided to employ "queer" to refer to the LGBTQ community, even though I know some people object to that term, and that others may not use it to describe themselves. I have nonetheless chosen it due to both personal preference and the obvious links to queer theory.

Tyson explains that "[q]ueer theory argues that human sexuality cannot be understood by such simple opposed categories as homosexual and heterosexual, which define our sexuality by the sex of our partner and nothing more" (2011:177). This helps explain the choice of "queer theory" versus, say, "homosexual theory"; queer is a larger category that covers more territory, plus it has the added benefit of reclaiming a word that sometimes has negative connotations or is used in a denigrating way. In addition, queer theory explores and often challenges the socio-cultural constructions of gender and sexuality, and considers why certain orientations, identities, practices, and so on are encouraged while others are discouraged, mocked, or even made illegal. Queer is also an approach, or a way of thinking. In my analysis of these texts, I try to queer them by not reading them only for what they say but also for what they suggest or teach. All this is to say that the term "queer" is essential to this book and will be used repeatedly, and I apologise if this grates on or offends any readers; I hope, however, that I have shown my rationale in choosing it.

Another vital term to define is "children's literature". It is such a broad term as to be nearly meaningless, so in the next section I explore that in more detail.

Children's Literature[4]

What is children's literature? And what is its function? As Robert Bator points out:

> Literature for children easily merits definition. Books have been written for them in England and America for at least 300 years, and a sizable publishing industry, almost as old, continually supplies that audience. One would expect, by now, critical consensus on what is a children's book. (1983:3)

One may expect it, but not find it, even thirty years after Bator wrote that. Ideas of what children's literature is have changed many times over the approximately three centuries that the field has been recognised (Taxel, 2002:152), and this has in large part been due to changes in the understanding of the concept of childhood. One can say that the easiest way to define children's literature is as anything that is read by or to children. However, not all critics agree with this, and this definition is not as straightforward as it may first appear. The intention behind the writing or publishing of some texts may be something else altogether from how the book is received and used, and of course an author or publisher's intention is not always known. Bator mentions the difference between "acceptance (what books children choose to read) [and] intention (what books were meant for children)" (1983:3). This useful concept, which he offered in just a sentence and did not return to, has been lost in most more recent discussions. An exception is Torben Weinreich, who points out that some texts are targeted towards children because they are viewed as a group of people "with particular ways of experiencing and perceiving and...[they] have special needs, partly because they are regarded as real or potential consumers of specific products" (2000:10). However, scholars are not always agreed on what these "special needs" might be. Since children's literature has changed so much over time, it seems that society's understanding of what children's needs are has likewise changed.

A simple way of defining the topic would be to say that children's literature is work read by children. For example, along the same lines as Bator, Riitta Oittinen defines children's literature as literature "intended for children or [as] literature read by children" (2000:61). This definition includes books that people consider to be for adults or both but which are sometimes read by children, too (see Reynolds, 1998:21 for more on this). Emer O'Sullivan writes that children's literature is literature "written or adapted specifically for children by adults" (2005:13), which, interestingly enough, is a definition that does not have room for any works written by children themselves, as uncommon as they may be, and again ignores what is read by children even if it was not specifically intended for their consumption. Also, writers may not always have a sense of whether they are writing for children or adults, and the perceived audience of a given book may change over time as well. Publishers and booksellers may define whether a work of literature is marketed and sold as being for children or adults or both, and teachers or schools may decide whether a book is purchased and taught in a classroom of children, but it is important to remember that their opinion may differ from that of the author or indeed the audience.[5]

One thing that clearly separates children's literature from that for adults is that it tends to be more audience-defined. There are no sections in bookstores or libraries that are devoted to books for adults in their twenties, say, or their sixties; rather, adult literature is defined solely by genre and topic while work for children tends to be separated by age and then by style or topic. This might suggest, then, that the function of children's literature is different from that of literature for adults. It is generally understood to serve as both education and entertainment, but different authors, publishers, and others prioritise one or the other in different ways.

An additional complication is the definition of a child (cf. Lathey, 2006:5), because what children need in terms of literature is based on what adults think children are, what they think they need to know, and how people believe children should be treated (see, for example, Travers and Travers, 2008, who explore the topic of children's literature in terms of developmental stages). Childhood itself is a relatively new concept; in western society, children are no longer viewed simply as small adults, as they were up through the nineteenth century. A typical view then was exemplified by John Locke. As Kornei Chukovsky describes it:

> For Locke a child was a mistake of nature...Naturally as a result of this presumptuous attitude toward the real needs and tastes of children, Locke condemned without mercy all existing children's books, ballads, poetry, fantasies, fairy tales, proverbs, and songs, which, in his opinion, were bad because they were neither geography not algebra. All of children's literature, vital to the child as air, Locke called triviality. (1963:110-11)

In other words, if children were simply to be shaped into adults, their "special needs", to quote Weinreich, were only pedagogical. Children thus had no need for creative, imaginative works. So texts for children initially were primarily didactic: books were one of the tools people could use to help form these little beings who were soon to be adults and would therefore need to know how to operate in adult society. To some extent, this is still the case today. As Peter Hunt writes:

> It is arguably impossible for a children's book (especially one being read by a child) not to be educational or influential in some way; it cannot help but reflect an ideology and, by extension, didacticism. All books must teach something, and because the checks and balances available to the mature reader are missing in the child reader, the children's writer often feels obliged to supply them. Thus it may seem that children's books are more likely to be directive, to predigest experience, to "tell" rather than to "show", and to be more prone to manipulation than others; but, in fact, it is only the mode of manipulation that is different. The relationship in the book between writer and reader is complex and ambivalent.
>
> Children's writers, therefore, are in a position of singular responsibility in transmitting cultural values, rather than "simply" telling a story. And if that were not enough, children's books are an important tool in reading education, and are thus prey to a whole area of educational and psychological influences that other literatures escape. (1994:3-4)

In contrast to the earlier view of children as needing only to be educated and developed into adults, in modern western society, children are seen as youths with specific needs beyond education, such as entertainment and identification, and childhood is recognised as a specific period in a person's life, with particular requirements. Children are now thought to need both pedagogical and imaginative literature. As Chukovsky puts it, "It took hundreds of years for grownups to realize that children have the right to be children" (1963:111). "The right to be children" might seem to translate into a right to specific kinds of material in specific styles, but this is in fact extremely variable. For example, children's writer Michael Rosen has a broad view of who children's authors write for, saying, "I don't think we do just write for children. I think we write as a way for adults to join the conversations that adults have with adults, adults have with children, children have with children – on the subject of what it means to be a child and live your life as a child" (2011:89). He adds that "children's literature has a magnificent history of saying important things to many people, often in a context where adults are caring for children. I think that's a good thing to attempt" (ibid.). Another children's author, Philip Pullman, has even been quoted as saying, "There are some themes, some subjects, too large for adult fiction; they can only be dealt with adequately in a children's book" (1996:n.p.). His view is somewhat different, in that he seems to reverse the usual scale of importance by putting children's literature above that for adults, but nevertheless, it seems to imply some sense of didacticism. Jacqueline Rose considers language to be the matter that books for children refer to: "the history of children's fiction should be written, not in terms of its themes or the content of its stories, but in terms of the relationship to language which different children's writers establish for the child" (1993:78). The word "establish" raises the suggestion that works for children are there to create ideas or set boundaries for the child readers. The reigning attitude is clear: for some people, no matter what children read and no matter what the author's apparent intentions, children's literature is inherently pedagogic. Whether it should be is a matter that will not be taken up here, but obviously writers, translators, editors, publishers, teachers, parents, and others who work on or use children's literature must keep in mind that "sociocultural and political forces have a perceptible, often public, impact on the books written and published for young people" (Taxel, 2002:146).

If childhood is deemed to be a particular period in one's life with its own requirements, then what one reads during that time should likewise be different from what one reads at other times. This is not to say that children's literature is a distinct genre, but rather that it might be set off from literature for adults, even if they share some characteristics in common. Myles McDowell offers a list of differences between fiction for children and that for adults:

> children's books are generally shorter; they tend to favour an active rather than a passive treatment, with dialogue and incident rather than description and introspection; child protagonists are the rule; conventions are much used; the story develops within a clear-cut moral schematism which much adult fiction ignores; children's books tend to be optimistic rather than depressive; language is child-oriented; plots are of a distinctive order, probability is often disregarded... (1976:141-2)

Children's literature, therefore, seems to be considered simpler and more conventional than works for adults. It also is apparently meant to "help" children first and, perhaps, to entertain them second. One would most likely not define literature for adults as work that primarily helps adults and then possibly entertains them as well.

Although children's literature often has its own section in libraries and bookstores and thus could be seen as an equivalent to, say, crime fiction or romances, one cannot say that there is a genre of children's literature, because within children's literature all the major genres of literature are represented. Children's literature is simply an overarching title for a large set of texts read to and by young people. It is not, however, simple in and of itself. As the Pullman quote above suggests, works for young people take on all the same themes as works for adults and sometimes even additional ones as well. One finds children's literature about death, depression, sexuality, gender identity, ethnicity, evil, and many other topics that some might consider inappropriate or too advanced for young people. As J.A. Appleyard discusses, for example, fantasy novels might be popular for children because they allow readers to explore their feelings (1991:36-7), even feelings that one might not expect children to experience. And as children get older, their way of reading changes, as does their need for different types of literature, and thus children's books change and develop too (1991:59, 74-5, 100, 108, 164, 171, 182, and others; also see Travers and Travers, 2008). In other words, children's literature reflects the development of children as readers. Hunt also points out that children's literature is often recognised by certain features, which he names as "strong nostalgic/nature images; a sense of place or territory; egocentricity; testing and initiation; outsider/insider relationships; mutual respect between adults and children; closure; warmth/security—and food; and, perhaps most important, the relationship between reality and fantasy." (1994:184) In many of the books discussed here, a sense of self is probably the most characteristic feature, which perhaps falls under some combination of his categories of "egocentricity; testing and initiation; outsider/insider relationships" and "security".

Meanwhile, at some point children's literature develops into young adult literature. Cart and Jenkins define young adult (YA) works "as books that are published for readers age twelve to eighteen, have a young adult protagonist, are told from a young adult perspective, and feature coming-of-age or other issues or concerns of interest to YAs" (2006:1). I think this is a useful starting point, but I do not agree completely. One could argue persuasively that YA books can be about issues that are not directly relevant to young adult lives. For example, young adults may be thinking of topics such as which university to attend or whom to date, but besides that, they may be concerned about illness and death, developing careers, getting married or having children, or other issues that we may not think are of direct interest to them at this stage in their lives. Books for readers of that age may well be told from an adult perspective or indeed even from a child's perspective. Nonetheless, the distinction between children's books and YA books is an important one. It could also be pointed out that sexuality and related topics appear more often in young adult literature than in books meant for younger readers.

In sum, then, children's literature is not easy to define, but for the purposes of this book, one can say that if a book is read by children, then it can be considered children's literature. Furthermore, it is essential to emphasise the power relations inherent in this field: adults are usually the ones who write, edit, translate, publish, market, stock, sell, buy, teach, and give books to and for children. They are the ones who decide what is appropriate for young readers or not, and how to depict certain topics. So children's literature is read by children but written by adults, thus creating a huge power imbalance. We must keep this in mind in later chapters, when we look at what messages young people are given.

As Lee Wyndham and Arnold Madison point out, "In the United States, between two and three thousand children's books are brought out annually by some one hundred sixty publishers...From the age of three and up, we have at least sixty million boys and girls..." (1968/1988:1). That is only in the United States, which suggests that the market for children's literature – whatever children's literature actually is – around the world is potentially huge. This in turn means that such literature is a subject worthy of attention and analysis.

Sexuality, Children and Children's Literature

It has only been fairly recently that sexuality has become an accepted topic in books for younger readers. As Joel Taxel writes, "This 'new realism' [i.e. in the 1960s] contributed to the erasure of longstanding taboos as authors broke dramatically from the conventions of previous generations by exploring themes that previously were deemed unacceptable (e.g., drugs, alcoholism, sex, and violence)." (2002:146) Capturing the same idea but in a somewhat more negative-sounding way, John Rowe Townsend writes, "Premarital sex, drug abuse, homosexuality, running away from home are hardly remarkable any more." (Townsend, 1990:276) In either case, the point is that what used to be "unacceptable" or "taboo" or "remarkable" in children's literature no longer is to the same extent, and this really started changing in the 1960s (cf. Cart and Jenkins, 2006:7-8). This is from a combination of factors, such as the change in the way that young people are viewed, a greater acceptance of sexuality in society more generally, and a developing perspective on what children's literature is and what it can do. For example, it seems to be the case that premarital sex is in general not considered an issue in today's society – with the acknowledgement that this depends on what subculture someone belongs to. At the same time, adults have begun to think that young people need information about sex and sexuality, and that literature might be a key way of giving them this information. In this section, I briefly explore sexuality and the usage of literature as an educational tool in regard to teaching children about sexuality.

Teenage sexuality has frequently been viewed as problematic (see Francis, 1995, among others), especially in relation to females (Moore and Rosenthal, 2006:24), but this has started to change in recent times. Now, many recognise that adolescents do have sexual feelings and do engage in sexual activities and that sexuality is an important stage of development. For example, "[a]ll theories of adolescent development give sexuality a central place in negotiating the transition from child to adult" (Moore and Rosenthal, 2006:2 and cf. Furman and Shaffer, 2003:3-22), so the issue of whether adolescent sexuality should or could be portrayed in young adult literature and, if so, how, has arisen. According to many, information about sex is essential for adolescents to have in order to develop healthy romantic and sexual relationships (see Moore and Rosenthal, 2006:2, for example), but what is perhaps more surprising is that a number of people view literature as the ideal way of giving children this information. Rather than solely relying on pamphlets, say, or sexual education courses, literature is sometimes used for the same purposes, in part because "many teachers are not trained to present sensitive and controversial topics, and indeed may feel uncomfortable or anxious about doing so" (Moore and Rosenthal, 2006:117). Hence, adults may turn to literature because they do not need to be so actively involved; a young person can read a novel and thereby "learn" about sex from it. Also, literature is seen as less cold than factual details. As Kimberley Reynolds writes, "many adults believe that the best way to protect children from premature, unwanted, or risky sex is by providing accurate but not clinical information in forms and formats young people enjoy and trust" (2007:117). She adds that "[f]iction offers a unique way to learn about and prepare for experiences to come, including sexual and romantic relationships" (2007:120) and also that children's literature in particular encourages "readers to approach ideas, issues, and objects from new perspectives and so prepare the way for change" (2007:1). Does all this then mean that literature has some sort of duty to give facts and information and to reflect reality? If that is the case, I wonder if the texts I analyse in this book fulfil that duty.

Pat Pinsent points out that writers in the recent past often felt they could discuss "issues" in YA literature but were hesitant about which issues and how. Some writers "seem to have felt that portraying their characters within a 'real' world was more appropriate to the consideration of immediate social problems such as drugs" (2005:202). But even once they started writing about sex, they mostly portrayed it in a negative light. Reynolds says that "although teenage sexual activity has become a commonplace of YA fiction, until recently the tendency has been to focus on the problems in can bring" (2007:115), so that "[w]here once 'doing' it in YA fiction meant boys and girls losing control and reaping the consequences – usually in the form of pregnancy – books for teenagers increasingly acknowledge that the sexual orientations of the young are just as varied and their desires at least as urgent as those of the adults around them" (2007:122). Some of this is due to the time period when authors were writing and some of it is due to other authors breaking the boundaries. But today, YA novels that feature sex "such books now emphasise the need for sex to be safe rather than the need to avoid sex" (Reynolds, 2007:122).

What all this means, then, is that adults use fiction as a way of, as Lydia Kokkola phrases it, "socialising teenagers into conducting themselves in a manner approved by adults." (2011:n.p.) Such fiction has changed over time, perhaps reflecting changing views of sex in general and adolescent sexuality in particular and also of what is considered acceptable to include in YA literature.

It was only in the 1960s that sex and sexuality began appearing in literature for children and young adults, and it was really only from the 1980s that non-heterosexualities began to be depicted.[6] Cart and Jenkins write that "private schools provide the setting for many of the homosexual novels in the early years of the genre–perhaps because, like English boarding schools, they offer a ready-made, same-sex environment for boys or girls away from home for the first time." (2006:9) One can add that this makes sense also because boarding schools are temporary experiences, so the books could imply that the characters would "return" to normal, heterosexual behaviour after leaving school. After these private school-based texts, one of the first LGBTQ YA books was John Donovan's *I'll Get There. It Better Be Worth the Trip*, which was published in 1969. Cart and Jenkins write:

> *I'll Get There. It Better Be Worth the Trip* remains tremendously important three-and-a-half decades after its publication, not only because it was the first book for young readers to deal with homosexuality, but also because it established–for good or ill–a model for the treatment of the topic that would be replicated in many of the novels that followed in the 1970s. The characters are male, white, and upper middle-class. The physical nature of what happens between them remains obscure.

> A cause and effect relationship is implied between homosexuality and being the child of divorced parents–more specifically, having an absent father and a disturbed and/or controlling mother. Homosexuality is presented both as a rite of passage experience with no long-term meaning or consequences...and also as a matter of conscious choice. (2006:14)

This means that some of the issues that I discuss later in the book, especially in the chapters on stereotypes and on sex and marriage, were present from the beginning: "male, white, and upper middle-class" characters, a lack of sexual interactions, there being a cause of homosexuality, non-heterosexuality being a choice and often one that can be temporary, and so on.

Throughout the 1970s, more such books were published (Cart and Jenkins, 2006:17), but I would contend that it is only quite recently that we have started to see a larger number of LGBTQ books for younger readers. Before I discuss which texts I will be analysing here and why, I would like to underscore just how recent a phenomenon it is to feature sexuality – especially non-heterosexuality – in books for children and young adults, and also how it appears to be the case that scholars, teachers, parents, and other adults seem to think these texts ought to be realistic and educational, so that children can learn about this topic through literature. I do think it is very possible to disagree with the concept that literature, especially that for children and particularly in regard to sexuality, ought to be educational and/or realistic, but as it appears that society today promotes this view, I will not argue with it here. It is worth considering further, however.

Corpus of Texts

In this book, I explore literature for children and young adults that features lesbian, gay, bisexual, transgender, and other queer characters. As stated above, it is only in the past few decades that we have begun seeing LGBTQ literature for young readers. It is claimed that around 200 such novels have been published, mostly in the United States, since 1969 (Cart and Jenkins, 2006:xv and Abate and Kidd, 2011:5). As Cart and Jenkins point out, "[a]lthough 200 books might appear to be a substantial number, this averages out to five titles per year, which seems hardly sufficient to give faces to unnumbered millions of homosexual youth" (2006:xv).[7] They also write that "the number of YA novels with gay/lesbian content has slowly increased, growing from an average of one title per year in the 1970s to four per year in the 1980s to seven per year in the 1990s to over twelve per year in the early years of the 21st century" (2006:xvi). Given this, I cannot hope to be comprehensive. Instead, I have read and analysed as many as I could access in libraries and bookstores in the U.S. and the U.K., and this amounts to thirty-two young adult works, eight middle-grade books, and twenty picture books,[8] most of them recent.[9] The total is thus sixty books. I focus on full books, rather than also including short stories.[10] This thus builds on other work done, such as Jenkins' s analysis of LGBTQ YA novels from 1969 to 1992 (2011:147-163). Clearly, I do not have the space to summarise or analyse all of them in detail, but I pick out the salient bits of each, and look for overall patterns.

My rationale for looking at as many of these works as possible, even if my analysis in some of the chapters may at times seem exhaustive, if not quite exhausting, is quite simply that I did not want this book to only be a case study of a couple of texts. Therefore I deliberately read as many as I could find, and I quote from or at least mention most of them throughout my analysis. Here, I make larger claims about LGBTQ literature for young readers than merely saying what one particular text or author seems to be doing. If a multitude of books has the same stereotype, for example, then there is a clear pattern, and it is these overarching patterns and messages that I am intrigued by. The idea is that with more texts, it is easier to make quantitatively verifiable claims (see Gilbert, 2006:69-70 for a brief analysis of why larger numbers help scientists more accurately measure information; I believe this can be applied to the study of literature as well). Despite this, however, I have not and cannot claim to have read every single LGBTQ book for children and young adults that exists. In order to restrict myself, I have primarily focused on recent, English-language books in a realistic style. The reason for the very modern focus is that contemporary texts were more readily available, whereas I generally could not access ones published in the 1970s or 1980s since they were out of print. I have been limited to what I have been able to get access to here in the U.K. and on trips to the U.S.; the occasional book from another English-speaking country, such as New Zealand or Canada, has slipped into the corpus as well. The reason for the focus on English-language books is because I think the English-language cultures, while not the same, are close enough to be grouped together. Furthermore, there needs to be additional research on texts from different cultural settings, and one book cannot attempt to cover all LGBTQ literature from all around the world. In a few cases, some books that were written in other languages are discussed in the following chapters. Where translations are used, I specifically refer to this, in order to show that I am not pretending that they are English-language originals that represent an English-language culture.[11] Finally, my focus is on realistic, literary texts, and this is because they more clearly represent society's views about young people and sexuality. Realistic texts often portray the world as it is, rather than the world as it could be, or once was. One might expect that some genre fiction, such as science fiction, might actually allow for more flexibility in regard to gender and sexuality and might be more accepting of non-norm genders and sexualities, and perhaps at some point another scholar will look into this topic. However, I stress that I have chosen primarily literary, realistic texts not out of a sense of high-brow, snobbish, canonical taste but rather because I feel they reflect our current society more clearly and reveal our views about topics today.

Where I have not limited myself is in regard to the audience of these books. In this analysis, I look at picture books, which are for readers of any age, although most often from newborns through about five or seven years old; middle-grade books, sometimes also known as junior books, which are suitable for readers from about eight and older; and young adult literature, which is generally aimed at people who are twelve and older.[12] Many young people read books about those who are a little older than they are themselves. In practice, most of the books I look at are picture books or YA literature; there are not as many LGBTQ middle-grade texts, which I think is because publishers and writers might believe that that audience is at a stage that is less interested in sexuality. There are many reasons why people read, but with LGBTQ literature, it is for some readers to learn about others, while others want to learn about themselves. Young children need picture books in part to see representations of themselves and their family lives, while pre-teens and teenagers need young adult literature in order to be reminded that they are not alone and that others feel the same way they do, and also to learn about the kinds of lives they might lead. Middle-grade audiences fall in between those two periods in life. Perhaps in the future more authors will write LGBTQ texts for that group of readers.

This is to say that, in this book, I analyse sixty literary LGBTQ texts for young readers, and most of these works are recent, realistic picture books or YA books from English-speaking countries.

Methodologies

It is also worth saying a few words about the methodologies employed in this book. In contrast to many other scholars or writers,

I do not use only one methodology or one field of study here; rather, I am interested in any methodologies or fields that can provide useful tools for the material at hand. This means, for example, that literary theories, sociological studies, history, anthropology, legal information, pedagogical materials, current events, interviews, and other types of material or documentation all are employed as background, context, and/or approaches. The aims are to try to understand the corpus of texts, to situate them in their respective time periods and locations, to see what they might suggest about contemporary situations and opinions, and to explore what their possible effects are on their readers, and that is why I use any material that can help accomplish these goals.

As for how such analysis is carried out, one of the major methods is to look at the characters almost as though they were real people and to thereby discuss issues such as how they are portrayed in regard to appearance, personality, characteristics, and life,[13] how they create their identity/ies, whether they seem realistic and in particular whether they reflect how LGBTQ people actually live their lives, what the authors might be saying about LGBTQ people and LBGTQ lives through the characters, and so on. I think of this as an ethnological approach, whereby I study a given context and the people within it to learn about their society and beliefs. I was inspired in part by Clifford Geertz's ideas about how to interpret culture, in which one analyses symbols and behaviours to "determin[e] their social ground and import" (1973/2000:9).

Richard Canning writes that academics "have mostly concentrated either on canonical works of literature or on nonliterary phenomena (opera, film, politics, philosophy)... The truly extraordinary cultural phenomenon of the burgeoning of gay literary production has gone relatively unexplored by the very people who are best trained to understand it." (2000:xiv) I would agree that it is important to look at non-canonical texts – such as for young readers – and, what is more, to use non-canonical methods to do so.

Structure of This Book

Finally, here I set out what is to come in the following chapters. Since I know that I cannot hope to cover every possible aspect of these books, I have chosen four major areas to explore here. They are issue books, portrayal and stereotypes, diversity, and sex and marriage.

The first chapter explores the ways in which LGBTQ books for young people are "othered" and seem to be written, published, and marketed as being for a niche audience with a distinct set of problems. The effect I believe this has is that being queer is portrayed as having an "issue" that could be problematic and that needs to be discussed, and also that it is an issue that is only of interest to people who are queer. That is to say, non-queers are apparently thought to have little interest in or desire to learn about queers. I therefore question the purpose and existence of LGBTQ issue books. This leads into the second chapter, which focuses on portrayal and stereotypes. Here, I discuss how LGBTQ people are depicted in stereotyped ways in many of these books, and I explore the possible impact that this can have on readers and thereby on society. Even positive stereotypes, I argue, can be unwelcome in that they can force people into certain ways of being that are not authentic. In the next chapter, I follow on from the discussion of the lack of a wide variety of LGBTQ people in these books by focusing more specifically on diversity, or, rather, its absence. I find that, as the Cart and Jenkins quote earlier intimated, many of the characters are "male, white, and upper middle-class" (2006:14). Indeed, they are even less diverse than that might suggest, in that the books also rarely feature diversity in regard to religion, able-bodiedness, size, or other aspects of identity. The final main chapter explores the sex lives and romantic prospects of LGBTQ people in children's literature. This deepens the discussion of stereotypes in that gay or bisexual men are frequently depicted as very sexual, while lesbian or bisexual women as not sexual at all, and marriage does not seem to be much of an option for any queer. Since these books can influence what young queer people might think about themselves and their futures, I chose to spend a chapter exploring what their futures might entail specifically in regard to their queer gender and/or sexuality. I close this book by summarising my findings and making some suggestions for the future.

Conclusion

This chapter has ranged over a lot of topics, trying to set the stage for what follows. I have explained my choice of terms; defined children's literature and referred to the power issues inherent in it; explored sexuality, especially in connection to young people and to literature for them; discussed how children's literature seems to employed in an educational way, particularly when it comes to sexuality, which perhaps suggests that it ought to be realistic; and explained the rationale behind the choices for the corpus of texts analysed here and the methods used to analyse them.

If it is true that the children of LGBTQ parents are likely to be "less conventional and more flexible when it comes to gender roles and assumptions than those raised in more traditional families" (Belkin, 2009:n.p.), then I would argue that this is something to encourage.[14] These young people deserve to have literature that reflects who they are and who their families are, literature that is positive about them and their lives and that helps them succeed. This is ultimately why I have chosen to analyse LGBTQ books for young readers: I want to know what messages society sends to LGBTQ young people and/or to children of LGBTQ parents, to see how it helps them understand themselves and make a life for themselves. Authors, teachers, publishers, editors, parents, young people themselves, and others can be – and maybe should be – activists, promoting fulfilling, successful lives for LGBTQ people.

Issue Books

In this chapter, I explore how many of the LGBTQ books for children and young adults are written, published, marketed, and/or employed as "issue books" or "problem books". What I mean by that term is that instead of just being viewed as works of fiction about people who happen to be queer, the texts discussed in this book tend to focus on queerness as a problem (see more on this in the chapter on stereotypes). These books have features that make them seem quite different from books with non-queer characters. This comes across in a number of ways. For example, there might be what I term "mini-lectures" in the books themselves, where one character educates another about queerness in a rather unnatural way, whereby the reader is also educated. There might also be peri-texts/paratexts[15] – that is, aspects of the book outside the fictional content itself, such as blurbs, afterwords, discussion questions, and so on – that suggest that a given book tackles or raises particular issues, some of which might be worth discussing in a pedagogical setting or learning even more about. Also, the placement of the books in libraries or bookstores and/or how the books are used in schools can reveal much about how these books are viewed. Thus, the issues I consider in this chapter are in regard to the audience and the goals of these works and can be described through the following questions: Who is the audience of these books? And what is the goal of these books? The existence of issue books suggests that they are meant to educate, and often in a less than natural, holistic way, and it can therefore seem as though the books are only considered to be relevant to those who are LGBTQ or are from LGBTQ families (cf. Robinson, 2002:426). All this then leads to the idea that LGBTQ people and topics are separate from others; if a group can be "othered", this may mean that other people do not view them as fully equal or as worthy of respect or rights.

There are two main, but related, types of problem novels or issue books, it seems to me. The first relates to something Suzanne M. Johnson and Elizabeth O'Connor wrote: "Estimates are that between six and fourteen million children in the United States are being raised by at least one parent who is gay or lesbian. Yet, very little is known about how gay- or lesbian-headed families function or whether they differ in any relevant ways from families headed by straight parents." (2002:1) This idea of normalcy or difference runs through many LGBTQ books for children. In such works, the issue of whether queer families are different is dealt with by attempting to confirm that they are not. This is what we might term a normalising approach, assuring readers that queer families are just as valid, just as loving, just as good, just as normal, as non-queer families. Often this type of book is a picture book, presumably aimed at young children in two-mother or two-father families; these children may worry that there is something different, and perhaps unacceptable, about their family.

The second type of book goes further and perhaps that is why it generally comes in a middle-grade or young-adult format. These books tend to try to teach readers about LGBTQ people and the LGBTQ community. Thomas Crisp has written, "As gay adolescent 'problem novels,' we may expect these books to didactically work against homophobic discourse. Problem novels as a genre rely upon intrusions that are clearly written to educate and inform readers." (2011:239) Vanessa Wayne Lee likewise writes that "educational plots...inform their audiences that lesbianism exists, whether the reader/viewer likes it or not." (2011:170) Johnson and O'Connor point out that it is only since 1975 in the U.S. that homosexuality has not been considered a disorder (2002:1). Jenkins writes that the "problem novel" first began appearing in the 1960s in the United States, and that "[h]omosexuality and the social prejudice against those who identify as gay or lesbian was one of the themes to emerge at this time" (2011:147). She adds that "[y]oung adults have many questions and much misinformation about homosexuality, and reading is one of the few private ways for adolescents to gather information about this subject." (2011:148) In other words, literature, especially that aimed at young adult readers, is meant to educate the audience about topics they might not be able to get information about from other sources. In regard to queerness, this has only happened in the past few decades, as LGBTQ people have become more accepted in society. The second main type of problem book, then, is educational, although it too may feature elements of confirmation.

Out gay writer David Levithan has been quoted as saying, "being gay is not an *issue*[;] it is an *identity*. It is not something that you can agree or disagree with. It is a fact, and must be defended and represented as a *fact*" (2004:n.p., italics original). However, it seems as though many who write, publish, market, sell, stock, and use these books do not see it that way. Rather, to them, queerness is not an identity but an issue. Solomon writes that "[t]he reasonable corollary to the queer experience is that everyone has a defect, that everyone has an identity, and that they are often one and the same." (2012:18) Many of these books seem to focus on the supposed defect rather than the identity. In what follows, I explore the ways these texts appear to be issue books. I do not discuss whether literature, and children's literature in particular, ought to be realistic and/or educational, as this was discussed to a certain extent in the introduction to this book, and it is also a topic that has been explored many times throughout the years. Rather, I take the texts that exist now and analyse the messages they offer readers and what the texts themselves seem to be doing, and I find that it appears that authors, publishers, and other adults feel that LGBTQ books for children ought to be educational.

Publishing and Practical Considerations

While for the most part we are not privy to what happens behind closed doors at a publishing company, we do know that for obvious reasons, most publishers have to consider the bottom line, and this may mean that they are more or less likely to publish books on certain topics or with certain sorts of characters; some research and authors' experiences confirms this. Also, of course, cultural norms influence which subjects are deemed appropriate or acceptable. All this in turn affects how books are marketed and for which audience/s.

Joel Taxel's analysis of the children's publishing industry provides much useful information in regard to this. He says that "editors are very aware of the audience for particular books and accept or reject a manuscript based on its marketability. Many editors, authors, and marketing people aspire to reach the widest possible audience since that means that more books are being sold." (2002:177-8) He adds that the "[f]ear of controversy undoubtedly has led some cross-cultural writers and their editors to stick to safer, simpler books or to avoid writing and publishing books with complex and divisive issues and themes (e.g., racial conflict, violence, sex and sexuality, etc.)." (2002:179) In other words, publishers have what some may say is a natural inclination to appeal to the greatest number of readers and to avoid anything that might be controversial. Unfortunately, this then leads to situations such as the recent one where authors claim that they were told by a literary agency that they could get a book deal "on the condition that we make the gay character straight, or else remove his viewpoint and all references to his sexual orientation." (Geen, 2011:n.p.) The authors added that "the agent said that [the character] could become gay in a sequel if the book was popular." (ibid.) This suggests that homosexuality might be viewed as one of the more challenging or controversial subjects. Taxel agrees that "[t]here is often a gap between the kind of books more informed readers celebrate and the books that sell in the numbers demanded by the new corporate managers. Editors and writers must be able to withstand the enormous pressure..." (2002:184). But writers, especially those who are new to publishing and have not yet built names for themselves, may not "be able to withstand the enormous pressure", as Taxel puts it.

The result of this cultural attitude towards and financial fear about queer topics is two-fold. Either publishers will not publish books that feature queerness at all or if they do publish them, they market them solely towards a niche audience, comprised of queers themselves. In regard to the former, Cart and Jenkins confirm:

> In 1994 Michael Thomas Ford stated that fear of controversy has often discouraged publishers from issuing gay or lesbian titles. A decade later we continue to be aware that while controversy can build a market for a title, it can also open publishers to criticism, boycotts, and public censure–particularly when a book is aimed at a young audience. (2006:xvii)

Dispiritingly, they point to the political situation, especially in the U.S., and the way people ban and challenge books, as a major issue.[16] In fact, they write, "[c]hallenges to books with GLBTQ content–particularly those aimed at young readers–are on the rise." (2006:xvi; cf. American Library Association's "Frequently Challenged Books Statistics" for more on this.) In this context, then, it is not a surprise that publishers may shy away from publishing such texts.

On the other hand, if publishers do choose to brave any potential fallout, they might do so by marketing their books for a very specific audience. As Taxel puts it, "[n]ovels...are believed by many to be suited for specialised (e.g., African American or gay and lesbian) audiences, thus further limiting the perceived marketability" (2002:179). So if it is the case that publishers are less likely to publish books that feature taboo or challenging topics, then it stands to reason that if they do publish such books anyway, they might assume that the books will be aimed at a niche audience, and will thereby have a smaller readership. In other words, if, for example, homosexuality is a challenging topic, a publisher might decide to publish a book with a homosexual character, but for that book to be marketed at a reader that is homosexual and/or has homosexual parents. This therefore strengthens the view that these are issue books, aimed at people for whom the particular topic is a relevant issue. People without that "issue" may not want or need to read about it, and if they were to come across such a book, they may even challenge it or request for it to be banned.

In short, then, writers, literary agents, editors, publishers, and others involved with the practical task of getting books out into the world have to consider how a specific book is going to be perceived and received. Either they do not publish challenging books at all in order to keep the literary world safe and comfortable, or they do publish challenging books but attempt to aim them only at a particular audience, thereby trying to avoid negative consequences, such as lawsuits or banning. Taxel sums up the situation by writing that the "ability of authors and editors to resist escalating pressures to commodify children's literature further and to maintain their independence in the face of relentless bottom-line imperatives will go a long way in determining the future of children's literature and will have a momentous impact on the social, cultural, and political life" (2002:184). At the moment, it seems as though publishers have to market LGBTQ books for children and young adults as issue books for a niche market.

Something interesting to consider in the future could be how the growth of self-publishing may have an impact upon which subjects and which authors get published. Self-publishing may undermine the traditional publishing houses and how they work, and this could allow for an increased number of texts published by and about LGBTQ people.

Paratexts

In this section, I explore paratexts because they provide keys to how the works are perceived and how they are expected to be employed. If, as suggested in the previous section, publishers aim certain texts at specific audiences, one of the ways they make the intended audience clear is through paratexts. Paratext is the term that covers all the extra information given on/by a book, such as the descriptions on the back and front covers, quotes from other authors, blurbs, a note from the author, a foreword/afterword, a list of discussion questions, the description of the author, and so forth. Here I also include any stickers placed on a book by a library or bookstore (such as rainbow stickers to denote queer content), and also what section in the library or bookstore a book is kept in. While the latter items are not strictly paratextual, they are close enough to be included, as they offer more information about what people judge a book to be doing and who they consider it to be for. I will not include the reception of the text here, such as how many copies the book has sold and to which groups, and how it has been reviewed, because although that is relevant and interesting, it is somewhat beyond the purview of this book and would require several additional chapters. Perhaps future research can explore this. Here, I focus on what extra information is offered by a text and what this suggests about the intended audience.

The Norfolk and Norwich Millennium Library is the busiest library in the U.K. (Norfolk County Council website, n.d.:n.p.). While it is obviously not in London, is not centrally placed in the country, and is not in the most culturally diverse city, it nonetheless can serve here as a representative for other libraries in the country due to its busyness and popularity.[17] Still, I would urge readers to go in search of LGBTQ books for children and young adults in their own local libraries and to analyse where these books are kept and why, if they are there at all. In Norwich, the picture books featuring LGBTQ families are housed in the "New Experiences" section.

In this area are books about sharing, getting a new sibling, divorce, feeling unhappy, being overweight, having asthma or diabetes, going to the hospital, toilet training, and starting school, among other topics. And, of course, the books about having a slightly different family set-up, such as two mothers or two fathers, are kept here as well. Such books include Ken Setterington's *Mom and Mum are Getting Married*, Sarah S. Brannen's *Uncle Bobby's Wedding*, Ed Merchant's *Dad David, Baba Chris and Me*, and Todd Parr's *We Belong Together: A Book about Adoption and Families*, which features a range of non-norm families.[18] Arguably, if a child is raised with two mothers, this is not a "new experience" for the child, but the library seems to suggest it is, on a par with getting diagnosed with allergies or feeling sad. One could then wonder whether the location in this section means that the books are aimed at people for whom same-sex families really are "new experiences", such as children from norm families. But unless a heterosexual parent is particularly liberal and interested in exposing their children to LGBTQ families, it seems rather unlikely that they would deliberately choose to look for these picture books.

When queried, a librarian there told me that this section was useful because parents then knew where to go to look for such materials if and when they wanted to find them. I would, of course, point out that it is very easy to use a library catalogue on a computer to search for books and that the general picture book section is arranged alphabetically, so literate parents would have no more trouble finding, say, Todd Parr's books under "P" than they would finding Dr Seuss's texts under "S". The bigger concern, I would argue, is that this effectively others LGBTQ people and LGBTQ issues, and puts them in a small box, or, rather, on a small shelf, that only some people might dare to approach. A parent would have to actively look for this section in order to find these picture books, rather than accidentally stumbling upon them amidst all the other picture books in the general area. Many parents go to the library and choose and/or allow their children to choose a stack of books to bring home, but LGBTQ books will not be part of that selection as long as they are kept in a separate area. Again, then, this suggests that these books are meant for LGBTQ families only. So the title of the section, "New Experiences," and the books' placement there emphasises that these are issue books, about issues/experiences that only a select audience would be interested in.

Meanwhile, young adult novels with LGBTQ characters are mostly (but not always) kept in Norwich in the "Loud and Proud Collection", and they have rainbow stickers on the spine. This collection also features adult books on LGBTQ themes, including romance novels, as well as some non-fiction, such as essays on being gay or a guide to planning a same-sex wedding. This location, too, is problematic for many of the same reasons that the "New Experiences" one is, in that it implies that LGBTQ topics are specialised and must be purposely sought out and in that it also keeps LGBTQ people and subjects separate from more general ones. But this collection is also worrying for another reason: it forces young people (or, indeed, older ones) who may be struggling with their sexuality or gender identity or who may not be out or those who may be interested in LGBTQ issues but not actually LGBTQ themselves to very publicly out themselves. These readers may not want to be "loud and proud", or they might be "proud" but not wish to be "loud". And yet the library insists that these readers go to a clearly marked part of the library that is separate from both the teenage section and also from most of the other adult fiction and to pick up books with a "loud" rainbow sticker on it. Not everyone will be willing to do this. Imagine a young, closeted teen with homophobic, biphobic, or transphobic parents: would this person bring home a book plastered with rainbow stickers? Somehow, I think not. So whether this "collection" is serving its purpose, I cannot say, but it does seem that together, the "New Experiences" shelves for picture books and the "Loud and Proud Collection" for books for older readers give the message that LGBTQ issues are for a select audience, rather than being of interest to everyone.

David Levithan writes:

> Teens read books to find themselves within the pages, and they visit libraries to find themselves on the shelves—a Dewey-decimal recognition of who they are and what they might be going through. It is not only a librarian's job to make this representation as welcoming and as accurate as possible. It is a librarian's *obligation* to do so. (2004:n.p., italics original)

His point can, of course, be extended to younger children as well. While he is only speaking in favour of the availability of these books, and not their placement in the library, I think his use of the word "obligation" is vital here. We have an obligation to young people to show them representations of themselves and also representations of others; shelving the books where they can only be found by those specifically searching for them shirks that obligation.

Another point in regard to materials on and in the texts is that some of these books come with a note saying that they are suitable only for a specific group. In some cases, the placement of the book in the library or bookstore also emphasises this; for instance, if the book is in the teenager/young adult section, then that suggests that younger (or older, for that matter) readers may not gain access to it, or may not want to. Whereas a book with a heterosexual love story featuring adolescents generally will not have a sticker on it saying which age group it is for (see the No to Age Banding website, n.d.:n.p., for more on labelling books by age), presumably because there is nothing shocking or upsetting about heterosexual love, unless it is too graphically sexual, a homosexual love story might have such instructions/warnings. Jacqueline Wilson's *Kiss*, which I would classify as being a middle-grade book, being suitable for readers from eight or nine and older, is in the young adult section at the Norwich library, perhaps because of the homosexual content. *Pink* by Lili Wilkinson is labelled as being "for secondary school age", as are quite a number of other such books. Meanwhile, Paula Boock's *Dare Truth or Promise* also promotes its "girl on girl" content (2009:n.p.), which trivialises and sexualises the book, othering it into what I might call "issue book territory".

The books themselves, it must be said, encourage the view that they are for a select group – usually those who belong to that minority but occasionally those who just want to learn more about that group. For example, a number have discussion questions in the back, names of LGBTQ organisations, and even listings of hotline phone numbers to ring should the readers need to discuss their presumed homosexuality with a professional. As is discussed in the chapter on diversity, in fact such lists are primarily for and about L and G people, with the B, T, and Q more or less ignored, except in two cases mentioned below.

Robin Reardon's *A Secret Edge* has a list of discussion questions, and they seem to be aimed at educating readers about homosexuality or at least getting them to reconsider their perceptions. For example, the questions encourage readers to think about whether the "rules for romance" are different between two people of the same sex (2007:262) and what it means to "be" a certain gender, as in the questions, "Why is being seen as male so crucial to most boys? Do you think the importance of this struggle could affect how adult men of any orientation view homosexual men? Do we see girls go through similar struggles to prove they're female?" (ibid.) Another discussion question seems to be aimed at getting readers to think about what would happen if a friend of theirs came out: "If you were good friends with someone you believed was straight, someone you had known a long time, and then you found out he or she was gay, would you find that confusing?" (2007:262-3) Of course the answer here could simply be "yes" or "no", but the intention is apparently to get a discussion going and to help "humanise" non-heterosexual people. This may be a noble goal – and it implies that the audience is not solely meant to be queers themselves, which is positive to see – but the problem, as I see it, is that it makes homosexuality an issue that needs to be discussed. In other words, including the discussion questions actually calls attention to LGBTQ topics as being different, problematic, and even worrying. Would books about heterosexual teens and their romantic relationships have such discussion questions?

Some of the discussion questions or phone numbers are specifically about HIV/AIDS, but as the topic of STDs is so prevalent, I mostly handle it below in its own section. Still, here I can mention the section called "For More Information About...", which is featured in all three of Alex Sanchez's *Rainbow* books. This section has twelve pages of information, including website links, telephone numbers, addresses, and encouraging summaries, under headings such as Violence and Hate Crimes Against Gays and Lesbians; Issues with Parents; HIV and AIDS; Teen Sexuality; Gay and Lesbian Teen Suicides; Gay and Lesbian Teen Services on the Internet; Youth Advocacy; and Youth Activism (*Rainbow Boys*, 2003:n.p.). The links are to the Gay, Lesbian and Straight Education Network; the New York City Gay and Lesbian Anti-Violence Project; the Human Rights Campaign; the Trevor Helpline; Parents, Families, and Friends of Lesbians and Gays; and the National AIDS Helpline (ibid.). The short texts accompanying the names of the organisations encourage young people to learn more and to get involved. For example, under Organizing a Peer Group, it is suggested that readers might like to start a Gay-Straight Alliance (GSA) at their own school. A typical line reads, "GSAs help eliminate anti-gay bias, discrimination, harassment, and violence by educating school communities about homophobia and the lives of youth" (ibid.). The last page in the book, right in front of the back cover, which has information about the author, looks like an advertisement for a website called Know HIV-AIDS. The inclusion of all these links and all this information again strengthens the idea that this work is an issue book, meant to support and educate young people. Of course, some non-LGBTQ people might consider themselves straight allies or might wish to contact these organisations, to learn more, to volunteer, to call a hotline, or to help run a Gay-Straight Alliance, but in general, one could argue that most likely it will be LGBTQ young people themselves who will find these materials useful and interesting.

Most of the works that have such lists or questions focus on lesbian or gay issues. Two young adult books also have resources on transgender topics. *Parrotfish* by Ellen Wittlinger lists references, including books by Leslie Feinberg and Kate Bornstein, as well as resources and websites, such as Advocates for Youth; Gender Education and Advocacy; Gay, Lesbian & Straight Education Network; Illinois Gender Advocates; TransGenderCare; and Youth Guardian services. Unlike most of the other young adult books, it also advertises other fictional books, including ones by Alex Sanchez, Todd Strasser, Sonya Sones, and Pete Hautman. Cris Beam's novel *I Am J* is about a transman and it too offers a resource list on queer, especially trans, topics. There is also a note from the author, who admits that she is not transgender herself, but knows and loves many trans people and that "I wanted to help give voice to all the dozens of brave, creative, and resilient kids I came across" (2011:n.p.). She writes "I can only know a kind of truth by proxy" (ibid.), which may lead readers to question the authenticity in Beam's book. Beam's novel also includes a note recommending *Luna* and *Parrotfish*.

Meanwhile, the "commemorative edition" of Nancy Garden's *Annie on My Mind* includes an interview with the author, where the first question is "When did you first know you were gay? How did you know?" (1982:239) That immediately imparts several pieces of information to the reader. One is that the author is herself gay, which, unlike in Beam's case, perhaps lends the story more authenticity or accuracy, or even makes a reader believe that the novel is based on the author's own life. Such a question and the way it leads the interview also suggests that Garden's authorship has her lesbianism as its very foundation; in other words, rather than first asking about Garden's career or about her experiences as a writer, it is implied that her sexuality is the key aspect of her life. This again problematises and others homosexuality.

These books, then, seem to be mostly aimed at an LGBTQ audience, particularly young people that have "issues" that need to be dealt with. The main issue often seems to be coming out, but HIV/AIDS and bullying are also prominent ones. These are all situations that have to be "discussed" and a reader may even need to phone a special hotline or join a group. In some cases, the issue is one that non-LGBTQ people might want to learn about and discuss, which again others it, as people seemingly do not need to discuss heterosexual or cisgender topics.[19]

In sum, these paratextual materials and the ways in which the books are housed in the library add to the idea that LGBTQ books for children and young adults are specialised, issue-centred, and mainly for a particular niche audience, namely LGBTQ people themselves or the children of LGBTQ parents. Non-LGBTQ people can simply live their lives, whereas texts that feature LGBTQ characters seem to imply that they live issue-filled lives (which relates to the analysis in the chapter on stereotypes) as well as that they need to be kept separate from others and that they need extra help/support/discussion. Of course, in some cases this may be true, but it is a worrying over-generalisation.

Confirmation of Normality

As discussed further in the chapter on sex and marriage, some of the research on LGBTQ parenting and related topics seems aimed at confirming that LGBTQ young people and children of LGBTQ parents can and do turn out "normal" (e.g. Johnson and O'Connor, 2002:3 and 36-53). The idea of normality is of course a concept that can and should be problematised, because it is very unclear. What does "normal" mean? Who decides who/what is normal? Why is normality something people should strive for? How does heteronormativity affect LGBTQ people? What is homonormativity? The questions could go on. For my purposes, as already indicated elsewhere, the norm can be said to equate to the majority, and to what is generally accepted and encouraged. As Christine Horne puts it, "[n]orms are most often seen as behavioral rules, about which there is some degree of consensus, that are enforced through social sanctions." (2001:305) She also points out that people may punish others for not following norms and although there may be "costs" for punishing people, norms may also come with more "benefits, such as support from others" or group cohesion (2001:321). Obviously, a fuller discussion of normality is called for, but this is not the place for it. For now, though, I can say that in children's literature, there is often a clear, acceptable norm that tends to link to what the majority does or believes in. In recent LGBTQ books for young people, interestingly enough, there is a regular theme that can be called the confirmation[20] of normality, wherein LGBTQ people or children of LGBTQ parents are told that they are just as okay, just as "normal", as the majority. I believe this fits with the idea of calling these texts "issue books", because they end up actually encouraging the idea that being LGBTQ means being different, and that is an issue that must be dealt with. Also, continually questioning whether such people are normal suggests they are not. As Suzanne M. Johnson and Elizabeth O'Connor put it, "Being a *lesbian* or *gay* parent is currently a highly marked category so the terms 'lesbian' and 'gay' are not usually associated with those to do with family, children or parenting…there are exclusionary practices that work to displace lesbians and gay men from imagined realms of lives involving family and parenting." (2002:3, italics original) In short, what many picture books in particular do is to mark the category of LGBTQ parenting and the wider category of being LGBTQ. They do this by attempting to normalise LGBTQ people, but this attempt merely calls attention to it, whereas simply featuring LGBTQ people and not commenting on how they are "normal" or "acceptable" would succeed more, I would argue.

Most LGBTQ picture books feature LGBTQ parents, rather than LGBTQ young people. Often, the parents explain to their children that they love each other, and the children, as much as heterosexual parents do. Another common theme is for the children to have to explain and/or defend LGBTQ relationships to other children or people at school or elsewhere. This draws attention to the difference between types of people or types of families, whereas featuring a variety of people who are just going about their daily lives would make a stronger statement, I believe. Lissa Paul calls such books "the crude 'just like us' versions" (2009:96); they attempt to show that LGBTQ people are "just like" the supposed norm. Examples of confirming (or conforming) texts include Robert Skutch's *Who's in a Family?* and Todd Parr's *We Belong Together: A Book about Adoption and Families*. These books both feature LGBTQ parents along with other types of families. Skutch starts his book with the line, "A family can be made up in many different ways." (1995:n.p.) He then goes on to look at different family set-ups, such as having two mothers, single parents, being an only child, and so on. One of his families is described thus: "Laura and Kyle live with their two moms, Joyce and Emily, and a poodle named Daisy. It takes all four of them to give Daisy her bath." (ibid.) Another is: "Robin's family is made up of her dad, Clifford, her dad's partner, Henry, and Robin's cat, Sassy. Clifford and Henry take turns making dinner for their family." (ibid.) Meanwhile, Parr's book is explicitly about adoption and has sentences such as, "We belong together because…you needed a home and I had one to share. Now we are a family." (2007:n.p.) Another is: "We belong together because… you wanted to learn and we had lots to teach you. Now we can discover new places together." (ibid.) The words do not explain what these family set-ups are, but the pictures do, and in the second of the foregoing examples, two women are depicted. There are two men shown with the sentences: "We belong together because… you needed someone to read to you and we had stories to share. Now, we all have someone to make us laugh." (ibid.) The book ends,

"There are lots of different ways to make a family. It just takes love. Share your home, and share your heart." (ibid.) While such books undoubtedly have positive intentions, in that the authors seem to want to show young readers that many kinds of families exist and are acceptable, I believe that they also have the effect of calling attention to difference in a way that may not always be helpful. Incidentally, both these books – and many of the others I mention in this section and throughout this chapter – are kept in the "New Experiences" part of the library in Norwich that was previously discussed.

For books that are not generally about "different" types of families but instead feature only LGBTQ parents, many seem aimed at comforting the children of these parents and confirming their "normality." *Josh and Jaz Have Three Mums* by Hedi Argent is a good example of this because the storyline is about confirming that being LGBTQ, or being the child of LGBTQ parents, is "okay", and some of the sentences are very explicit about this. For example, the character of Mummy Sue says:

> Families come in all shapes and sizes...Some children live with a mother and a father. Some children live with a mother or a father. Some live with their grandparents or aunts or uncles. Some children have stepfathers or stepmothers. Some have lots of sisters and brothers, some have only one or two, and some have none. (2004:n.p.)

To refer back to the previous section on paratexts, the back of the book says, "A heartwarming story for young children that encourages an understanding and appreciation of same-sex parents, as well as showing that families come in all shapes and sizes." (ibid.) This seems to focus on the difference of LGBTQ families, and the need to explain to young people that despite being different, these families should be accepted. Other examples along these lines include *Daddy's Roommate* by Michael Willhoite. This story is a typical example because it includes the line, "Being gay is just one more kind of love. And love is the best kind of happiness." (1990:n.p.) But "gay" is never defined, and the euphemism "roommate" is used; it seems to be assumed that either children would already be familiar with what being gay means, or that they would have adults reading to them who could explain. Ed Merchant's *Dad David, Baba Chris and Me* has a similar theme, even if it is much more recent. In the story, the protagonist is teased by his classmates. His teacher comforts him: "Miss Patel said it was very wrong of my classmates to tease me about my dads[21] being gay. She said they hadn't learn that being gay meant that two dads could love each other just like their mums and dads did." (2010:12) Merchant's book includes a biographical note about the author and how he himself is a gay parent, and also states that "[t]his book has been written to help and support children who are being parented by gay men, and also as an acknowledgement of the great work that all foster carers and adopters are doing." (2010:n.p.) So the story itself is a confirmation, an attempt to "help and support" the children of LGBTQ parents, which again others such families and makes the topic an issue that needs discussion, confirmation, and support.

A similar example of a book that seems meant to support children and confirm that they are not alone is Cheryl Kilodavis' s *My Princess Boy*, which is based on her young son. He wanted to wear dresses, so Kilodavis wrote a picture book about that. "It's not acceptable for us to sit back when children are taking their lives because they're not accepted for who they are," Kilodavis is quoted as saying (in Van Meter, 2010:n.p.). The implication seems to be that cross-dressing or transgender issues – whichever is the appropriate description for her "princess boy" – should be tackled in literature in order to help young people.

A long quotation from Steven Bruhm and Natasha Hurley gets all this across nicely:

> The fictional children of gay and lesbian parents, by contrast, are children without many desires at all. In books like *Heather Has Two Mommies*, *Daddy's Roommate*, *Uncle What-Is-It Is Coming to Visit!!*, and *Gloria Goes to Gay Pride*, we find sanitized middle-class worlds where children are evacuated of any desires but those of creature comforts–Who will pick me up from my politically correct day care? or Why do I have to eat Brussels sprouts? These children do express some anxiety about their queer domestic configurations–Why don't I have a daddy like other kids? What does it mean that my uncle is "gay"?–but these anxieties are quelled by the assurance that they are just like everyone else, that love makes a home, and that Uncle What-Is-It is not a drag queen but a Princeton letterman. These children live perfect lives, evidence of homosexual respectability. They exhibit a pronounced absence of sexual curiosity: they don't play at imitating their homosexual elders in the way typical of "dolls-and-trucks" children's culture, and they *never* wonder about their own sexual tastes or consider their own erotic identities. Granted, the authors of these books are writing in a climate where panic about (at best) recruitment and (at worst) pedophilia in gay and lesbian culture is rampant. But their bland children throw into high relief the truism that sexuality is otherwise omnipresent in children's culture. (2004:xii-xiii, italics original)

In other words, many of these books seem to elide or erase difference. In attempting to confirm that all is normal, they ignore what is unique, and what perhaps should be discussed and even celebrated.

Cart and Jenkins argue that LGBTQ books for young readers are important because they "assur[e]" young people that they are not alone and show them how they could live their lives (2006:xviii). This is true, but constantly emphasising the difference of LGBTQ people, especially LGBTQ parents, through the guise of confirming their normality despite their difference, is arguably not the best way to do this. I would suggest that writing books about LGBTQ people going about their daily lives is better than repeatedly saying that LGBTQ people are acceptable and normal. Having to say that queers are normal puts the question in readers' minds about whether these people actually are normal. It emphasises that they diverge from the norm and that they have lives that may be different, abnormal, and problematic. This relates to the chapter on stereotypes as well, which discusses how LGBTQ lives are often portrayed as difficult. In sum, focusing on the ab/normality of queer people makes their sexuality/ gender identities an issue that needs discussion.

HIV and AIDS

The topic of sexually transmitted diseases was briefly mentioned above in the section on paratexts, but because it is such a common feature in LGBTQ books for young readers – especially books that feature gay men – it is important to analyse it separately. Here, the focus will be on HIV/AIDS, because that is the main infection/disease that appears in this books, and also because, as Richard Canning writes, in some ways, AIDS defines gay men (2001:xv):

> Like Jews who must imaginatively and morally view the exodus from Egypt as an event that they personally experienced despite the intervening millennia, the gay man is a person who must imaginatively and morally view AIDS as something that has defined him directly. If nothing else, it is this crucial event that not only justifies the singling out of gay authors as a category but also demands that they speak. (ibid.)

This is a rather worrying idea, because it suggests that a disease that has struck the gay male community hard is what defines that community and that identity. Whether this is true is not something I can discuss here in more detail, though I hope it is not, but what I can discuss is how AIDS is depicted in books that feature young gay males.

A number of the books, particularly those by Robin Reardon and Alex Sanchez, are quite pedagogical about safe sex and STDs, and especially about HIV/AIDS, which may increase young people's concerns about sexual interactions and also underlines the idea that this is an issue for queer people. Interestingly, Robert McRuer writes, "I argue, however, that because of the lack of representations of gay men, frank speech is disallowed and information about AIDS is consequently not disseminated in these books in the ways that have been most successful, over the past decade and more, in gay and lesbian communities." (2011:185-6) I would disagree with him, because queer characters do appear in literature and, as this section will show, information about AIDS is disseminated. I am not always convinced that this is the best way to do it, though. As Cart and Jenkins write, when homosexual men engage in sex, HIV/AIDS is often shown as a consequence (2006:84-5), which suggests that AIDS is an issue that young people need to be aware of, and frightened of. In other words, HIV/AIDS is yet another problem that needs to be tackled, often in a pedagogical way, and, again, it is linked in particular to homosexual men.

As the chapter on sex and marriage discusses, the use of protection is not that common, and when it does appear, it is in relation to gay men. Characters might tell other characters that they need to use condoms in order to "stay safe". For example, in *A Secret Edge*, by Robin Reardon, the protagonist's aunt, a nurse, gives him condoms, saying, "This isn't just a health issue. It has to do with your own self-respect. You are worth keeping safe. Your life is worth every bit as much as anyone else's and a lot more than a few minutes of pleasure." (2007:111) This sort of conversation indubitably sounds awkward and may be accurately reminiscent of a parent's tone, but it does have the effect of reminding readers – who may roll their eyes at the lines – of the need for protection when engaging in sex.

Alex Sanchez's *Rainbow* trilogy goes even further, generally educating readers through the guise of the "out and proud" character of Nelson. In the first book, Nelson has a one-night stand without protection and thus must go have an AIDS test. As Thomas Crisp writes, Nelson's HIV test "provides an opportunity to make explicit the process of HIV testing (as well as to clarify how the virus is spread)" (2011:243). In the second book in the trilogy, Nelson and Kyle go to get tested, and the doctor asks them if they have unprotected sex or have been exposed to body fluids, then tells them that they might want to stop "fooling around with this sex business" until they are older (2003:20-1). Nelson also has a boyfriend who is HIV-positive, and he must consider whether and how to have sex with him. And in the final book, while on a road trip, Nelson wants to sleep with a man he and his friends meet at a gay "sanctuary". His friend Kyle rather piously stops him, informing him, "It's *never* just sex. You're trusting a guy with one of the most special parts of you—and you need to know him first...Even with a condom, he might've had some disease besides HIV. Every day the news reports some new drug-resistant STD." (2005:83, italics original) Later in that book, Nelson goes on a date with another young man, and his monogamously coupled friends Kyle and Jason warn him to "be safe" (2005:213). When Nelson and the man he went on a date with decide to become a couple, Kyle says they must discuss their HIV status immediately (2005:234). The chorus of "be safe" and "use condoms" is repeated throughout the trilogy, generally by Nelson's mother and his friends, and sometimes by lecturers in the LGBTQ youth group the three protagonists attend. Whether young people actually talk this way is a question; it does seem unexpected that teenaged boys would use terms such as "making love" and "being safe" as Kyle and Jason often do, and this makes the books seem more like a mouthpiece for adult views than a realistic depiction of young men. Strangely, there is no mention of Jason and Kyle using condoms, but perhaps the implication is that since they are a serious and (mostly) faithful couple, they do not need to do so, while Nelson is promiscuous and sex-crazy and therefore is more at risk.

Crisp writes that some schools use literature or films as a way of teaching about same-sex issues, and those that do that rely mainly on one text. As he points out, Sanchez's *Rainbow Boys* has become a prime of example of that sort of "problem literature" (2011:223), and Sanchez is quoted as being pleased that his books are helping readers (2011:224). Of course one can discuss whether literature should be used to teach and, if so, whether these books in particular should be used in that way. The real problem with these problem books, however, is that "[a]lthough Sanchez undoubtedly has the best intentions in attempting to educate young adult readers about the virus, it feels as if gay men are reduced to a stereotype through the equating of being gay with having AIDS." (Crisp, 2011:243) They thus "rely upon and reinforce heteronormative and stereotypical constructions of gender and sexuality." (2011:246)

In analysing how sexual education is taught in the U.S., Laurie Abraham discusses a teacher who does things differently, choosing to teach "good sex" rather than – or alongside – "safe sex". Abraham writes:

> His main premise is that young people will tune out educators if their real concerns are left in the shadows. And practically speaking, pleasure is so braided through sex that if you can't mention it, you miss chances to teach about safe sex in a way that young people can really use.
>
> For instance, in addition to pulling condoms over bananas — which has become a de rigueur contraception lesson among "liberal" educators — young people need to hear specifics about making the method work

> for them. "We don't tell them: 'Look, there are different shapes of condoms. Get sampler packs, experiment.' That would be entering pleasure into the conversation, and we don't want that." (2011:n.p.)

It is worth keeping this in mind in connection to how young adult novels portray and/or teach about sex. It seems quite possible that Sanchez's and Reardon's readers might begin to "tune out" the messages they offer because they can seem didactic, with little attention paid to pleasure. Although Nelson in the *Rainbow* trilogy prioritises pleasure over safety in having unprotected sex, the outcome is worrying, because the reader of the first book is left uncertain about whether Nelson did in fact get HIV from this one-night stand. If using condoms was shown as just one part of a pleasurable sexual experience, the message would be much subtler and arguably more effective.

The queer books for young adults that mention HIV/AIDS or other STDs are often quite pedagogical, with characters lecturing one another and thereby lecturing the reader. As discussed previously, the paratexts emphasise the idea that these are issue books by suggesting websites and phone numbers where readers can get more information about these topics. As already mentioned, the very last page Sanchez's *Rainbow Boys* is even an advertisement for Know HIV-AIDS, so readers are left thinking that sexually transmitted diseases are an issue for gay males in particular. Rather than decreasing homophobia through knowledge, these books may increase it by suggesting that gay men can get and spread diseases, and that STDs are not relevant to people outside that particular community.

Teaching Through Characters

Although the previous section analysed the topic of HIV/AIDS specifically, other subjects are also problematised and/or taught about in many of these books, often via mini-lectures. The books, in other words, can be pedagogical or didactic, and they treat queer topics as issues that must be learned about, studied, and dealt with. Cart and Jenkins ask rather plaintively, "Could these books perhaps play a positive didactic role in acquainting young readers with realistically portrayed gay/lesbian characters?...Could a young reader not simply feel *for* gay and lesbian people but *with* them?" (2006:xx, italics original) This would certainly be an ideal to strive for, but many of these books treat LGBTQ people as a topic that has to be learned about, not as people readers might empathise with, relate to, and perhaps even be. Characters learn about queerness through books and/or give or receive lectures about it, and thereby pass on their knowledge to the reader at the same time.

A common plot device is that a character goes to the library, looks up homosexuality in an encyclopaedia or dictionary, and learns something about it. For example, Ellen in Garret Freymann-Weyr's *My Heartbeat* goes to a gay store called A Different Light and gets a discount that is "the price break we give to all straight people who want to educate themselves." (2002:45) She reads about Michelangelo, Oscar Wilde, and other gay men (interestingly, she learns nothing about lesbians), and reports her findings to the reader:

> It used to be against the law for men to have sex with each other. People got arrested, lost their jobs, were abandoned by their friends, were put in mental homes, or killed themselves...Now it's not a big deal. There's AIDS to worry about or getting attacked by a redneck, but that's about it. Only people who don't know better still think it's shameful or wrong to be gay, but not people we know. Not smart people. (2002:46)

Ellen is depicted as an innocent young woman, perhaps quite like the reader, so she can be educated throughout the course of the book, which means that the reader can too. She is rather naïve when she says gays have few problems today other than AIDS and "rednecks". This again links gays to AIDS. Ellen later argues with her father about homosexuality, when he says "gay people are forced to live outside the mainstream of society," because he seems to think that they should be, and she disagrees (2002:110-11). Her father says that gay people are in "life's margins" and that "[f]rom there, they are able to make unique observations. Most art – dance, music, poetry, what have you – is an expressed observation." (ibid.) Ellen thinks about what he has said and her reflections also enable the reader to reflect on homophobia and on whether LGBTQ people ought to stay in "life's margins".

Ellie in Leanne Lieberman's *Gravity*, an Orthodox Jew who has had some sexual interactions with another young woman and is uncertain about her sexuality, also heads to the library to learn about LGBTQ issues. She looks up "homosexual" in the encyclopaedia and learns that some people just experiment. "I leave the library somewhat relieved. Maybe we just experimented, maybe I'll grow up and learn to like men. Maybe." (2008:96) But she continues to feel attracted to women, so she returns to the library. "I've done some research on gay people at the library, and being gay doesn't sound too good. Besides being an abomination according to Jewish law, all the famous gay people I've read about had tragic ends, or at least disappointing sex lives." (2008:126) Although Ellie eventually decides to choose her sexuality over strict interpretations of Jewish law, her initial findings are worrying. Both she and Ellen learn about what possible lives LGBTQ people might live by reading books in the library, and what they learn is not necessarily that positive. It is also a reminder that the young people reading these books (i.e. Lieberman and Freymann-Weyr's novels and other such texts) will be learning as they read, so it behoves the authors to show a variety of lifestyles and situations, and also to accurately portray LGBTQ people and issues, but this often does not happen.

Jody in Hayley Long's *What's Up With Jody Barton?* also visits the library, although he is more interested in films than books (2012:201-3). After having been rejected by the boy of his dreams and threatened with exposure in school, Jody takes to skipping school. He goes to the library for help and support and is told to watch a film because films can "heal" (2012:202). Watching movies makes him remember that he is not so strange and not so alone. Elsewhere in this book, reading material plays a role. Jody gets the nerve to tell his doctor that he got a black eye because he tried to kiss his sister's boyfriend and the doctor says, "You're not the first person to experience these feelings and you certainly won't be the last." (2012:161) Then he gives Jody a pamphlet called "Am I gay/lesbian/bisexual?" (ibid.) Although Jody does not read this pamphlet until quite a bit later on, when he is ready, what he learns from it does help him. While this book is more positive in that Jody finds comfort and knowledge from his reading and viewing, it again suggests that being queer is an issue that must be studied or read about.

J in *I Am J* by Cris Beam also uses a brochure as a way of learning about being queer; in his case, the information is on getting testosterone, and J hands it to his mother instead of orally coming out to her (2011:155). Another form of research is using the internet, and J Googles terms such as "women who want to be men" and chest binding, and learns about hormones (2011:52-7); the reader can learn along with J.

Besides going to the library, the characters in these books might learn by receiving what I term a mini-lecture from another character, or they in turn might offer one, even if simply through their thoughts. Often, these lectures do not sound authentic to the way youthful characters might actually speak; they may not reflect how young people talk to one another, although they might well reflect how adults talk to children when trying to educate them. Examples from Reardon and Sanchez's books were given above. Another book, Ellen Wittlinger's *Parrotfish*, has a very long but apt example of this as well. Grady, the protagonist, is transgender, but struggles to get everyone to accept this. He thinks about gender and his thoughts can be said to be rather didactically phrased:

> What made a person male or female, anyway? The way they looked? The way they acted? The way they thought? Their hormones? Their genitals? What if some of those attributes pointed in one direction and some in the other? And some of this stuff had to do with the way you were raised, right? It's not as if we'd managed to stamp out stereotypes in this culture. In many places sugar and spice were still considered the opposite of snails and puppy-dog tails. When I decided I was a boy, I realized that if I wanted to pass, I'd have to learn to walk differently, talk differently, dress differently, basically act differently than I did as a girl. But why did we need to act at all? A quick glance around Buxton High provided numerous cases of girls acting like girls and boys acting like boys—and very few people acting like themselves. Eve was a perfect example: She'd been a great girl until she hit Buxton, but now she was a high-pitched, low-self-esteem, capital-G Girl who couldn't relax and be Eve anymore.
>
> So maybe it was silly for me to try to be somebody else's idea of a boy. I didn't need to swagger around and punch guys in the shoulder—that wasn't going to prove anything. There were still people who didn't succumb to the stereotypes. Sebastian certainly didn't punch or swagger, and he was a boy, although one who couldn't get a date to the Winter Carnival dance.
>
> And why was changing your gender such a big honking deal anyway? People changed lots of other personal things all the time. They dyed their hair and

> dieted themselves to near death. They took steroids to build muscles and got breast implants and nose jobs so they'd resemble their favourite movie stars. They changed names and majors and jobs and husbands and wives. They changed religions and political parties. They moved across the country or the world—even changed nationalities. Why was gender the one sacred thing we weren't supposed to change? Who made that rule? (2007:131-2)

One could argue that a transgender person him- or herself might not use words, phrases, or ideas such as "deciding to be" male or female or "changing gender" but rather would discuss "confirming" gender; besides the authenticity or lack thereof in regard to that, it also seems unlikely that a teenager would sit at home thinking about gender in this way. It feels as though the author wants to get these ideas across to the reader and wants to challenge the reader's views on gender, rather than this mini-lecture/reflection genuinely coming from Grady himself.

A conversation between Sal and Carlos in Alex Sanchez's *Getting It* is likewise lecture-like rather than teenager-like. Sal is gay and wants his straight friend Carlos to help argue for a gay-straight alliance at their school. Sal says:

> "I need you to talk—as the straight guy in the group—about how homophobia hurts everybody."
>
> Carlos pondered that. "But I don't know what to say."
>
> "Sure you do! You get called 'faggot' too, don't you?"
>
> "Yeah. Everyone does sometimes."

> "Exactly! And do you like being called 'homo' or '*maricón*'?"
>
> "No."
>
> "Then why don't you do something about it?"
>
> "Because it's like being called '*pendejo*'—it doesn't really mean anything."
>
> "Oh, yeah? If it's the same as being called '*pendejo*,' then why are you scared to be seen with me? Why are you so afraid people might think you're gay?"
>
> Carlos bit into his lip, unsure how to respond. Sal continued. "Homophobia means that, any time you say or do anything the least bit different, you risk getting called queer—whether you are or not. You think that doesn't hurt you? You think that doesn't keep you from being an individual?" (2006:66-7, italics original)

Here, then, the reader is educated about homophobia and bullying along with Carlos. Carlos has to confront his feelings about this issue, just as the reader is encouraged to.

A number of other books also feature the library visit or the lecture format, such as Carol Plum-Ucci's *What Happened to Lani Garver*, where Claire's repeatedly emphasised naivety allows for her to be told things in a rather pedantic way, and thus for the reader to learn at the same time. As Vanessa Wayne Lee points out in regard to lesbian novels in particular, some of the texts "position[s] lesbianism as a threat or a problem. As such, they do not attend to the formation of a lesbian identity but are designed to educate audiences unfamiliar or uncomfortable with lesbianism and/or to eroticize the lesbian as a facet of male heterosexual pleasure." (2011:165) This seems true for many LGBTQ books for children and young adults. That is to say that they seem "designed to educate audiences unfamiliar or uncomfortable with" queer issues, as well as to educate queer young people themselves. They do not generally "interrogate received wisdom", as Lee puts it (ibid.), but rather teach in a non-challenging way, and they can be quite didactic about queerness and/or about society's homophobia (Lee, 2011:169). This situates these texts squarely in the "problem books" or "issue books" category.

Controversy

A final indication that LGBTQ books for young readers are considered problematic is the extensive controversies surrounding many of them. This clearly shows that these books are thought to be issue books on specific topics that may not be appropriate for certain, or even all, children and young adults. This is different from reception because here I do not explore how young people themselves think about these books, but rather how adults view them. The American Library Association keeps detailed records about challenged and banned books in the U.S. Over a twenty-year period, from 1990-2010, nearly 11,000 challenges were recorded. Of these challenges, a large number (over 3,000) were in regard to books deemed "sexually explicit"; 300 challenges were about books that were "anti-family" (and one can guess that "anti-family" may indicate "non-heterosexual, nuclear family"); close to 900 were about "homosexuality" specifically; over 600 were in regard to "nudity"; over 300 were about "sexual education"; and more than 2000 were "unsuited to age group" (all statistics from the ALA website, n.d.:n.p.). One has to keep in mind that some books were challenged for multiple reasons and also that not all of these challenges have to do with LGBTQ matters (for example, an "anti-family" book might show a single parent, or grandparents raising a child). Still, there were approximately 7,100 challenges related to sexuality or similar subjects, and out of 11,000 challenges, that means that over 60% had to do with such topics. This staggering statistic reveals how controversial such texts really are considered to be.

It is important to remember that the ALA information comes from the U.S. There is no similar organisation in the U.K. that keeps track of such information, but it would be interesting to know whether the statistics are along the same lines in other English-speaking countries and indeed in other parts of the world. Abate and Kidd write that:

> common conservative rhetoric in the United States asserts that lesbian teachers, same-sex parents, or gay Boy Scout leaders are intent on "recruiting" or "indoctrinating" the nation's children into sexual deviancy. Such language casts childhood and LGBTQ identity as mutual exclusive. Since children are ostensibly devoid of LGBTQ thoughts, feelings, or actions then, by extension, so are the narratives intended for them. (2011:13)

In the United States, and potentially elsewhere, then, consumers, readers, parents, teachers, and other adults are afraid of these books, because they believe they might teach children about topics that they ought not learn about, and might even "recruit" children into a queer identity. As Abate and Kidd write, this assumes that children are not already aware of queer feelings or actions. It also assumes that childhood is, and should be, an "innocent" time, and that adults can or should protect children from certain information, feelings, or experiences. Both assumptions are faulty, of course.

One of the first picture books for children to feature LGBTQ characters was *Mette bor hos Morten og Erik* by Danish writer Susanne Bösche (1981 in Danish, 1983 in English, as *Jenny Lives with Eric and Martin*; the translation of Mette into Jenny is an issue worth exploring elsewhere). Bösche has written:

> I wrote Jenny lives with Eric and Martin back in 1981 because I became aware of the problems which some children face when meeting family groupings different from the ones they are familiar with, i.e. mum and dad, possibly mum and dad divorced, maybe a step-parent. It's not possible to go through life without meeting people living in different ways, and they shouldn't come as a shock to anybody. (Bösche, 2000: n.p.)

In other words, she chose to write this book to give children a window onto other family set-ups and to educate them about what might be considered normal. As an analysis of the English version of the book and its effects has shown, Bösche's work was considered "homosexual propaganda" and "vile" and may have helped lead to the passing of Section 28 in the U.K. (Smith, 2008:n.p.).[22]

Lesléa Newman's *Heather Has Two Mommies* was likewise controversial, although in the U.S. rather than in the U.K., and it features on ALA's list as number nine out of the ten most challenged texts in the 1990s, while Michael Willhoite's *Daddy's Roommate* was number two on that list (ALA website, n.d.:n.p.). A CNN report from 2011 shows that Justin Richardson and Peter Parnell's *And Tango Makes Three* – a book based on the true story of two male penguins who form a relationship and parent a baby penguin – topped the list of most challenged books in 2006, 2007, 2008, 2009, and 2010 (2011:n.p.), and the ALA lists it as number four on the ten most-challenged books from 2000-2010. Michael Alison Chandler writes that "a parent complained that [*And Tango Makes Three*] promoted a gay agenda" (2008:n.p.). Kate Kelland notes that both the penguin book and Linda de Haan and Stern Nijland's *King and King*, which is about a prince who marries another prince, "sparked anger among some religious groups who say [such books are] homosexual propaganda" (2007:n.p.). One person was quoted in Kelland's article as calling LBGTQ books for children "child abuse" (ibid.). He went on to say that the texts could make young people think "that two boys fiddling with each other...is perfectly normal...Parents should be able to have the peace of mind of knowing that school is a safe place...And to have their children indoctrinated with pro-homosexual propaganda is an abuse of the trust parents place in schools." (ibid.) Clearly, then, adults are very worried about the existence of these books and wonder if children would be "indoctrinated" into a homosexual lifestyle by them.

Marcus Ewert's picture book about a transgender girl, *10,000 Dresses*, has also been criticised by adults who find the material inappropriate for children. Ewert writes:

> The Right Wing has decried the book as 'teaching and promoting your children to cross-dress' – which to me misses the point entirely: Bailey's not a transvestite, she's transgender – but I think some conservatives can't even conceive of that: a child who doesn't identify with the gender they were assigned at birth. To them, ideas such as 'assigned gender' vs. 'affirmed gender' are so alien to their viewpoint as to come off as totally nonsensical, if they even register such themes at all. So instead my book becomes 'the book about the boy who wants to be a drag-queen.' Um, no. (personal correspondence, 2013:n.p.)

Some people, it seems, find the subject matter of Ewert's book uncomfortable, while others are concerned that it might encourage young people to experiment with gender in ways that are unacceptable.

As for young adult books, Nancy Garden's *Annie on My Mind* makes the top fifty on ALA's list for the 1990s and *Rainbow Boys* by Alex Sanchez does the same for the following decade.

Both books feature non-heterosexual characters, non-heterosexual love stories, and non-heterosexual sexual interactions. They are deemed upsetting for their subject matter, and some adults try to prevent young people from accessing and reading them by challenging them or requesting a ban of them.

All of the foregoing suggests that some people are deeply concerned about the existence and goals of books with LGBTQ characters. Some adults feel that queer topics should not be portrayed in books for young readers because such books might educate children, change their beliefs/morals, and even tempt them into being queer themselves, and while one could argue that books, however important they are, do not have the power to transform readers into something other than who and what they already are,[23] the fact is that some people refuse to accept that. The controversies surrounding these texts push them even further into the realm of "issue books". The issues are ones that many adults do not want young people to have access to, even if it is not possible to keep children "innocent" – if they ever are truly innocent – forever.

Conclusion

In this chapter, I have explored the many ways in which in which LGBTQ literature for young readers is turned into or treated as "issue" or "problem" literature. This primarily happens through what I term the confirmation of normality and through the pedagogical function. Richard Canning writes, "One of the ways that gay authors have been ghettoized is by people overlooking their achievements as writers and viewing them as merely spokespersons for a social movement." (2000:ix) In a strange way, we are ghettoising LGBTQ literature by treating the books as issue/problem books, or even as spokespeople (or spokesbooks) for the greater LGBTQ movement. Canning has a point in regard to how queer authors might write their texts, as evidenced by Alex Sanchez, among others, as discussed above, because they choose to focus on "problem" topics, rather than showing LGBTQ people in all their complexity and variety. Elizabeth A. Ford agrees:

> Authors who chose gay themes and who write for children must also choose whether or not to be commercially viable. Those who want to sell books must learn, as Lesléa Newman seems to have learned, to maintain a "safe" distance between child and gay adult characters. More like a wall than a comfort zone, distance problematizes the treatment of gay themes in children's literature and may keep the genre from reflecting the growing cultural acceptance Lopate identifies as a contemporary reality. (2011:202-3)

What Ford and Canning are getting at is that merely by writing about queer issues and characters, authors are "choos[ing] whether or not to be commercially viable", and this relates back to the earlier discussion about practical considerations when it comes to publishing. Of course, as I have discussed here, it is also a matter of how authors write about these topics. For example, mini-lectures, didactic tones, and educational information play a big role in turning these works into problem texts. I believe it would be possible to write such literature in a way that would not make the book an issue book and that would allow for commercial viability, but as these examples suggest, this is not so common. But it is not only authors themselves who make the texts into issue books, nor is it just down to critics or scholars who treat the books in these ways. As I have tried to show here, the books are "ghettoised", to use Canning's term, in libraries and bookstores, and by consumers. Placing LGBTQ books in particular areas of the library or challenging them for their content ensures that they are viewed by the general public as only about and for a certain minority group. This suggests that the audience is either LGBTQ themselves (or the children of LGBTQ people), or else is a small subsection of non-LGBTQ people who want or need to learn about queer issues for some reason.

As David Levithan was quoted as saying earlier in this chapter, "being gay is not an *issue*[;] it is an *identity*. It is not something that you can agree or disagree with. It is a *fact*, and must be defended and represented as a fact" (2004:n.p., italics original). Unfortunately, however, queerness is still being treated in many of these books and in their paratexts, and in the discussions about and surrounding them, as an issue, rather than as a fact or an identity. I would argue that it is time for this to change.

Portrayal and Stereotypes

In this chapter, I analyse the ways queer characters are portrayed in books for children and young adults. Although I applaud the existence of books for young readers that feature LGBTQ characters, as I read them, I frequently am concerned about how these characters are depicted. Their non-normative sexuality and gender identities tend to mark them apart and define them, rather than simply being just another aspect of their personalities. That is to say, they are LGBTQ first and everything else second, instead of being, say, people who have multiple interests and personality traits and just so happen to also belong to the LGBTQ community. They are portrayed as being readily recognisable and/or as having very specific characteristics, such as gay men being camp and humorous or gay women being serio http://www.rtve.es/alacarta/videos/pienso-luego-existo/pienso-luego-existo-beatriz-preciado/1986547/ us and feminist, and this allows for little flexibility or variety, which therefore makes LGBTQ people appear to be monolithic.[24] Furthermore, the very fact of their queerness is often depicted as being difficult; for example, a queer character might be represented as very stressed and unhappy due to being queer. The experiences of recognising one's queerness, coming out to oneself, one's family, and one's friends, finding and participating in sexual and/or romantic relationships, and living a queer life are frequently shown as causing stress and depression, with the implication being that it is close to impossible to be an out queer who is happy and healthy. This, of course, follows on from the discussion in the previous chapter about issue books in that being queer is viewed as having an issue. In short, queer characters are stereotyped in ways that I consider limiting and problematic. If stereotypes were employed in order to be challenged or played with, that would be interesting and it could make readers think. But this is generally not the case.

In this chapter, then, I first discuss the concept of stereotypes in order to explore what they are, why they come about, why they are used, and what the dangers and pitfalls of employing them are. After that, I analyse some of the stereotypes that recur throughout LGBTQ children's and young adult literature in regard to the portrayal of queer characters. One could even begin to call these frequently seen plots or characteristics tropes. My aim is to understand what the common stereotypes are, why they exist, and if anything can be done about their regular appearance and the messages they offer to young, impressionable readers. Finally, I close by discussing the importance of reducing prejudice and the role literature can serve in regard to this.

Prejudice and Stereotypes

In this section, I explore prejudice and stereotypes in some detail, as it is important to understand what prejudice is, where it comes from and what consequences it has, before I focus on homophobia, biphobia, and transphobia specifically and then move on to the portrayal of queer characters in literature. As I show here, what common sense suggests is backed up by the research on the topic: prejudice causes problems for those who have to face it, as well as for those who hold prejudiced views. I would therefore argue that we need to find ways of reducing prejudice in general, and that against LGBTQ people in particular. Since the media encourages stereotyped views, the media might actually be a potential solution to this problem, if books, TV shows, films, magazines, and so forth would start showing people in all their diversity.

So the first question, of course, is what is prejudice? As Bruce Blaine puts it, "**Prejudice** is unjustified negative judgment of an individual based on his or her social group identity" (2007:61, bold original). He points out that "negative categorical evaluations are unfair because they are applied indiscriminately to all members of the group." (2007:62) In other words, prejudice comes about when a whole group of people – whether the group is based on a shared religious or ethnic identity, sexual orientation, appearance, ability, or other feature – is viewed negatively simply by dint of their identity. In this case, the LGBTQ community faces prejudice because many people do not understand gender identities or sexualities outside of the heterosexual, cisgender norm. Many writers on prejudice point out that prejudice can be positive – for example, someone might have a particularly positive and open-minded attitude towards a specific group – but in most cases, it seems, prejudice causes problems and is unwelcome. Rupert Brown writes, "the kind of prejudice that besets so many societies in the world today and which so urgently requires our understanding is usually the negative variety: the wary, fearful, suspicious, derogatory, hostile or ultimately murderous treatment of one group of people by another." (2010:4) In other words, "prejudice is not to be regarded as just a cognitive or attitudinal phenomenon; it can also engage our emotions, as well as finding expression in behaviour." (2010:7) If prejudice moves beyond being "just" a bad attitude or a vague dislike of a group and creates a situation where people behave badly and even abusively towards a group or particular members of a group, then something indeed must be "urgently" done, as Brown suggests.

One aspect of prejudice is stereotyping. Stereotyping means having fixed views of a group of people based on their group identity; again, such views generally are negative, but they can be positive as well. For example, Jewish people are frequently viewed as being stingy and greedy, but they are also often seen as clever.[25] While some claim that positive stereotyping is welcome, I would argue that it can be just as damaging, because it still puts people into defined boxes rather than seeing them as individuals, and also it may promote some groups over others (i.e. one group that is seen as less clever may be discriminated against in favour of a group considered more clever). The stereotyping – both positive and negative – of LGBTQ people that often seems to serve as characterisation in the novels discussed here may lead to more entrenched prejudice in the long term.

Diane M. Mackie, David L. Hamilton, Joshua Susskind, and Francine Rosselli explore how stereotypes are acquired. They discuss a range of different mechanisms, such as categorisation, which comes about "when an aggregate of persons is perceived as comprising a group, an entity", and then that group is thought to have distinct characteristics that differentiate them from others (1996:44); correspondence, which is "the tendency to see behaviour as reflecting an actor's inner dispositions, even if the constraints of social roles or situational contingencies are readily apparent" (1996:48); conditioning, "when a person or object that is repeatedly paired with a particular emotion itself comes to elicit the emotion" (1996:52); and exposure (1996:53-5), although this is thought to "contribute to positive stereotypes about *in-group* members (to whom one is frequently exposed), rather than to positive feelings about out-group members" (1996:54, italics original). While this all might sound rather technical, it is clear that stereotypes and prejudice do serve sensible evolutionary purposes, in that, at their simplest, they help to differentiate between friend and foe, between safe and unsafe. The issue is that they become and remain ingrained even when no longer required, and they are then passed down from one generation to the next as a matter of habit, creating often unnecessary boundaries between groups. Children are exposed to stereotypes at an early age and such prejudice can be reinforced through information they receive from relatives, friends, teachers, other authority figures, and the media, including, of course, literature. In short, "[t]o participate in a culture means, at least in part, learning and accepting what the culture believes about one's own and other groups. Thus, stereotypic conceptions of groups are often socially transmitted: stereotypes are acquired readymade and prepackaged." (1996:60)

As already insinuated, stereotypes can be useful in some situations in that they can enable us to quickly make judgments about particular people or places (categorisation seems to be a useful trait because it helps people understand what is dangerous and what is safe, who might help them and who might harm them). As Sam Gosling puts it:

> we use stereotypes to fill in the gaps when we are unable to gather all the information. And most everyday opportunities for perception are riddled with gaps. If you didn't use stereotypes, you would be overwhelmed, because every item, person, and experience in life would have to be treated as though it were a totally new experience, not part of a broader class. Thinking about stereotypes this way—as assumptions about things (people or objects) in the absence of direct experience of those particular things—allows us to see how common they are and how often we use them in all manner of impression-formation contexts. Without them, we couldn't take a walk down the street or bite into a sandwich. (2008:138-9)

Blaine adds that we sometimes use prejudice in order to "maintain a positive social identity" about ourselves (2007:66) and to defend ourselves and/or our group (2007:66-7). All this suggests that humans need some amount of prejudice/stereotyping in order to survive. For an author, of course, this sort of shortcutting can be beneficial, because a writer can assume that their readers know something about the issue/group they are referring to. But this can go too far and stereotyping can have serious consequences.

The consequences of prejudice and stereotyping affect both those who hold the prejudiced views and those who are the target of such views. In regard to the former, Brown writes that prejudice can be faulty, inflexible, or inaccurate (2010:4), thus giving people incorrect information. Gosling says that "even when stereotypes have some validity, the information they convey is often dwarfed by specific, case-by-case facts." (2008:165) Blaine takes this idea further. As he puts it, a consequence of stereotyping is that we think groups are more different from other groups than they are and also that people in groups are more alike than they actually are (2007:36). This leads us to not recognising people as individuals and instead assuming that we know what they are like simply because they happen to be from a particular background, have a certain gender or sexual orientation, have a specific set of beliefs, or appear one way as opposed to another. Also, because of this assumption, we may expect people from these groups to act or look in a certain way, pressuring them and not recognising them for who they are. The examples below back up these ideas.

As if these consequences were not enough on their own, there are also severe consequences for those who have to face prejudices. Some research has shown that if people are reminded about negative stereotypes about their group, they perform worse on tests and exams (Aamodt and Wang, 2011:208), and of course this is especially relevant for the young people who might be reading the books discussed here because they are more likely to be taking exams than adults. Sandra Aamodt and Sam Wang suggest reminding groups of positive stereotypes instead (ibid.), but again, even positive stereotyping can have detrimental effects. On a larger scale, if a group is expected to behave or look a certain way, people from that group may feel forced to actually do so, thus creating inauthentic versions of themselves, and making stereotypes into self-fulfilling prophecies (cf. Blaine, 2007:42-3, 51). This is a stressor that can take a mental and emotional toll. Blaine writes that there is now "the recognition that there is a greater psychological burden associated with being a member of some social categories than others and some of this burden *is* attributable to past oppression and injustice." (2007:9, italics original) In other words, if a group is oppressed, or mistreated, or if group members cannot be their authentic selves, they are understandably experiencing undue stress. Blaine says that "minority stress refers to the chronic experience of being stereotyped (e.g., disliked, feared, judged) and socially alienated (e.g., excluded from social institutions)" (2007:148).

In regard to prejudice and the LGBTQ community in particular, there is less research on this. Even in works that focus in depth on prejudice, there is often little mention of homophobia (such as Brown, 2010) and if there is a reference to homophobia, there rarely is one to biphobia or transphobia (such as Blaine, 2007), and of course it is important to remember that these prejudices are not interchangeable. Blaine writes that gender is "by far the most-researched aspect of diversity" (i.e. in regard to how women are oppressed), followed by race, while sexuality is the second-least researched, only above weight (2007:3). While such an analysis ignores intersections of diversity (see the next chapter for more on this), it does highlight that how members of the LGBTQ community are stereotyped and discriminated against is under-researched, as is the issue of how such prejudice affects them. And yet, there is more physical hate crime against LGBTQ people than any other group (Blaine, 2007:77).[26] Brown has slightly different statistics, but likewise comes to the conclusion that this is a serious matter when he writes that "after anti-black crime, **homophobic** incidents are the second most frequent form of hate crime in the USA. There is evidence to suggest that being a victim of hate crime on the basis of one's sexual orientation has more serious psychological consequences than being a victim of a comparable crime without the hate elements." (2010:221-2, bold original) So it is rather puzzling that homophobia, biphobia, and transphobia are not more analysed and problematised than they currently are.

Homophobia in particular is defined as "fear, disgust, and aversion" towards homosexual people while homosexism "involves stereotyping, prejudice, and discrimination directed at people because of their homosexual orientation" (Blaine, 2007:143). Texts on the topic often do not give specific definitions of biphobia and transphobia, but one could give an oversimplified explanation of these terms by replacing "homosexual" with "bisexual" or "transgender" though "transgender" is not an "orientation" (and cf. Ochs, 1996 for more on biphobia). Homophobia and homosexism, biphobia and bisexism, and transphobia and transsexism can have the types of effects on members of the LGBTQ community that were discussed above in relationship to prejudice more generally. For example, Brown discussed a study where people posing as applicants for a job went into stores wearing either "Gay and Proud" or "Texan and Proud" hats and found that when they wore the former, they had shorter, more negative interactions with staff in the stores (2010:205). In other words, people perceived to be gay were less likely to receive positive responses in regard to potential jobs than if they were perceived to be heterosexual and proud of the state they came from.

Since facing prejudice and stereotyping is known to be stressful and harmful to one's health, it stands to reason that this is the case for LGBTQ people as well. "Coping with the stereotyping and discrimination that is directed at gay men and lesbians exacts a price in terms of decreased psychological and physical well-being." (Blaine, 2007:149) Brown adds that "lesbians and gays reported greater depression, stress, anxiety, anger and perceived vulnerability to future crime if they had experienced a hate crime in the past five years than if they had experienced a non-hate crime." (2010:222)

One difference between prejudice towards LGBTQ people and other types of prejudice is that queers are often thought to deserve whatever difficult things happen to them. While other groups may be disliked, they are not often blamed for the random fact that they happen to have been born to a certain ethnic or religious group.[27] LGBTQ people, on the other hand, are thought to have chosen immoral, perverse, or ungodly lifestyles and this supposed choice therefore is seen as warranting them being discriminated against. Blaine writes how "perceived control over one's sexuality is an important predictor of homosexism; people who hold negative attitudes toward gay men and lesbians tend to see homosexuality as controllable and changeable" (2007:143). What this suggests is that those who think homosexuality can be chosen will be less sympathetic towards homosexuals. For example, gay males are viewed as sexually (over)active and to thus deserve the risk of getting AIDS or other sexual transmitted infections (Blaine, 2007:144). Mackie, Hamilton, Susskind and Rosselli write that for many people, "[i]t is comforting to believe that bad things happen only to bad people—that AIDS is a punishment for taking drugs or for a gay lifestyle" (1996:59-60). As the chapter on issue books shows, AIDS is often depicted in young adult literature as being a problem for gay men, and this may strengthen people's beliefs that gay men deserve to be at risk of AIDS. So an additional issue for LGBTQ people is that they have little recourse against prejudice and little support in their fight against it, because they are in some circumstances considered to earn it through their own choices and behaviours.

Finally, it is worth emphasising a point that was briefly made earlier. The portrayal of a particular group in the media does encourage and strengthen the general public's opinion of that group. Most of the research on this topic focuses on television (such as Blaine, 2007:156-69), seeming to scarcely recognise the existence of literature, much less its possible influence on readers, particularly young ones. Nonetheless, the discussion of television can perhaps help set the stage, as it were, for my own exploration of literature. Blaine writes that "[h]istorically, gay and disabled characters have been both infrequently and negatively portrayed on television. In the early TV decades, gay men and lesbian characters typically appeared as mentally unstable, morally corrupt individuals whose lives ended tragically before the end of the show—often by suicide." (2007:163-4) In more recent times, he writes, the situation has changed to a certain extent. "However, the portrayal of those gay characters is mixed. Some male characters act out the effeminate gay male stereotype...Stereotypic portrayals of gay men typically overemphasize their sexuality and sexual behaviour" (2007:164). This is quite similar to my own findings, as discussed below. If gay men are portrayed as being "effeminate" and overly sexual, this both promotes the idea that gay men have to be like this, which puts pressure on gay men to conform to this stereotype, and also means that those outside the LGBTQ community do not get a whole picture of what gay men, and other queers, might be like, further entrenching their stereotyped views and endorsing, perhaps non-intentionally, homophobia and homosexism. I come back to the role of literature and the media later in this chapter.

As an example, I can describe how I submitted an academic article that discussed the issue of how gay males tend to be portrayed as camp and witty in young adult fiction. In response to this analysis, one anonymous peer reviewer wrote that they did not see why this was an issue or why it was worthy of an article, because as far as they could see, gay males *were* in fact camp and witty, and thus young adult novels were realistic. I suppose to me this exemplifies just what the problem is. We categorise people and assume that categories of people are monolithic and unchanging. We assume that since we have seen some camp and witty gay men, all gay men must be like that, when in fact that is only one type of gay man, and of course straight men and bisexual men – and one could argue women – can be camp and witty too. To present the message that gay men are camp and witty is to force gay men into a narrow box and to allow people to just assume they know what all gay men are like rather than getting to know them in all their individuality.

Stereotypes do not just have to do with behaviour or appearance, such as being camp and witty, however; they can, of course have to do with other aspects of life. What seems to be the case for many of the books discussed in this chapter is that both the people and the plots are stereotyped; in other words, queers are thought to have specific personalities and specific types of lives solely because they are LGBTQ. Frequently, these lives are portrayed as stressful and the personalities are not fully fledged. What this section about stereotypes has shown is that this sort of portrayal is limiting and can lead to inaccurate information, stress, depression, an inability to be oneself, discrimination, and, in the worst-case scenario, violence and homophobic, biphobic, and transphobic crime.

A Brief History of Stereotypes in LGBTQ Literature

Clearly, stereotypes and prejudice can be very detrimental, which is why it is important to analyse the specific stereotypes or prejudiced messages that are offered by many contemporary queer children's books. I would like to first point out, however, that in my research, I have again and again come across scholars who write about just how stereotyped LGBTQ books for young readers have always been. For example, Cart and Jenkins claim that early LGBTQ books "perpetuate stereotypes in their portrayal of homosexual characters. Some are pictured as unfortunates doomed to either a premature death or a life of despair lived at the darkest margins of society." (2006:xvi) They add that "too many of these [books] were marred by stereotypical characters and predictable plots centered on the inherent misery of gay people's lives." (2006:17) In addition, these books show that:

> the consequences of being gay include:
> 1. being hideously injured in a car wreck
> 2. becoming an embittered, tormented recluse
> 3. being rejected by a boy whom you have sought only to mentor, comfort, and reassure
> 4. exiling oneself to a life among strangers
> 5. dying prematurely of a heart attack no doubt brought on by 1, 2, 3, and 4. (2006:20-1)

Christine Jenkins carried out an analysis of gay and lesbian YA novels from 1969 to 1992 and notes that some of the stereotypes they include are that "gay/lesbian teachers commonly los[e] their jobs" (2011:150); gay people are either promiscuous or else have no sex lives (2011:152); gay men in particular die often in these books (2011:154-5); gay males show no connections to females, whether as friends or relations (2011:157); and that "[o]ne-note portrayals of gay/lesbian characters as tragic outsiders continue to appear in contemporary young adult fiction, but they are no longer hegemonic." (2011:159) And, finally, Melinda Kanner finds that the LGBTQ characters in young adult novels are frequently lonely, unhappy, and distrusted (n.d.:n.p.). In what follows, I show that although there have been some improvements to the field, not as much has changed as we might like.

Queerness as a Problem

In this section, I explore how being non-heterosexual or non-cisgender is portrayed as a problem in many of these works.

For many queer people, coming out to themselves and to others is one of the first steps they take as they embark on living a queer life. This can be a difficult situation for many, as they may face fear, anger, disappointment, or other negative reactions from friends and family. Most people move beyond this and either limit their interactions with those who are not accepting, or learn to ignore such responses. In either case, queer people go on to get an education, find jobs, have partners and/or children, make friends, enjoy travel and hobbies, and otherwise live their lives. Coming out, then, does not define a queer life; it is merely one part of it. While there is definitely a need for coming-out stories, the fact that such a large number of LGBTQ books for children and young adults focus on coming out and related stresses encourages readers to believe that for queer people, coming out is difficult and upsetting, and also is one of the main issues that they face, and that it is a defining feature of LGBTQ lives and personalities. As Kanner puts it, "the lives of the gay and lesbian teen and adult characters revolve almost exclusively around the issue of their homosexuality; and gay and lesbian characters are included simply because of their gayness rather than because of their intrinsic interest or complexity." (n.d.:n.p.) One could easily figure out, however, that for queers, just like for any group of people, life is comprised of many challenges and many accomplishments; there are issues to do with education, health, finances, family, friends, romance, and more.

Therefore, as Table 1 shows, out of the thirty-two English-language young adult novels I discuss in this book twenty-three, or 72%, deal with coming out. Out of the twenty-three, twenty-one, or 91%, show difficult things happening to LGBTQ people as they come out. This in turn suggests that being LGBTQ (or being in the same household as someone who is LGBTQ) is stressful. In the other books, either the LGBTQ person is a side character – often there for comic relief, it seems, in the case of gay men – or the story starts after the person has already come out and instead focuses on the character finding a boyfriend/girlfriend or other matters or the person never actually comes out (as in Perihan Magden's novel, where the potentially lesbian character is portrayed as obsessive and crazy, and never admits to her sexuality). I only include YA novels here in these statistics instead of also including picture books and middle-grade due to the differences in style and subject matter. However, it is worth pointing out that out of the thirty-two total young adult novels, twenty-three include stress, whether due to coming-out or being bullied or teased, having feelings of shame or worry, having problems with relatives and/or friends, and so on. Sometimes the stress comes from having a queer relative and being teased about that or wanting to hide it. In other words, over 70% of these texts suggest that queerness is a problem or causes problems.

Total number of YA novels	Total number that feature coming out	Percentage of coming-out stories	Number that suggest that coming out is stressful	Percentage of stressful coming-out stories
32	23	72%	21	91%

Table 1: Stressful coming-out stories.

What this focus on coming out suggests to a reader is that accepting oneself as LGBTQ and being accepted by friends, relatives, and society is one of the main aspects of queer lives, and that this is a particularly stressful situation. This emphasises the idea that being non-norm is upsetting, difficult, and problematic, and it may make young readers think twice before coming out themselves. It may also highlight to young non-LGBTQ readers that something is wrong with those who are LGBTQ and that they deserve any stress or pressure they feel.

In what follows, I give many examples from some of these books that features stressful coming-out stories. This may feel like a relentlessly negative section, but I feel all the examples are important to show just how pervasive this problem of depiction really is.

In Maureen Johnson's *The Bermudez Triangle*, Mel finally begins to label herself as gay. The narrator says, "She'd absolutely known. The only thing she'd never done was write the word in the caption of the self-portrait that she kept in her head. That kept it from being real – because if it was real, she would have to deal with *reality* – and who even knew what the reality of being a lesbian was? That meant coming out and all kinds of complicated things that she really hadn't felt like thinking before." (2004:44-5, italics original) This quote suggests how difficult coming out can be; it is "complicated" and it means "deal[ing] with reality", which is not something all teenagers – or indeed all people of any age – are prepared to do. For Mel, the ramifications are mostly in relation to her friends, because they are not quite sure how to relate to her anymore.

Nina, for example, worries that she might be gay since her two best friends are (2004:111), and she is uncertain whether she can point out her outfit to Mel, or whether that will mean that Mel then looks at her body in a lascivious way (2004:117). Mel's girlfriend, Avery, is unwilling to come out, or at least she is unwilling to label herself; she sees herself as being with Mel, rather than as having a particular sexuality (as on 2004:152). This also causes stress for Mel, because she seems to want a girlfriend who will commit wholeheartedly. In fact, Avery cheats on Mel with a boy, because she views their relationship as an "experiment" (2004:184). The description of this is, "She'd only wanted to test it out, just to see how it made her feel. The way she saw it, her whole relationship with Mel was one big experiment, so the rules didn't always apply. She wasn't cheating – she was checking her homosexuality quotient." (ibid.)[28] So Mel has trouble with her friends and her girlfriend, and she also faces stress at home when she comes out. Her mother tells her, "I'm not going to support this kind of lifestyle. Neither is your father, and neither is Jim. Don't expect us to pay for your college or for your living expenses. If this is how you're going to be, then you'd better be prepared for some reality, little girl." (2004:325) In this novel, then, coming out brings about a whole set of problems, many of them stressful and difficult to handle; interestingly, a number of them seem to have to do with facing "reality", as though the reality of being queer is always an unhappy one.

Kim in Julie Burchill's book *Sugar Rush* falls for her best friend and the novel can be read as a coming-out tale. However, Kim seems to refuse this, willing to admit that she has a crush on Maria, but not that she is a lesbian. She instead mocks "[p]oor gay teenagers", never considering herself one of them. This long quote sums up her feelings:

> I suppose you're wondering why I'm not more het up about my new feelings for Maria. Well, I told you I was level-headed, didn't I, and naturally as a good little library-ticket-holding girl with liberal parents

> I've read all those novels which bend over backwards to reassure you that it's perfectly normal for your haywire hormones to make you believe that you're in love with your same-sex role model. Whatever.
>
> It was 'only natural', wasn't it, to get a crush on someone of the same sex who seemed to have all the qualities – beauty, confidence, absence of parent who brought oversized jars with French words written on them into the house, thus driving away other parent, that you wanted for yourself? If you really WERE a proper gay teenager, you'd get so much I-hear-you-and-it's-only-natural-at-your-age eyewash from parents and agony aunts about loving someone of the same gender that you could easily end up totally confused and isolated, in fact more so than years ago, when they were telling you it was a filthy sin.
>
> Poor gay teenagers! I thought smugly as I eyed my treacherous, respectable self in my bedroom mirror. So lonely, so sad, so…stuck. Not like me, who's totally on top of her totally temporary pash for the naughtiest girl in the school. (2004:49-50, capitals original)

Here, Kim emphasises how stressful it must be for gay teens, while simultaneously distancing herself from them, though she is obviously also mocking herself to a certain extent. The novel does turn into a coming-out tale of sorts, but her "pash" for Maria only leads to distress, as Maria says that Kim is "perving" on her (2004:118) and is a "pervy" person (2004:165), they scarcely have sex (2004:180-1, 189), and Kim is forced to watch as Maria flirts with and sleeps with a range of boys (2004:121, 207). Meanwhile, she sees bullying in school but says it is just part of life and young people will grow out of it (2004:191-3). This may be a healthy attitude in that she does not allow herself to be upset by it, but it seems to accept that LGBTQ young people – and, as she puts it, people with red hair or glasses, or people who answer questions in class – should and will be bullied, which is a defeatist attitude. Stressful is probably an understatement in terms of Kim's life.

Another example is Aidan Chambers's *Dance on My Grave*, where the main character's love for another young man wreaks havoc, including infidelity, death, parental rejection, trouble at school, a break-in at a funeral home, and more. While Hal does not ever to say to his parents that he was having a relationship with Barry or that he is, as he puts it, "a bosom-pal freak" (1982:45), they suspect and seem to keep themselves apart from him. Barry's mother at first seems to think that Hal is a different sort of young man from the "other boys he knows [who] lead him astray" (1982:76). Later, after Barry has died, his mother seems to acknowledge the relationship and she will not allow Hal in the house because she blames him (1982:183), calling him a "vicious nasty boy…[who] should be put away" (1982:189). Here, too, then, a teenager exploring his non-norm sexuality is portrayed in a very difficult situation, with many extreme, upsetting experiences.

In Ellen Wittlinger's *Hard Love*, Marisol, a teenage lesbian, tells her friend about what coming out involves: "It means you stop lying. You tell the truth even if it's painful, especially if it's painful. To everybody, your parents included." (1999:27) For her, it was painful to a certain extent, particularly in relation to her father. She says:

> When I opened the closet door my mother assured me I could always count on her support, but she cried for days with the bathroom door locked. She was mourning expectations, I think: dresses and a wedding, boyfriends and babies, things she was looking forward to. (One of those things even I had been looking forward to. I still am.)

> My father didn't say anything to me for several days, but I heard the two of them talking at night in their bedroom. She was trying to convince him that it would be all right, that it was not perverse, that I was still their beloved child. It's been more than a year now, and my father has never discussed my lesbianism with me, but he speaks to me again and pretends nothing has changed.
>
> My mother, within a week, had joined PFLAG (Parents and Friends of Lesbians and Gays) and announced to me that the two of us would march together in the Gay Pride parade. I know this makes me lucky. I know there are parents who would rage and scream and throw their children out of the house after an admission like mine. And still I resent them. One denies and one embraces. My father wears a blindfold, and my mother wants to out-gay me! I barely know what it means to be homosexual myself, and she's racing ahead of me, reading all the literature, consulting experts, wanting to "explore my feelings." I don't want to explore lesbianism with my mother, at least not now. (1999:43-3)

For Marisol, her mother initially mourned the daughter she had expected and wanted, but now is supportive, although perhaps too much so. Her father, on the other hand, pretends that his daughter's sexuality is either asexual or heterosexual, refusing to acknowledge what she told him. So Marisol does "stop lying" and does thereby experience pain, but luckily for her, the end result is not quite as extreme as it is for some of the characters in other texts mentioned here.

In another text by Ellen Wittlinger, *Parrotfish*, coming out is again described as equalling freedom and honesty. Grady, the transgender protagonist, says he came out "[b]ecause I was tired of lying.

And the truth was, inside the body of this strange, never-quite-right girl hid the soul of a typical, average, ordinary boy." (2007:8-9) Again, there is a strong emphasis on honesty as being the reason for coming out. But here too, what sounds like a positive move leads to some challenging situations. Grady comes out as transgender and has to face discrimination and bullying at school, plus a distinct lack of support from some family members and teachers. One of the big issues revolves around naming, and the right for Grady to choose his own name, and thereby his own identity. When Grady tells his family that he would prefer to be called Grady instead of Angela, his sister says, "It's a stupid name...what if we all decided to go and change our names? What if I decided I'd rather be called Cinderella or something?" (2007:6) A teacher likewise shows disdain in regard to the name change: "Angela, it seems to me that changing one's name is nothing more than an attention-getting device. I see no reason to disrupt my classroom just because you've made a rash, momentary decision. You may decide by tomorrow that you want to change your name back again!" (2007:45) The principal agrees with the teacher, telling Grady, "You don't understand what you're letting yourself in for, Angela. There's no need to go overboard. We're a liberal community—dress boyishly if you like—but to change your name and announce it to everyone? What's the point of that? Terrible idea." (2007:53) Beyond the issue of his name, Grady is also subject to verbal abuse and to mean tricks in school (2007:57-9, 79-80, 94, 179).

Another trans character, J, in Cris Beam's *I Am J*, tries to present as male before officially coming out as trans and being affirmed male, and also faces problems. "Other girls, of course, rejected J, saw only the most superficial aspects of him-the way he was so butch and tough-looking-and they'd run away, thinking he was a freak or a dyke or both. Something predatory, something hard and impenetrable." (2011:23) Others call him a "faggot" and ask what gender he is (2011:48-9). When he tries to explain to friends that he is trans, the response is often confusion (as on 2011:192-4 or 288-9), although confusion about what being transgender means is certainly better than his father, Manny, saying that he "thinks we did something wrong raising you." (2011:220) J eventually runs away from home and ends up switching schools and going to live with a friend and her mother rather than returning home. Neither of his parents are supportive, although his mother does improve by the end of the novel. Luna, too, in Julie Ann Peters's novel has to leave home because she is unable to be fully herself while residing with her parents. See the chapter on diversity for more on transgender characters and the focus on problems in novels featuring them.

Another novel that features problems at school is *Annie on My Mind* by Nancy Garden. The novel is dated, in that it was published thirty years ago, so some of the scenarios are less likely now. Nonetheless, impressionable readers might feel that Liza goes through an awful lot due to her love for Annie. She gets in trouble at school initially for an ear-piercing fundraiser but then because she is caught with Annie. The reaction might seem to us to be extreme: Liza is threatened with losing her position as president of the school's student council. The teacher who found them says to another student, in front of Liza, "Sodom and Gomorrah are all around us...There is ugliness and sin and self-indulgence in this house...And to think... that the president of student council is a—a..." (1982:167). She cannot bring herself to finish the sentence. Liza is told by the head of the school, "I do not understand the—the pull of...abnormal sex" and she refers to Liza's "unwise and intense out-of-school friendship." (1982:183). Liza is suspended, asked to give up her position as president, and removed from the student fund drive. Someone leaves a note in her locker that says "Liza Lesie." (1982:197) Even when the case goes to the tribunal in school, Liza does not come out to her parents or her brother, because she is attempting to protect them (as on 1982:187-8). Her father tells her, "Liza, damn it, I always thought I was—well, okay about things like homosexuality. But now when I find out that my own daughter might be...I want you to be happy in other ways [not just becoming an architect], too, as your mother is—to have a husband and children. I know you can do both." (1982:191) He thinks she cannot have children if she is gay and that she will not be happy, and this is clearly the same view that her teachers and classmates have.

Charlie in Sara Manning's *Pretty Things* says that his friends dumped him when they found out he was gay:

> I came out, announced to the world that I was here, queer, and they could bloody well get used to it. And all those friends who I used to play football with just dumped me. There was a little bit of name calling, an incident after school where someone tried to throw me headfirst into the path of an oncoming car, but mostly my big gay announcement was a cue for everyone to move on. Like I was the handrail in a disabled toilet – something that was there but that they'd never need. Well, that and I might as well have had a sign painted on my head that I fancied boys. Even the fat, ugly ones who smelled of stale perspiration. Which, actually, not so much. (2005:105)

As in some of the other books, there is some dark humour here; Charlie tells his sad tale while also making light of it, but this does not hide the pain he must have experienced.

Jody in Hayley Long's *What's Up With Jody Barton?* also has trouble as a young gay man. He comes out gradually and in fact his gayness is used in a way that suggests the author finds it to be a shocking or humorous plot device. The reader is initially led to believe that Jody is a female, because his twin is Jolene and they are called "sisters" by friends and he subtly states that "[e]ven I'm not as flat[-chested] as her [Jolene]" (2012:37). Jody is even referred to as "sulky Sue" by their father, which perhaps makes readers of a certain age think of Johnny Cash's "boy called Sue", but this is not likely to occur to the target audience of young people. Jody and Jolene each have a crush on the same boy and it seems for the first one hundred pages as though they are simply sisters who want the same boyfriend. There is then the big reveal where the reader learns that Jody is in fact male (2012:108), and this perhaps is meant to challenge the reader's assumptions, but it has the effect of making homosexuality seem surprising or weird. Jody kisses his sister's boyfriend, who taunts him, calls him "bent", and spits phlegm on his bedroom carpet (2012:110), and later threatens him (2012:176). Other classmates call Jody "Battyman" (2012:194) and he gets bullied on Facebook with comments such as "WASSUP GAY BOY?" and "LOOK AT ME FUNNY AND U R DEAD." (2012:198, capitals original). When Jody stands up to his father, his father is pleased and says, "My boy is turning out to be a right proper geezer! There ain't nothing Fairy Mary about that one, thank God!" (2012:143) Eventually, Jody's parents come around and his sister and friends accept him, and a rainbow even appears in the sky "[w]here just a moment earlier I'd seen only varying shades of grey" (2012:249), but for most of the book, Jody's homosexuality is a stressful aspect of his identity.

In *Thinking Straight* by Robin Reardon, Taylor, the protagonist, does not exactly come out but rather is found out. As soon as that happens, his parents pack him away to a Christian programme to be cured. Needless to say, much suffering ensues, and he does not get cured. One of the other participants in this programme commits suicide, and it is hinted that he is far from the first (2008:134). The preacher even says, "Better a boy like Ray should take his own life than return to his gay lifestyle. Homosexuality leads to death of the spirit. If he dies before he commits himself to that pit, God may still take his soul." (2008:133) What this suggests is that modern society has not moved far beyond the idea that to be LGBTQ means ending up dead far sooner than one should. Reardon's work may sound anti-gay in some ways, but as a long essay on her website, "The Case for Acceptance", makes clear, she seems to feel that LGBTQ people are not accepted or treated well by society and should be. She appears to consider herself an ally and her work a form of activism (Reardon, n.d.:n.p.). While I do not doubt her good intentions, I find that her work can be quite stereotyped in its portrayal of gay men, and it can sometimes reflect the belief that being queer is difficult.

Reardon also wrote another YA book about a young gay male, *A Secret Edge*. In this text, when Jason comes out, he is called a "faggot" and is physically threatened by schoolmates (2007:15). His aunt and uncle are raising him, and his aunt is positive when she receives the news, and says she had suspected that that was the case (2007:82). She says:

> I wanted so much to let you know it would be okay, that you were okay, regardless. But I was afraid even to say things that were obviously accepting. Of homosexuality, I mean. I was afraid you might think I was pushing it on you. So I decided you'd have to discover it for yourself, and then there'd be something to talk about...It is okay, you know. And you are the same boy you always were. (ibid.)

Jason's uncle, on the other hand, is deeply disappointed. He says to his wife:

> I've failed...I couldn't give you children, and when fate gave us Jason—I've let my brother down, Aud. I've failed him, and I've failed Jason...No one should have to live like that. He'll be hated, ostracized. He won't be able to marry or have children...I know what it's like not to be able to have children. But at least my reason isn't something everyone around me disapproves of. They don't think it's what I deserve. (2007:90)

Jason overhears this and finds out how his uncle feels, which obviously does not make him feel positive about his life.

Also, in this novel, Jason has a girlfriend and when he comes out to her, she sarcastically tells him, "Jason, I can't tell you how delighted I am that I was the one who helped you figure that out. You've made me feel like a real woman." (2007:144-5) He tries to comfort her by saying that him being gay has nothing to do with her attractiveness to men, but she does not accept his explanation (ibid.). So for Jason, the people around him tend to make his gayness about them rather than about him, and they are not always as supportive as they could be.

Jason's boyfriend, Raj, has parents who are not very accepting of his gayness (2007:65), and he eventually is mocked and beaten up by other young people (2007:233). While the text ends positively, in that Jason saves Raj and also Jason's uncle eventually becomes more accepting, coming out is portrayed as very stressful, and society as closed and unwelcoming.

The reaction of Liza's father in *Annie on My Mind* and Jason's uncle *A Secret Edge* – i.e. that their children will not have children or be able to get married – is a common response to a teen coming out in these books (see the chapter on marriage for more on this). Another example is when James' father in *My Heartbeat* by Garret Freymann-Weyr says that while life "outside the mainstream" offers some opportunities, such as helping people be better artists, he would rather his son be straight because being gay is "a limited way to live" (2002:110-1). A number of these books do indeed suggest the queer lives are limited.

A parent who goes even further than that is in Perry Moore's *Hero*. Thom Creed's father is virulently homophobic, saying of queers: "They are the ultimate downfall of our society, too, because if it were up to them to proliferate, there wouldn't be any reproduction and we would fail to continue as a species." (2007:31-2). Thom is afraid to tell his father. He thinks, "In that brief glimpse [into his father's thoughts], I could see what he was thinking behind that fixed stare. There would be no grandkids, there would be no more Creed family bloodline, nothing else to look forward to. From that point on, I'd become the last, most devastating disappointment in what he thought his life had added up to—one overwhelming failure." (2004:27) Being LGBTQ is considered to equate with being single – or at least not being openly in a relationship – and with being childless, so for many of the characters who come out, they receive responses similar to those that Thom, Liza, Jason, and others get. Incidentally, when Thom comes out, he is dropped from the basketball team (2004:39) and it is implied that his father is stuck in a low-level, manual job because of his son's sexuality, or, as it is put in the novel, because "[h]is kid likes dick" (2004:369). Moore was quoted as saying:

> I have always been enthralled with comic books and superheroes, and I've always believed there should be a gay superhero. Not as a joke, not as a supporting character, not as a victim, not as a token, but as a real front-and-centre hero. I've always been surprised by how few gay heroes there are in comic books, and I decided I would write the definitive coming-of-age story of the world's first gay teen superhero. (in Geen, 2011:n.p.)

While Moore certainly did write a novel about a "gay teen superhero", it is nonetheless a little disappointing that his superhero has so many difficulties to overcome. On the other hand, of course, it creates an appealing and typical narrative arc. In general, it can seem as though parents are protective of and scared for their children and their "limited" futures.

In yet another text, Carol Plum-Ucci's *What Happened to Lani Garver*, the gay character Lani is teased and tormented and at the end, it is unclear whether he has been killed or whether he has escaped. The main character is naïve and shows little understanding of Lani, but the message is once again that queerness is a problem.

As Kanner writes in her short piece on "Young Adult Literature", "the assumption that being a lesbian or a gay man is physically dangerous and sometimes life-threatening pervades these books. More than half of the lesbian and gay protagonists in young adult literature meet with physical harm or tragedy" (n.d.:n.p.).

Most of these works take place in contemporary times, so it may be unfair to compare those set in earlier periods. Still, it is worth pointing out that upper-class Louisa in Victorian London in Jane Eagland's *Wildthorn* is put in a mental institution when her proclivities are discovered. In part, some of her problems stem from her wanting to have a career, which was not acceptable in that time and place (as on 2009:283-5), but she is deemed insane because she kisses her female cousin in an inappropriate manner.

For some characters, the difficulties and/or abuse is so extreme or so painful to handle that once they come out, they have to leave their hometowns and/or their families in order to find peace and acceptance. J in Beam's novel, as mentioned above, moves in with his friend and her mother. H.F. and her best friend Bo in Julia Watts' *Finding H.F.* leave their small, Baptist town in the south of the United States, because they find it too prejudiced. H.F. fears coming out, not least because she is being raised by her Christian grandmother. H.F. says, "At least I'm not boy-crazy. If Memaw knew the truth—that I'm girl-crazy instead—I don't know what she'd do. Pray and cry and try to get me 'cured,' I reckon. One thing's for sure: She'd never understand it, and neither would most people in Morgan, Kentucky, which ain't exactly San Francisco, if you know what I mean." (2001:4-5) So she knows that her grandmother would not understand her lesbianism, nor would other people in their hometown. Although she has not yet explicitly come out, her homosexuality is suspected, as is Bo's. The two of them are repeatedly made fun of (as on 2001:26). H.F. says, "The sissy boys have it harder than the tomboys. If you're a boyish girl, other girls just snub you, but if you're a girlish boy, other boys beat the living hell out of you. Believe me, I've picked Bo up off the pavement more times than I can count." (2001:8) The first young woman that H.F. kisses gets "scared", "scared because I was [a lesbian] and she might be one too" (2001:61). Hence, H.F. and Bo eventually leave their bigoted town.

Another protagonist who chooses to leave is Ellie in Leanne Lieberman's *Gravity*. Ellie cannot reconcile her sexuality with her Judaism (see the diversity chapter for more on this), and not only faces potential rejection from her family, but also from her wider ethnic group. She is told by the rabbi's wife that being a lesbian is unacceptable and that should she feel herself tempted, she should recite a psalm or pinch herself (2008:97). Ellie worries about coming out because it means "being an abomination according to Jewish law" (2008:126). Besides this stress, she also must deal with an indecisive girlfriend who toys with her, creating additional worry. The anxiety causes her to rip her hair out until she begins to get a bald spot (see, for example, 2008:168). Ultimately, Ellie has to choose between her Orthodox religion and her sexuality, and she decides to leave.

In a few of the books, it is the parents of the protagonists who are LGBTQ (usually lesbian and sometimes gay; I have not found a single bisexual, transgender, or otherwise queer parent), rather than the young people themselves. For example, Holly in Nancy Garden's middle-grade book *Holly's Secret* gets tangled in a web of lies by trying to hide her mothers' lesbianism. She attempts to impress the popular girls in school and to be someone other than who she truly is. Eventually, she does tell the truth, but only after having been through significant stress. The book could be read as reminding readers that lying and hiding only cause problems and are not worth the pain they cause and the havoc they create. Julie Ann Peters' *Between Mom and Jo* is similar in that the main character suffers prejudice due to having lesbian mothers, but this is complicated further when his mothers separate; as Jo is not his biological mother, she has no legal right to him. This highlights the issues regarding legal rights in the U.S. and elsewhere (see more on this in the chapter on marriage). It is worth mentioning that both of these books seem aimed at pre-teens rather than young adults, so although they still include stress, it is clear that the stress is on a different level and is not related to the protagonists' own sexuality or gender.

Alex Sanchez's *Rainbow* trilogy is much more upbeat than some of the other texts referred to here, although it has other issues with stereotyping, as explored below in great detail. Nonetheless, coming out is not a simple matter for his three main characters. Two of the three main characters are athletic and both are on the receiving end of bullying and derogatory homophobic remarks from their teammates (2003:26, 87, 176, and other places). The school principal even accuses Jason of not caring about the team and of "jeopardiz[ing] [his] future" (2003:96) because of wanting to be open about his sexuality. Jason loses his scholarship to attend university (2003:212) and faces rejection from his father, while Kyle's parents react with confusion, especially when Kyle suggests he might turn down Princeton in order to go to the same local university as his friends (2003:115-120). The young men are asked what they might do in bed and they are told that that is "disgusting" (2003:205). Nelson's mother, on the other hand, is supportive and goes to meetings of Parents and Friends of Lesbians and Gays.

It is important to note that, as for Nelson in the *Rainbow* books, coming out to parents is not a bad experience for all queer young people in these books. One of the rare positive depictions of parental approval is in *Pink* by Lili Wilkinson. In this text, Ava's liberal parents are so pleased that she is a lesbian that they have a party for her. "When I first told my parents I was a lesbian, they threw me a coming-out party. Seriously. We had champagne and everything. It was the most embarrassing thing that'd ever happened to me." (2009:3) While this seems to be good news, Ava's parents are mocked for their extremely liberal attitudes, almost to the point of comparing them to conservative, homophobic people for the strength of their beliefs. Despite her parents' acceptance of her and the fact that she has a girlfriend, when Ava switches schools, she does not tell her new peers that she is gay, because she is unsure about what their reaction might be. Throughout the course of the book, Ava wonders if she might actually be attracted to men as well, but she is afraid to come out as bisexual in part because of the lack of approval. So although she is accepted to a certain extent – and of course familial acceptance is very important – she is not honest with everyone and also worries that there would be more acceptance for a homosexual than a bisexual person. Ava does not seem to have truly accepted herself – whether as bisexual, homosexual, or something else entirely; she plaintively tells a friend who accuses her of being ashamed that she just wants to be "normal" (2009:227). She immediately wonders if normality exists, but the fact that she longs for this state regardless shows her confusion and angst.

In still another text, classmates, friends, teachers, and relatives are all more or less accepting of a wide range of sexualities and gender identities. However, although it is a fun read, *Boy Meets Boy* by David Levithan is so over the top and unrealistic that rather than leaving the reader with a positive view, it instead highlights just how difficult it is to be LGBTQ in most of the world. For example, the novel takes place in the U.S., and the quarterback of the football team is a drag queen who regularly wears women's clothes to school, but receives no flak for it. This seems highly unlikely, so the book can be read as a utopian wish-fulfilment, but then again, it could show readers what society ought to be aiming towards. About this novel, Levithan has said, "I basically set out to write the book that I dreamed of getting as an editor - a book about gay teens that doesn't conform to the old norms about gay teens in literature (i.e. it has to be about a gay uncle, or a teen who gets beaten up for being gay, or about outcasts who come out and find they're still outcasts, albeit outcasts with their outcastedness in common.)" (n.d.:n.p.) Cart and Jenkins write that Levithan's *Boy Meets Boy* is "the first feel-good gay novel for teens" where the characters are "truly–even blithely–accepted and assimilated" (2006:145) and that "it represents a near-revolution in social attitudes and the publishing of GLBTQ books" (2006:146). And Abate and Kidd note that whereas early LGBTQ books were mainly written by non-queers, now they are more likely to have been written by queers, and that Levithan even "launched his writing career as such." (2011:7) In many cases, writers' own experiences and knowledge influence how they write, so perhaps an out author such as Levithan would be likely to write a different sort of book than a non-LGBTQ author.

A final example of a positive coming-out story is *Absolutely, Positively Not* by David LaRochelle. In this novel, Steven is a nice guy who goes square-dancing with his mother and is working on getting his driver's license. He thinks his male teacher is very handsome, but he tries to collect pictures of girls in bikinis and goes out on lots of dates. He also tries to get to know the jocks, so he can be inspired by them. However, his best friend Rachel and her parents seem to have figured out that he is gay and they are very laid-back about it when he finally realises it himself and tells them. His parents have a little more trouble initially, but everything ends up okay. He gets his license, goes to a gay youth group, and so on. It is a very easy path for Steven in the sense that everyone is accepting of his sexuality before he even realises it or accepts it himself. Few of the books are along these lines, however.

Wide Awake by David Levithan is one of the few YA books to not be a tale about coming out. It is about politics, but the main issue is whether it is possible to elect a gay Jewish president of the U.S. This still suggests that non-heterosexual people have problems because of their sexuality (i.e. if the American public is unwilling to vote for a gay person, this means that gayness is seen as different and problematic).

In sum, these texts tend to offer the message that coming out is a dramatic, stressful experience that may involve rejection, verbal and even physical abuse, problems in school or with friends or peers, and potentially even death.[29] As Jenkins writes, "Many of the gay/

lesbian characters in these books, particularly those who are young, lead isolated and lonely lives." (2011:155) While coming out is something that most LGBTQ people go through and thus there is a need for coming-out stories, this is a very restricted view of LGBTQ lives. Also, of course, being queer after coming out is shown as difficult. Cart and Jenkins write, "too many of these [books] were marred by stereotypical characters and predictable plots centered on the inherent misery of gay people's lives." (2006:17) In the online Encyclopedia of Gay, Lesbian, Bisexual, Transgender and Queer Culture, Kanner sums it up well:

> The greatest failure of gay and lesbian young adult fiction as a genre is that the works are generally plotted around the "problem" of homosexuality. Consequently, the lives of the gay and lesbian teen and adult characters revolve almost exclusively around the issue of their homosexuality; and gay and lesbian characters are included simply because of their gayness rather than because of their intrinsic interest or complexity. (n.d.:n.p.)

Queerness is not a problem, and ought not be treated as such in these books. But as the extensive examples show, it frequently is.

Causes of Queerness

Interestingly, it is not only coming out that creates stress for LGBTQ people in these books. In fact, many of the characters are portrayed as having other difficulties, generally related to their families of origin. This seems to imply the old notion that homosexuality (or bisexuality or transsexuality) is "caused" by something, such as a bad relationship with parents. This in turn leads to the erroneous idea that if queerness has a cause, it can also have a cure (as in *Thinking Straight* by Robin Reardon, or as suggested in Watts's

Finding H.F.). Or that it can be prevented. This is also a prejudicial message to give to readers.

For example, in Julie Burchill's book *Sugar Rush*, the main character's mother has just walked out on the family. It is after this that Kim switches schools and then meets the young woman she falls in love with. Thus there is implication that her lesbianism is "caused" by her absentee mother, which is strengthened by Kim saying that it is natural that she would be attracted to someone who has a mother in residence (2004:49-50). She also says that she had to play mother to her mother and now is playing mother to the woman she has feelings for (2004:156-7), which suggests that Kim is unable to form healthy relationships due to her mother.

Nelson in Alex Sanchez's *Rainbow* trilogy is raised by a single mother and Jason has an abusive, alcoholic father, so again this might lead to readers believing that only people from broken, unhealthy families might be LGBTQ. As Crisp puts it:

> T.C.J. [an acronym for "Tragic Closet Jock"] Jason's construction as the quintessential unemotional man comes as a result of his internalized homophobia; he desperately seeks the attention of his alcoholic father: a physically violent and verbally abusive man who consistently calls him names like "Stupid, Dummy, Fairy-Boy, Pansy." Although the novel distances itself from Jason's father (as readers, we are supposed to disagree with his viewpoint), it routinely implies that if his father were more affirmative of his "masculinity" as opposed to identifying him as "feminine," Jason may not have "turned out" gay. (2011:226-7)

Crisp does not recognise that Jason may have "turned out" bisexual, not gay, but other than that, he is completely right about the depiction of Jason.

H.F. in Julia Watts's *Finding H.F.* was raised by her single grandmother after her mother got pregnant and ran off. When H.F. as a teenager takes a road trip and finds her mother, her mother rejects her because of her lesbianism, and makes it clear that she wants nothing to do with her. Her mother says, "I mean, I'd understand it if you was some kind of famous teenage model or if you'd won the lottery and you came to find me to say, 'Look how rich I am, look at how great I turned out.' But coming down here the way you are, with your friend the way he is? Are you trying to embarrass me? You and your little faggoty little friend want to make me ashamed, to make me feel like it's my fault you turned out to be—." (2001:150) It is indeed hinted that it might be her mother's fault that she turned out to be gay.

J, in Cris Beam's *I Am J*, is told by his father that he is "sick" (2011:316) and when his mother lies in order to hide his being trans, J blames Carolina for not being home enough when he was child and maybe causing this in some way (2011:221). Although J may just be lashing out in anger, this does promote the idea that there can be a reason for queerness that stems from the parents and how they raise their children.

Disturbingly, there is even an insinuation in *Thinking Straight* that being sexually abused can cause gayness. As mentioned previously, Reardon seems to want to produce works that are supportive of the LGBTQ community, but perhaps because she focuses on gay males and is not a gay man herself, her books do not always succeed, and they can be quite problematic. The writing and the plot are overly simplistic, and while the overall message in this book is that such treatments do not in fact work, the fact is that there are people who believe in this aversion therapy. As some survivors of this sort of treatment recount, it can be hugely damaging (Millington, 2012), and while it is likely beneficial to raise awareness of aversion therapy/ex-gay treatment, especially its dangers, authors need to be careful how they do it, so as not to actually suggest that it might work or that it is possible to "cure" queerness. A quote in the book says, "And his [Ray's] uncle used to, you know, hurt him—when he was younger. He was all mixed up about it. He *really* wanted not to be gay, I think partly because he thought that made him safe." (2008:224, italics original) This suggests that because Ray was raped by his uncle, he turned to gay behaviours for comfort and familiarity. Meanwhile, in that same book, a reverend tries to "cure" homosexual young men by anally raping them, which he considers aversion therapy. The reverend says, "What we're going to do, my special boy, is teach you not to eat cookie batter. It's interesting, you know? You can't get too much of God's love, but you can get too much of Satan's lustful sin. And just like the cookie batter, when you've finally had too much, you won't want more." (2008:256) And lest young Taylor think the creepy reverend is enjoying the "cure", he is told, "Remember I'm doing God's bidding. What happens next gives me no pleasure. No pleasure at all. If it weren't for God's instructions, I'd be risking my own soul to save yours. But God has commanded me." (2008:256-7)

In other words, several of these books promote the idea that one can clearly identify reasons for someone to be queer, and that these reasons are negative life experiences rather than genetic or random. Absent parents, abusive or alcoholic parents, or traumatic sexual experiences can all cause someone to be LGBTQ. Readers might thus come to believe that if this is known and understood, then it should be possible to prevent and/or cure queerness.

An additional issue in relation to this is that if queerness is a sort of disease that can be prevented and/or cured, it is possible that others can be "infected" by it. In *Dad David, Baba Chris and Me* by Ed Merchant, the protagonist wonders if he will turn out gay like his two fathers (2010:16), as though being gay is a vertical rather than horizontal identity (Solomon, 2012:2). And when Nina in *The Bermudez Triangle* finds out that her two best female friends are having a relationship with one another, she has a momentary sense of panic:

> What were the chances that both of my best friends would be gay?
>
> This was a good point. After all, didn't that say something about her? And she was part of a *triangle.*
>
> Hello!
>
> She was so gay.
>
> No, she wasn't. She had a boyfriend. She was writing to him now to get advice about her gay friends.
>
> A boyfriend who lived three thousand miles away. How convenient! Unconsciously she had been setting herself up for this all along because she must have known that deep down, she was *a total and complete lesbian*, part of a lifelong lesbian trio. (Johnson, 2004:111, italics original)

Obviously, this is humorously extreme, but for readers with less experience with the LGBTQ community, it is certainly possible that they might believe they could catch queerness from friends or relatives.

In short, many of these books may "infect" readers with false beliefs about LGBTQ people. In some cases, they suggest that there are clear reasons for someone "turning out" queer and/or that there could be a cure. This is likely to promote stereotyped ideas of queerness rather than to encourage readers to see LGBTQ people as more or less the same as anyone else, except for their sexuality and/or gender identity.

Looking Queer

Another way in which many of these books endorse stereotypes is in how the LGBTQ characters are depicted in regard to how they look and act. While it is in some cases hard to separate appearances from behaviour, here I am going to attempt to do just that, in order to show just how inescapable and omnipresent the stereotyped portrayals of LGBTQ characters are. Still, I am doing this with the proviso that I am aware that there are no clear-cut divisions in someone's character in regard to how they talk, look, interact with others, feel, and live. In this section, I look briefly at picture books first, then move on to young adult novels, focusing first on gay males then females.

One of the issues that comes up most often in these books in regard to stereotypes is that if there is an LGBTQ person, they look a particular way. In picture books, the stereotyped appearances tend to be shown through the illustrations rather than through the words, so this quickly and visually gets across the stereotyped ideas. For example, the cover of Ken Setterington's *Mom and Mum are Getting Married* shows two women, one with longer hair and a skirt and the other with short hair and trousers. The one in the skirt is depicted throughout the book itself as having larger breasts, while the other one is fairly flat-chested. In other words, this is a fairly typical butch-femme dynamic. Meanwhile, as Ford discusses, the pictures in Lesléa Newman's *Heather Has Two Mommies* portray Heather as androgynous, while the mothers look as though they are from the 1970s in terms of their haircuts and clothing styles (2011:205), and they "resemble composites assembled from a butch/femme stereotype clip-art file" (2011:204). Encouraging readers of any age to think that lesbian pairings come with one butch and one femme in turn strengthens the incorrect assumption that all couples – regardless of sexuality – include one "male" and one "female".

The novels tend to go further than the picture books because they verbalise what is only implied, albeit implied very strongly, in illustrations. People, both LGBTQ and not, seem to hold a range of assumptions about the appearance of those of non-norm sexualities and gender identities, and they show no compunction in announcing them regularly, even if this encourages others to believe the stereotypes as well.

As previously mentioned, Taylor in Robin Reardon's *Thinking Straight* is in a programme meant to "cure" homosexuals. A new young man at the programme asks him, "You here because you're a fairy?" (2008:288) Taylor seems to find this offensive, because according to him, he does not "look" gay. He thinks:

> Now why would he ask that question? Even when I'm at home, there's nothing femme about my appearance, my voice—no giveaways. And in here, where every guy dresses in almost exactly the same boring khaki crap, there's really no way to tell a gay guy unless he's outright swishing. (ibid.)

Even though Reardon's book is gay-positive, she encourages readers to believe that most – or at least a significant proportion of – gay men are "femme" and "swish". Does this mean that any man who swishes is gay? Does it mean that homosexual men should avoid appearing femme so that they are not recognisably gay? Similarly, when Jody thinks his mother knows that he is gay, in *What's Up With Jody Barton?* by Hayley Long, he worries because "[i]t's not as if I go *gaying* around or anything. At least, I don't think I do." (2012:131, italics original) "Gaying around" perhaps can be defined as swishing and being effeminate.

Carlos in Alex Sanchez's *Getting It* is not gay, but he has turned to his gay friend Sal for advice on clothing and getting women. Sal recommends that Carlos wear a pink shirt, but Carlos is not keen on this idea:

> "I'm not wearing pink. What's wrong with the black one?"
>
> "First try this. Girls *love* guys in pink. It makes you look sensitive."
>
> "It'll make me look like a—" He started to say something but changed his mind. "Like a wimp."...
>
> He took the pink shirt into the dressing room, giving it a precautionary sniff. When he stepped out to the mirror, he thought the shirt looked totally gay. (2006:60, italics original)

Carlos thinks that wearing pink makes him look gay, and this idea is confirmed when his father tells him that he looks like a "*maricón*" (2006:62, italics original), which is Spanish for "faggot". Carlos finds that he actually feels comfortable in the shirt, but then his friends mock him too (2006:64). Sanchez's work tends towards the message-heavy, so of course Carlos does wear the shirt and does become comfortable with both his own sexuality and Sal's and does get an inner makeover, which perhaps may suggest that the author tries to demolish stereotyped ideas, but the way he highlights them first encourages readers to think that certain clothes and certain appearances are indeed gay.

In Sarra Manning's *Pretty Things*, Walker says about Charlie, "He's not really gay. I mean he is but he isn't. He's not all nudges and innuendo like Graham Norton on speed. In fact, apart from the Gayer T-shirt, you'd never know it to look at him." (2005:53) The implication here is that it is usually easy to tell a queer person from their appearance, and that a "really" gay male is "nudges and innuendo like [comedian and talk show host] Graham Norton".

In Lili Wilkinson's *Pink*, Ava also connects appearance to being gay. For her, black is what a proper lesbian should wear, and her desire for pink suggests that she may not be quite as homosexual as she had believed. There is also a distinct gay appearance for men, in her mind. She switches schools and at the new school, she meets Jules, a gay young man who is a member of the stage crew, and hence is one of many artistic homosexuals that appear in these books. When Ava finds out that he prefers men, she thinks, "He didn't *look* gay." (2009:61, italics original) Presumably, a young woman who is herself unsure about her sexuality and about how she fits into various categories might be a little more thoughtful before making such reductive comments, but this book never seems to challenge such ideas. Jules goes on to elucidate Ava by saying:

> There's two kinds of gay...There's normal-gay, which is people like me who happen to like boys, but are otherwise functioning members of society. And then there's ghey-with-an-h. Gheys-with-an-h have shiny, shiny skin from too much exfoliating. Gheys-with-an-h constantly apply lip gloss – not lip *balm*, but lip *gloss*. Cherry-flavoured. And they wear women's jeans...Oh, and they walk like ladies. Not women. (2009:64-5, italics original)

He, of course, is a "gay", but not a "ghey", and he is quick to point out, "just because I'm a homosexual, it doesn't mean I'm a mincing queer." (2009:66) So Jules places gay men into two types and distances himself from what can be considered the feminised type. He even seems homophobic.

Some authors seem to view the feminine and the feminised types as two different categories. Alex Sanchez's *Rainbow* trilogy is one example of that. The series trades in stereotypes, both in terms of appearance and behaviour. There are three main characters, and they are each a distinct "gay" archetype. Jason is a jock, whose body is athletic and admired; Kyle is the somewhat softer, more feminine type; and Nelson is the camp, feminised character. He dyes his hair "flaming pink" (Sanchez, 2005:4), has green-painted toenails (2005:24), has rainbow beads and a hula girl in his car, along with a sticker that says "I Can't Even Drive Straight" (2005:28), wears women's glasses (2005:36), and eventually dresses up as a woman (2005:71). The three young men's behaviour likewise reinforces the idea that there are three very different but recognisable types of gay men, as will be discussed below.

In a short story in a collection of romance-related stories for teenagers, "The Young Stalker's Handbook" by Sarah Rees Brennan, the following is one of the very first sentences: "'Just because he's wearing skin-tight gold trousers doesn't necessarily mean he's a homosexual.'...In a way, I feel like that sentence summed up my personality completely. Anyone who overheard us would have known immediately that I was optimistic, a dreamer, and utterly clueless about men." (2011:17) The main character is a "clueless" "dreamer", and this suggests that it should be obvious to most people that a man "wearing skin-tight gold trousers" must be gay.

There are many stereotyped depictions of the young lesbians as well. In *Sugar Rush*, Sugar asks Kim if she is gay and says that since she is pretty "it's not creepy [or] sad" (2004:94), thus implying that it would be if Kim were not pretty. Sugar further encourages the idea that it is a disgusting, depressing problem when unattractive women are lesbians by saying, in reference to some women who apparently fit that bill, "[r]eally tragic...Imagine ever being like them women. Growing up to be some sad, ugly dyke. I'd rather be dead." (2004:194)

Strangely, the idea that lesbians are unattractive is not uncommon. In *Pretty Things* by Sarra Manning, Brie says "being a lesbian is kinda cool as you can eat what the hell you like 'cause other lesbians don't mind if you're a chubster." (2005:78) In other words, lesbians are heavy, but that does not matter (see the chapter on diversity for more on weight), possibly because there is the implication that women do not have sex, so sexual attractiveness does not come into the equation (see the chapter on sex for more on this).

Also, Brie does not want to spend time with Daisy, and she explains this as being because Daisy "looks" gay and this might rub off on her. "One, she's a lesbian. And two, she looks like a lesbian. So people might think if I'm with her that I'm one too and it's hard enough to think of anything to say to boys without them not bothering with me at all 'cause they think I'm gay." (2005:59)

In *Pink*, which was referred to above, the lesbians are not unattractive; on the contrary, they are portrayed as attractive and of a very particular type. Ava's girlfriend Chloe is a stereotypical angry lesbian, who wears all black, and smokes, and is too cool for everything. Chloe likes to hang out in a lesbian bar, about which Ava says, "I'd just always called it the Lesbian Batcave because it was dark and cavelike, and full of serious-looking lesbians wearing black." (2009:27) Everyone there, including Chloe, is "artsy" and "very cool and intellectual", but Ava "didn't really get their art, and I didn't like the thick black coffee that they drank constantly." (ibid.) As already mentioned, the premise of the book hinges on the fact that Ava wants to wear pink, and is ashamed of and confused by this. It is apparently wrong, somehow, for a lesbian to wear bright colours and to be uninterested in art or to not want to drink coffee. While the book eventually seems to suggest that it is possible for there to be many kinds of lesbians, just as there are many kinds of straight women, the impression it gives throughout much of it is that if a young woman does not want to look and act like the other lesbians, she must be doing it wrong.

The short story "Never Have I Ever" by Courtney Gillette features a young woman who has a boyfriend but is also attracted to other females. Amber considers which women she finds attractive and she likes one who "had short messy hair and a mean face. She was wearing combat boots and cargo pants, vaguely boyish..." and Amber then says "she looks like she could be gay or something." (2011:155) So again, there is the implication that it is easy to tell who is queer just by clothes and appearance.

In *The Bermudez Triangle*, Avery is called a "dyke"

(as on Johnson, 2004:159) and feels she has a typical dykey appearance:

> She [Avery] looked down at herself. Jeans, a grungy vintage T-shirt for some plumbing company, heavy shoes and a leather cuff bracelet. She could feel her cropped hair brushing against the back of her neck. The only make-up she had on was some dark liner around her eyes. Why didn't she just put on an I'm Not Gay, But My Girlfriend Is shirt and get it over with?
>
> ...Only Avery would be seen as the rough dyke who lusted after the cheerleaders and couldn't be trusted in the locker room after gym. Other girls would put their books up over their boobs when they passed her in the hall, and they'd stop fixing their make-up when she walked into the bathroom. They would see her as a predator trying to sneak a peek or cop a feel, even if she just bumped into them in the doorway or as she squeezed in between rows of desks. (2004:161)

In other words, Avery's clothes, hairstyle, jewellery, and minimal make-up signal that she might be a lesbian, and this would make other young women wary of her. A queer woman, after all, cannot be trusted to be near other women without "trying to sneak a peek or cop a feel", and if Avery is recognisably queer, she will be seen as this creepy "predator". The idea that people can figure out who is LGBTQ simply from the clothes, hairstyle, or other aspects of the appearance recurs throughout the book. One character says, "You don't...look gay. I know gay doesn't look like anything – but sometimes you can tell, right? With some people you can definitely tell." (2004:80) And Nina tries to scope out possible girlfriends for her friend Mel, but she only points out young women with short hair (2004:239). When Mel mentions this, Nina asks, "But how else can you tell?" (ibid.) While Johnson's book is funny, even bordering on the silly, and is rather light-weight, it too encourages readers to think that it is easy to "tell" who is queer simply based on appearance. Still, there are places where she questions stereotypes. For example, Mel tells a friend that she thinks she is butch, and the friend scoffs, "I always think that when I see your sparkly T-shirts." (2004:337) Mel responds, "It's not the clothes…It's the attitude." (ibid.)

If only more of these books showed the "attitude" and stopped focusing on appearances. Instead, they continue to promote the belief that LGBTQ people look a certain way. And if they have a particular way of looking, then it must be easy to recognise them, and if you can recognise them, you can avoid them.

Acting Queer

In many ways, these books, along with other materials, such as media descriptions, give the impression that there are very few options for behaviour if someone is gay. A typical example comes from an article in an international magazine, *Time*. In this piece, Joel Stein describes going to a gay-run and gay-friendly hotel. As a self-described straight man, he seems to find it amusing to try to "pass" as gay. He repeatedly refers to the idea that gay males are all waxed and thin. He seems to consider himself to have many gay characteristics because "I love the catty banter, the brunches, the gym workouts, the modern aesthetic, the not having to deal with women." (2012:n.p.) Apparently, according to Stein and to many others like him, gay men do not have female friends, colleagues, or relatives, and are all into working out and staying fit. He also suggests that in a gay hotel, "without straight people holding them back, they [gay men] would act in some kind of supergay way so incredibly gay, I couldn't even imagine it." (ibid.) In other words, there is a gay way of acting, and even potentially a "supergay" way.

Later, looking for this "incredibly gay" way of being, Stein thinks, "I guess I'm going to have to go to the Sound of Music sing-along." (ibid.) In short, a gay way of being means being appearance-fixated, loving musicals, being catty and gossipy, and not having much to do with women. In many ways, this is what is shown in the young adult novels too. As Jenkins discusses, in YA novels, few gay men are shown as having interactions with women (2011:157). Although she is specifically discussing works published between 1969 and 1992, this appears to be the case to a certain extent in the modern texts as well. And being witty and fashionable are still heavily featured stereotypes today, as is being either "feminine" or else what can be considered masculine or even "hypermasculine".

Blaine points out that people view gay males as falling into three categories:

> *Cross-dresser/leather/biker* gay men were combined into a group linked with traits such as make-up wearing and flamboyant. A second group consisted of *effeminate gay men*, who were described with traits such as dramatic and soft-spoken. The third subtype consisted of *artistic/straight-acting/masculine gay men*. Not surprisingly, the cross-dressing subgroup was rated low on both competence and warmth. Of the three subtypes, these individuals would be most likely to be perceived as threatening traditional male sex roles and being sexually active. The effeminate subtype was regarded as warm but not very competent, stereotype content that is similar to stereotypes held about disabled and elderly people. The artistic/straight-acting/masculine subtype of gay men was stereotyped as highly competent but cold, in much the same way as wealthy people and Jews are. (2007:145-6, italics original)

Interestingly, all three types appear in young adult literature, although I found no leathermen or bikers. Instead, I would actually put cross-dresser together with effeminate in a category in which men have stereotypically feminine traits, sometimes including wearing make-up or women's clothes or having no body hair. And I would also add in an athletic/butch category. Blaine does not offer categories for lesbians. As Jenkins writes, "[o]ne of the most noticeable patterns in the young adult novelistic portrayal of gay/lesbian people is the predominance of males, both as teens and as adults. This trend has become even more pronounced in recent years." (2011:150) In fact, 75% of the books in her sample featured men (ibid.). Cart and Jenkins write that of the "forty books published in the 1980s, twenty-nine (73%) included gay male content and eleven (38%) included lesbian content. Of the seventy GLBTQ YA novels of the nineties, 48 (69%) included gay male content, 18 (26%) included lesbian content, and only four titles (6%) included both gay males and lesbians." (2006:90) Similarly, there are fewer lesbians in my corpus than gay men, and the statistics over the years seem to be staying about the same, with around two-thirds of the texts featuring gay men. See Table 2.

Number of YA Books	Books with Female Queers	Percentage with Female Queers	Books with Male Queers	Percentage with Male Queers
32	12	38%	21	66%

Table 2: Number of books with female and male queer characters.

As Table 2 shows, there are significantly more male characters in this corpus than female, with 38% featuring female LGBTQ people and 66% including males; these statistics are very similar to Cart and Jenkins's. I included transgender people based on the gender they identify as.[30] Note that that a few of the books have both female and male characters, which is why the total is over 100%. Also, of course, some books have multiple queer characters of one gender, but I only counted that once. For example, Sanchez's *Rainbow* series has three main queer male protagonists and additional, usually male, queer characters, but I counted each book only once rather than listing each queer character. When I added in the middle-grade books as well, the percentage of books with male queers went down slightly to 65% and the percentage with female queers rose to 43%; I think this is because more of these texts included LGBTQ parents, and they were always female couples, rather than male couples.

What both my work and Cart and Jenkins's findings suggest is that there are more YA novels with male characters than female characters. Hence, it may make sense that there are fewer types of female queer characters. If lesbians are less often written about, thought about, or analysed, it follows that lesbians have not been categorised to the same extent. The categories I would suggest based on my findings are the *butch*, who is athletic and short-haired, and may use a male name, and the *feminist/intellectual*, who is often angry and may rant about the oppression of women and enjoys discussions about art, philosophy, and/or literature. With all this having been said, I now turn to the texts to explore just how the characters are portrayed, and I start with the gay men.

H.F., the "wiry little butch" (2001:127) in Julia Watts' *Finding H.F.*, is best friends with Bo. Bo is described as a "sissy" (2001:8), among other such terms, and although Bo has not officially come out, H.F. is certain he is gay:

> Come to think of it, Bo has never come right out and told me he likes boys. He'll say things like, "bein' the way I am" or "not bein' a real masculine type of person," but he's never plainly said he likes boys in general, let alone one boy in particular. Instead he rattles on about stuff like how much he just loves that new Celine Dion song. I don't know who he thinks he's kidding. If you're a boy who lives in a place like Morgan, and

> you just can't stop talking about how *fabulous* that new Celine Dion single is, guess what, buddy: You've done come out of the closet. (2001:14, italics original)

Here, a young man who is not "masculine" and who appreciates the music of Celine Dion must be gay.

Along the lines of the Celine Dion fan, a common stereotype in regard to behaviour is that gay men are interested in music or theatre. In *Pink*, the gay male works on the stage crew in the theatre. There is an implied gay male in Esmé Raji Codell's *Vive La Paris*. Michael is said to like cooking, singing, and acting, and he is described as "like that" and "a girl" (2006:160). In Jacqueline Wilson's *Kiss*, Carl is in a play and Paul teases him, "We're going to have to watch you, Carl, you might turn gay on us" (2007:180). Carl does turn out to be gay, not surprisingly, as he also describes himself as "arty and swotty and not too good at football" (2007:233). Generally, if there is a gay male in YA books, it is fairly likely that he will be a fan of music or theatre or even – in a shocking development – musical theatre. As Jenkins found as well, "An interest in some sort of creative art is commonly portrayed as part of a gay/lesbian person's interests." (2011:150) I would suggest that this is more common for gay males than for females.

Besides the taste for music and acting, another common theme in these books is that gay men all have fantastic fashion sense. There are multiple scenes throughout the corpus where gay men go shopping with their female friends or relatives or where they advise them on clothing or make-up. Examples include stylish Ely in *Naomi and Ely's No Kiss List* by Rachel Cohn and David Levithan, who borrows Naomi's clothes, and Jason in *A Secret Edge*, whose aunt goes shopping with him: "because I'm gay, she seems to think it will help my mood" (Reardon, 2007:229). In Manning's *Pretty Things*, Brie admires how Charlie knows how to dress and he replies, "That's because I'm gay, sweetie. Being a style icon is all part of my genetic coding." (2005:11)

Sometimes the gay men even help other men, nearly always straight ones, to improve their hygiene, fashion sense, and dating technique, in a sort of "Queer Eye for the Young Adult Male". Jason in Reardon's *A Secret Edge* teaches his friend Robert how to flirt with women and ask them out (2007:30). As mentioned above, in Alex Sanchez's *Getting It*, Carlos, a straight male, goes to Sal, a gay male, for advice on fashion and getting girls, emphasising the idea that homosexual men have a sense of style that is far beyond that of anyone else and that they really understand women, perhaps because they are "feminised" and womanly themselves. Carlos thinks, "Maybe that's why gay guys existed: to help straight guys figure out women." (2006:100) Despite being grateful to Sal for his knowledge, Carlos is puzzled that Sal is not "weak and girly" (2006:19), because as far as he knows, that is how gay men should be. Still, he seems to think that Sal certainly acts gay, even if he is not "girly", because he understands women and has great fashion sense. Later, Sal suggests that Carlos' friend Toro is gay. Carlos rejects this idea, but:

> as they drove home, he thought about how Toro was always looking at muscle mags and hanging out at the rec center. And yet he didn't look or act gay like Sal, or Javier, or the *Queer Eye* guys. And hadn't he had sex with that girl, Leticia? Toro couldn't be gay. No way. (2006:89)

It turns out that although Toro does not "look or act gay" and though he may have had sex with a girl, he is in fact gay. In a sense, perhaps this challenges stereotypes to a certain extent, because it shows that anyone can be gay. But it also seems to encourage them, because it reminds readers what the stereotypes are, and seems to set up people such as Toro as the exception.

Campness is also common in these books. By this I mean the feminine attributes that people tend to link to gayness: limp wrists, swishing walks, using a female name or referring to oneself as "she", witty jokes, and catty behaviour. Ely in *Naomi and Ely's No Kiss List* by Rachel Cohn and David Levithan is a good example: he always has a perfect one-liner as a response and he is catty and, of course, he has a great sense of fashion, as already mentioned. Wilson's Carl finds himself "clown[ing] around with limp wrists, going *whoopsie* all the time to try to be part of the joke" (2007:233, italics original), trying to act gay as though this will protect him from people making fun of him. Acting in an over-the-top stereotypically gay way – campness, lisping, and generally being "feminine" – is often depicted as a way for gay men to identify themselves and others, and, perhaps strangely, also as a form of protection. Just as Carl tries "to be part of the joke", mocking himself before others can, Jason in Reardon's *A Secret Edge* pretends to lisp and speak in a falsetto in order to get the attention of bullies off his boyfriend. He says, "Oh! My heav-enth!...What are you boyth doing? Oh, oh!...Oh, thith ith terrible! I mutht get help! Oh!" (2007:234) This scene in Reardon's book is particularly unbelievable, as though bullies would stop beating up one gay man just because another gay man was lisping and acting very camp. At one point Jason ponders, "What does it mean if I'm gay? Does it mean I'm not normal? Does it mean I have to run with my feet going out to the sides like a girl and call myself Jessica?" (2007:54) His sole model for being homosexual, it seems, is the "femininised" type, and though he seems to feel no urge to "swish", as Taylor in Reardon's other novel put it (2008:288), or to use a female name, he does not appear to realise that it is possible to be gay in any other way. Unfortunately, based on this corpus, it appears that Jason and Taylor are not alone in this belief.

Another distinct gay male type is the athlete. This boy is rather "butch", with a muscular, fit body, and he usually pretends to be heterosexual, which sometimes involves dating girls, in order to get along with his coach and teammates. He is accepted due to his seeming strength and maleness. Examples of this type include Jason in Robin Reardon's *A Secret Edge* and Jason in the three

Rainbow books by Alex Sanchez. Both Jasons are star athletes and they shock people when they come out, because of the perception that "masculine" boys cannot be gay. Once such a male comes out, there is usually what I term a "shower scene", where the boy is showering with his teammates after a match or practice, and he is bullied and/or the teammates make comments about how he is a pervert and is watching them and desiring them, and/or someone else asks if he gets "horny" while showering with his teammates. For example, Reardon's Jason is told by his coach that he will not be removed from the team "unless you're accosting the other boys in the showers" (2007:173). And Sanchez's Jason is asked, "So what's it like spending so much time with guys in the locker room? Don't you get totally horny?...Have you ever gotten a woody in the locker room showers?" (2005:88)

As mentioned previously, Sanchez's three *Rainbow* books are filled with stereotypes about gay men, including the butch athlete, the camp queer, and the feminine male. Here I quote extensively from Thomas Crisp's detailed and careful analysis of the series, because he appears to view the books exactly as I do. It is especially worrying that the first book in Sanchez's trilogy, *Rainbow Boys,* is, as Crisp points out, "as close to a canonical work of GLBTQ fiction as any other book." (2011:215) This means that more people are likely to read this book in school or on their own than many other queer books for young readers, and thus it would seem to behove Sanchez to question stereotypes rather than to confirm them or have his characters conform to them. Alas, this is simply not the case. Crisp writes:

> Although the protagonists of the *Rainbow Boys* series identify as homosexual, they embody characteristics that reinforce normative conceptions of gender and, by extension, sexuality...it seems that the books rely upon stereotypes of what it means to be "male" (i.e. aggressive and dominating) and "female" (i.e., submissive

> and self-sacrificing) to depict men in homosexual relationships as embodying either a "masculine" or "feminine" counterpart (perpetuating the fallacy that in gay relationships, one partner is the "man" while the other is the "woman"). (2011:216)

Crisp rightfully says that a relationship with one "man" and one "woman" might feel realistic to some readers but "it is precisely the familiarity with such tropes that leads to the perpetuation of myths and misconceptions." (2011:217)

As Crisp writes, "Jason, a stock character who appears in many gay young adult novels, is identified by Alex Sanchez as the "Tragic Closet Jock" (or T.C.J.), a "masculine" young man whose status as an attractive star athlete permits him to discover his sexuality at both his girlfriend's and co-protagonist Kyle's expense." (2011:226) Meanwhile, Kyle is "the Sympathetic, Understanding Doormat" (2011:227) and Crisp says that though Kyle is a swimmer, "[t]he sports played by "masculine" athletes (like Jason) and that carry positions of social privilege are exclusionary of those who don't identify as male, while sports like the swim team on which "feminine" Kyle participates are coeducational." (2011:227) Although both Jason and Kyle are male, the story reads as familiar as it is "the story of the athletic dream guy who eventually falls for the intelligent, self-conscious, introverted wallflower." (Crisp, 2011:228) Kyle appears happy to play the role of the "female", who allows his man to check out other people and even to kiss them (as on 2005:128), and Kyle even considers giving up his dreams of attending Princeton to stay behind in their hometown with Jason, who does not have the same intellectual prowess (as Crisp discusses on 2011:230-1).

The third main character is Nelson, who is "[t]he *Queer* and *Proud* Homosexual" and "Sexually Insatiable Target" and "is presumably supposed to show gay young adult males what it means and looks like to be openly and comfortably gay" (Crisp, 2011:233, italics and capitals original). However, as Crisp points out, Nelson is also shown to be "someone with deep-rooted self-hatred" (2011:235); he chain-smokes, has bulimia and "abus[es] diet pills in an attempt to slim down even though those around him insist to him that he is slender." (2011:235) This is to suggest that the "queer and proud" character may in fact be anything but proud and self-confident. He is also sex-fixated, or "sexually insatiable" (Crisp, 2011:237), always lusting after men and wanting sex with them (as on 2005:46 and 52, among other places). And, as mentioned above, Nelson is very feminised, as opposed to "female" like Kyle. He refers to other men as "she" or "girl", and is accepting of his "female self", as Crisp puts it (2011:234). Crisp discusses how Nelson has a one-night stand with a very masculine man, and behaves in a "feminine" way during it:

> Here we have the "Queer and Proud" homosexual embodying the negative, stereotypically "feminine" stance of wishing for the use of protection during sexual activity and the subsequent abandonment of that protective instinct in order not to risk rejection and to satisfy the "masculine" male: in this case, the motor-cycle-riding, muscular "HotLove69" Brick. (2011:236)

In short, Crisp writes, "[o]f all the protagonists, it feels most important that we see him grow, and it is unfortunate that he changes little across the three books." (2011:237)

Besides the three main characters serving as archetypes of gay males – i.e. masculine, feminine, and feminised – secondary characters are used to suggest tensions between different types of gay men, such as the "faeries" at the "Radical Faerie sanctuary" in the last book in the series (2005:68-9). They are polyamorous and are confident in their queerness. One is called Lady-Bugger and another is Horn-Boy, and Jason calls them "freaks" while Nelson says they are "just gay people like us" (2005:69). Jason, the masculine jock, is unwilling to accept more feminine gay men, and in fact it is only in the last book of the series that he starts to approve of Nelson, who has been one of his closest, most loyal friends throughout the three books.

Sanchez's popular books "work to heteronormatively construct what it means to be gay" (Crisp, 2011:225). In other words, they cater to a heteronormative view of queerness, and reinforce stereotypes. As Blaine points out, "There is evidence that people subtype gay men into at least two types: those that are effeminate and have female-stereotypic qualities (e.g., emotionally sensitive) and those that violate traditional sex roles for men (e.g., have sex with men)...People like the first type of gay men better than the second" (2007:145). This is to say that effeminate gay men are more acceptable or more "liked" possibly because they are more obviously gay. They can be recognised as such since they seem like "inverts", with traditionally female characteristics. Men who are masculine, athletic, and/or butch are less easily recognised and less easily understood, and thus are likely to be more challenging. This is one possible reading. The opposite is that less masculine gay men are more challenging because they are not truly like men.

As mentioned above, the female characters are stereotyped as well, but they tend to fall into either the butch or the femme stereotypes. Within those types, of course, there are common sub-types, so there are serious, angry lesbian feminists or masculine dykes, for example, just as there are artsy gay men or athletic gay males.

Mike, in Julie Ann Peters' *Far from Xanadu*, is a stereotypical butch dyke. What I mean by this category is a young woman who plays sports, might use a male name, probably has short hair, and is not too concerned about fashion or style. Mike is a star softball player at her high school and she runs her father's plumbing company after he commits suicide. She, as one might suspect, falls for a femme woman, and her best friend, Jamie, is a stereotyped gay boy. Others who fall into the category of butch dyke are the tough, independent H.F. in Julia Watts's *Finding H.F.* (who also has a feminine gay male best friend), or Avery in *The Bermudez Triangle* by Maureen Johnson, who is called a "rough dyke" because she wears grungy clothes and little make-up (2004:161).

The other main type is the angry, humourless feminist. This young woman often thinks seriously about heavy matters, the way Ellie in *Gravity* by Leanne Lieberman tries to understand Judaism so she can decide whether it is possible to be both gay and Orthodox (see, for example, 2008:56 or 2008:126). In Sarra Manning's *Pretty Things*, one character is described as "the angry dyke girl" (2005:36) and Ava's girlfriend Chloe in *Pink* is also depicted as a typical angry lesbian. Another example of this type is Behiye in *2 Girls* by Perihan Magden, although this was translated from Turkish by Brendan Freely, and thus should be viewed with a slightly different lens than an original English text. Behiye rants about fashion magazines and the way women are raised to serve men and to make themselves appealing to men. Another such character is in Jane Eagland's *Wildthorn*. Although the book is a historical novel and thus must also be considered from a different perspective, part of what defines Louisa, besides her woman-loving, is that she is angry about women's oppression. She longs to be educated, rather than to "be patient, cheerful and obedient and do boring ladylike things" (2009:77). However, her mother insists that if she were to receive education, "[i]t will spoil her chances of marriage. Do you want her to become *mannish*?" (ibid., italics original) The feminist type can, in many texts, especially the contemporary, English-language ones, be labelled as the stereotypical man-hater.

Besides the butch and the feminist, there are few other lesbian characters, and they are categorised through the use of stereotyped jokes or other descriptions, often with the suggestion that one type of lesbian is more acceptable than another. For example, in Johnson's novel, there is this quotation:

> Avery remembered a joke she'd heard somewhere: what does a lesbian bring on a first date?

> Answer: a U-Haul.
>
> What if there was some truth in that? What if Mel wanted to get married and have a commitment ceremony and play Ani DiFranco and k.d. lang songs and have cats as bridesmaids? That would be great for Mel, but it just wasn't something Avery could picture. The thought scared her. A lot. (2004:204-5)

This suggests that the kind of lesbian who might want to have a commitment ceremony and who might like cats and music by Ani DiFranco might be less tolerable or desirable than one who does not. Similarly and as already discussed, in *Pink*, there is one type of acceptable lesbian, and this is the intellectual, artistic one dressed in black, who drinks a lot of coffee and smokes. Though Ava does not act like that, and this worries her, she is certain that she is nonetheless a particular type of lesbian. Her room is grey because pastel colours are not allowed for lesbians, and "[t]here wasn't even so much as a rainbow flag; as Chloe said, we weren't *that* sort of lesbian." (2009:6, italics original) Here, there seems to be a hierarchy of lesbians, or perhaps of lesbianness, where wearing all black and smoking and wanting to discuss art and philosophy is at the top, and while Ava knows she does not quite fit in there, she is still higher on the hierarchy than the type of lesbian who might fly a rainbow flag and like pastel colours.

In other words, as in the texts that feature gay males, the gay females have a limited array of feelings and traits. Perhaps not surprisingly and as hinted at above, the non-gay characters in these works do not seem to be depicted in such narrow ways, nor are non-LGBTQ characters in non-queer YA books. See Table 3 for an overview.

Type of Queer Male	Explanation	Type of Queer Female	Explanation
Masculine	Butch, athletic, manly, not gay-seeming	Butch	Butch, athletic, often uses a male name, stereotypically lesbian, often friends with men
Feminine	An in-between type, softer than masculine, but with stereotypically feminine traits, such as doing what his (usually masculine) boyfriend wants and being a supportive partner	Femme	Often attractive, feminist, serious, perhaps man-hating
Feminised	Stereotypically gay, may wear make-up or women's clothes, may have dyed hair, sex-obsessed, may use a woman's name		

Table 3: Types of queer characters in YA books.

It would be interesting to see a straight male who was camp and witty or a straight female who used a male name and played sports, or indeed queer characters who did not fall into the above categories at all, or who were a mix of characteristics from a variety of types. While here I have focused on gay males and females, see the chapter on diversity for an exploration of the depiction of bisexual, transgendered, and otherwise queer characters.

Sex and Marriage

While sex and marriage are both discussed in more detail in a chapter of their own, and that chapter looks at the stereotyped ideas of LGBTQ romantic relationships, here it is worth mentioning just a couple of things in regard to these topics. First of all, marriage is not really seen as an option for LGBTQ people. This encourages the stereotyped idea that queers do not want long-term relationships or cannot commit and also that their relationships are not of equal value. Along the same lines, this idea is emphasised through the strangely large number of unfaithful queers in these texts. While I would not argue that monogamous relationships should be the ideal, my point is that in these books, when characters have agreed in principle to be monogamous, they do not always follow through.

I have not carried out a scientifically quantitative survey, but informally it seems to me that cheating is very common in LGBTQ YA books, perhaps even more so than in non-LGBTQ YA books. Examples include the novel by Johnson, as already mentioned; as well as novels by Wilkinson (where Ava flirts with and kisses a young man without telling her girlfriend); Sanchez (where Jason flirts with and kisses a young woman without telling his boyfriend); Freymann-Weyr (where James sleeps with his boyfriend's sister at the end of the novel); and Burchill (where Sugar sleeps with several men, not minding if her girlfriend sees); as well as the short story "Never Have I Ever" by Courtney Gillette (where the main character, Amber, has a boyfriend but writes stories and poems about wanting to have sex with her female best friend, and eventually kisses another young woman; she asks herself if she is cheating and decides that "[i]t seemed a whole different plane. I was 400 miles, a six-hour train ride, three states from home" (2011:153)). There are several possible reasons for this plethora of cheating. One might be that LGBTQ people are considered overly sexual, so it seems appropriate that they would cheat on their partners, although it is interesting that many of the examples feature women, and generally women are viewed as less sexual than men. Along these lines, then, the authors could have been inspired by ideas about sexual fluidity (cf. Diamond, 2008), which suggest that women's sexuality is more fluid than men's and that they are therefore more likely to have relationships with both men and women. However, as Cutler points out, men's sexuality has traditionally been viewed as fluid too, so the belief that it is not is a recent one (2012:15-16). Another possibility is that some authors may feel that LGBTQ relationships are not as serious as heterosexual ones, and that therefore it would not be out of the ordinary for LGBTQ people to cheat. A final possible reason is that these novels are in some way a throwback to earlier LGBTQ works, including pulp fiction, when queers had to go straight, die, or end up in a mental hospital, and could not live happily ever after as out queers. No matter what the case, the prevalence of cheating is an odd stereotype. Whatever the reason, these books seem to suggest that LGBTQ people are incapable of being in long-term, monogamous relationships.

The Gay Boyfriend

Another common stereotype in YA books is the idea of what I term the "gay boyfriend". Although, as previously mentioned, many gay males are called upon to help their female relatives and friends pick out clothes and improve their fashion and style sense, they also serve another role: love object. This might seem strange, as women would surely understand that they cannot hope to get or "convert" gay men, but it is nonetheless a recurring theme. Perhaps it is their very unavailability that renders them appealing.[31] Young women in these works tend to fall for their gay best friends and hope that they will somehow tempt those gay males away from men. In her review of LGBTQ YA books from 1969-92, Jenkins talks about two books that "portray boys who are loved by the female narrators. When the boys come out, both narrators react with dismay and anger at the 'injustice' of a gay male being attractive but attainable" (2011:151) She adds that "men are never shown falling for lesbians. It appears that a man without a woman is attractive and valued, but a woman without a man is not." (2011:151-2) However, I would say that her findings differ from mine in two ways. The first is that in many, though not all, of the cases I discuss below, the young gay males have already come out or at least have implied that they are gay, so the young women who have feelings for them do generally know, or should know, that they do not have a chance. The second difference is that I have found one example where a young male possibly falls for a lesbian.

In two of the books that are aimed at slightly younger, possibly pre-teen readers, the young women do not know that the males they are attracted to are gay. In Philip Pullman's *The Broken Bridge*, Ginny has a crush on Andy. In one scene, they are both at a party, they dance, and Ginny feels she is in love with him (1990:156). Andy has a big piece of smoked salmon that he calls Gertie and he jokes he should have brought Gertie to the party. Another friend, Eryl, says:

> "Who's Gertie?...You changing your spots, Andy?"
>
> "No spots on me. I'm an Ethiopian."
>
> "First time I've heard it called that." (1990:154)

This is quite subtle, but the implied comment is that Andy is gay (i.e. an "Ethiopian") and has not "chang[ed] [his] spots" or turned straight for a woman (Gertie the salmon). Ginny does not understand that he is gay until much later and then she feels ashamed that she cared for him and did not realise who he was. There is a similar situation in *Kiss* by Jacqueline Wilson. Sylvie does not know that her love object, Carl, is gay, though he spends much of his time with Paul and others suspect that he is homosexual. When he finally tells her, she thinks, "This was it. The end of all my dreams." (2007:231) So these two books do follow the pattern Jenkins outlined, where the young straight women "react with dismay" to the news that their best male friends are gay; it is worth noting again that they are for younger readers, whereas in the books for older readers, the female characters know that their "gay boyfriends" are indeed gay. Instead of anger, however, it seems to me that they often also experience shame: shame that they did not know or guess, and shame that they were in love with people who could never love them back. A slightly different take on this is in Garret Freymann-Weyr's *My Heartbeat*. The main character, Ellen, has a crush on a young man who is in many ways the best friend of both her brother and herself, but who also seems to be her brother's secret boyfriend. Ellen is aware of this, but also seems to hope that the best friend, James, might in some way choose her, and indeed he ends up sleeping with Ellen when she is just fourteen (2002:134).

The YA books show the main female character aware of her best friend's homosexuality but obstinately refusing to accept it and subsequently continuing to subject herself to unrequited longing. Naomi in *Naomi and Ely's No Kiss List* by Rachel Cohn and David Levithan is straight and is in love with Ely, her gay best friend. She longs to have sex with him. Her thoughts on this matter include, "*Gay* doesn't change that – our shared past, our committed future. *Gay* doesn't mean I shouldn't wait for that one moment when he won't be." (2008:12, italics original) She also says, "Just because Ely is attracted to boys doesn't mean he couldn't want to push our mind-meld into body-meld. I refuse to believe it's possible he couldn't want that, too, on some level, whether he knows it or not." (2008:44) No matter how many times Ely emphasises his gayness to her, she is unwilling to believe it or accept it. A character who is very like Naomi is Brie in *Pretty Things* by Sarra Manning. Brie has a crush on her gay best friend, Charlie. She says:

> [T]he one thing I want more than anything in the world is for Charlie to not be gay. It would be the best thing ever. One day he'd just look at me and he'd stop

> being gay. Or else he'd realize that he never was actually gay at all, he just hasn't had a girlfriend, which is not the same thing. Anyway, he wakes up and he's, like, straight. (2005:61)

Charlie tries to convince her that he really is gay and that he will never be attracted to her, by saying things such as, "I'm gay. I'm a pouf. I'm a fairy. I'm a nancy boy. I'm a big old queen. An arse bandit. A fudge packer. A friend of Dorothy's" (2005:98). But Brie still will not believe him. She repeatedly shows little or no understanding of his sexuality and she angers others by saying that he is just going through a phase.

Cart and Jenkins also discuss another book "depicting a straight girl's falling for a gay boy", *The Other Side of the Fence*, from 1986 (2006:68), and though this is not one that I was able to access, it is worth mentioning it because it shows just how prevalent this concept is.

These books seem to emphasise the idea that women are "fag hags" who like to spend time with gay men and they may also encourage the belief that females find sex and sexuality frightening and thus would rather be in love with unavailable gay males than to look for those who might be able to love them back. This is to say that straight women's sexuality and sexual maturity is apparently looked down upon, in much the same way that lesbian women's sexuality is (as is discussed in the chapter on sex and marriage).

While Jenkins found no examples of straight men falling for lesbian women, I might have found one, although it may not be a particularly strong example. John in Ellen Wittlinger's *Hard Love* is unsure of his sexuality and develops a crush on Marisol, a lesbian. But, as he explains, this is possibly because she is not really a "girl", to which she replies, "For your information, dickhead, lesbians *are* girls. Don't they teach sex ed in your school system?" (1999:24, italics original) It is unclear whether he is really attracted to her or whether he is just trying out his sexuality. Some people who were aware of my research thought that I might find more stories of males in love with their lesbian best friends in part because contemporary pornography suggests that men find the idea of two women together sexy, which perhaps might lead to men even finding single lesbians sexy, but this has not proven to be the case. I think that there the appeal is two women engaging in sexual activities for the male viewer while a lesbian on her own just seems to be uninteresting and not worth the time.

In a couple of texts, young women who identify as lesbians end up dating men, but this seems different, in that they are not pined after obsessively by men but rather find that their sexuality is more fluid and allows for them to have relationships with males. One example is Lili Wilkinson's *Pink*, as discussed elsewhere, and another is *Pretty Things* by Sarra Manning, in which the lesbian character Daisy falls for Walker, although she still wants her girlfriend, Claire, too. This would imply that such characters are bisexual rather than lesbian, but this is not how they describe themselves.

What these examples suggest is that gay men are extremely appealing to women. Gay males do not only "get" women on an emotional level and can thus help straight men understand women, as discussed above, but they also just "get" women, whether they want them or not. Straight women are portrayed in some cases as desperately sad because of their longing for these unbelievably smart, funny, fashionable, and generally lovely and loveable gay men. Lesbians are apparently not as smart, funny, fashionable, lovely, or loveable, according to these texts.

Positive Stereotypes and Challenging Stereotypes

As discussed earlier on in this chapter, stereotypes are not only negative, and also even stereotypes that are negative can be challenged by someone highlighting them. This is not common in this corpus of texts, unfortunately.

There can be positive stereotypes, and some of the ones mentioned above can be viewed in that light. For example, adjectives such as stylish, artistic, funny, or intellectual are all positive and have strong connotations. Being described as witty, for instance, would seem to be a good thing. In other cases, the attributes refer to more than just single adjectives. For instance, in Wilson's *Kiss*, when Carl comes out to his mother, she is accepting, although she admits that his father will find it difficult. When Carl asks if she minds, she says no, and adds, "It's maybe a bonus for me. Gay sons are always lovely to their mums." (2007:272) However, it is worth pointing out that even positive stereotypes are stereotypes, and they continue to pigeonhole LGBTQ people and may lead to self-fulfilling prophecies.

Some of these young adult novels question stereotypes or show characters fighting against them. In *Parrotfish*, which is discussed more in the chapter on diversity, Grady sometimes muses on gender and his situation in ways that can feel rather didactic, as though the author is using Grady to comment on society and our understanding of gender. An example is where Grady wonders what makes someone male or female. He complains about his friend Eve, who has transformed into a "high-pitched, low-self-esteem, capital-G Girl who couldn't relax" (2007:131). He also points out, "maybe it was silly for me to try to be somebody else's idea of a boy. I didn't need to swagger around and punch guys in the shoulder—that wasn't going to prove anything. There were still people who didn't succumb to the stereotypes. Sebastian certainly didn't punch or swagger, and he was a boy, although one who couldn't get a date to the Winter Carnival dance." (ibid.) Grady talks about having to learn to "pass" as male and finds this odd: "I'd have to learn to walk differently, talk differently, dress differently, basically act differently than I did as a girl. But why did we need to *act* at all? A quick glance around Buxton High provided numerous cases of girls acting like girls and boys acting like boys—and very few people acting like themselves." (ibid., italics original) And yet, clearly Grady has an idea of what being male is and feels that this is more appropriate to him than being female, even while also apparently balking at the very idea of maleness (and, for that matter, of femaleness). So Grady questions stereotypes of gender and the concept of "doing" gender (perhaps linking back to Simone de Beauvoir's idea of "becoming" a woman (1949/2009) or Judith Butler's troubling of gender (1990/2006)), which is unusual in these YA novels, but then ultimately he does seem to look for a way of being/becoming/doing male.

Charlie, the beloved of Brie in *Pretty Things* by Sarra Manning, says, "Automatically girls expect me to act like Graham Norton, go shoe shopping with them and act as confessor for their gruesome sexual secrets...It's stupid. Just because I fancy boys, I'm expected to come with this complete list of gay interests. I hate Kylie. I wouldn't be seen dead in leather trousers and I have absolutely no desire to get myself up in drag." (2005:154) I cannot help but wonder, though, if such sentences or phrases often end up emphasising stereotypes rather than arguing against them. I sometimes think it would be better to have characters acting differently rather than verbally grumbling about or arguing against the stereotypes.

In short, while some books do feature positive stereotypes or while the authors apparently attempt to challenge stereotypes in their work, I think in many cases they end up encouraging the stereotypes they are fighting against and/or continuing to put people in easily labelled boxes rather than seeing them as individuals.

Reducing Prejudice and Literature's Role

It seems that many of these texts rely on stereotypes and thereby even encourage readers to believe in them. While this has not been researched much in regard to literature and thus I have not found any texts specifically on the stereotyping of sexuality and gender identity in literature, research on children and television programmes reveals that this is not unusual. As David J. Schneider writes, "[l]ike childrearing practices and roles within the home, television both reflects and reinforces prevailing cultural tendencies." (1996:435) As mentioned earlier, LGBTQ characters on TV are often stereotyped, and as I have shown here, this is the case in books for children and young adults too. The question here then is whether it is possible to use literature – and other media – to counteract stereotypes and to help readers see LGBTQ people as individuals rather than as types defined solely by their sexuality or gender identity. I would argue that it is and that authors ought to try to look beyond stereotypes as they write LGBTQ characters. The issue thus is, then, how prejudice can be reduced through literature (see Brown, 2010:243-80 for more on reducing prejudice more generally, and Robinson, 2002:415 for the importance of counteracting prejudice early in children).

Several scholars who research prejudice discuss the contact hypothesis (cf. Blaine, 2007:210-12, and Brown, 2010:243-4). Brown writes that the "central premise [of the contact hypothesis] is that the best way to reduce tension and hostility between groups is to bring them into contact with each other" (2010:244). But, as he points out, contact alone is not enough (2010:244) and integration (ibid.) and friendship (2010:245) are essential features, too. Another requirement is that both or all sets of people have to have "equal status" (2010:247), so, for example, one group is not in a subservient position to another. This is where programmes such as Schools Out, where LGBTQ people go into schools to tell students about themselves, can be helpful as a first step (see Brown, 2010:250-7 for the importance of contact in schools). However, hearing a lecture by, say, a transgender lesbian will only go so far, as young people still should, according to research, form friendships and integrate with those who are different from them, and not just have occasional, tangential contact with them. As Brown writes, mostly in reference to racial prejudice, "however well designed the curriculum and its accompanying pedagogic activity may be, if children from different groups return daily to a world outside the school gates which is still largely segregated and dominated by prejudiced values, it would be surprising indeed to find much general change in their intergroup attitudes" (2010:253). I would like to suggest that literature could be a second step or it could be used in conjunction with school visits. It cannot replace friendship with or being related to someone who is LGBTQ, but it can enable a young person to empathise with and learn more about being queer. In other words, I would argue that reading non-stereotyped portrayals of "others" in literature might be a way to develop contact, since research suggests that people do feel close to characters in books. An LGBTQ character can thus serve as an example of an LGBTQ person, a safe way for a young reader to explore LGBTQ issues. Although Kerry H. Robinson points out that "[s]exuality and sexual orientation issues are controversial areas that are fraught with many obstacles and cultural taboos that operate to silence, marginalise, and/or limit any dialogue or representation of this form of difference" (2002:416), she also acknowledges that this is starting to change and that, more than ever, we need to help reduce prejudice, make people aware of discrimination, and generally fight "the perceived irrelevance of broader social, political and economic issues to the 'child's world'." (2002:417)

For LGBTQ young people themselves, not having to read stereotyped portrayals of who and what they are will have many important effects. Obviously, it may help them be treated better by their peers, since their peers will have seen a wider range of LGBTQ people in literature and will ideally feel they know more about being queer. LGBTQ people themselves may feel less pressure to fulfil the stereotyped ideas about how they should look and behave. As Blaine writes, "the self-fulfilling prophecy can be eliminated by efforts to understand and know, rather than please, other people. This insight can be put to practical use in social contexts involving high- and low-status groups (such as parent-child interactions) by fostering mutual understanding rather than one group's approval of the other." (2007:51) Imagine a situation where a young gay male does not feel he has to be camp or to pretend to enjoy shopping and fashion;

the freedom to be oneself, whatever that means, is what could be encouraged and enjoyed if stereotypes were not engendered as often in literature.

So if authors – and journalists, and anyone working in the media – would start to describe LGBTQ people in non-stereotyped ways, this may help young people learn more about queer issues and being queer, and it may eventually help reduce prejudice.

Conclusion

In sum, the books in my corpus of texts tend to suggest that LGBTQ people have very particular ways of being/looking/acting/living. The books are filled with clichéd ideas about being queer and these clichés have turned into tropes, tropes that may have normative roles. Stereotyping might lead young readers to believe that it is easy to recognise LGBTQ people and/or that living a non-heterosexual life involves a particular set of activities, appearances, experiences, or feelings. The obvious point to mention here is that stereotypes come from somewhere and often have some basis in reality, and therefore that portraying characters in a stereotyped way means that those portrayals will be true for some people; the problem, as I see it, is when stereotypes are the main portrayals one sees in literature. I would apply this to LGBTQ children's and YA literature as well; stereotypes are understandable to a certain extent, but I think it would be hugely beneficial and preferable if we were to see a wider range of behaviours and appearances. A reader of YA fiction that features heterosexual characters would not see the males limited to three major types or the females to two or three types, and yet this is the case for LGBTQ YA novels, albeit with a few exceptions. Also, few heterosexual characters in these books are stereotyped.

For an audience that is not familiar with LGBTQ people or even for a young LGBTQ audience that is going through the coming-out process, these stereotyped views of lesbians and gays and their lives give the following messages: if you are a lesbian or a gay male, there are particular ways of being, and you ought to fit into one of those categories, and also that being queer means having a traumatic, anxiety-ridden life that can include rejection by one's friends and relatives. Some of these books suggest that being queer means living a constrained, and therefore sad and difficult, life. While there are of course sad and difficult aspects to everyone's lives and sympathy is generally a more useful feeling than disdain, it seems unlikely that overwhelming pity is the best emotion with which to view LGBTQ people. Showing a broad range of characters – from the femme to the butch and everything in between and beyond – and a broad range of situations – including but not limited to rejection by parents – could help rectify this.

One point that may be worth pausing on is that while some of these authors are themselves LGBTQ, some of them are not (Robin Reardon is one example of a non-LGBTQ writer; her website includes some discussion of this matter. Ellen Wittlinger is another example). While I would not argue that only LGBTQ authors should write books about LGBTQ people or that only LGBTQ people can truly understand LGBTQ people, it may be the case that some non-LGBTQ authors are unaware that gay, bisexual, and transgender people, just like straight people, come in a wide range of personalities and with many different hobbies and experiences. They may not have accurate information about what it means to be queer and to live a queer life. This idea might be worth exploring more at some point, because educating authors or at least suggesting particular resources to them could help how they write about particular groups.

Clearly, research suggests that contact is one of the most important ways to start tackling prejudice – in this case, prejudice and stereotyping about LGBTQ people. I would like to suggest that some contact can be made via literature. That is to say that young people can be exposed to queers through literary texts that feature them and "normalise" them. This can be extended outwards into "real life" by having queers go into schools to give talks to children. Reading about and meeting LGBTQ people is a way for children and young adults to get to know queers, which helps reduce confusion about or prejudice against the "other" and can also reduce feelings of self-hatred and depression in those who are LGBTQ. And media portrayals, including literature, should be as non-stereotyped as possible so that people do not get the erroneous idea that, for example, all gay men are slender and funny or that all lesbians are serious and humourless man-haters. Also, of course, it behoves as many queers as possible to be out in their daily lives, so that all people, no matter their age, can recognise that they do know and like LGBTQ people. This will have a big impact on acceptance and understanding. As Abate and Kidd write, "understanding children's literature as queer means embracing trajectories and tonalities other than the lesbian/gay-affirmative and celebratory" (2011:9). What I think is missing from many of these books are those "tonalities" and even the "celebratory" aspects; instead, these books rely on stereotypes, often negative ones, as shortcut methods for depicting LGBTQ people, and they thereby unfortunately suggest that LGBTQ lives are much more limited than they actually are.

Diversity

Diversity is often understood to mean primarily or solely ethnic diversity (Robinson, 2002:425), but here I mean the term in its broader sense. Within the large umbrella that is called "diversity", there are two issues that I explore in this chapter, although both have to do with invisibility. The first issue is that some of the letters within the alphabet soup of queerness are missing from children's literature. More specifically, there is a distinct dearth of bisexual, transgender, and otherwise queer characters.[32] Those who are portrayed in books for young readers often are done so in a problematic way that raises more questions than it answers. For example, bisexuality is completely missing from picture books and is depicted as an in-between stage in young adult literature, a stage that people have to go through in order to decide whether they are gay or straight. Bisexuality is not itself seen as a valid identity.

The second issue to be discussed here is that children's books do not seem to recognise that it is possible to have multiple identities and, in particular, to have multiple minority identities, i.e. that many people live at the intersections of identities.[33] Characters may be lesbian, gay, bisexual, or transgender, but they seemingly cannot be both that and also, for example, Muslim and/or Chinese and/or dyslexic and/or working-class. It is as though children's books can only handle one deviation from the supposed norm at a time. It seems to be thought to be impossible for young readers to understand what it means to create a coherent identity out of two or more minority characteristics, or to be multiply marginalised. In what follows, then, I analyse these two issues, trying to make sense of this clear lack of diversity in books for children and young adults. In other words, which types of queers are visible in literature for children and young adults and why might this be? And who is invisible and why?

Missing Pieces

As stated, in this chapter I explore who and what is missing from LGBTQ children's books. As Daniel Gilbert points out, we must attend to absence, and yet so often we focus on what is present; to analyse what is missing and why could therefore offer much information (2006:96-104).

In children's picture books, it is most often the parents who exhibit an LGBTQ identity, and not the children, who are frequently portrayed as not sexual and/or not aware of sexual matters. All the queer parents are gay or lesbian (Epstein, 2012[34]). In books for older child readers, there are queer young people, but they too are primarily gay or lesbian. In other words, where are the bisexual, transgender, or otherwise queer characters in children's books? Note this quote from a review: "The subject of lesbians and gays in children's literature is one that will not 'go away' no matter how many debates, controversies, or protests accompany the subject." (Pizurie, 1994:n.p.) This comment only refers to "lesbians and gays" and not to "lesbians and gays and bisexuals and transgenders and other queers", and the books analysed here do indeed tend to ignore the other colours in the queer rainbow, which may mean that authors, publishers, and members of society in general are able to accept queers as long as they are monosexuals and as long as they are not too queer.

Bisexuality

Bisexuality is most often understood as meaning that someone is attracted to both men and women.[35] It is a complicated term and a complicated identity, one that troubles many. As Jonathan Dollimore points out, "bisexuals have been variously characterized as promiscuous, immature, undecided, treacherous, cowardly, and carriers of AIDS into the straight community. Conversely, and even more recently, they are being hailed not only as one of the most politically radical of all sexual minorities, but provocatively postmodern as well." (1997:250)[36] Which is it then? Are bisexuals immature? Or are they radical and postmodern? Can they be both? Or are they something else altogether?

A major issue here is that bisexuals are generally not easily, visibly identifiable. As Robyn Ochs discusses, they are not visually recognisable in the way some ethnic groups are (1996:219), and if they are visually recognisable at some point, it is usually due to, for example, holding hands with or kissing someone of the same sex, which would mean that they are seen as lesbian or gay, not bisexual (Ochs, 1996:225). If they are holding hands with or kissing someone of the opposite sex, then they are identified as heterosexual (ibid.). Hence, unless bisexuals regularly proclaim their bisexual identity and/or wear bisexual flag jewellery or t-shirts, they are not a visible minority.

To become visible is to challenge norms and perhaps to face a lot of negative stereotyping and discrimination. Loraine Hutchins writes that:

> [s]tereotypes and misinformation about bisexuality and bisexual behavior—that bisexuals are "really gay," that bisexuality "doesn't exist," and that bisexuals are "confused, can't make commitments or have mature relationships"—all take their toll... Many bisexual people concede to social pressure and

> "choose"—often depending on whom they're partnered with or the community or group of people they identify with most easily. (1996:241)

Also, sex columnist Dan Savage points out that it is, unfortunately, easy for bisexuals in opposite-sex relationships to pass as heterosexual (2011:n.p.). He writes, "most adult bisexuals, for whatever reason, wind up in opposite-sex relationships. And most comfortably disappear into presumed heterosexuality" (ibid.). Thus, there may be more bisexuals in this corpus of books than I recognise. They could, for example, have previously been in same-sex relationships but are currently single or in opposite-sex relationships and just never happen to come out or to be outed in these novels. But such situations simply contribute further to bisexual invisibility. While it may feel forced for someone in an opposite-sex or same-sex relationship to mention that they are bisexual, it could nonetheless be extremely beneficial.[37] This creates visibility for this frequently invisible group and could remind people that sexuality is not a binary between straight or gay but rather is a continuum, with multiple possibilities.

In her analysis of the "bisexual plot" in literature and films, Marjorie Garber finds a number of what she calls "distinguishing characteristics". She writes that they include:

> [t]he "phase," which can be "outgrown" on the way to safely heterosexual (or sometimes gay or lesbian) "maturity"; the mode of "indecisiveness" or "confusion"; the rivalry between a man and a woman, both erotically interested in, and interesting to, a third party; a love relationship with a couple, in which jealousy and rivalry are transmuted into some version of "having it all," or else directed at winning away one member of the couple as one's own lover. Very often...the erotic tension is not acted upon...The bisexual plot, as I conceive it,

> is a mode of erotic triangulation in which one person is torn between life with a man and life with a woman. (1995:456)

While Garber only explores works for adults, her list is useful here too. Young adult literature is not quite as full of "erotic tension" as some of the adult work she looks at, but "erotic triangulation" does come up, as when characters – who may or may not identify as bisexual – cheat on their partners with someone of the opposite gender. In addition, confusion and indecisiveness are regular features of these works, particularly when a character cannot or will not "decide" whether they are gay or straight, as though those are the only options. The bisexual plots she finds exist in literature for young adults as well, except with less tension, rivalry, and jealousy.

Before looking at those young adult novels, it is worth saying a few words about books for children. In picture books, there are some characters who could conceivably be read as bisexual, but only by a knowing reader. For example, in Michael Willhoite's *Daddy's Roommate* (1991), it seems as though the main character's "Daddy" was previously in a relationship with his mother, and now is with the euphemistically referred-to "roommate". Whether Daddy identifies as bisexual or whether he came to the realisation of a homosexual orientation later in life is not clarified. Some authors may prefer for the characters to "just be" and for their sexuality to be so normalised that no discussion is needed, but this of course contributes to what Savage calls the "bisexual closet" (2011:n.p.).

Cart and Jenkins write that the first young adult novels featuring bisexuality were published in the late 1990s. "Although labels may seem simpler, a teen's self-definition may well resist an either/or sexual identity and instead insist upon claiming *both*." (2006:134, italics original) It is unclear why this should be true only for teens, as it is – or should be – well known that bisexuality is a valid identity for people of all ages. Unfortunately, in LGBTQ literature for young people, when there are bisexual characters, they are not always described positively, nor are they shown living contented bisexual lives. For example, there is a bisexual main character, in *Boy Meets Boy* by David Levithan (2003). Kyle is portrayed as unhappy because of having a supposedly divided sexuality, as in this discussion with an ex-boyfriend:

> "I'm so confused."
>
> "Why?"
>
> "I still like girls."
>
> "So?"
>
> "And I also like guys."
>
> I touch his knee. "It doesn't sound like you're confused, then."
>
> "But I wanted to be one or the other. With you, I wanted just to like you. Then, after you, I wanted to just like the girls. But every time I'm with one, I think the other's possible."
>
> "So you're bisexual."
>
> Kyle's face flushes. "I hate that word," he tells me, slumping back in his chair. "It makes it sound like I'm divided." (2003:85)

Here, then, Kyle is "divided," which he clearly views as a negative word and a negative situation. He does not see bisexuality as a coherent whole identity. Also, the way he describes himself as liking both guys and girls reflects the stereotype of bisexuals as being "indecisive and promiscuous" (Ochs, 1996:218). Although Kyle's ex-boyfriend does not chastise or criticise Kyle for being bisexual, Kyle seems to have internalised societal biphobia; he does not want to be seen as someone who wants anyone and everyone. As Ochs explains, "[m]any people privately identify as bisexual but, to avoid conflict and preserve their ties to a treasured community, choose to label themselves publicly as lesbian, gay, or straight, further contributing to bisexual invisibility" (1996:233). Kyle is struggling with whether to identify – publicly or privately – as bisexual; his isolation and unhappiness are evident from his usage of the word "divided" and his unwillingness to accept the label that best seems to describe his sexuality.

In another book, *The Year They Burned the Books* by Nancy Garden (1999), Jamie and Terry call themselves "maybe"s, because they are not certain about their sexuality yet. They talk about shades of meaning and "probably maybes" or "maybe probablys", but they do not see bisexuality as a possibility. They must go one way or another. So bisexuality is shown as a state of confusion, one that a person will "come out" of, so to speak, by going one way or the other, i.e. gay or straight. A more charitable reading of this is that they are aware that, as Hutchins puts it, "[m]any bisexuals identify first as heterosexual and then as lesbian/gay, back and forth several times, before settling on a bisexual identity" (1996:241). Perhaps Jamie and Terry are talking about people who will identify back and forth for a while before "settling on a bisexual identity". This sort of deeper understanding seems unlikely, however. What I would guess is more likely is that Jamie and Terry feel unable to choose a bisexual identity and they do not see the possibility of being "sexually postmodern" (Dollimore, 1997:253) or of helping to "trouble", to use Butler's term, or de-stabilise binary systems.

The premise behind *Pink* by Lili Wilkinson (2009) is that the main character, Ava, has come out as a lesbian and been accepted as such, but now finds herself wanting a boyfriend. She spends much of the novel debating whether she is a lesbian or heterosexual, when a simple solution would have conceivably been to accept herself as bisexual. For some reason, this seems to be impossible for her until the very end. This may reflect a common trajectory for someone with internalised biphobia. This is somewhat similar to Daisy in *Pretty Things* by Sarra Manning; Daisy is not the main character, so her story does not receive as much attention in the novel, but she is a self-described lesbian with a girlfriend who also finds herself wanting a man.

In Maureen Johnson's *The Bermudez Triangle*, one character is described as "Felicia Clark, the outspoken 'If you have a pulse, I'm interested' bisexual sex addict" (2004:121), and this perhaps explains why the character of Avery, who is in a relationship with Mel, is unwilling to describe herself as bisexual.

> 'I'm not gay.' Avery said it again, very clearly and sternly.
>
> 'Okay,' Mel said, trying to be conciliatory.
>
> 'You're bi.'
>
> 'Stop trying to tell me what I am!' Avery snapped.
>
> Mel stepped back in shock. She could understand that Avery might not feel comfortable being labeled gay – Mel still had trouble with this sometimes – but being bi wasn't exactly something she could deny.
>
> 'This isn't the same as other people,' Avery went on. 'The bi girls, they go back and forth. We're just...together.'
>
> 'So?'

> 'It's more serious with us. We act like lesbians. Real ones.'
>
> Avery was shaking her head as she spoke, as if the concept of 'real lesbians' wasn't something she could quite comprehend.
>
> 'I am a real one,' Mel said. 'But you can be whatever you want. I don't care. It doesn't matter.' (2004:152)

Avery, perhaps understandably, does not want to label herself, but she does show negative feelings about bisexuals, who, she claims, "go back and forth" (ibid.). Later, though, Avery thinks about herself, "Gay. Gay as the day is long. Except that she wasn't. Despite all the evidence, she was not gay. She knew it. Because gay women don't have sudden, overwhelming and (she had to admit it now) *constant* urges to make out with guys." (2004:185, italics original) Avery recognises that she is attracted to both men and women, but she seems disturbed by this idea. She tells her friend, Nina, who asks, "You like guys too?" (2004:186) Avery's response is to blush and to think, "Something about that question made her feel like...a glutton. Like she wanted *everyone*. Guys, girls, dogs, cats, populations of whole cities." (ibid., italics original) In short, then, Johnson's novel quite clearly shows the negative ideas surrounding bisexuality in YA literature.

It may seem surprising that some of the young queer characters are biphobic; one would hope that minorities would not be phobic of or oppressive towards other minorities, but these books show that it does nonetheless happen. When J switches to an LGBTQ high school in Cris Beam's *I Am J* (2011), in his English class, the students read work by Walt Whitman, and some of the young people say it's "nasty" to be bi (2011:179). J "didn't expect this from queer kids" (ibid.), but these books suggest that people – queer or not – do have negative feelings towards bisexuals.

The only YA novel that I found that was more open and accepting of bisexuality was Aidan Chambers's *Postcards from No Man's Land* (1999). The protagonist, Jacob, goes to Amsterdam and meets young people who are openly bisexual or gay and who are fully accepting of themselves; this in turn makes him rethink his own sexuality and become aware that sexuality can be seen as a continuum. It could in part be the novel's setting in the Netherlands that allows for this (see the chapter on sex and marriage for more on the influence of location on attitudes towards sexuality), but I certainly wish that there were more YA novels that feature such positive views of bisexuality.

Again quoting Hutchins, "claiming a bisexual identity takes great courage, especially in the absence of role models and validation… The open assertion of a bisexual identity affects everyone, not just the person identifying as bisexual, because it disturbs the set of assumptions that sexual orientations and attractions are binary, exclusive, either-or categories" (1996:241). Perhaps this sort of courage is too much to expect from teenagers. Maybe the lack of support for LGBTQ people in general and bisexuals specifically affects young people so that it is too hard for them to come out as bisexual until they are older. Assuming that, then, we are still left with the question of why there are no openly bisexual adult characters in these books; as already mentioned, queer adults are always gay or lesbian. Being openly bisexual can "transgress the either-or paradigm" and thereby "open up conversations about sexual diversity and promote sexual education in a way that doesn't pressure people to take sides or close off dialogue" (Hutchins, 1996:243)

Ochs writes that a "primary manifestation of biphobia is the denial of the very existence of bisexual people" (1996:224). In this case, most of the books in this corpus of texts seem to manifest biphobia. Savage writes, "Yes, lots of people judge and condemn and fear bisexuals. If those were good reasons to stay closeted, no gay or lesbian person would ever come out. And if bisexuals did come out in greater numbers, they could rule...well, not the world, but they could rule the parallel LGBT universe." (2011:n.p.) What we need is for more bisexuals in literature to come out and to be recognised for who they are; then they might rule the literary LGBT universe.

Transgender

Andrew Solomon writes:

> Western culture likes binaries: life feels less frightening when we can separate good and evil into tidy heaps, when we split off the mind from the body, when men are masculine and women are feminine. Threats to gender are threats to the social order. If rules are not maintained, everything seems to be up for grabs, and Joan of Arc must go to the stake. If we countenance people who want to chop off their penises and breasts, then what chance do we have of preserving the integrity of our own bodies? (2012:599)

A transgender identity is thus a threat to western ideas of the self; Solomon also points out that "[b]eing trans is taken to be a depravity, and depravities [particularly] in children are anomalous and disturbing" (2012:600). Jay Prosser writes that the "trans" in "transgender" can mean "across" and also "beyond", so those who are transgender can be either moving from one gender to another or they can be moving beyond gender completely (1997:310). Prosser says, "the one [across] conjures mobility, the other stasis, one a trajectory in material space, the other a transcendence of it" (ibid.). This means there are potentially many different transgender identities and experiences. While this is not the place to discuss the medicalisation of transgendered people and the impact on how they are viewed, treated, and depicted, it is important to point out that "transgendered subjects [are now] speak[ing] for themselves" (Prosser, 1997:317) and that the transgender movement has been developing and increasing in strength since the 1990s (Love, 2010:149). Interestingly, not one of the authors whose works are discussed later in this section has been labelled or has chosen the label of transgender, so perhaps the transgendered are not yet speaking for themselves in children's literature. Heather Love writes that "[e]stablishing a transgender tradition means addressing the crucial distinction between literature about transgender people and literature by transgender people. Transgender individuals have long exerted a fascination for non-transgender people – as symbols of transgression, enlightenment or degeneration" (Love, 2010:150). This suggests that we need more works by transgender people and not just about them.

As Prosser points out, although gays and lesbians traditionally have been stereotyped as being cross-gendered (in that gay men are thought to be like or want to be like women, and lesbians to be like or want to be like men), oddly, "transgendered subjects [have been marginalised] *within* lesbian and gay culture" (1997:311, italics original); there has been a lack of understanding about what it really means to be transgender. Hence, transgendered people have not been included in LGBTQ groups contexts as long as lesbians, gay men, and bisexuals have. Even today some groups do not want to include them. Although "[m]ost lesbian and gay movements, publications and community centres in the United States now include transgender people at least nominally...questions remain about how fully integrated trans people really are in such organizations" (Love, 2010:150). Stonewall, for example, lobbies for the rights of LGB people, but explicitly says they do not work on issues of gender. This distinction between gender and sexuality is something that confuses many. For example, Joane Nagel, in her work on ethnicity and sexuality, calls transgender a "sexual identity" and links it to homosexuality, heterosexuality, and bisexuality (2003:46, 48), although many would argue that being transgendered is about one's gender identity, and that one can be transgender or transsexual and also homosexual, heterosexual, or bisexual, or have another sexual identity. I personally agree with that and I also feel that the "T" belongs in LGBTQ, which is why I am discussing it in this book. With that being said, there are in fact few books for children or young adults that feature transgender characters.

These days, we see some trans and intersex people in the media, although there is often an emphasis on the problems they face. News reports discuss bullying and suicide. Films such as *Boys Don't Cry* (1999) or *XXY* (2007) depict struggles and pain. Novels often do a bit better in terms of nuance (such as Jeffrey Eugenides' *Middlesex* (2003) or *Annabel* by Kathleen Winter (2011)), but are not always in print or easily available (one thinks here of Leslie Feinberg's *Stone Butch Blues* (1994/2004)). So it is not surprising that adults do not always get accurate information or positive ideas about trans issues, which explains in part the scarcity of children's books featuring them.

Jody Norton created the term "transreading", which he defined as:

> intuiting/interpreting the gender of child characters as not necessarily perfectly aligned with their anatomies. Transreading may involve as simple a move as locating a male identity in a female body (for example, the practice of casting female actresses in the role of Peter Pan). Or it may constitute itself as a much subtler imaginative enactment of a much wider range of identities. (2011:299)

There are now several young adult books about transgendered young people, which one can try to analyse through transreading, or one could even transread books that are not explicitly about trans characters. Love writes that "[m]any of the fiercest gender battles are fought on the bodies of newborn infants, elementary school children and adolescents – it is during childhood that the violence of making gendered individuals imposes itself with greatest force" (2010:159), which suggests that there is a need for literature for children and young adults that explores this. The Human Rights Campaign estimates that transgendered people make up at least 0.25 – 1% of the U.S. population (see the HRC website), so this means that there are fewer transgender people than there are lesbians or gay men or bisexuals, but I am still concerned about how few YA books there are that feature transgender characters. Three of the most remarked upon young adult novels on this topic are *Luna* by Julie Ann Peters (2004), Ellen Wittlinger's *Parrotfish* (2007), and Cris Beam's *I Am J* (2011). Cart and Jenkins write that *Luna* is the first "YA novel to address transsexual/transgender issues." (2006:138) And Margaret Talbot writes that *Parrotfish* "along with books like '*Luna*' and '*I Am J*,' is a touchstone for trans kids." (2013:59) She mentions a trans teen who read *Parrotfish* and it gave him "a flash of recognition; a few months later, after a bout of Internet research, he told [his parents] that he was trans." (ibid.)

Luna is about a transwoman, Liam, who was declared male at birth and wants to be affirmed female and become known as Luna.[38] The novel is told from the point of view of Regan, Luna's younger sister. In a way, the story is primarily about how Luna's identity affects Regan; Liam/Luna comes across as self-involved and selfish. She routinely wakes her little sister up in the middle of the night to talk, to show off her latest outfits, and to use her mirror/room, and she also causes trouble for her at her baby-sitting job, so Regan loses the job. In return, Regan seems to get little from the relationship. So the reader might be forgiven for getting a sense of transgender people as being egocentric and only interested in their own issues. Love agrees that Luna "treats both the difficulties of being trans (and, in this case, in the closet) and of being intimate with someone who is. In protecting her brother Liam (who at night becomes Luna), Regan shares in his secret, and is isolated from her parents and her peers." (2010:159) Regan's isolation and trouble might thus paint a negative picture of transgender people.

The novel also seems to imply that being trans is necessarily stressful and must involve leaving home, which might suggest to a reader that there are few or even no happy trans stories. On the other hand, if it is true that over 40 per cent of trans people have attempted suicide (Petrow, 2013:n.p.) and that "[w]orldwide, a transgender person is murdered every three days" (Solomon, 2012:654), then perhaps it makes sense that trans novels can be depressing.[39] Love is more appreciative of Peters's novel than I am, in that she feels "Peters offers a sensitive account of the experience of a transgender adolescent, clearly distinguishing Liam/Luna's experience from homosexuality and portraying the violence of compulsory gender" (2010:160) and she praises the fact that Peters, as a lesbian author, "is able to capture the specificity of transgender experience so well" (ibid.), which returns to the earlier idea of needing more works by transgender people as well as about them.

Parrotfish is a stronger book, in my opinion, and also shows that it is possible to be transgender and to receive support, encouragement, and respect, and to have a positive life. Wittlinger's novel is about Grady, who is declared female but feels male, and it is told from his perspective. This book is much more positive in that while Grady does encounter some difficulties, he is supported by his family to the best of their ability, and also by one particular teacher. Wittlinger's book focuses on Grady's identity as a whole and not just on the gender aspect, which is why I believe that it is more successful, although, as I discuss elsewhere, I am not always convinced by the depiction of Grady and sometimes find it didactic (see the chapter on issue books for more on this). Grady has a number of things going on in his life, and being transgender is simply one of them. In a sense, this is the way literature about any minority is done best; that is to say, having a particular race, religion, sexuality, ability, gender identity, class, and so on is just one part of a character and not all there is about them.

Cris Beam's *I Am J* (2011) is my favourite of the three young adult books that feature trans characters, in part because it shows more diversity. J has one Jewish parent and one Puerto Rican Catholic one, and although gender is undoubtedly the main topic and J's best friend, Melissa, even points out how gender-obsessed he is (2011:275), J is a well-rounded young person who also has hobbies, is dating, and is trying to decide what university to go to. J was declared female and is attracted to women, but does not identify as a lesbian. J's parents would prefer to have a lesbian as a child rather than a trans son (2011:162), but J gets upset when people assume he is a lesbian: "Dyke, aggressive, AG, butch. Whatever the names, none of them fit." (2011:2) J much prefers being called "dude" (2011:3). "In J's mind, if not in anyone else's, he was a *he*. He couldn't go so far as to actually think of himself as male anymore; he had let that dream go at puberty...Still, saying *she* felt like something close to blasphemy." (2011:3, italics original) J wears multiple layers of shirts to try to cover his breasts but "[e]ven with two sports bras and the extra shirts, you could see their roundness, their adamant shout: *I am a girl.*" (2011:14, italics original) He also feels discomfort when showering and tries not to look at his body (2011:38). J's suffering eventually comes to a crux, so he begins doing research on trans issues (2011:52-7) and using a chest binder (2011:62). Since he believes his parents will not accept him being trans, he runs away from home, goes to live in a shelter for LGBTQ teenagers, changes high schools to one that is likewise aimed at LGBTQ teenagers (2011:141), and starts attending "masculine spectrum" meetings (2011:241). While all this is going on, he has a fight with Melissa, because he has a crush on her and kisses her, and though she is attracted to him too, she seems unable to see past his female body (2011:26-7). J also begins a relationship with another girl, Blue, who accepts him as male (2011:104-9) but is later angry that he did not tell her that he was trans (2011:288-9), because she feels he lied to her. J's father tells him that he is "sick. You need help" (2011:316) and J also discovers that his mother has been lying to him (2011:318). Despite all these problems, J is a creative person with a passion for photography, he is able to accept himself and knows what he wants to do with his life, he finds a queer community, he meets friends and family friends who like him for who he is (as on 2011:292-3 or 160-1), and he gets accepted to university (2011:326). His mother, Carolina, always called J "m'ija", which is Spanish for "my daughter", and at the end of the novel, she changes it to "m'ijo", or "my son" (2011:321), and this shows a new level of understanding and acceptance on her part. J is in most ways a typical teenager, which is why it is easy to relate to him.

In Alex Sanchez's *Rainbow Road* (2005), the main characters meet an assortment of queer people on the road trip across the U.S., including a transgender teenager with the unfortunate name of B.J. Jason assumes that B.J. was born female and when Nelson asks her, "So what's it like out here in the sticks growing up gay?" (2005:106), Jason is confused, and it is implied that this is because he would not have guessed that such a pretty girl would be a lesbian (ibid.). B.J. goes on to say, "I never really thought of myself as gay…Not that I have anything against gay people. But for as long as I can remember, I've always known I was a girl." (2005:106-7) Jason then notices B.J.'s Adam's apple, and all is clarified when B.J. says that "[t]he problem…was I'd been given the body parts of a boy." (2005:107). Jason starts to think of B.J. as a "boy/girl" and feels "curious and a little repulsed." (ibid.) What is interesting about the portrayal of B.J. is that the focus is primarily on the three protagonists (Jason, Nelson, and Kyle) and their feelings about her rather than about her own experiences, although B.J. does talk about her unhappy home life, how her father beat her (ibid.), how Social Services placed her with her grandparents (2005:108), and how she went to a Christian school where the principal told her to "repent or I was going straight to hell." (ibid.) In other words, the character of B.J. is there to serve a certain role, perhaps an educational one, and does not develop in her own right.

Jason is the one out of the trio who struggles the most with transgender issues. He thinks, "Why would a guy dress up like a girl except as a joke?…This wasn't joking. Jason felt the urge to wipe off B.J.'s makeup and tell him to stop it. But at the same time, she looked so beautiful." (2005:107) The switch between "him" and "she" is very telling regarding Jason's confusion about the "boy/girl". Meanwhile, Nelson is much more accepting. He "had met a couple of transgender teens before, at the queer youth group he sometimes attended. But they'd been superbutch girls who dressed as boys, with baseball caps and baggy jeans. He'd never met a male-to-female tranny, especially one who loves Britney [Spears]." (2005:110) Still, he meets two of B.J.'s friends and wonders "Were they truly women?" (ibid.), where the "truly" suggests that Nelson is not fully accepting either. He also thinks back to when he was a child and dressed up in his mother's clothes, but the reason why he did this was because of "the *illusion* of being female (and freaking out his dad)" (2005:111, italics original) and he "had never seriously desired to become a *real* girl" (ibid., italics original).

In Sanchez's work, the transgender character has had difficulties but clearly accepts herself now and is attempting to live her best possible life, while it is other people who find her troubling. By the time the three young men leave B.J., they seem more open and more accepting, but there is an unspoken implication that even in the queer community, transpeople are somewhat beyond the norm.

A book for young readers that possibly features a transgender character is Meg Rosoff's *What I Was* (2007). The main character, Hilary, shares a hut with a character called Finn. It is only some time later that Hilary is told that Finn is actually female, although Finn was ostensibly living, dressing, and behaving as a male.[40] The news comes as a shock to Hilary, but the story never clarifies whether Finn feels male and is thus transgendered or whether Finn was simply trying to have a better life by living as a boy.

Luna, *Parrotfish*, and *I Am J* are all for teenaged readers, but since we know that pre-teens, school-aged children, and even some pre-schoolers are recognising that their psychological gender does not match their physical body (Tanner, 2012), and also because children will meet trans people, there ought to be some trans books for young children too. I am unfortunately aware of no texts about transgender characters for readers between five and twelve or so. However, there are a couple of picture books, which at least can be used with children up until the age of five or six, regardless of whether they are themselves trans or know any trans people.

My Princess Boy, which is by Cheryl Kilodavis (2011), is about a boy who likes pink and enjoys wearing tiaras and other princess clothes. While there is no indication that this boy is transgender, in that he seems to identify as a boy and of course the title suggests he is and will remain a boy, the book is positive because he is accepted for who he is and how he likes to dress. This is a strong message to pass on to children. It does not matter if the princess boy is transgender or not, if he will grow up to identify as a transvestite, if he will be straight or gay or bisexual or something else; for now, he is a little boy who likes pink sparkly dresses, and it is implied that that is completely fine with his relatives, classmates, and teachers.

10,000 Dresses by Marcus Ewert (2008), which is another picture book, is, in my opinion, one of the best transgender books. The main character, Bailey, dreams about beautiful dresses and longs to make them and wear them. One strong aspect of this book is that Ewert uses female pronouns when referring to Bailey, even though Bailey's relatives repeatedly say, "You are a boy, Bailey." (2008:n.p.) This suggests that the narrator has accepted Bailey for who she is and that therefore so should the reader. While this might potentially bewilder some young readers, it can be easily explained by an adult reading besides them, and also is a good starting-point for discussion. This shows respect for the character and for trans people more generally. On the other hand, young people might be more willing to accept Bailey as she is. When I asked Ewert if he thought using female pronouns despite Bailey's family's insistence on her maleness might confuse some young readers, he replied, "No, I don't at all. To me it boils down to this: a person's gender is what they themselves say it is. A young child can get that, no problem." (personal correspondence, 2013:n.p.)[41]

Ewert's book also has strong, symbolic illustrations by Rex Ray that emphasise which characters see Bailey for who she is and which do not; Bailey's parents and brother are depicted as larger than Bailey, but their faces are never shown, while Laurel, Bailey's friend, is shown in her entirety and on the same scale as Bailey. Bailey's relatives quite literally turn away from her, but only Laurel can and does see her. In addition, the ten thousand dresses of the title are creative and fun and can inspire other readers. Ewert points out that his book is about art as much as it is about gender: "What's it like to be an artist, and what do you do if the people around you don't share your vision?...Bailey [is] not a single-issue character. That's too reductive, plus inaccurate: people are never just one thing. Sure, Bailey's a transgendered girl, but equally, she's an artist." (ibid.) However, in Ewert's book, Bailey's family is not understanding or supportive and they do not "share [Bailey's] vision", because Bailey was declared male at birth and her parents and brother refuse to accept her as a young girl. Although Bailey faces some problems, she is still a confident person who believes in herself and who looks elsewhere for support. Some readers might find the ending upsetting, in that there is no resolution with Bailey's family – the only person to be accepting is a young friend who lives nearby – but perhaps in the follow-up book that Ewert is currently writing, this will change. As Ewert notes:

> people on the Left have sometimes criticized the book for how harsh and dismissive Bailey's mother, father and brother are portrayed. And I think that's actually a very valid point. Certainly, rejection such as I've depicted is all-too-common; nevertheless, I wish I had been able to show a little more hopefulness vis a vis Bailey & her family. In my own mind, I'm quite clear that they will come around, and become amazing

> allies – I've always known that – I just wish I could have hinted at that outcome (at least a little!) in 10K D. I don't like to leave things on a bleak note, and I absolutely do believe people can open up and change for the better. (ibid.)

Ewert writes that in the sequel, he will show that Bailey gets the support and love she needs:

> It's very important to me…to show just how far Bailey's family has come in terms of loving and supporting her. Extremely important. The sequel also deals with Bailey at school: midway through the school year, she announces her affirmed gender to everyone, with the support and blessing of her family.
>
> And finally, there's a new character, Regis, the King of All Valentines, who's an African-American transgendered guy, from an earlier era in American history (circa the 1890s). It's really important for me to show Bailey as part of a much a larger lineage – she's clearly not just one idiosyncratic individual – she's someone who has a place – along with hundreds of thousands of other people! – in a very intricate, ornate tapestry: History, in a word. (ibid.)

Despite the fact that some readers might find the ending "bleak" in regard to Bailey's family, it is still quite positive, as Bailey is able to find some acknowledgement of who she is, and she is able to express herself as an artist by designing and making a dress.

Solomon points out that "[g]ender is among the first elements of self-knowledge" (2012:607), and that often this knowledge comes through clear feelings about what clothes to wear, including underwear and swimwear, as well as how to play and how to urinate

(2012:607 and 616). Most of the books mentioned in this section do tend to focus on clothes as an indicator of gender. I cannot help but wonder if this is problematic to a certain extent, as clothes are not all there is to gender. Perhaps in an era when clothes are more gender-neutral, literature will instead focus more on an internal sense of self, or maybe ideas about gender will shift completely. As Julie C. Luecke writes, books with transgender characters do offer "bibliotherapeutic relief for young people who are transgender or questioning whether they may be" (2012:n.p.) – and one can note that this again makes them into issue books, aimed at those who are or might be trans rather than at the general reading public – but they also show that "we still want to separate people into clear-cut groupings: either you're transgender, or you're not. We believe we can embrace transgender children and a male/female dichotomy simply by reassigning these children to the appropriate gender role — swapping Captain Underpants for Babymouse." (ibid.) In other words, they can still be quite gender-normative.

As Victoria Flanagan discusses extensively, there are quite a few books for children that feature cross-dressing. It is not the same thing as transgender, but it is worth looking briefly at the three models Flanagan finds in literature and films for young readers/viewers. The first is the male-to-female cross-dresser, "which is often used for comedic purposes, drawing inspiration from 'drag,'"; then there is the female-to-male cross-dresser, "the most common paradigm, which generally facilitates a critique of gender through the protagonist's ability to give a successful performance of masculinity"; and finally there is the transgender model, "which occurs only rarely and offers the closest approximation to the contemporary adult transgender experience." (2008:2) As this section has shown, the third model is indeed quite rare. Flanagan adds, "The relationship between cross-dressing and subversive sexualities (transvestite, transsexual, homosexual) remained unacknowledged in children's texts until only recently. The recent proliferation of literature directed at adolescents, however, has demonstrated an unprecedented willingness to embrace adult concepts previously considered off-limits to younger readers" (2008:213-4). I would not say there has been a major "proliferation", but I would agree that the works being published recently do represent a change in what people think is appropriate to discuss with children and young adults.

Transgender identities can destabilise and denaturalise gender binaries and the ways in which people other others (cf. Butler, 1990/2006, Prosser, 1997:312, and Solomon, 2012:599). As Dierdre Keenan puts it, "[t]ransgender and transsexual identities serve as the ultimate challenge to all assumptions about gendered experience and constructed borders between sexualities." (2004:123) If transgender is not only an identity but also "a methodology, a subjectivity and a community" (Prosser, 1997:313), then we clearly need more books that explore this, particularly books for younger readers, so that they can begin to think about issues of gender more broadly than they are currently socialised to do. Interestingly, Prosser calls for "specification" in the transgender community, i.e. "more specific subject categories to account for these different identities within transgender and transsexual" (Prosser, 1997:320), although I am not convinced that small communities need to be fractured into ever more specific subsets. Robert E. Nye also explains how developments in the field and recent work on gender "has resulted in an important corrective to the temptation to see sex and gender in exclusively binary terms, endlessly reinvented as a series of polar oppositions. Third sex and third gender models and even more complicated schemata have been developed recently to account for the great diversity of body types, gender identities, and sexual practices that have thrived in the West and throughout the world." (2004:11-2) I agree that we should recognise and accept many gender identities and sexualities and that we need more acceptance and depiction of these "specific subject categories". Perhaps more works such as Ewert's will signal such a move, because clearly, transgender literature for children is rather mixed at the moment in terms of how it portrays transpeople and trans issues. Also, the fact that there is such a small number of texts suggests that there is much more work to be done in the field.

Other Shades of the Rainbow

When I say "otherwise queer", as I briefly discussed in the introduction to the book and earlier in this chapter, I include those who define themselves as questioning, intersex, asexuals, sadists, masochists, fetishists, polyamorous, and anyone else who would like the label of queer and/or would like to belong to the queer community or communities. As stated previously, while others prefer the "Q" in LGBTQ to strictly refer to those who are questioning, I find that limiting, and I personally know many people who call themselves queer but are not lesbian, gay, bisexual, transgender, or questioning; thus, having the "Q" stand for "queer" is a more open, accepting use of the letter.

Few books for young readers even touch on the Q in LGBTQ. In Julie Burchill's *Sugar Rush*, Sugar is depicted rather unsympathetically as a young woman who is unwilling to be monogamous in or open about her relationship with Kim. Sugar wonders why she cannot like boys as well as Kim (2004:120) and she implies a polyamorous attitude when she say:

> But say I got a favourite CD – a single. Can I only EVER play that single, because it's my favourite? Can't I ever play another single or…not even PLAY it, say, cos that implies, you know DOING IT, but more to the point can't I ever HUM another song? Can't I have it as my mobile tone? Can't I be happy when it comes on the radio and go "Oh I really love that song!" (2004:121, capitals original)

Kim does not want to accept Sugar playing, humming, or otherwise enjoying any other song, but it will perhaps surprise no one that Sugar later cheats on Kim with multiple male partners. This could suggest to readers that LGBTQ people cannot be monogamous or that their sexual relations are not satisfying (see the chapters on stereotypes and on sex for more on this). It may have been better to show Sugar and Kim talking about and enacting an open relationship.

Alex Sanchez's *Rainbow Road* (2005) is certainly not the best written of the LGBTQ corpus for children and young adults, but it is arguably the most inclusive, as its protagonists are three gay male teenagers – although one has had a girlfriend and also cheats on his boyfriend by kissing another girl so perhaps should be termed bisexual, even if he does not use that label himself – and the three boys go on a journey where they meet a variety of other queers, including a transgender girl, as already referred to above, young gays living in a sort of commune, some "heteroflexible" girls, an older gay male couple, and the students at a high school for LGBTQ youth in California, among others. Interestingly, few lesbian or bisexual girls feature in the story, so the characters are predominantly male. At the commune, there are two young men who go by the names of Horn-Boy and Lady-Bugger. The character Nelson asks if Horn-Boy and Lady-Bugger are a couple and the latter says, "Mostly." (2005:70). Horn-Boy explains they have an open relationship and Nelson's response is, "Wow" (ibid.). The narrator says of Nelson, "He realized he sounded like a kid, but he'd never met anyone in an open relationship before." (2005:71) Nelson is tempted to sleep with Horn-Boy but his best friend Kyle does not let him, as Nelson is stoned and Kyle generally plays the overprotective mother figure to Nelson's irresponsible teenager (2005:77). The next morning, Nelson and his friends leave the commune and some days later, Nelson meets a boy that he starts what seems to be an exclusive relationship with, so there are no further mentions of open relationships.

Although in reference specifically to bisexuality, Hutchins points out that the polyamory/polyfidelity movement "includes many varieties of negotiated relationships, ranging from triads to group marriages, primary and secondary partners, and so on." (1996:251) Perhaps some of these relationship forms will be portrayed in children's literature in the future, so as to reflect lived experiences.

As a final example, a potentially asexual character is depicted in Ellen Wittlinger's *Hard Love*. The character of John, who is unsure of his sexuality, speaks with Birdie:

> "I'm not even sure myself if I'm gay or not. I mean, I've been thinking maybe I am."
>
> "You *have*? Are you attracted to *men*?" Birdie asked.
>
> "Well, no. But I'm not attracted to women either."
>
> "Oh, *well*, that's just dysfunctional, not *gay*," Birdie announced confidently. I was lost for a comeback. (1999:52-3, italics original)

While John could be asexual, in that he is apparently attracted to no one, he is told that he is "dysfunctional". This sends quite a harmful message to young readers by suggesting that there is something wrong with asexuality.

Beyond these characters, I have not yet found any children's books that feature other types of queerness, including heterosexuals who define as queer. This may be because there is a fear of discussing sex with children (Lepore, 2010), and there is an erroneous assumption that discussing sexuality necessarily means discussing sexual practices, and a further assumption by some that discussing sexuality and/or sexual practices with children or in children's books is inappropriate. Another reading of this lack is that society is less accepting of certain aspects of queerness and therefore the "trickle-down effect", wherein a topic gradually becomes less taboo, first in literature for adults and finally in literature for children, has not yet taken place.

In sum, this section has aimed to show that "otherwise queer" characters are absent from books for young readers, and the first half of this chapter more generally has looked at how the BTQ in LGBTQ is either missing from children's literature or is portrayed in problematic ways. As the next section will discuss, it is not just BTQ people who are the invisible missing pieces in books for young readers, however. LGBTQ people are generally represented as being solely queer, without the possibility of having intersecting identities.

Multiple Identities

One of the many effects that Judith Butler's book *Gender Trouble* has had on feminist and gender studies is that it highlights how no group is monolithic. As she points out, feminism itself is problematic because it assumes "women" to be a group with similar experiences, similar backgrounds, similar needs, and similar goals (1990/2006:5-6). Dierdre Keenan has written that the "notion of a *global sisterhood*, in a sense, refused the category of race and other differences that separate women" (2004:111, italics original). Clearly, such a global sisterhood – or a global group of anything, whether gay men, Jews, people with cerebral palsy, redheads, the depressed, and so on – unites people only on one level of identity, and ignores or irons out differences on all the other levels. One can apply this to queerness in that even homosexuality is heterogeneous, despite the prefixes on the words. Later theoretical work has continued this line of thought, exploring how identity is in fact the intersection of multiple identities – race, religion, sexuality, class, size, level of education, marital status, ability, profession, to name just a few – although some people might choose to create a hierarchy within that, so that, for example, one person might prioritise their race and belong to racially identified groups, while someone else might focus on their religion and spend much of their time and energy on related activities and with others from the same religious organisation (Sullivan, 2011:58). Many communities built on having something in common, such as sexuality, often fail to recognise that their members may have more dissimilar features than similar ones, and most likely will not agree with one another on all matters. All this is to say that although there is now more recognition of the fact that people can and do belong to a variety of different groups and can and do create coherent identities, there is still a problematic assumption that occurs more often than one might like, namely that one identity is more important or overarching than the others.

The impetus for some of the analysis that takes place in this part of the chapter builds on this sort of work and comes from the understanding that people are in fact comprised of intersecting pieces of identity (cf. Sullivan, 2011:58). Often, it seems as though people feel they must have a hierarchy of identity, where one aspect takes precedence. But one need not prioritise one part of one's identity to the detriment of others (Sullivan, 2011:67): for instance, would a person be a gay black or a black gay? Are these two different ways of being? Sullivan points out that ignoring issues of race turns all queers white (2011:58), and of course we know that queers come in all colours, even if whiteness seems to be the assumed norm in queer communities. As Georgio discusses, those who are white and LGBTQ still enjoy some white privilege (2011:n.p.) and this needs to be acknowledged; one can add that those who are Christian and LGBTQ enjoy some aspects of Christian-majority privilege, and those who are able-bodied and LGTBQ enjoy some aspect of that ability-based privilege, and so on. People can be racist and LGBTQ, or sexist and LGBTQ, and so on, because belonging to one minority does not necessarily make them understanding or accepting of all minorities. As Georgio puts it, "Homosexuality is not a race. I am black. I am also gay. I am not gayack or blagay. Being in one minority group doesn't excuse being insensitive to another minority group" (ibid.).

Hence, we need to pay attention to race, and other attributes, but not in such a way that we are looking to see which group is the most oppressed or has the worst situation; this is not a competition. Instead, I am interested in how people create a coherent identity out of the various parts of their identity. Clearly, people do live as, for example, anorexic, Hispanic, agnostic, married, bisexual men with learning difficulties; the issue is how they bring these seemingly disparate features together. Sullivan refers to this as "interlocking systems" (2011:71), and here I to explore how such interlocking systems or intersextions of identity are portrayed in books for young readers. Are there queer characters who think about other aspects of their identities? Do these books suggest that one can be queer and also non-norm in another way? Or do these books assume that all queers are white, able-bodied, middle-class, and nominally Christian?

In children's literature, my findings suggest, this latter assumption does unfortunately reign. While there are now some LGBTQ characters in books for children and young people, which is progress, their queerness tends to be their defining feature and their defining identity. It is very rare to see a character who is both queer and from another minority group and who rates these two or more aspects of their identity as being of equivalent importance, or who explores what it means to create an identity out of more than one sub-group. Most queer characters in these books are at least nominally Christian, white, middle-class, able-bodied, and fairly well educated, or in the process of being educated. While one could argue that it is complicated enough to be, say, white and queer, or that those identities do not always fit neatly together, and I would agree with that, I would also assert that it is easier – both in reality and in literature – to deviate from the norm in only one characteristic. Hence, it is fascinating to explore why there is such an absence of characters in children's books who deviate from the norm in two or more ways at the same time.

Race/Ethnicity

I start looking at intersectionality and identity by exploring race/ethnicity. As Keenan points out, this is a challenge because "there exists no coherent or stable meaning for the terms of race. Outward appearances certainly cannot account for the meanings attributed to racial difference or for the hatred and oppression scripted by racism." (2004:111) In other words, is race defined by "outward appearance"? Is it actually defined by ethnicity? Is it some combination? And who has the right to label someone's race – the individual in question or other people or the government or someone else? Does it change depending on context? Here, I rely on Nagel's definitions of ethnicity and race. She writes that ethnicity refers to "differences between individuals and groups in skin color, language, religion, cultural, national origin/nationality, or sometimes geographic region. Ethnicity subsumes both nationalism and race." (2003:6) Nagel explains that "[c]urrent notions of *race* are centered exclusively on visible (usually skin color) distinctions among populations, although its historical origins and usage were broader and included religious and linguistic groups (such as Jews or the Irish) who were considered to be 'races.'" (ibid., italics original) Hence, as "ethnicity" is the broader and perhaps clearer term, I generally employ it, although it is interesting to note that much of the research relies on the word "race" rather than on "ethnicity". In regard to who decides what someone's ethnicity is, for these books, I am going by how the characters are labelled or label themselves, or by what can be assumed based on their names or other features; for example, if a character speaks one language at home and another in the public sphere, then I assume this person is at least bilingual and bicultural. As Nagel writes, "[e]thnicity is not merely a feature of one's ethnic ancestry. The social definition of an individual's race, ethnicity, and nationality is decided and given meaning through interactions with others. An individual's ethnicity is a negotiated social fact—what you think is your ethnicity versus what others think is your ethnicity." (2003:42) For the most part, I rely on whatever "negotiated social facts" are offered in the text, through how people refer to themselves or others.

Ethnicity, as with gender or sexuality or religion, is a way of identifying and othering people. Obviously, ethnicity can be used to "unify women and men in categories" (Keenan, 2004:117). Nevertheless, it is still a category, among many, that both divides and unites, possibly doing more of the former than the latter. LGBTQ as a category can be said to do the same, and yet of course I am focusing on it in this book. I suppose that my awareness of this is one reason why I think it is so essential to look at intersections between/among identities. I like the term intersectionality, but Nagel also refers to "positionality", by which she means someone's position, sometimes at the intersection of multiple identities (2003:ix).

Interestingly, many texts seem to ignore these intersections/positions. Donnellan's non-fiction book *Homosexuality* (1998), which is aimed at young readers, has nothing at all on ethnicity. Nagel's work, which is on how sexuality is used in racial discussions/discourse, scarcely mentions non-heterosexualities. Nagel even says that "[d]espite the visceral power of sexual matters in general, especially those involving race, ethnicity, or the nation, the connection between ethnicity and sexuality often is hidden from view." (2003:2) However, her awareness of this does not seem to extend beyond heterosexuality for the most part (a rare example is when she discusses LGB (not TQ) Irish-Americans (2003:26)).

Some texts, such as *Lesbian Studies* (1982), edited by Margaret Cruikshank, do indeed look specifically at issues of the intersection of sexuality and race or ethnicity. Her book includes chapters on black lesbians, Latina lesbians, and Jewish lesbians, although the main focus of the work seems to be about academia, rather than on how such people create or perform their identities or how they are portrayed in literature, and it is in any case thirty years out of date now. Nonetheless, if ethnicity can be performed (cf. Nagel, 2003:54), in the way gender or sexuality can, what would that mean? What would a performance of, say, Chinese lesbianism look like? More specifically, what would this involve in books for young readers?

Sadly, this is very difficult to answer, for the simple reason that few of the books in this corpus are situated at ethnosexual intersections. David Levithan's utopian, futurist young adult novel *Wide Awake* includes a variety of mixed-race characters with different sexualities (2008). It is atypical of LGBTQ fiction for young readers in that it is set in the future; the United States portrayed in Levithan's work is a positive place where nearly everyone is accepted, no matter what religion, ethnicity, or sexuality.

Perhaps a better example is Jason, one of the three protagonists in Alex Sanchez's *Rainbow* trilogy.[42] Jason's parents occasionally use a word in Spanish while speaking but Jason never mentions being bilingual or bicultural. The only real reference to his ethnicity comes in the last book in the trilogy, *Rainbow Road*, when Nelson says, "I've never done it with a Latino guy." Jason responds, "Dude, we're the best!" (2005:213) His background is thus a positive feature in this situation but is otherwise unacknowledged in any explicit way. It is not clear whether Jason's parents are recent immigrants or whether his family has been in the U.S. for generations, nor where their roots are. One could argue that it shows how assimilated Jason is and/or how comfortable he is as a young man of Latino origin in the U.S., which would mean that it is progressive that this is scarcely referenced. But one would also be hard-pressed to claim that it is always easy and perfectly acceptable to be Latino/a and LGBTQ in the United States. As Nagel points out, "The writings of Native American, Asian American, and Latino gay men and lesbians resonate with those of African Americans reporting feelings of exclusion both from their home communities and from the white gay world. Lesbians of color express similar experiences of isolation and make similar criticisms of white lesbians and feminists for insensitivity to the differing needs of lesbians of color" (2003:125). In other words, for many people who are not white, it is a challenge to integrate these various aspects of themselves and to feel at home both with other members of the LGBTQ community and with people from their own ethnicity.

The only picture book I have found with a Hispanic LGBTQ character is Rigoberto González's *Antonio's Card* (2005), where the protagonist has two mothers. The book is interesting in that it does not explicitly discuss the ethnicity but is a bilingual text – again, the only one in my corpus – and the main character, Antonio, has a name that would be easily recognised as Spanish. Bilingual LGBTQ books are a wonderful idea, in my opinion, and I hope publishers will consider producing more.

Black characters are also strangely absent. In her research, Christine Jenkins found that "[a]ccording to both the earlier and the more recent novels, most gay/lesbian people are white and middle-class. Only three of the sixty books portray people of color as gay or lesbian, all of them African-American." (2011:149) Melinda Kanner writes, "Only three titles feature African-American characters: Guy's *Ruby*, Jacqueline Woodson's *The Dear One* (1992), and Rees' *The Milkman's on His Way*. In the field of young adult lesbian and gay fiction, there are apparently only three authors of color, Alice Childress, Rosa Guy, and Jacqueline Woodson." (n.d.:n.p.) In my own research, I also have found the dual-heritage (half-African-American and half-Caucasian-American[43]) Staggerlee (formerly known as Evangeline) in *The House You Pass on the Way* by Jacqueline Woodson (2003), and there is a secondary character, Andy, in Philip Pullman's *The Broken Bridge*. In the latter novel, the main character, Ginny, has a crush on Andy. She also feels a close connection to him because they are the only two black people in their rural town in Wales (Ginny is mixed-race and lives with her white father). Ginny does not realise that Andy is gay until quite late in the novel and although she is disappointed, she decides that the relationship she has with Andy is one of "siblings, kindred, blood relatives" (1990:179). In other words, she feels that their connection is strong because of their shared ethnic identity, and that this surpasses their different sexualities and the fact that they cannot have a romance. Andy is otherwise assimilated into their community as Welsh and white.

Nagel refers to Eldrige Cleaver's famous attack on James Baldwin, on how he is "somehow un-black" because he is gay (2003:122). This, of course, stems from the idea that black men cannot be homosexual, as though being queer is a white "attribute" or problem. This suggests that having both a non-norm ethnicity and a non-norm sexuality is impossible, with the two identities being incompatible (2003:123-5). A gay black man is not "black enough", to use Robyn Ochs' term (1996:228, where she relates it to the idea of bisexuals not being queer enough). Nagel sums this up well by saying that the "homophobia at worst, indifference at best that face lesbians and gays in the black community, combine with the racism of gay whites, to further isolate black homosexuals." (2003:125) Indifference might be a good word to use to explain the missing non-white characters in these books.

Beyond black and Latino, there were very few other ethnicities recognised. Although being Jewish can certainly be considered an ethnicity and thus is a relevant category here, I actually discuss this more in the following section, on religion, so here I can simply say that there are a couple of Jewish queers in these works. It is worth mentioning, however, that in Cris Beam's *I Am J* (2011), the main character, J, has a Puerto Rican Catholic mother and a Jewish father, and J seems equally interested in both aspects of his background, which is actually to say equally disinterested. It is refreshing to read a book where the queer character has other features of diversity and does not struggle with them; J appears to just accept that this is his background. Raj, Jason's boyfriend in Robin Reardon's *A Secret Edge*, is an immigrant from India and there is some discussion in the book of homosexuality in an Indian context, but he is not the main character and his feelings about being both gay and of Indian origin are not explored. Also, there is *Swimming in the Monsoon Sea* by Shyam Selvadurai (2007), which takes place in Sri Lanka, so the setting allows for, and insists upon, Sri Lankan characters. Similarly, Magden's *2 Girls* is set in Turkey and the main characters are secular Turkish Muslims, as will be referred to more below. But for the most part, books written and published in the U.K. and the U.S. have white characters.

It is worth mentioning that nearly every example that was referred to here came from a young adult novel. Picture books seem to be an even whiter world. Perhaps some of the white characters are meant to stand as a sort of general person, the way males are presumed to represent all people, male and female. But this does not allow queers of other ethnicities to feel represented, nor does it remind readers that many people do indeed live on the intersections (or the "[e]thnosexual frontiers", as Nagel puts it (2003:14)). Keenan quotes Audre Lorde, who "asserts the multiple dimensions of her identity that separated her from others" (2004:121), i.e. "black lesbian mother in an interracial relationship" (ibid.), and one could add writer and activist as well. I would say that Lorde is right to declare and insist upon all the aspects of her identity, which is what I would hope all the young characters in my corpus of texts would do. As Nagel says, "[s]exual identities, desires, and practices are defined and constructed by sexualized expectations attributed to one's own and one's partners' racial, ethnic, and national membership." (2003:255) I would change her word "membership" to "memberships" in order to recognise the intersectionality that I have attempted to discuss here. Regardless, we have not yet seen literature for children and young people that explores the intersections and multiple positions that various memberships would entail, nor how people can create coherent identities out of these multiple memberships.

As Doris Davenport points out, the absence of texts with racial minorities (in her case, she notes a syllabus that includes "no Blacks and/or wimmin" (1982:9)) might be because such people/groups are viewed as a "threat" (1982:11), and the result of this "visible invisibility" (ibid.) can be harmful and hurtful. She calls for changes "in the way Black lesbians are viewed and treated in academia, and the rest of the un-real world" and "[c]hanges in the way we are presented and perceived" (ibid.); this call can and should be extended to many people whose identities are at the intersections. In an article on civil rights and marriage equality, Gary Yonge writes:

> To compare these two struggles is not to equate them. To say homophobia and racism are the same would be ridiculous. As Quentin Crisp once said: "The difference between being gay and being black is that you don't have to come downstairs one day and say, 'Mum, Dad, I'm black.'"
>
> It goes without saying that there are major differences between race and sexual orientation. It also goes without saying that the existence of many black lesbians and gays makes the binary opposition of the two issues redundant. The problem with Crisp's joke is that it contains the implication you can't be both at the same time. (2012:n.p.)

The problem with Crisp's joke is the same problem with many of the LGBTQ books for children; we know that logically you can be "both at the same time", but these works do not recognise that. Hence, we need to cross ethnosexual frontiers and see more intersectionality in children's books.

Religion and Spirituality

It can be difficult to define religion, as it is such a large term, and it can be used in multiple ways (for example, someone can call herself Jewish, but be an atheist, so is this person a Jew in the religious sense?[44]). Thus, it is worth clarifying that religion here refers to religious communities, including world religions (Buddhism or

Christianity, say), movements, and even cults. Spirituality or faith here means belief in something, but not necessarily membership in a particular religious group, and thus is a broader term. Regardless of which term is in focus, my findings suggest that being queer and religious or spiritual is not common in literature for children and young people. Perhaps this means that the general belief or understanding is that religions are not open to LGBTQ people and that in turn a god or gods who is/are the basis/bases of any religion might not be accepting of LGBTQ people either. The books studied here seem to suggest that if a person is LGBTQ, they must either hide that part of their identity/self and can thereby still be religious/spiritual, or else they have to leave religion behind in order to have an LGBTQ life.

As Helen Cosis Brown and Christine Cocker note, "the influence of many religious leaders and the power of religious teaching are heavily influential in some countries in the world where religion, particularly fundamentalist religious beliefs, are closely associated with significant political and legal influence." (2011:78) And, as they discuss, such political and legal influence includes treatment of LGBTQ people, and this can create a very unpleasant or challenging environment. They write that "Amnesty International estimates that there are in excess of seventy countries where homosexuality is illegal" (2011:80), and many of these countries are religiously fundamentalist.

In terms of the connections between gender/sexuality and religion, there has been research carried out into that topic in distinct periods of time (such as the Middle Ages, as in Brozyna, 2005) or in specific cultures (such as India, as in Leslie and McGee, 2000). Furthermore, some people within particular religions have looked at whether there are ways of reconciling their religious beliefs with their sexualities, as in Elizabeth Stuart's gay and lesbian prayer book (1992) or in Alison Webster's analysis of Christianity and female sexuality, which discusses how lesbians and feminists feel marginalised by the Christian religion and invisible within it (1995). Webster seems to ultimately suggest that it can be a challenge for lesbians and/or feminists to find a place for themselves in Christianity, which is, of course, one of the main religions in the world today. Along those lines, some of the research on religion and sexuality or gender explores the religious oppression of women (cf. Harrison and Heyward, 1994:131), and this can be expanded to the LGBTQ community as well, so perhaps this is why religion is not often raised as an issue in these books. On the other hand, clearly there are religious LGBTQ people, just as there are religious feminists, and they may need to work on reconciling their religious beliefs with their sexuality or gender identity (for a discussion of religious feminists, see Harrison and Heyward, 1994:131-148).

Ursula King explores why it is so important to analyse these issues. She writes that "[g]ender issues are ubiquitous in religion, but also highly complex – local and particular as well as universal at the same time. Their relationship is subtle for here, probably more than anywhere else, the profound ambiguity and ambivalence of all religions becomes evident." (2004:71) She also says that "dynamic patterns of gendering are deeply embedded throughout all religions, fused and interstructured with all religious worlds and experiences. This *embeddedness* means that gender is initially difficult to identify and separate out from other aspects of religion" (2004:71, italics original) Although she focuses on gender, much of what she says is applicable to sexuality. As she writes, "throughout all previous history, there has been a sharp gender asymmetry in the hierarchy of knowledge, and nowhere is this more clearly institutionalized than in religion." (2004:73) Indeed, this is true of sexuality as well. When King discusses how women read and reread religious texts, trying to understand them from other perspectives, i.e. not biased by "lenses of gender" (2004:77), perhaps this can be extended to LGBTQ people. If women are looking at how religions have treated women, or whether women have been able to participate in religious ceremonies, or how women can create religious communities, or how religions portray women (cf. King, 2004:77-9 for examples of topics women might study), the same could perhaps be suggested of LGBTQ people, who might similarly try to find a place within religious tradition(s). In other words, we can start queering religion by thinking about how religions have treated and included LGBTQ people, or whether LGBTQ people have been able to participate in religious ceremonies, or have same-sex marriages in houses of prayer, and so on, or how LGBTQ people can create religious communities, or how religions portray LGBTQ people, among many other interesting topics. Hence, it is worth exploring how the intersections of religion and sexuality/gender are portrayed in children's literature, but I have so far found no research on this and/or in regard to young people in particular.

Since Judaism and Christianity are the two religions that appear most often in children's books with LGBTQ characters, I start with the former, as it, obviously, came first. As Farley writes:

> Judaism traditionally has shown a concern for the "improper emission of seed." Included in this concern are proscriptions of masturbation and homosexual acts. Both are considered unnatural, beneath the dignity of humanly meaningful sexual intercourse, and indicative of uncontrolled and hence morally evil sexual desire. The source of these prohibitions seems to be more clearly the historical connection between such acts and idolatrous practices of neighboring peoples than the contradiction between sexual acts and the command to procreate. (1994:56)

As one might guess from this quote, traditional Judaism might be assumed to be against male homosexuality, but it seemingly does not recognise female sexuality, much less female homosexuality. This indeed is a problem for Ellie, the main Jewish character in this corpus of texts and the protagonist in Leanne Lieberman's *Gravity* (2008). Ellie is the only Orthodox Jewish character I have found and this is also the only book where religion and sexuality are given equal weight and where the protagonist attempts to bring her religious beliefs and her sexuality together to create a coherent identity.

Ellie thinks of Judaism as being like a taxonomy in that it helps make order out of chaos. And yet, once she realises that she is attracted to other girls (as on 2008:39), she begins to worry about how she can reconcile this with her religion. She reads the Chumash (the Torah, or five books of Moses) and sees that a man is not supposed to lie with a man, but also notes that there is nothing about women lying with women (2008:78). Confused, she gets advice from the rabbi's wife at school, and is told that it is forbidden to be with a woman, but that many girls get "schoolgirl crushes" (2008:97). At the same time, she is instructed to recite a psalm or pinch herself if she finds that she is tempted to behave in a way that is not appropriate to an Orthodox Jewish girl (ibid.), i.e. being sexual with another girl. For Ellie, coming to terms with her lesbianism means that the previously orderly life she lived as a Jew is no longer possible; the chaos that religion had staved off has closed in again. During the course of the novel, she goes back and forth; she takes off her star of David (2008:56), but then prays on Rosh Hashanah, "Please forgive me for girl lust." (2008:108). She looks at Hustler magazine (2008:114) and seems to masturbate (2008:180), but also tries to tell herself that she was just "experimenting" and that "maybe I'll grow up and learn to like men." (2008:96) Ellie's sister Neshama tells her, "I say, go be gay and screw the Torah. Screw it all." (2008:140) Towards the end, Ellie begins to question the existence of a god (2008:143) and to become a non-believer, and the final outcome is that she chooses her sexuality over her religion. Interestingly, her mother suffers a breakdown that is implied to be due to religion and her sister leaves home behind, including her Judaism, in order to study at university and live a secular, and seemingly happier, life. What all this suggests is that it is not possible to be an Orthodox Jew and a lesbian, or even an Orthodox Jew and a woman; Ellie struggles to make sense of the chaos that is her life and ultimately feels that either she can deny her sexuality and be religious or she can leave her religion behind and be a lesbian, and she chooses the latter.

This might seem to be a strong decision, but the question it raises is why Ellie – and others like her – cannot find a way to reconcile both parts of her identity. A film about queer Orthodox Jews, *Trembling Before G-d* (2001), similarly suggests that it is not possible to be Orthodox and queer. Either they find ways around the restrictions in the Torah (for example, one man would not have anal sex, since that is what is specifically forbidden, but he would engage in mutual masturbation, oral sex, kissing, and hugging) or they have to leave one or the other, i.e. live a queer life and become modern Orthodox or leave Judaism entirely, or pretend not to be queer and get married heterosexually.

Beck discusses how "the patriarchy is especially good at fragmenting the loyalties of those of us who are members of more than one minority group" and notes that it can be a "struggle" "to keep all components of our identities intact...both within the minority groups to which we belong and against the dominant culture" (1982:81). She asks where such difficulties "leave the Jewish lesbian/feminist who is dedicated to being heard in Jewish as well as feminist contexts?" (1982:82). Beck also draws parallels between "Hitler's persecution of the Jews and his treatment of homosexuals" (1982:83), both as a way of discussing power and oppression, but perhaps also to suggest links between these different aspects of identity. Thirty years on, Beck's question is still relevant: where does this leave the Jewish queer who is dedicated to being heard in both Jewish and queer contexts?

There are a few other Jewish characters in LGBTQ books for young readers, but generally either they are secondary characters or their Jewishness seems cultural rather than religious and is not problematic in the story. No other characters that I have found are strictly Orthodox, so perhaps this reveals how much easier it is to be modern Orthodox, conservative, or liberal and queer than it is to be Hasidic or Orthodox and queer. One book with Jewish queer characters is *Wide Awake* (2008), by David Levithan, which was already referred to. There is also Barry from *Dance on my Grave* by Aidan Chambers (1982) and Nelson in the *Rainbow* series by Alex Sanchez (2001, 2003, 2005), although neither of these characters discusses being Jewish, and only an astute reader would recognise them as Jewish due to their last names and some of their other features. For example, Nelson uses Yiddish words such as "shtick" (2005:8) and "kvetch" (2005:156) and Barry has a stereotypical Jewish mother with whom he is possibly too close (see 1982:30-1 for an example), plus he says "shalom" (1982:112) and later is buried in a Jewish cemetery (1982:232). However, neither Barry nor Nelson, nor the characters in Levithan's work, seem troubled by their religious identities, particularly in relationship to their sexuality. As Crisp says, in regard to Sanchez's work, the books are supposedly about "rainbow boys" but their diversity is scarcely mentioned, though Jason is Latino and Nelson is Jewish (2011:252-3, note 130). Crisp argues, and I agree, that "this is troubling because it seems to reduce these characters to ethnic stereotypes." (2011:253)

As mentioned above, in Cris Beam's *I Am J* (2011), J is half-Jewish. While J does not practise either his mother's Catholicism or his father's Judaism, when he goes to get his first testosterone shot, he does recite the vaguely remembered shehecheyanu prayer (2011:296). This prayer is a common one, said at special occasions and to give thanks. This seems to be the moment when J feels most connected to his Jewish ethnicity/ancestry.

The single picture book that I am aware of that features queer Jewish characters is the recently published *The Purim Superhero* by Elizabeth Kushner. Kushner's book centres on the holiday of Purim, and she has said:

> It always seemed weird to me that there were lots of great read-aloud stories about Chanukah and a good

> number of Passover books, but there were, at that time, almost no books about contemporary Jewish kids celebrating Purim. It seemed like such a natural theme for a children's book, with many of the appealing qualities of Halloween and April Fool's Day (Costumes! Silliness! Carnivals! Treats!), but most of the books I found, while wonderful, were basically retellings of the story of Esther. I wanted a book to share with my library classes that would reflect and expand on their present-day experience of celebrating Purim. I thought a kid with a costume crisis might be a good hook for a story. A few years later, when I heard about Keshet's contest for a picture book with both gay/lesbian and Jewish content, I thought, wait, I'm a Jewish lesbian, I'm a parent, I'm a writer, and I've read lots of Jewish picture books. If I don't enter this contest, I'll never forgive myself! (Kramer, 2013:n.p.)

In Kushner's picture book, Nate, the protagonist, loves aliens and wants to dress up as one for Purim but all the other boys are dressing up as superheroes, so he feels torn. Nate looks to his two fathers and his older sister for advice. One father, who is called Abba, which is the Hebrew word for "father", says, "Sometimes showing who you really are makes you stronger, even if you're different from other people." (2013:n.p.) Instead of this being a simplistic lesson about individuality, the narrator then tells the reader, "Nate didn't think being different would make him stronger. He thought it would make him lonely." (ibid.) Abba says that "not all boys have to be the same thing" (ibid.) and eventually Nate chooses to blend his own desires with what everyone else is doing by dressing up as a "super alien", i.e. a superhero alien. At the end of the Purim party at their synagogue, the other boys agree that Nate's costume is original and that "[n]ext Purim, let's be whatever we want" (ibid.). The queer aspect is subtly done; there is no discussion about whether Judaism allows homosexuality or whether Nate and his sister Miri have had any trouble with their peer group due to having two fathers. Rather, the issue for Nate is whether he dares to stand up for what he wants and whether he is accepted by his friends for doing so; his two fathers are merely part of his background, which, one could argue, is how it should be. Within the narrative, there are no explanations of what Purim is or about Judaism, but the illustrations hint at the Jewishness of Nate's family. In one picture by illustrator Mike Byrne, the family eats chicken soup with matzoh balls, and the two fathers wear yarmulkes on their heads. In two pictures, Nate and the other boys from his Hebrew school class also wear yarmulkes although they do not do so during the Purim party. At that party, they are also shown eating hamantaschen cookies, which are traditional during the Purim holiday. The final page of the book has short biographical notes about the author and illustrator, along with a paragraph explaining what Purim is. In short, Kushner's book does not suggest any sort of conflict between religion and queerness, nor does it over-explain; Nate just happens to be a little Jewish boy with two fathers, and the biggest issue in his life appears to be what costume to wear to his synagogue's Purim party. Unlike many other LGBTQ picture books, as discussed in the chapter on issue books, the reader is not told how being gay is "normal" or "acceptable" or how Nate's dads love him just as much as non-LGBTQ parents love their kids. Kushner's book is successful because it is different and does not problematise ethnicity or sexuality.[45]

In most of the texts I look at in this book, the characters are Christian. This may not be said explicitly, but they might, for example, celebrate Christmas (as Grady does with his family in *Parrotfish* (2007)), which implies at least nominal, cultural Christianity. Few characters seem to struggle with their Christian beliefs, however, in relation to their gender or sexuality. As Margaret Farley writes:

> Overall, Protestant sexual ethics is moving to integrate an understanding of the human person, male

> and female, into a theology of marriage that no longer deprecates sexual desire and sexual pleasure as primarily occasions of moral danger. For the most part, the ideal context for sexual intercourse is still seen to be heterosexual marriage. Yet questions of premarital sex, homosexuality, masturbation, and new questions of artificial insemination, genetic control, and in vitro fertilization are being raised by Protestant theologians in Protestant communities. (1994:66)

Her text, now almost twenty years old, could explain why Christianity is not often viewed as a challenge for the protagonists in these books, the way Judaism was for Ellie in *Gravity*. Perhaps Protestant sexual ethics have moved on and may be more accepting these days, or maybe this is because there are so many denominations of Christianity and thus there is a "something for everyone" approach. Interestingly, however, some research suggests that Christianity and non-heterosexuality do not get along quite as well as Farley and many of the authors of the LGBTQ books for children might suggest. For example, Mary E. Hunt, in a very problematic analysis of lesbianism, seems to imply that to be a Christian and a lesbian, one can only have "friendships" with women, i.e. not sexual relationships. Hunt returns to the earlier feminist movement idea about how one could be a political lesbian but need not have sexual or romantic relationships with women. For example, she claims that gay men "have emphasized their sexual lives as the locus of their liberation" but that lesbian feminists "have defined ourselves according to certain relational commitments to other women, or what I am calling female friendship." (1994:172) She goes on to say that "we are reclaiming the word *lesbian* for what it has always meant, namely, women loving women without fixating on the presence or absence of genital activity to define it." (ibid., italics original) This is to say that Hunt argues that one's sexuality is private, but that one's relationships (friendships) with women are public and political, and that that is what lesbian feminists should focus on. She goes on to say that "it is important that *lesbian* not be forced to carry the symbolic freight of sexuality for all women" (1994:173, italics original). Such an argument has several negative effects; it weakens the word "lesbian" and its meaning, and thereby weakens the LGBTQ movement and community, but also, in this spiritual/religious context, it suggests that one need not fight for various religious communities to accept lesbians. This means that if "lesbian" is just a political label having to do with a supposed sisterhood ("a sister in the struggle" (Hunt, 1994:174)) or a belief in female friendships, women's sexuality is once again hidden and oppressed, and there is thus still little space in religious movements for women who identify as lesbians in the sexual/romantic sense. Therefore, such a move diminishes the work of organisations such as the Lesbian and Gay Christian Movement or Keshet Ga'avah (the World Congress of Gay, Lesbian, Bisexual, and Transgender Jews).

Hunt argues that "lesbians" need to focus on "women's friendships", and says such friendships involve "embracing one another in a deep, life-giving way" and are "a major contributor to Christian culture" (1994:175). The characteristics of these relationships are "*mutuality*, that quality of a mature friendship when giving and taking are possible between equals"; "*community*"; and "*honesty*" (ibid., italics original). She writes that it "is these characteristics which will transform our culture and create the preconditions for the possibility of the reign of God" (1994:179), and she goes on to explain their connection to Christianity (1994:179-181). She is not the only critic to view sexuality and religion – Christianity in particular – as exclusive. Similarly, J. Michael Clark excoriates gay male culture with its "glory holes" and AIDS (1994:216-7) and recommends intimacy in that a "truly liberated sexuality is one that affirms the wholeness of our being as persons-in-relation" (1994:219). He argues that gay men's sexuality "should *in no case* be reduced to "merely genital functions."" (1994:220, italics original) Unlike Hunt, Clark seems to find a possible way for someone to be gay and Christian, but only through monogamy (1994:224-227). This suggests that to be a religious/spiritual gay man, one must commit fully to each relationship, not have flings or purely sexual relationships, and be monogamous. Of course, while "friendships" or monogamy may work for some religious LGBTQ people, such ways of reconciling religion and sexuality may not suit all.

One of the few young adult texts to explore Christianity as a religion rather than using it as cultural backdrop is Julia Watts's *Finding H.F.* (2001), where "H.F." stands for "Heavenly Faith" and is the name of the main character. The protagonist is being raised by her religious Baptist grandmother in the poor, rural South of the United States. Mab Segrest, for example, discusses the confusion and difficulty of being Baptist and a lesbian and says that she worries that when she is found out (by other Christians), she will be "fired, maybe prayed to death" (1982:16), though she does not say what might happen if she is discovered by other lesbians to be a Christian, particularly a Baptist. In other words, the challenge for her is in "lead[ing] two lives" (ibid.) and not in trying to bring them together. That seems to be the challenge for H.F. too.

H.F. and her best friend, the "sissy" Bo, leave their hometown to try to find H.F.'s mother in Florida. On their way, they meet other LGBTQ young people and begin to see that they could in fact have queer lives, but they suspect that this means that they will have to stop being religious. In Atlanta, Bo says, "Lord…no wonder the preachers back home always talk about big cities bein' hotbeds of sin and fornication. I reckon you could do pretty much whatever you wanted in a place like this." (2001:96) You can do whatever you want, but not if you want your preacher's and church's approval, is the implied message.

The revelation comes when they see a church that has a cross and a rainbow flag outside it. H.F. says, "It's hard for me to say how I feel seeing these two signs mixed together. All my life I've heard gay people preached against as perverts, and now finding out that there's such a thing as a church for gay people…well, it's awful to say, but it feels like I just found out that the Ku Klux Klan started accepting black members and working for racial equality." (2001:118) The church has a female priest, which startles H.F. as well. "I can't stop thinking, *She's a woman, she's a preacher, and she likes girls just the same as me.*" (2001:119, italics original) H.F. and Bo begin to talk about their feelings about religion and homosexuality with some older members of the LGBTQ community that they meet. One of them says, "What did Jesus say in the Bible about homosexuality? Not one word. Now, sure, homosexuality is prohibited in the Old Testament, but so is wearing mixed-knit fabric and eating shellfish. And I don't know about you, but I've seen plenty of supposedly devout straight Christians wearing polyester and chowing down at the Red Lobster." (2001:122)

Through meeting older people who go to church and are openly LGBTQ, H.F. and Bo begin to believe that they can be queer and Christian, although they realise that they would have to belong to a different denomination of Christianity than the one they were raised in. They do not make the switch in the novel itself, but they seem to consider it possible. The book ends on a rather hopeful note, at least in regard to religion, which makes it stand out among books for young readers:

> Memaw would say I was blaspheming if she knew I was comparing something in the Bible with my own experience of being queer. But I think the way I do because of who I am: a teenage dyke from small-town Kentucky, raised by my memaw on Bible stories and old-timey hymns. And to me, the rainbow sign God put up in the sky for Noah said pretty much the same thing as the sign I saw at the gay bookstore, at the church, and in the faces and hearts of the rainbow of people who are my gay family: "Here you were, thinking it was the end of the world, when it turns out it was only the beginning." (2001:165)

In regard to Islam, the one book I have read that features Muslims is *2 Girls*, which differs from all the other works mentioned in this chapter in that it is a translation. The novel is set in Turkey and has been translated from Turkish to English by Brendan Freely. It also trades in stereotypes, as the apparently lesbian character seems psychologically disturbed, is passionate about her heterosexual friend to the point of awkwardness and tension, and has an unhappy ending. The "two girls" of the title are not religious and there is no discussion of religion affecting their sexuality; however, it is worth mentioning because they are nominally Muslim, in the way that most of the characters in the corpus of texts here are nominally Christian. It would be interesting to find a book for young adults that features queer Muslims who are religious.

For a final example, the main character's boyfriend, Raj, in Robin Reardon's *A Secret Edge* (2007), is from an Indian family that immigrated to the U.S. and they seem to have fairly devout Hindu beliefs. This is not explored in any great depth, because Raj is not the main focus of the story. But Raj does tell Jason, the protagonist, a bit about his background and when Jason asks, "You said your folks aren't happy that you're gay. Are they angry? Do they try to convince you to go straight? Do they think it's some kind of perversion, or sin, or—" (2007:65), Raj responds by explaining the Vedic tradition of appreciating the third sex. However, he also says that Hindus these days think that homosexuality is wrong (ibid.). The topic is then more or less left there.

I have not found any LGBTQ characters in children's books who are Buddhist, Quaker, or pagan, or who believe in voodoo or spiritism, to name just a few other religious and spiritual traditions. For that matter, I have not found any who are strongly atheistic and who discuss their feelings about that. It seems that most characters are nominally Christian or at least assumed to be Christian as the norm. Furthermore, what this section has attempted to show is that in books for children and young adults, it appears to be the case that a character cannot be both a person of faith and someone who is LGBTQ (cf. Cart and Jenkins, 2006:100 and 106, where they discuss how religion generally is depicted negatively). This might give the readers the message that if you are LGBTQ, either you will have to leave your religion, or you will have to repress your sexuality or gender identity in order to comply with your religion. However, given the organisations and religious communities that exist for people who are LGBTQ, this seems to be an erroneous and potentially harmful message.

Dis/Ability[46]

As Maddie Blackburn points out, "sex is still regarded as one of the great taboos of modern society, a subject regarded by some as not to be talked about, at any time, in any place and least of all among disabled people." (2002:1) For this reason, there is very little research done on the intersections of dis/ability and sexuality, and even less on those between dis/ability and non-heterosexuality. Even in Blackburn's own study, homosexuality is scarcely mentioned, and other aspects of queer identity are not referred to at all. In her work, she is interested in whether "the disabled person's relationship experience (whether sexual or platonic) [is] any different from their able-bodied peers" (2002:2-3), but the only mentions of homosexuality are in brief reference to a couple of the cases she studies. When she discusses disabled people's definitions of "sexual intercourse" and their understanding of this term, not one offered a definition of anything between two people of the same sex (2002:69). Another text on sexuality and disability only refers to homosexuality by saying that heterosexual sexual positions can be adapted for homosexual couples (Cooper and Guillebaud, 1999:24). Similarly, in Donnellan's review of homosexuality, which is aimed at younger readers, there is a short discussion of how disabled lesbians can have sex (1998:30) but in regard to gay men, only AIDS is mentioned, which perhaps suggests that AIDS is seen as a disabling disease for homosexual men, but otherwise, disability is not something one needs to discuss much in regard to non-heterosexuals.

Not surprisingly, then, in my large corpus of books for children and young adults that feature LGBTQ characters, I could not find even one character who was both queer and disabled. I did not read a single discussion about what it might mean, for example, to be bisexual and have spina bifida, or to be blind and transgender, or how one might have sex when one is in a wheelchair.[47] As for mental health, there are certainly teenaged characters who exhibited what might be termed stereotypical teenage moodiness and there are those who are depressed due to, for example, being rejected by friends, but there is no clinical depression, even though "new research shows that lesbians and bisexual women are more likely to experience depression than heterosexual women" (Czyzselska, 2012:n.p.). I could not find learning difficulties, such as dyslexia, or other related issues such as attention deficit disorder.

Keenan claims that "[p]erhaps the most marginalized difference in feminist discourse is disability" (2004:124), and this can be extended to other areas of discourse as well. It may be that disability is marginalised in the queer community as well. Keenan goes on to argue that "[j]ust as feminist work must reintegrate race, gender, and sexuality, it must also reintegrate considerations of disability if it is to speak to and for all women." (2004:125) This is a problematic way of putting it, because a question I am attempting to raise here is whether anything can actually speak to and for all women or indeed to and for all of any group, but the general issue is an important one. Disability is currently missing from the discourse regarding non-heterosexualities and particularly from books for young readers, and this is something to challenge and change in the future.

Age

Matile Poor defines "older lesbian" as "lesbians over fifty" (1982:165) and Merryn Gott likewise defines older as being over fifty (2005:82), so perhaps this definition can be adopted here, although fifty does not seem old, especially given today's higher standards of living. Nonetheless, the specific number perhaps does not matter much, as I have not found a single "older" LGBTQ character in any of these books. Most LGBTQ characters in these books are either young people discovering their sexuality or else parents of young or teenaged children. Poor explores how the "older lesbians" she refers to have learned to hide their identities and thus may not want to be out; in other words, they have been assimilated into mainstream culture (1982:165). Dana Rosenfeld also discusses how some members of the LGBTQ community might not want to have been "liberated" by Stonewall and might not want to be visible (2003:179-80 and 191-3). This might explain why there are so few older LGBTQ characters in books for young readers; if older members of the community are not that visible, authors might not think to include them.

Interestingly, Poor mentions that it is easier to find older out gay men and wonders if this is because "lesbians, having been oppressed not only as lesbians but as women, feel more fear about being open than gay men" (1982:166). On the other hand, Gott discusses how ageing is harder on gay men than on lesbians. She writes that:

> older gay men face more pressure to maintain a youthful physical appearance than their same-age heterosexual counterparts. Indeed, the youthful, muscular 'adonis' represents the central image to aspire to within the gay male subculture. However, by contrast, lesbian women seem to a certain degree, to escape the age-defying culture that can be so oppressive for heterosexual women. (2005:83)

This is a fascinating point of discussion that may become more relevant to literature in future years, but I will not go into it any further here, as the main concern is why there are few older LGBTQ characters in children's literature.

This could be because children's books generally have children as their main protagonists, so it could be seen as inappropriate or pointless to feature, say, a gay grandfather; I can quickly demolish this argument by pointing out how many children's books do feature a visit to a grandparent or other interactions with older relatives or older people in general. Another possible argument then could be that if LGBTQ people were not as able to come out until more recently, then we are not likely to see them in books; however, since there have been at least a couple of generations in the U.S. and the U.K. of LGBTQ people being more out (i.e. since the late 1960s, with Stonewall (cf. Gott, 2005:83 or Rosenfeld, 2003:175), as mentioned above), it stands to reason that these people have aged and could have children or grandchildren by now or have other connections to and with young people. What this suggests is that older LGBTQ people are missing from these books for another reason, and this may be due to a general discomfort with ageing and prejudice against the aged combined with discomfort with and prejudice against the queer community.

Class

Cherríe Moraga says that she feels it is important to discuss and teach about the kinds of intersections of identity under analysis here because for her, political issues related to race and class need to refer to queerness, since her "politics feel so Lesbian-identified", while, for example, "women's studies classes and Lesbian-related courses...were so completely white and middle-class" (1982:55). She and Barbara Smith agree that they are not interested in "Rich White Women" but rather need a place for their own identities as lesbians, women of colour, and definitely not upper class (ibid.).

In other words, class is another important issue to analyse; the experiences of, say, a working-class, white lesbian will not be the same as an upper-class, white lesbian, which, as already pointed out, is one of the problems Butler raised in regard to the feminist movement. Loraine Hutchins writes that it is essential to discuss class because economic privilege or lack thereof can affect "how an individual's ability to be an out activist relates to his or her employment, family, and economic status; and how changes in the health professions, such as managed care, make sliding fee scales and alternative therapies less likely and sexuality or relationship counseling less accessible for many people." (1996:253) Class can, of course, affect many other areas of life as well.

In literature for young readers, class is another mostly ignored issue (although it does appear sometimes in literature for older readers, as Heather Love points out in reference to Feinberg's *Stone Butch Blues*, in discussing how middle-class lesbians create a community at universities, excluding working-class lesbians (2010:155)). Kanner writes that in her research, she has found that "[w]orking-class characters appear in only five of the seventy titles that feature gay and lesbian characters and themes. These include Guy's *Ruby*, Garden's *Annie on My Mind*, and Rees's *In the Tent*." (n.d.:n.p.)

Annie in Nancy Garden's *Annie on my Mind* (1982) is from a lower class than her girlfriend, Liza, and this is a noticeable difference between the two young women, although it is not discussed much. Liza attends a private school, while Annie goes to the local state-run school, and when Liza goes to visit Annie there, she is very aware of how different the experience there is from her own (1982:132). Similarly, Liza lives in a nice house with her parents and brother, while Annie is in a cramped flat with her parents and grandmother. Though the girls are conscious of these dissimilarities between them, they do not discuss them. They both go to university after finishing high school, which suggests that Annie's family's financial situation does not stand in the way of her getting an education.

Indeed, most of the characters in this corpus of texts are solidly middle-class, with few references to financial woes, and all who are of the right age go on to some sort of institution for higher learning after completing secondary school. Jason in Sanchez's trilogy does lose his scholarship to a state university after coming out, but he is still able to attend community college. In short, money or class consciousness are seldom issues in these works.

A possible exception is Julia Watts' *Finding H.F.* (2001), which was discussed above as an exception in regard to religion as well. The characters in this book are working-class and from the South in the U.S., and this is important to the story, because they long to get out of their poor, conservative town. Their tale is a road trip of discovery, where H.F. and Bo try to find H.F.'s mother, and they gradually start to realise that they can have queer lives. When they find H.F.'s mother, she is not pleased to see them, especially because they are gay, and says she would only have been glad to meet them if H.F. were "some kind of famous teenage model or if you'd won the lottery" (2001:150). H.F. and Bo never do "win the lottery" or otherwise strike it rich, and they are very conscious of their class. When they see a fancy hotel, H.F. thinks, "I bet there ain't one person staying in that hotel whose permanent address is a trailer on the side of a strip-mine-scarred mountain, like where Bo lives. And I'm sure there's nobody in there whose momma took off and left her to be raised by her memaw neither." (2001:94) There is no resolution to their money problems, but then that is arguably not the point of the book. Rather, H.F. and Bo accept their sexuality and begin the process of considering how they can integrate these various aspects of their identity – homosexual, working class, Christian, Southern.

Thirty years on from Moraga's complaint that "women's studies classes and Lesbian-related courses...were so completely white and middle-class" (1982:55), one can sadly say that LGBTQ literature for children is still almost completely white and middle-class.

Weight/Size and Body Image

Unfortunately, although perhaps not unsurprisingly, I found no LGBTQ books for young readers that featured queer people who also had non-normative weights; instead, they feature solely people of average weights and with no body image problems.[48] Eating disorders and depression are fairly common within the queer community, especially for men, so I had hoped to see a character struggling with weight, and, of course, having characters of varying weights would have reflected the diversity of everyday life. The field of fat studies, as it is known, looks at, among other things, how "the fear of being or becoming fat tyrannizes average-size and relatively thin women, limiting their quality of life and often leading to eating disorders" (Saguy, 2011:600), and how "sexism, racism, sexual abuse, and weight-based discrimination…contribute to eating problems among minority women" (ibid.). But as these two quotes reveal, this rather conveniently ignores how all this affects LGBTQ people as well as how it affects men, and also how issues such as homophobia, transphobia, and biphobia contribute to eating problems among both women and men. Fat studies explores issues of weight, body image, and self-esteem, often in connection to women and feminism (as in Orbach, 1988), but more research is needed in regard to LGBTQ people in particular.

Sarah Grogan refers to the fact that some scholars think "lesbian culture downplays the importance of conventional physical attractiveness…[while others argue] that lesbians are socialised to conform to the same societal standards as heterosexual women" plus must also comply with the standards within the lesbian community (1999:152). Esther D. Rothblum points out that studies show that lesbians are "liked most when their physical appearance conformed to heterosexual standards for women" (2002:258), which suggests the pressure put on them to be feminine, with all that that entails. Meanwhile, "[s]tudies of body satisfaction in gay men have generally suggested that they tend to show higher levels of body concern than heterosexual men" (Grogan, 1999:155) and also that "gay men weigh less than heterosexual men" (Rothblum, 2002:259). As for bisexuals, Rothblum writes that data on how they feel about their bodies and their size is lacking (2002:257), and I have been unable to find material on transgender people and weight, although there is of course plenty of research on transgender body issues more generally.

What is important to note is that LGBTQ people have to face two sets of norms in regard to body image and weight: general societal norms and also the norms within their own communities (cf. Rothblum, 2002:263). "Physical appearance has been a major vehicle by which lesbians and gay men have identified 'like others,' and it continues to provide a sense of group cohesion and identity." (ibid.) Thus one would expect that it would come up as an issue in LGBTQ books, but my findings suggest that actually this issue is not reflected in queer literature for young readers. The only real references to weight come from Nelson in Alex Sanchez's *Rainbow* trilogy, as Nelson seems to have a mild version of bulimia, although this is scarcely discussed. Nor were there any anorexic gay men, although "[g]ay and bisexual men may be at far higher risk for eating disorders than heterosexual men" (ScienceDaily, 2007:n.p.). Beyond health problems related to weight, there were no characters who were of non-average sizes and where this was just another aspect of their identity. Body size does not appear as a topic in this rather corpulent, so to speak, corpus of texts, although one would certainly expect and hope it to.

Conclusion

In this chapter, I have attempted to cover a lot of ground, with the aim being to explore diversity and intersectionality in LGBTQ literature for children and young adults. This may seem like a fast trip through various types of diversity, but the goal has been to acknowledge the existence of all those types, with the awareness that there are still others that could have been included here, and to then show that they are generally missing from literature for young readers.

What these research findings suggest is twofold. First of all, these books imply to child readers that sexual minorities are acceptable, but only to a certain extent, so that while lesbian and gay male characters appear in these books, bisexual, transgender, and otherwise queer characters are missing, perhaps because they are deemed too challenging or inappropriate. This propagates a binary system in regard to both sexuality and gender, and does not allow children to learn about other ways of living or to see representations of themselves or their families. When these characters are visible in the texts, they are often depicted negatively or as having limited and limiting lives, which encourages readers to have stereotyped ideas about what it might mean to be, say, bisexual, transgender, or polyamorous.

Secondly, the texts discussed here give the incorrect impression that one cannot be LGBTQ and another sort of minority (or at least that to have a character who is both queer and something else is too much for YA and children's literature to handle at this time). While it is positive that there are books that feature sexual and gender diversity, other kinds of diversity (in terms of race, religion, ability, class, size, and age) tend to be ignored. When there is a character who is a minority in some other way, this is often not explored in any great detail, which may lead readers to believe that issues of sexuality are more problematic or stressful than other issues of identity, such as class. Furthermore, LGBTQ books for young readers offer the message that most LGBTQ people are white, middle-class, able-bodied, norm-sized, and Christian (or at least from a technically Christian background). This might cause young people to get an erroneous idea about who can be LGBTQ, which might in turn make – to take a random example – a young, working-class Hispanic woman who believes she is a lesbian feel that something is wrong with her and that it is not possible for her to be gay. No literature can represent all possible combinations of personalities and experiences, but it can at least provide a variety, so readers can see characters that are somewhat like themselves. To give the message that a person cannot incorporate two or more minority identities is flawed and possibly dangerous.

What is more, not only do the books ignore these issues, but many academics do as well, as evidenced by the analysis of scholarly texts woven throughout the analysis of literary texts above. This suggests a systematic ignorance or unawareness of the realities of positionality; the underlying assumption seems to be that life is more simplistic and more often lived on a binary than actually is the case. Continuums and intersections are strangely absent.

Where I would like to leave this analysis is with a simple call for authors and scholars to become aware of these absences and to begin to make currently invisible LGBTQ identities more visible in both academic literature and literature for children and young adults.

Sex and Marriage

In this chapter, I focus on two aspects of LGBTQ life: sex and marriage. While the one topic does not always have a lot to do with the other, here I am connecting them because they both fall under the larger category of romantic and sexual relationships. What I am interested in is how books for young readers portray the sex lives and romantic prospects of LGBTQ people, because this gives us some information about what society thinks is possible or even desirable for the queer community. Some of what follows connects back to the discussion in the chapter on stereotypes, in that it seems to me that men and women's sexual feelings, desires, and actions are expressed differently in these works, which may be due to stereotyped ideas about gender and sexuality.

As Nicholas Tucker writes:

> In former, traditional, fiction sexual interest between children was non-existent or minimal. The 1960s, however, saw an explosion in sexual awareness among all generations. Information picture-books designed to accompany the newly compulsory sex lessons held in school began to name parts and state facts in a more robust and easily digested way. Stories written for adolescents started to recognize the existence of sexual feeling as right and desirable. A few authors such as

> Judy Blume, Aidan Chambers and David Rees went further, describing actual adolescent sexual encounters with sympathy rather than shock. The increasing treatment of parental divorce also highlighted the role of sexuality in adult lives; hitherto a taboo subject in children's literature. (1998:17)

In other words, it is only since the 1960s that we have begun to see sexuality tackled in literature for young readers. It seems to me that if adults believe that fiction can and does teach young people about life, as was discussed in the introduction, then it is essential that we analyse it and see what messages it sends. Also, we must consider whether portrayals of sexuality in particular are "authentic" or "realistic", with the acknowledgement that these are tricky concepts; this matters because if young readers get some of their information about sex from novels, then we ought to ensure that they get information that keeps them healthy, safe, and happy. So this is a brief defence of why I think young adult literature should include sexual scenes, which is something not all people agree with.[49] I would then go even further to say that YA literature should include non-heterosexual sex scenes and relationships. I agree with Tony Grima, who complains that:

> [y]oung heterosexual love is ever-present on the big and small screens and in books, but young gay or lesbian love is rarely seen...gay and lesbian teenagers and children are denied these images of themselves, and they therefore never receive the comforting messages and reassurances that what they're feeling is normal. Even worse, when they see all the straight love stories on TV and in movies, they may feel even more different, more isolated, and terribly alone. The virtual nonexistence of gay or lesbian images tells these kids that they do not count. It's time that we started to fill the void by

> creating books, movies, and television shows that deal plainly with gay and lesbian teenagers and the issues they face. (1994:7-8)

Almost twenty years after Grima wrote that, young LGBTQ people are still getting the message that they "do not count", because their romantic possibilities and sex lives are not always featured in a positive way in these books. Young people deserve accurate information and representations.

Hence, here I first compare how teenage lesbians and teenage gay males[50] are portrayed in YA literature in regard to their sex lives, using three key areas: masturbation, the use of protection, and sexual interactions. Among other things, my findings suggest – perhaps not surprisingly – that society is still uncomfortable with gay female sexuality. The discourse regarding male sexuality suggests that it is wild and uncontrollable, and that men need to have a lot of sex, whereas women are not encouraged to express their sexual feelings.

In the second half of the chapter, I look at same-sex marriage in picture books and YA novels in order to see whether it is shown as a possibility or even a desired outcome for queer couples. While I do not argue that marriage is a state that all same-sex couples should or would want to enter, I do believe that as long as there is marriage, it should be an institution open to all people, regardless of their sexuality and gender identity. Hence, it is of significant interest to analyse whether books with queer characters refer to this institution and if this varies depending on the country where the book was written and published.

In short, this chapter focuses on teenagers and older LGBTQ people (i.e. those who are or potentially could be sexually active and/or married) and the ways in which their sexual and romantic identities are represented in books for young readers.

Masturbation

To start with, how teenagers are shown to enjoy sex with themselves is important to study. Although spatial and thematic constrictions mean that the history of masturbation cannot be discussed in detail here, it is worth pointing out that perspectives on young people masturbating have changed significantly over time. Since this book focuses on contemporary works of fiction, I will not write much about the earlier history of masturbation, but instead focus on the current period. Still, I can briefly mention that generally, masturbation was viewed negatively, as unacceptable or inappropriate, or else as practice or second best compared to the "real thing", i.e. sex with another person. In the early twentieth century, Freud, among others, accepted that children have autoeroticism, i.e. that they masturbate (Brenot 1997:46). This change in views towards masturbation and young people reflects larger shifts in how people understand sexuality. In the twentieth century, there has been a move towards accepting a broader range of sexual identities and practices, even though we could argue that this has not yet gone far enough.

As Laqueur points out, masturbation then became seen as something natural for young people to do (2003:73). He continues:

> Adolescence, in particular, became the crux, a fraught time between "natural" infantile autoeroticism and its sad holdover into maturity, the period when masturbation went from being a sign of "budding sexuality" full of promise to being an indication that its practitioner was unable to have a proper love object and, more generally, to make peace with the demands of society. One's relation to masturbation tracked precisely one's willingness to go with the flow of the civilizing process. (2003:73-4)

In other words, it is acceptable for young people to masturbate, but as they get older, they are supposed to leave masturbation behind in order to have "mature" sex, which apparently means sexual interactions with other people. Regardless of one's opinion of this particular perspective on masturbation and maturity, the fact is that in the twentieth and twenty-first centuries, it has become more common to acknowledge and accept the autoeroticism of young people.

Obviously, one of the first sexual activities that people engage in is usually masturbation. Some scholars refer to the importance of masturbation as a way for young people to experiment with and learn about sexuality. For example, Susan Moore and Doreen Rosenthal write, "masturbation can help inexperienced youngsters learn how to give and receive sexual pleasure and allow for the expression of sexual feelings without entering into a relationship for which the teenager is not emotionally ready." (2006:19). Others are less positive about adolescent masturbation, such as Francis who writes that masturbation is a problem if it includes fantasies and/or if it becomes addictive (1995:114), and he also calls it "self-centred" (1995:110), although he acknowledges that the feelings that lead to masturbation are normal, even if the act itself, in his view, is not acceptable in many or even most circumstances (ibid.).

Still, Moore and Rosenthal, among others, discuss how widespread masturbation is among young people. They write that "[m]asturbation is the most common source of orgasm in teenagers of both sexes and the source of a boy's first ejaculation in two out of three cases" (2006:15) and they say that "young girls begin to masturbate at an earlier age than boys (on average about age 12 compared with age 14) but fewer girls than boys admit to this practice" (2006:16). All this is to say that even if some adults believe masturbation to be inappropriate, shameful, or wrong, it is nonetheless a common practice. It is no surprise, then, that if it is so common, it is featured in books for young readers.

In literature, how teenage lesbians are portrayed in regard to masturbation is quite different from how teenage gay males are portrayed. Teenage gay males masturbate regularly and this is described frankly and openly. There are frequent mentions of tissues. For example, in *Naomi and Ely's No Kiss List* by Rachel Cohn and David Levithan, there is a scene with Ely masturbating. This activity is summarised as follows: "Mono-hand maneuver…Discard Kleenex under bed." (2008:29) Ely clearly has a quick and easy method.

In Robin Reardon's *Thinking Straight*, Tyler regularly masturbates. Several times he does so while pretending to be praying. This long quotation is a typical example, and it too includes the usage of tissues:

> I grabbed a handful of tissues from the box on my desk...I knelt there, facing the corner like some naughty kid doing time-out, thinking of Will.
>
> I closed my eyes. I must have looked very penitent... as I imagined running my fingers down the side of his naked body, seeing the wicked grin on his face that turned slowly into something else, his mouth and eyes half-open as my hand explored other parts of him. With my other hand, the one not touching Will, I undid my belt—only not just in my imagination. I stopped and listened carefully, then undid the button. Oh so slowly I pushed the zipper down, tooth by anxious tooth, until I was touching both of us—me and Will, at least in my mind—one hand for each.
>
> My ears strained for anything like a quiet footfall, a voice in the distance, the creak of a door. Nothing. I bent my head. And I pulled.
>
> Fortunately I'd gotten very good at keeping quiet doing this at home. It's true my breathing was a little—well,

> raspy. But other than that, the only thing I heard was in my mind, when Will came, that rich "ah" sound he makes at the very end. And a little grunt of my own. I gritted my teeth and clamped my lips shut so I would be as silent as possible.
>
> I got the tissues into position just in time. (2007:55-6)

A later quotation from the same novel again shows the character masturbating and cleaning up the evidence with tissues, and this passage ends with the pun "head cleared (as it were)" (2007:171).

In Perry Moore's *Hero*, the main character discusses his rules for looking at porn and masturbating. One rule is "there couldn't be anyone in the house when I did it. The last thing I needed was to get caught jerking off to an oiled muscle stud." (2007:40-1) Another rule is that he will not look at any porn with animals or children, among other items (ibid.). So he knows what he likes and is unafraid of enjoying it.

"Lost in Translation" is a short story by Michael Lowenthal where the main character is a gay male with a crush on a guy called Pat who is together with Stacy, "a girl known for her bouncy, precocious breasts." (2011:40). The main character "was miserable, and envious, and turned on. For days after I would jerk off to the vision of them doing it, then get so fraught I couldn't finish, then finish anyway, pretending I was Stacy." (2011:40) Here, he is jealous of the girl who is with his crush, and masturbates while pretending to be her.

These examples show how gay males are shown to masturbate in YA novels quite frequently and to do so with no shame or compunction. The young men look at porn, have rules for how they masturbate, ensure that people cannot see or hear them, and know how to clean up after themselves.

In all the YA books I have read with LGBTQ characters, there have been almost no descriptions of gay teenage females masturbating. In Cohn and Levithan's novel, Naomi, who, as it happens, is heterosexual, says, "I've tried, but masturbation turns out to be hella time-consuming with not very satisfactory results. Or maybe I'm just doing it wrong. My work ethic has always been weak." (2008:47) This suggests to readers that females do not want or need to masturbate, or that they cannot figure it out even if they try.

In *Gravity* by Leanne Lieberman, there is a mention of the main character, Ellie, putting a pillow between her legs (2008:180), but there are no details beyond that. It would be quite possible to read that scene innocently and to assume Ellie was doing something else, such as getting comfortable while resting in bed. There is no description of what she is thinking about, what actions she might be performing, or how she cleans up or removes any evidence after she is finished, as there is for the teenage boys (as a reminder, references are made to tissues and towels when males masturbate, such as Cohn and Levithan 2008:29, and of course females might use lubrication or indeed might even ejaculate, and thus they too might need to clean up after they masturbate). So this might imply that some people (or at least some authors) believe that teenage girls do not masturbate, or that lesbians do not masturbate. It could also suggest that readers might not want to read about it.[51]

As historians on masturbation make clear, masturbation is a particularly complicated subject when it comes to females. Laqueur writes that:

> for girls the process was especially treacherous, because their early rehearsals were for the wrong show. In becoming adult, they had to give up not only masturbation but also the kind of orgasm procured by their infantile efforts. Giving it up meant, in this account, giving up clitoral for vaginal sexuality, fantasies of active masculinity for the reality of passive femininity. (2003:72)

This implies that some thinkers, including of course Freud, believe masturbation to be practice for the "real" thing, i.e. intercourse, and also that there is only one "right" sort of orgasm. If a female is to be mature, masturbation should have little or no place in her life, as she is to become passive. Clearly, this is an extremely debatable view and it is especially inappropriate when applied to lesbians, who are unlikely to want or need to be passive partners to males. Nevertheless, the lack of female masturbation in YA literature could reflect the view that masturbation is somehow inappropriate or wrong for teenage girls because it is too active at a point where they should be learning to be passive. As Laqueur comments, "Shame had to be mobilized to make young people, especially girls, behave chastely and modestly." (2003:231) This mobilisation of shame could involve not showing young females that it is natural and normal to masturbate. If a girl does not see a reflection of her own behaviours in the literature she is reading, she might come to the conclusion that she is doing something wrong or that she herself is wrong in some way. The difference between how self-pleasure is portrayed for boys versus for girls may lead readers to wonder whether people believe that teenage girls do not masturbate, or that lesbians in particular do not masturbate, or that they do masturbate but that society is not prepared to accept this or to read about it.

Protection

After solo-sex, many adolescents begin to engage in sexual activities with others. Due to the prevalence of sexually transmitted infections/diseases (STIs/STDs) in society today and the possibility of pregnancy as an outcome of heterosexual sex, one can wonder whether various types of protection are shown in YA novels. As Moore and Rosenthal explain, "[a]larmingly, whether we take as a measure contraceptive use at first intercourse or the extent to which contraceptives are ever used, there is evidence that many adolescents are ignoring (or not receiving) sexual health messages" (2006:28). According to their findings and others, adolescents frequently do not use protection/contraception except in casual encounters (2006:29) and although "[w]ith increased exposure to messages about contraception, particularly condoms, in the media and through sexual health programmes in schools, and with increasingly easy access to contraceptives, at point of sale and through family planning clinics, we might expect to see most teenagers acting responsibly in their contraceptive behaviour", this is unfortunately not the case (2006:34). Moore and Rosenthal suggest that this might be because teenage sexual encounters are not planned for and thus the young people might be unprepared (ibid.).

Another relevant point in regard to protection is that many YA novels show pregnancy and/or disease to be a consequence of indulging in sexual activity. In other words, the concept of getting pregnant or getting someone pregnant or getting a sexually transmitted infection is employed in many books as a punitive measure that apparently is meant to warn readers off "trying it at home". See, for example, Cart and Jenkins, where they mention that heterosexual sex often leads to pregnancy, and homosexual sex leads to AIDS for men (2006:84-5); there is no discussion of the consequences of homosexual sex for women, although Lee writes that some women are punished for being sexual by being forced to come out (2011:164-182), which is presumably meant as a form of shaming. So this might lead one to believe that protection would be emphasised in YA texts, in order to remind young people that if they are going to have sex, they should avoid pregnancy and/or disease.

Worryingly, however, in YA literature, using protection when engaging in sexual activities is rarely mentioned. While I do not think that literature needs to be educational or should take the place of sex ed courses (according to the Guttmacher Institute, over 95% of sexual education in the U.S. discusses STDs and almost that same amount specifically mentions HIV, 2000:n.p.), it does seem to me that it could reflect reality. And the reality is that there are sexually transmitted diseases out there and that sexually active males and females, no matter what their sexual orientation or sexual practices, can be exposed to those infections and diseases. Another aspect of reality is that homosexuality, in particular male homosexuality, is often linked to death (see James, 2009:89-96), and is viewed as being "fraught with danger" (James, 2009:91), especially because of the connection to AIDS. Hence one might expect to find many mentions of protection from disease and from death in literature featuring homosexuals. The topic is starting to become somewhat more common in texts featuring gay male teenagers, but it is far from the norm. Examples include novels by Alex Sanchez and Robin Reardon.

In Reardon's *Thinking Straight*, the main character's friend gives him condoms and lube and also an old Die Hard VHS cover for storing them in (2007:79). This is positive, in that it shows the importance of protection, but the spectre of AIDS comes up elsewhere in the book, when Will and Tyler threaten bullies by saying they will spit on them and give them AIDS. The bullies then run away (2007:148-9). Here, the connection between LGBTQ people and STIs is made explicit and is used as a potential weapon against those who would hurt the young gay men. One could argue that Reardon is challenging homophobic views by having her gay male protagonists use AIDS against straight men, but on the contrary, this seems to emphasise that AIDS is a gay disease and that heterosexuals have a right to fear homosexuals.

In *A Secret Edge*, also by Reardon, the protagonist's aunt is a nurse. She leaves him condoms and a note saying, "Just in case. Besides, won't it feel kind of cool just having them?" (2008:94) She also says, "This isn't just a health issue. It has to do with your own self-respect. You are worth keeping safe. Your life is worth every bit as much as anyone else's and a lot more than a few minutes of pleasure." (2008:111) Even if this sounds rather didactic, the message is an important one. The main character, and thereby the reader, is reminded about how condoms are a necessary part of a sexual experience for gay men. But I wonder whether a teenaged reader is likely to skim over this, the way a teenager might tune out an adult giving a lecture on safe sex; perhaps a stronger way of sending the same message would be to just show young people buying protection or putting it on before sex.

Rainbow High by Alex Sanchez even features an AIDS scare, when Nelson is worried that he might have gotten it from a one-night stand with someone; in a related storyline, his current boyfriend is HIV-positive. Nelson says he knows he should use condoms, but that he does not want to (2003:223), and he is encouraged by his friend Kyle to get an HIV test (2003:9; also see 2003:20-1, where the doctor they go to see gets frustrated with Nelson and Kyle and tells them "wait till you're older before you start fooling around with this sex business" [2003:21]). Again, such storylines might seem to be overly obvious and they include a lecturing adult, but they nonetheless show awareness of the very real issue of sexually transmitted infections and the need to use protection (see the chapter on issue books for more on this). Incidentally, Brick, the man Nelson has a one-night stand with, is quite a bit older than Nelson, and they meet online. Brick uses the screen name "HotLove69" and, as Crisp puts it, he "provides YA readers the only glimpse into what their lives as an adult gay male can be like" (2011:236). The character of Brick might therefore suggest to young readers that gay men are often predatory, extremely sexual, and dominating, and that they will often not bother with protection, or care about the sexual pleasure of their partner. In short, this is a disturbing message to give readers, especially those who are gay males themselves, as well as those already prone to stereotyped ideas of gay men (see the chapter on stereotypes for more on this, and the chapter on issue books for more on HIV/AIDS).

Interestingly, as Ford writes, "[p]aradoxical though it may seem, disease and death—even death caused by AIDS—are safer territory for authors of children's fiction than the theme of lesbian love and commitment" (2011:207). This suggests that lesbian sexuality is perhaps still too challenging to be featured in literature for young readers, while AIDS is more acceptable. This may seem surprising as death and disease are often taboo in children's literature.

In YA literature that features teenage lesbians, there is not a single mention of girls using dental dams, or plastic wrap, or anything else. This is the case even if they are sleeping with females who have previously slept with males or if they themselves have previously slept with males. While it is rare for women to pass on STDs to other women through sexual activity, it is certainly not impossible, although these books give that impression.

In Lili Wilkinson's *Pink*, the main character, Ava, has a girlfriend, but now wants a boyfriend. She says:

> I *wanted* a boyfriend. I did. I wanted to be normal and go to the school formal and wear a dress and for him to wear a tux and give me a corsage. But I hadn't actually considered that I would *kiss* a boy, let alone have *sex* with one. I mean, Chloe and I had done plenty of...stuff, but it seemed *different* with a boy. Dangerous. Fooling around with boys led to scary things like STDs and babies. (2009:33, italics original)

In the book, Ava questions her sexuality and her way of being a lesbian; in terms of the latter, she views her beloved pink cashmere sweater as a betrayal of the lesbian community and something she can only wear when among straight people so she can pass as straight. Regardless of her limiting and limited view about what it means to be a lesbian and her attempt to perform heterosexuality (cf. Butler, 1990/2006:183 fwd., on performativity), the quote mentioned above is very problematic. It suggests that being gay is not "normal" and that to be normal she has to have a boyfriend. But it also implies that it is not possible to get STDs from lesbian sex. Both of these messages are erroneous. They may also be harmful to young readers.

This is the only text that I have found that has a teenage lesbian (or possibly a teenage bisexual girl) who seems to consider the need for protection, but she does so only in the context of having sex with a male. It may be that authors, editors, or publishers are unaware that gay females might also need protection or it may be that it is not considered relevant or appropriate as a topic in literature. Again, while protection does not occur frequently in LGBTQ literature featuring either young men or young women, it is much more common in the former, although in a didactic but, luckily, not so punitive way. Hence, the lack of protection for females suggests discomfort with and/or unawareness of the fact that women, too, engage in sexual activities and that they also need to be protected from diseases.

Sex

As the previous sections have shown, there is a patently obvious difference between male and female characters in these novels, in particular between how they engage in sexual behaviours. Researchers point out that there is discourse around a male sex drive – one that say that it is uncontrollable (Moore and Rosenthal 2006:139) – but not as much discussion of a female sex drive (see, for example, Moore and Rosenthal 2006:54), whether controllable or not. Moore and Rosenthal write that "[t]here are no safe ways for women to express their sexuality other than those approved of by this masculinized culture, and indeed there is not even an appropriate language to enable women to express sexual feelings (without risking the label of 'slut')" (2006:54). Given that our culture seems to be "masculinized" in regard to sex, one can analyse these novels more closely to see if that is reflected in the books.

Moore and Rosenthal write that in terms of why people engage in sex, "men attached significantly more importance to pleasure, pleasing a partner, conquest and relief of tensions than did women who were significantly more likely to rate emotional closeness as an important reason for having sex" (2006:133). Young adult books that feature LGBTQ men and women seem to reflect this idea of male versus female sexuality. Young men show feelings of pleasure, "conquest and relief", while young women are more likely to be depicted as wanting to be close to one another.

As was the case for masturbation, descriptions of sex for gay teenage males tend to be quite detailed. The young men often have multiple partners and engage in a range of sexual activities. There are references to lubricant, swear words are employed to describe the sexual interactions, and the sexual encounters generally end with an orgasm. Gay men may even be depicted as sex fiends, as discussed in the chapter on stereotypes, or at the very least they are often eager to "mak[e] out like crazy", as it is described in Sanchez (2007:14).

In *Naomi and Ely's No Kiss List* by Rachel Cohn and David Levithan, Ely talks in a positive, self-accepting, perhaps even self-satisfied, way about how he always "fucks and runs" (2008:197), not staying in any relationships for very long. He expresses surprise about how slowly one relationship is moving: "Bruce and I are taking it slow. Like, nursing-home slow. Doing the things that end with –alking instead of the ones that end with –ucking." (2008:85) For Ely, and for other young gay males in literature, sex is a major focus of relationships; it seems that they would rather be fucking and sucking than walking and talking.

Pleasure in being sexual with another male features highly in these works. In *Wide Awake* by David Levithan, Duncan says with no shame or compunction that he likes Jimmy being inside him (2008:65). Similarly, passion and pleasure are important in *Rainbow High* by Alex Sanchez when Jason and Kyle have sex:

> [Kyle] hurled the shoes to the floor as Jason yanked his jeans off. Free at last, they pressed close together, the contours of their naked bodies molding perfectly, smooth and hard.

> Jason climbed on top of him, all his anguish about Tech and Kyle and his sucky life swelling inside him. And then they were heaving and moaning, as Jason clung to every part of Kyle, running his hands up to the curves of his shoulders, along his lean muscled upper arms, across his chest and down his back, wanting never to let go.
>
> Kyle's hot breath whispered into his ear, "Let it out, boy." Jason clutched him closer and harder, blood pounding in his ears, tighter and faster, until they were gasping and groaning, one following by the other.
>
> When it was over, they slipped beneath the sheets, their naked bodies sticky against each other. Jason pulled the sheet over their heads, wishing they could stay this way forever. (2003:217)

Although the protagonists enjoy the sex they share, other characters find it "disgusting" and even ask, "Which one of you is the girl?" (2003:205) So it is important to note that while the books themselves are positive about gay male sex, they do also recognise the lack of understanding that gay people may face about their sexual relationships.

Robin Reardon includes descriptions of blow jobs, hand jobs, and more in her novels. For example, in *A Secret Edge*, Jason and another boy masturbate one another:

> I massage myself while he fetches something from the rear compartment. Then he undoes his pants and tells me to do the same, and he hands me a small towel like the one he has on his legs.
>
> Now he's looking at me, hard, and he flips open this plastic bottle. He takes my left hand and oozes

> something into it, and then into his right. Then he reaches for me, and with his left hand he guides mine onto him, and suddenly there's this marvelous mutual thing going on. Moksha. Nirvana. Heaven. I don't care what you call it. I am in another world. I'm just barely with it enough to remember what the towel is for when the time comes. When I come. Norm comes right after me. (2007:154-5)

Interestingly, the word "heaven" also appears in her novel *Thinking Straight* in relation to sex, as though Reardon is making the point that sex can be practically a religious experience and can even lead the participants to a deeper relationship with one another or with a deity. She writes:

> I could have just told him about some of the things Will and I have done, the ways we've come to know each other, the way he makes me feel when he's holding me, teasing my hair, kissing my neck. I could have described those "baser" needs, how the energy would move through me like lightning bolts seeking the ground of Will's body, and how it felt afterward like heaven and hell had met and clashed and canceled each other out so that we floated in a sea of total calm. I could have said that I love Will so much that it seems like a window into the love God offers, as though I could follow this path to the source of all Love. (2008:31)

Since sex is shown as so meaningful, even beautiful, it also is portrayed as blameless and even acceptable. Some of these descriptions are more romantic than one might expect of young men, based on research such as by Moore and Rosenthal. Young men sometimes talk of "making love" and say that the experience is spiritual.

In Reardon's work, there is also oral sex:

> His tongue in my mouth feels so sweet. I could have sat there kissing him forever. Except—well, except that he reaches for my belt. And then his tongue feels even better someplace else.
>
> The windows are closed, and it's a good thing. I scream with pleasure. (Reardon, 2007:106-7)

In another scene with oral sex, one of the characters even "swallow[s] my cum" (2007:132), which highlights both the orgasm and the intimacy.

And there is phone sex: "I have to say that although I preferred his hand on me, when his "ah" sounded right in my ear it was still great." (Reardon, 2008:59) Finally, there is exciting sexual action in the shower too:

> He moves forward until we're both under the pelting hot water, and he uses his hands like they're washcloths. He caresses my arms, my back, my ass, my legs, the insides of my thighs until I'm embarrassed by the obvious effect he's having on me. It feels so wonderful and so terrible all at once.
>
> Then he's behind me, holding me, leaning his face into the back of my neck. I've had the same effect on him, it seems, but he doesn't do anything about it. He just holds me. I swear I'm ready to faint. (Reardon, 2007:79)

What these examples show is that young men engage in quite a lot of sexual activity with other males. They do not express confusion about what to do, nor do they show hesitancy or shame. Their sexual adventures tend to climax in satisfaction. The authors describe these sexual interactions in detail, allowing a reader to be part of them. And, as already stated, there is a clear emphasis on pleasure and relief. As one gay teen says to his boyfriend in one of these novels, "We have to [move fast sexually]. We won't get much time, and we won't get any encouragement." (Reardon, 2008:48) And in these novels, they do indeed move fast and enjoy doing so.

In contrast to the way gay teenage males are described having sex with one another, teenage lesbians have fewer partners and fewer sexual interactions with those partners. I found no descriptions of oral sex or mutual masturbation or sex in a variety of locations, such as the shower, as I did for gay males. This implies less variety in lesbian sex lives. Females also show more uncertainty about the very idea of being physical with one another.

Annie on My Mind by Nancy Garden was an early YA novel with lesbian characters. In it, the two main characters, Annie and Liza, spend more time together, but avoid touching, and get very nervous when alone together. Annie says this makes her feel they are doing something "wrong, or dirty" and Liza says she is scared of the physical parts of loving (1982:121). Teen boys do not show or discuss this same fear. They simply express their attraction and then get on with having sex. In Garden's novel, however, the girls are scared, and when they do eventually engage in sexual activity, they are, as Lee puts it, "punished… The ultimate punishment for transgressors is a forced coming out." (2011:174) Liza has no choice but to come out to her relatives and classmates, and she must take all the consequences that come with that.

This concept of shyness and hesitancy is quite common when it comes to young gay females. In Jane Eagland's *Wildthorn*, there is this description:

> Without quite knowing how it's happened, we're kissing. Her lips are dry and warm and I feel shy at first, tentative…and then I can't help myself…I melt into her soft, moist mouth, taste honey. My bones are turning to liquid, I feel breathless, dizzy with longing…and, floating into my head, with absolute certainty, comes

> the knowledge – this, this is who I am, this is what I want. (2009:326)

Although the character does feel more certain by the end of the scene, she starts out feeling "shy" and "tentative". Nancy Garden relies on a similar description in the following scene:

> I remember so much about that first time with Annie that I am numb with it, and breathless. I can feel Annie's hands touching me again, gently, as if she were afraid I might break; I can feel her softness under my hands…I can close my eyes and feel every motion of Annie's body and my own—clumsy and hesitant and shy—but that isn't the important part. (1982:146)

The girls are "clumsy and hesitant and shy" and then there is no more detailed description of what goes on. *Dare Truth or Promise* by Paula Boock uses some of the same words: "Louie was shy, Willa scared they would get caught, and both hesitant at first." (1997:67) When the two do have sex, the description is very euphemistic (1997:69). The repeated emphasis on teenage lesbians being fearful and tentative could reflect authors' or publishers' or society's views about what is sexually appropriate for young women.

Descriptions of teenage lesbian sex also rely on words such as "gentle", "slow", and "soft". This scene from Jane Eagland's *Wildthorn* features the latter two words:

> I didn't mean to…but I had only to move my face an inch or two and my mouth found hers. Her soft lips were a surprise and my heartbeat quickened. A slow fuse lit inside me, the heat spreading from the pit of my stomach, until my whole body was suffused with it… (2009:291)

Another quote from Garden uses "soft" and "gentle":

> Without thinking, I put my arm across her shoulders to warm her, and then before either of us knew what was happening, our arms were around each other and Annie's soft and gentle mouth was kissing mine. (1982:92)

Besides the use of such words, what I term "fading to black" is also widespread in YA lit that features teenage lesbians; by this phrase I mean that a sex scene is set up, but then not followed through in any detail. The scene might end or switch abruptly rather than continue to describe the sexual experience. An example is in *Finding H.F.* by Julia Watts. Laney kisses H.F.:

> It's not a shy, little getting-to-know-you peck either. Her mouth is open, her lips are wet, and the tip of her tongue touches mine.
>
> "I wanted you the second I saw you," she whispers when we pull apart. "You wiry little butch, you."
>
> I have no idea what a wiry butch is—it sounds like some kind of dog to me—but I've got no time to ask questions because Laney is on me like a duck on a june bug, kissing me and sliding her hands all over me. I keep feeling like I ought to be doing things to her, at least at first, but I figure she knows what she's doing and I don't, so I might as well lay back and enjoy the ride. (2001:127)

That is the entire sex scene; there is not much specification, even though it is actually somewhat humorous. While it is true that H.F. is inexperienced and thus the reader would not expect her to know exactly what she is doing, it does not follow that the reader cannot or should not hear what happens to H.F. and what she learns from the experience. In other words, there is little description, although there could have been more. In an earlier scene, H.F. kisses her friend Wendy and feels "shot through with electricity" (2001:57), which sounds dramatic and exciting, but the reader is told no more about it until the next morning when Wendy says what they did was a "mistake" (2001:59). The reader is left wondering if this "mistake" involved only kissing or something more.

Eagland also has the "fade to black" portrayal:

> As we climb on to my narrow bed, the springs creak, making us giggle. And we kiss, gently at first, my hands moving over the smooth warm curves of her body, her hands hot on my skin. But then our hands become fierce, urgent, hungry, and soon we are dancing, my love and I, dancing together in a rhythm that's easy, sweet and easy... (2009:358-9)

The two females are "dancing" in a "sweet" and "easy" way, but unlike in many of the scenes that feature gay males, readers of books featuring lesbians are not told if anyone is on top or what exactly is happening or if lubricant, towels, or any other items, such as dildos or other sex toys, are employed.

Besides fading to black, some books rely on euphemisms. As John Ayto writes, euphemisms are "the set of communicative strategies we have evolved to refer to a topic under a taboo, without actually contravening its term" (Ayto, 1993:1). He adds, "there are some experiences we would rather not conjure up quite so vividly... [d]eath and killing, disease, sexual activity, dishonesty, drunkenness, nakedness, fatness, ugliness, old age, madness – in short, anything that we are ashamed of" (ibid.). An example is the quote mentioned above in Lili Wilkinson's *Pink*, where Ava says she and her girlfriend have done "stuff" (2009:33). Jane Eagland's "dancing" (2009:359) is another euphemism. This avoidance of direct description is generally reflected in the words chosen. As mentioned above, the themes of shyness, hesitancy, and clumsiness are common; this is revealed by the words employed but also by the fact that the reader is not allowed to really experience what is happening in the story, the way the reader of a book featuring gay males often is.

Besides these rare and discreet descriptions of females sexually interacting with one another, sometimes nothing is said at all beyond implication. In Maureen Johnson's *The Bermudez Triangle*, readers know that Mel and Avery are in a relationship, but it is never clear whether this is a sexual one or exactly how much they do together. At one point, a young man offers the two of them ten dollars to kiss in front of him (2004:28-9); they do not take him up on it, but later Avery tells Mel that she would have done it. She says, "Ten bucks? Why not? Guys are *ridiculous* that way." (2004:33, italics original) This kiss, it seems, would only have been carried out to appeal to a man and to make money, although a most unimpressive sum, one could add. This suggests that lesbian sexuality is somehow for men, and even for sale.

Descriptions of lesbian sex are also unlike the descriptions of gay male sex in that the sexual activities generally do not culminate in orgasm, or at least if they do, that is not depicted. This is not to say that all sexual interactions do or should include orgasms, but it is nonetheless worth pondering how in YA literature gay males have orgasms while gay females do not seem to. Lee writes that "[o]f critical importance is how adolescent lesbian sexuality is articulated by adults for adolescents in popular literature and culture, because whether the adolescent reads for truth, experience, identification, or pleasure, she reads what the dominant culture deems publishable." (2011:165) Clearly, the message young women are getting is that females may not have satisfying sex lives.

One of the few books that shows young women enjoying their sex lives is Julie Burchill's *Sugar Rush*. There are no real descriptions, but as this quotation shows, the sex at least seems to be passionate:

> Except this was PROPER sex, in a way that a boy and a girl our ages could never have had. It was sex without the rubbish, without the fear, without the you-made-your-bed-young-lady-and-now-you're-going-to-have-to-lie-in-it punchline; the pregnancy, abortion, disease, boy-boasting, bad rep, whatever. It was as ceaselessly gratifying as checking out your swimsuit straplines in the mirror at the end of each day and knowing that your tan gets deeper, sweeter, stronger every day. (2004:113, capitals original)

However, this is problematic in a number of ways. For example, it suggests that sex between two people of the same gender is "without the fear", but as many of the other examples have shown, there can be fear no matter what the gender of the participants, so this does not seem authentic. Also, just as Wilkinson's novel does, Burchill's ignores the fact that lesbian sex can indeed lead to disease, even if that is less likely. A further quote hints at but gives no detailed description whatsoever of what the young women's "PROPER sex" is like: "When we were alone, when we were naked in my single bed, or lying in the dark with our skirts up and our knickers in our handbags in Peter Pan's Playground or on the beach, life was perfect at long last" (2004:115). But these two quotations hinting at passionate sexual activity are quite solitary in Burchill's book, because the two main characters quickly fall into the old stereotype of "lesbian bed death".[52] Sugar begins to say that she does not want Kim to touch her and that Kim is "perving" on her (as on 2004:118). As for being active herself, Sugar "never ever touched me [Kim] in public any more, and wriggled away whenever I touched her" (ibid., and cf. 2004:189). Soon they are having no sex at all (2004:180-1), unless Sugar is very drunk (2004:187), and if they do, it is only so they can have "a wriggly, gasping epiphany" (2004:118). Although it is positive that the characters are clearly in search of orgasms at one stage in their relationship, which is unlike the situation for young women in many other books, it seems sad that that is the sole source of their connection. Eventually Sugar cheats on Kim with a number of men. So despite the momentary flaming of passion, their relationship burns out quite quickly.

As mentioned, descriptions of lesbian sex in YA books have a strong tendency to rely on words such as "shy", "clumsy", "hesitant", "soft", "gentle", and "sweet". Other words used are "kiss", "honey", "softness", "hands", "sliding", "mouth", "tongue", "liquid", "moist", "easy" "beautiful", "longing", "stuff", "abnormal", "wrong", and "dirty". A high percentage of these words seem to express feelings of uncertainty and fear and they suggest that sex between women is either something "wrong" and "dirty" or else something "sweet" and "easy". There is little passion in these words and there is no sense that being physical together is something two females desperately want or need to do. In contrast to this, some of the words employed in depictions of gay male sex in YA books include "fuck", "naked", "behind", "hard", "muscles", "curves", "gasping", "groaning", "ass", "tongue", "thighs", "arms", tighter", "sticky" "ooze", "inside", "faster", and "come". This suggests a higher acceptance of and comfort with gay males having sex. The words in scenes featuring gay males relate more to body parts and to actions. The males "gasp" and "groan" and "fuck" and "come", while the females "long" but are "shy" and "clumsy". As a point of interest, only one word is used in both sets, and that is "tongue". "Make love" appears at times, but I was surprised to find it only in books in reference to young men (as in Sanchez, 2005:219), although I had anticipated that this soft term might be used by and about women; likewise, the talk of spirituality in connection to sex only arose in descriptions of men. In general, as already stated, all this seems to reflect ideas about male versus female sexuality. Men are sexually confident and are interested in passion and satisfaction and even, in some cases, romance, whereas women are fearful and seem unable to show their sexual feelings, lest they be labelled sluts, as Sugar is in *Sugar Rush*.

Another difference is that texts for young adults show friends or acquaintances being more confused about what might happen when two females are in bed together than they are in books where the characters are gay males. Although there are some scenes of teasing and name-calling in regard to gay males (such as in Sanchez 2001:21, 35-6, 190, or 2003:205), few question why two boys might be sexually attracted to one another and what they might do when they are together. This happens more often in books with young women, with the teasing being harsher; perhaps bullying is a better term for it. In Garden's book, a classmate teases Liza by asking, "I just wondered...if you could tell me, from a scientific standpoint, of course, just what it is that two girls do in bed..." (1982:218) This is said in a way that implies that what two females do in bed is difficult to imagine or understand. A teacher in the same book says, "Sodom and Gomorrah are all around us...There is ugliness and sin and self-indulgence in this house...And to think...that the president of student council is a—a..." (1982:167) The teacher cannot bring herself to say "lesbian", even though she can clearly bring herself to reference the Bible and to criticise non-heteronormative practices. The head of the school, too, refers to "abnormal sex" (1982:183). In Eagland's book, the main character is sent away due to her homosexual feelings and behaviours (2009). Such examples imply that no one can understand what two girls would do together sexually and also that this is not deserving of respect in any case. Lee writes that "[h]olding hands is used so often in lesbian fiction, specifically adolescent lesbian fiction, that it can be considered a trope of the genre." (2011:171) Perhaps holding hands replaces the sexual activities that no one can or wants to imagine.

In sum, this section suggests that to a certain extent, the books are realistic according to research on sex and gender, in that men are shown prioritising pleasure while women are shown looking for "emotional closeness" (Moore and Rosenthal, 2006:133), although it is true that some young men are also interested in emotions and romance. However, the books seem to give the message that women cannot and do not have passionate, sexually satisfying encounters with one another, and this clearly is not realistic and is a problematic comment to make on the sex lives of lesbians. Lee writes that "[t]he sex, however, is not the source of tension in these coming-out stories. Rather, the girls' verbal and physical articulations become meaningful with the threat of public knowledge." (2011:173) In other words, she is arguing that the sex matters less than what the relationship as a whole represents, and how the young women are received by others. This may be the case, but that still leaves readers with the belief that sex is not of as much importance to young queer women as it is to young queer men.

BTQ Sex

All of the above has focused on gay males and females. A few might possibly be labelled as bisexual, but as is discussed in more detail in the chapter on diversity, bisexual, transgender, and otherwise queer characters are for the most part notably absent from LGBTQ books for young readers, which means that their sex lives are also mostly missing. I found no examples of characters who call themselves bisexual having sex. Sometimes those who could be labelled bisexual are shown to kiss someone other than their girlfriend/boyfriend, as though to say that bisexuals cannot or will not be faithful (see more on this in the chapter on stereotypes). In novels with transgender characters, such as *Parrotfish* and *Luna*, the focus is mostly on other aspects of identity, and not sex, although J in *I Am J* does have a girlfriend for part of the novel. In regard to other aspects of queerness, in Alex Sanchez's *Rainbow Road*, the character of Nelson is tempted to sleep with a polyamorous guy he meets, but this does not end up happening (2005:77). Other than these few examples, readers do not see BTQ characters engaging in sexual activity, whether alone or with others. Perhaps this is thought to be too titillating or too shocking, or maybe it is not something most writers or publishers or indeed even readers are aware of.

Summary of Sex

In the foregoing sections, I have focused on young adult literature to explore how queer sex is portrayed. There is an obvious absence here in that queer sex in not depicted in picture books, so I have only analysed works for older readers. I would not argue for graphic sex scenes in picture books (I am not suggesting a Kama Sutra for five-year-olds), but I would argue that sex can be written about or depicted to a certain extent. For example, there are many picture books about where babies come from (see Lepore, 2010, for more on this or Cole, 1995, for an example), so I think there could be books that discuss in-vitro fertilisation, or egg sharing, or finding a sperm donor, or similar topics, which may well be relevant to the children of both LGBTQ and non-LGBTQ parents. Similarly, as Steven Bruhm and Natasha Hurley write, the children of LGBTQ parents are portrayed as being "without many desires at all" (2004:xii), possibly as though to avoid suggesting that LGBTQ parents raise children in an unhealthy way that oversexualises them. So even in YA books that feature LGBTQ parents, readers do not see them engaging in sex; on the other hand, this makes sense to a certain extent, because young adults themselves rather than their parents are usually the focus in YA literature, although this absence contributes to the general lack of anything other than gay male sex in these works.

As shown above, teenage lesbians do not seem to masturbate, to know about or consider using protection, or to have much passionate sex. When they do have sexual interactions with one another, the sex is described in very hesitant, often euphemistic terms, with little detail offered to the reader, and other characters might question or criticise it. Meanwhile, in YA texts such as by Levithan, Reardon, and Sanchez, gay teenage males masturbate regularly; show an awareness in regard to employing protection, even if they are sometimes averse to doing so; and have a lot of sexual intercourse, which is often described frankly in the books. Some of this may reflect stereotypes about promiscuous gay men versus lesbian bed death and/or stereotypes about male versus female sexuality. Society may be uncomfortable with portraying females, whether homosexual or not, as having active, healthy, satisfying sexual lives. It has been, and in many cases still is, acceptable for females in literature to have close, intense friendships and for there to be gentle kisses and cuddles, perhaps as "practice" for later heterosexual relationships, but anything beyond that is considered inappropriate and disturbing. These young adult books seem to represent the ideas that women should not be overtly sexual creatures, and that lesbianism is especially challenging to western society's ideas of sexuality. Also, BTQ sexuality is conspicuously absent.

Michael Cart and Christine A. Jenkins likewise have noted the lack of sexual activity in these books. They write:

> Of course, one argument made against including sexual explicitness in YA novels was that it is merely voyeuristic. Real life voyeurism is inappropriate, to say the least, but no matter how realistic a work of fiction may be, the reader is in a different relationship with a text than the observer is with the people observed in one's immediate surroundings. Teens who pick up a book are often reading with questions… (2006:34)

I am not sure that voyeurism is as inappropriate or wrong as some might suggest, because, as Cart and Jenkins acknowledge, teenagers have questions, so there is no reason why their questions cannot be answered in part by a realistic novel. So it is a concern that queer teenagers may not get their questions answered through these books or that they might get inaccurate answers.

I believe that young adult literature shows teens what is possible, provides models for them, and reflects society's views of them and their lives; here, then, such literature suggests that young homosexual women cannot and should not have satisfying sexual relationships. Even in the twenty-first century, female sexuality, and especially female homosexuality, is still too challenging and upsetting to be included in YA literature. "Gentle", "shy", and "soft" kisses are acceptable, but anything more than that is "wrong" and "abnormal". Meanwhile, young gay men are sometimes oversexualised, which may make male readers feel pressured to have uncontrollable sex drives (cf. Moore and Rosenthal 2006:139). Thus, portrayals of non-heterosexual sex are quite limited in a number of worrying ways.

Marriage

In this section, I explore marital relationships in LGBTQ books for young readers. Here, however, the emphasis will mostly be on how older characters' marital situations are depicted, since it is less likely that young people will be married, but I do look briefly at whether young people are portrayed in these books as being interested in marriage or as hoping to get married one day.

As of June 2013, it looks likely that the U.K. Government will soon offer civil marriage for same-sex couples. After Barack Obama was re-elected U.S. president in 2012, several states voted for same-sex marriage. This may have helped usher in new feelings about, and potentially new laws for, same-sex marriage throughout that country. Considering the changing political views of same-sex marriage in a couple of English-speaking countries (New Zealand recently voted for it, for example), I wondered whether and how gay parents and their children were reflected in children's literature, and whether the amount of books that feature same-sex marriage would map onto how common same-sex marriage is in a given country. If there is cultural momentum in some countries towards allowing full marriage, or even just civil/domestic partnerships for same-sex couples, this might mean that we start seeing more same-sex couples in books for young readers. It also might be the case that young LGBTQ people could start seeing marriage as an option for their futures. In other words, do books for children and young people suggest that we are seeing a move towards what can be called the nuclear gay family?[53] Below, then, I analyse a number of American English-language children's books and books for young adults with LGBTQ characters in order to explore the nuclear gay family and whether it exists, and I compare this to a small corpus of British English-language of children's books[54] and several northern European[55] children's books with LGBTQ characters. What the findings suggest is that marriage or civil/domestic partnership is not particularly common in the American books, but that it is more accepted in European and more specifically northern European children's books. This makes sense, given that there are more options for same-sex couples in northern European countries, as will be discussed in more detail below. Hence, children's books appear to reflect the current political situations where and when they are written, and in this case, that means that they either see same-sex marriage as part of a way of creating a gay nuclear family, or they do not recognise it.

First, I will offer some background on LGBTQ parenting and on same-sex marriage, and this will then lead into a discussion of the children's books.[56]

Background on LGBTQ Parenting

There has not yet been a huge amount of research into LGBTQ parenting. What research there is generally focuses on lesbian and gay parenting (i.e. not bisexual or transgender parenting[57]), although actually it tends to focus on lesbians, rather than gay males, perhaps because it is easier and/or more common for gay women to have children than it is for gay men (cf. Belkin 2009:n.p.). Stephen Hicks suggests that this lack of research into LGBTQ parenting may be because those who work on LGBTQ issues feel that parenting is not as "queer" or does not allow for as much "queering" as do other aspects of LGBTQ life (2011:17). Also, much of what research does exist frequently looks at the question of whether children raised by such parents turn out "normal" and whether their family lives can be compared to "normal", heterosexual families (cf. Johnson and O'Connor, 2002:3 and 36-53, and for literature, see Epstein, 2011, for example, or the chapter in this book on issue books), which seems to presuppose that something will go wrong with the children of lesbian or gay parents. Often, such work seems to attempt to reassure readers that children can be raised into healthy, happy adults by LGBTQ parents. As Suzanne M. Johnson and Elizabeth O'Connor suggest, it would be better to focus on parenting techniques, say, or values, rather than on using heteronormative approaches to the topic of parenting (2002:3).

Other research on the subject sometimes takes an opposing viewpoint, in order to prove that children should not be raised by LGBTQ parents. A typical example is Patricia Morgan's book, *Children as Trophies?* (2002). The title together with the publisher (the Christian Institute) suggest Morgan's ultimate conclusion. A sample line from her book is:

> Procreation is tied to marriage. Children are not to be spawned in random relations but begotten in arrangements in which their parents are bound to their offspring by the ties of law as well as nature. The intention is for parents to be as committed to the nurture of their children as they are committed to each other as husband and wife. (2002:11)

This sort of comment, which is very typical of the argument against same-sex parenting, refers to "nature" and to someone or something's "intention"; one can perhaps assume that given the publisher, the reference is to a god, who has created nature in a particular way with specific goals or intentions in mind. The comment also uses dramatic language to suggest that LGBTQ people only have "random relations", rather than committed ones, and that they would want to "spawn" children in order to use them as "trophies".

It is somewhat tautological, in that she seems to think it is wrong for children to be raised by parents who are not "tied" together by law, but of course if committed LGBTQ couples are not allowed to legally get married, then they cannot be "bound" to each other and to their "offspring by the ties of law". So the law should be seen as the problem, not the queerness. But, naturally, critics such as Morgan refuse to recognise that.

Regardless of this sort of argument, which of course is not the focus here, the fact is that same-sex couples are indeed having children; as Kathleen Hull puts it, "gay and lesbian couples increasingly seek to form viable family units of their own, either by acting as co-parents to children from previous marriages or by becoming parents together" (2006:5). Also, laws in the U.S. and in some other countries are seemingly designed to help them achieve this through the legalisation of LGBTQ fostering, adoption, insemination, and other relevant procedures.

As far as I am aware, there has been little research into how same-sex parenting is portrayed in children's literature. One interesting example is from Jane Sunderland's book *Literature, Gender and Children's Fiction*, in a chapter co-written with Mark McGlashan on two-mum and two-dad families. One of the analyses she carries out there is to look at the visual representations in picture books in order to see how much physical contact is portrayed (2010:142-172). But beyond such work, this is still fairly unchartered territory.

Background on LGBTQ Marriage

In this section of background material, I explore same-sex marriage in general terms. As this is not the place to rehash the arguments for and against same-sex marriage (see "Arguments For and Against Same-Sex Marriage", in Eskridge, 2001:113-132, for a brief review of the discussion), I simply assume an accepting stance towards the subject. I personally find it regrettable that I have to say "same-sex marriage" when it should simply be "marriage".

Whether marriage is something that same-sex couples aspire to is not necessarily certain. As with any group, LGBTQ people are not monolithic, and some couples may prefer to live together, or indeed to live separately, and not under the aegis of marriage. Some may feel it is too heteronormative and that they do not wish to partake of a heterosexual institution (e.g. Hull, 2006:100), while others may feel it was not an option when they were younger and thus they no longer think about it, and still others may not wish the government to be involved in their relationships, and so on. Stephanie Coontz claims that "[o]nly a small minority of gays and lesbians are interested in marrying at this point." (2005:275) Coontz does not say where she gets her statistics, but one could point out that the rush of same-sex couples who got married in California and elsewhere in the U.S. suggests that she is wrong and that many gay and lesbian couples do indeed wish to get married. Coontz does say that marriage "remains the highest expression of commitment in our culture and comes packaged with exacting expectations about responsibility, fidelity, and intimacy." (2005:309) If this is the case, then it stands to reason that same-sex couples, too, might want to express their commitment in the same way, notwithstanding Coontz's previous assertion that only a "small minority" do.

The reasons for this desire are both cultural and legal. Hull writes that "marriage is increasingly available to American gay and lesbian couples in *cultural* terms, but remains mostly inaccessible in *legal* terms." (2006:2, italics original) In her research, among other topics, she explores how same-sex couples can create commitment ceremonies or marriages, even without legal sanctions, which again puts pay to Coontz's heteronormative claim. Coontz also refers to the cultural importance of marriage, when she writes that the "relationship between a cohabiting couple, whether heterosexual or same sex, is unacknowledged by law and may be ignored by the friends and relatives of each partner. Marriage, in contrast, gives people a positive vocabulary and public image that set a high standard for the couple's behaviour and for the respect that outsiders ought to give to their relationship." (2005:309-10)

The legality clearly matters to many couples, and some of the research into this topic specifically refers to how legal marriage can affect children (obviously, the lack of legal marriage can affect the partners themselves in many ways, as in Spilsbury, 2001:15). Hull discusses how couples with children or plans to have children are often more concerned with legal protection, insurance, financial protection, and other legalistic issues (2006:121), and she writes that one argument for same-sex marriage is that children get legal recognition and protection, plus they feel more societal acceptance (2006:155 and 190-1). She writes that parents refer to "three distinct concerns about the impact of lack of marriage rights" on children with same-sex parents (2006:177). The first is that a child in such a relationship "lack[s] full legal protection within their family without marriage. This frames marriage as a legal issue that impacts both adults and children." (ibid.) The next is that children might not "understand a marriage substitute such as domestic partnership." (ibid.) The third concern is that having "parents who could not marry would mark [the child] as different and therefore not "equal" and "part of a larger community."" (ibid.)

What all this suggests is that some same-sex couples wish to get legally partnered or married, and that this is especially the situation for those who have or intend to have children. The reasons are both cultural and legal. But this discussion mostly refers to adult LGBTQ people. Since I am analysing young adult works as well, it would be interesting to see whether young LGBTQ people hope for or strive towards marriage. In one book that looks at "emerging adulthood", or that stage when people are in their late teens to early twenties, the author discusses marriage in detail, but never in connection to LGBTQ emerging adults (Arnett, 2004:97-118). Jeffrey Jensen Arnett writes, for example, that "[t]oday's emerging adults spend more years single and dating than young people in previous generations, but the great majority of them eventually make their way to the altar." (2004:97) He later reassures the reader again that "[n]early all emerging adults want to get married eventually" (2004:100), but his entire discussion refers to male-female couples, especially in connection to their supposedly differing desires and opinions about marriage (also see Jay, 2012, for a similar discussion, which never once mentions non-heterosexual couples). A question here is whether such researchers and writers simply do not consider the LGBTQ community or whether their research suggests that LGBTQ young people do not hope to get married; if the latter, then one assumes that this would be stated in the findings, so the former seems more likely, and this leaves one wondering why researchers ignore LGBTQ young people.

Despite changing laws, then, perhaps society still does not think same-sex marriage is acceptable or of equal value or something that can be held up as a possible route for young LGBTQ people. Some non-fiction texts aimed at young readers, such as Craig Donnellan's non-fiction book, *Homosexuality,* which seems intended for readers aged 12 and up, do not even mention marriage as an option for same-sex couples. Donnellan's work, for example, talks about discrimination, laws, and rights, but the only discussion of marriage is in reference to the Christian bible (1998:34-5) and how it is against homosexual couples, and in reference to gay men who came out after having previously been married to women (1998:38-9). I am not trying to argue that a twelve-year-old would be eager to get married, but only to make the reader aware that legal ceremonies for LGBTQ couples are not even mentioned as an option, especially when it comes to younger people. Young people do imagine their future lives, including relationships, but most books do not acknowledge this in regard to queer youth.

This section has shown that many LGBTQ people want to have civil partnerships or marriages for both cultural and legal reasons, but this idea has seemingly not yet trickled down into the younger LGBTQ community, or at least if it has, this is not recognised by researchers. This could be due to society's discomfort with the topic or with an unwillingness to see younger LGBTQ people as sexual beings who might one day want to get married, the way other "emerging adults" seem to. What the next sections will show is whether these ideas are borne out in literature.

U.S. Books

The U.S. is a particularly interesting and contradictory place to study, because many of the English-language LGBTQ children's books I have found were published there, which suggests a certain level of acceptance of LGBTQ people, and several states have instated same-sex marriage, even while other states have redefined marriage as being between a man and a woman only (Pinello, 2006:20). In 2004, Congress passed and former U.S. President Bill Clinton signed into law the national Defense of Marriage Act, which declared that marriage is between a man and a woman (Pinello, 2006:29), so even though the individual states have some independent jurisdiction, the overall attitude in the U.S. seems to be against same-sex marriage. However, as mentioned previously, the current political situation is transforming to a certain extent. Evan Wolfson suggests that "opponents are antigay, not just anti-marriage equality. What's transforming the country is coming to terms with, and accepting, gay people and their love on terms of equality" (quoted in Pinello, 2006:23). And as Bruce E. Blaine says, "Given the disliking and moral judgment of gay people prevalent in the broader culture, surveys show that most Americans are surprisingly willing to support some legal recognition and protections of gay men and lesbians, such as shared health benefits and civil unions" (2007:144). However, this shift – and the legal ramifications it entails – seems to be a slow process.

When it comes to children, Nancy D. Polikoff explains that the "number of planned lesbian and gay families skyrocketed in the United States in the 1990s, bringing unprecedented visibility in the media, in schools, in churches and synagogues, and in the courts." (2001:165) More specific statistics come from Daniel R. Pinello, who writes that the "2000 [U.S.] census reveals that 34 percent of lesbian couples and 22 percent of gay male couples have at least one child under the age of eighteen living in their home, compared with 46 percent of married opposite-sex couples having minor children at home" (2006:156). Interestingly, there seems to be more legal support for same-sex parenting in the U.S. than there is for same-sex marriage, which suggests a child-centred culture without support for marriage equality. One could ask how genuinely child-centred that actually is. As Yuval Merin writes, "[d]espite the general shift toward delinking procreation and marriage in the West, the United States is still very much a child-centered society." (2002:261) He also explains that in the United States, "same-sex couples enjoy many rights concerning parenthood: various levels of courts in almost half the states have recognized second-parent adoptions, some jurisdictions allow same-sex couples to jointly adopt unrelated children, and nowhere in the United States are artificial conception services for lesbians prohibited." (2002:254) This information may explain why there is a largish number of children's books featuring LGBTQ couples and their children published in the U.S., but few children's books with same-sex marriage, as the next paragraphs reveal. On the other hand, we still have to be aware of the discrimination that LGBTQ people who want to be parents or who are parents face. Blaine refers to the institutionalised discrimination that they encounter; what he means is that since they cannot get married in most states, this "is a big obstacle for couples hoping to adopt a child…[s]imilarly, the US Census Bureau defines a 'family' as involving two or more people who are related by birth, marriage, or adoption. Gay couples, therefore, are not recognized as families." (2007:148) Hence, they will not receive the same rights and privileges that other families do.

Many of the characters in LGBTQ literature for children are parents, as already mentioned. So a question is how these parents are portrayed and if any of them are married or engaged.

Most LGBTQ picture books, such as Michael Willhoite's *Daddy's Roommate* – which relies on the euphemism of "roommate" rather than employing "boyfriend", "partner", or, yes, even "husband" – do not seem to consider the possibility that the two mothers or two fathers could actually be wife-and-wife or husband-and-husband.[58] Regarding Willhoite's work, one might want to recall that as Ayto was quoted as saying above, a euphemism may be employed in order to avoid referring to something openly because it is shameful or unacceptable. The euphemism "roommate" might, therefore, suggest shame and taboo.

Other picture books with same-sex parents mostly have storylines about bullying or confirmation of a two-mother or two-father family as normal (as discussed in the chapter on issue books), and do not mention marriage. Examples include Rigoberto González's *Antonio's Card* (2005) or Elaine Wickens' *Anna Day and the O-Ring* (1994). Despite the fact that many of these books with two mothers or two fathers have a clear titular reference to one or more "mommies" or "daddies" (for example, Lesléa Newman's *Heather Has Two Mommies* (1989); *Mommy, Mama, and ME* (2009); and *Daddy, Papa, and ME* (2009)), these same-sex parents are rarely married or planning on getting married. Whether this is because authors believe that LGBTQ couples should not get married or because they think that there is no need for it or for some other reason is hard to say.

If one looks at preeminent queer writer for children Lesléa Newman's oeuvre of picture books, it is only in her most recent book, *Donovan's Big Day*, which was published in 2012, that one finds marriage. In this book, the focus is on the main character, Donovan, as he prepares for his mothers' wedding. It is thus told from the child's perspective, perhaps enabling child readers to better imagine themselves in that situation. It is not didactic or overly explanatory; rather, Newman's book just accepts the possibility of same-sex marriage, allowing a reader to do so as well. Newman writes, "I wanted to write a book that was a true celebration, capturing all the joy and excitement of the day without any issues whatsoever. All families deserve a wedding day of pure joy, and I wanted to give that to kids who have two moms. I hope that there will be many more books featuring kids with two moms or two dads in years to come." (personal correspondence, 2012:n.p.) Perhaps there will be more books from the U.S. that are "true celebration[s]" in the future, if same-sex marriage becomes more widely legalised.[59]

Sarah S. Brannen's picture book *Uncle Bobby's Wedding* shows a same-sex wedding. The book is about Chloe and her much adored Uncle Bobby. However, they are guinea pigs, which thus distances them from people, although using animals as characters is a common trope in children's literature. Chloe and Bobby spend a lot of time together. But when Bobby announces that he is marrying "his friend" Jamie (2008:n.p.) (as it is euphemistically phrased), Chloe is not happy. As the narrator puts it, "Everyone was smiling and talking and crying and laughing. Everyone except Chloe." (ibid.) Chloe asks her mother why Bobby is getting married and receives the response, "When grown-up people love each other that much, they want to be married." (ibid.; sic, since the text talks about "people" while the pictures clearly show guinea pigs). Chloe says, "Bobby is my special uncle. I don't want him to get married." (ibid.) Chloe and Bobby then go for a walk and Chloe expresses her fears; when Bobby tells her that he and Jamie want to have children "just like" Chloe, she gets even more upset (ibid.). Bobby reassures her and then he and Jamie spend more time with Chloe, taking her to the ballet, going sailing, and playing board games (ibid.) Eventually Chloe accepts Jamie and the relationship and agrees to be the flower girl at the wedding. All ends happily. One could note that Jamie is a gender-neutral name and he is not described as male until much later in the story when Chloe says, "I wish both of you were my uncles" (ibid.), but the guinea pigs are stereotypically gendered in the pictures from the beginning, with the females in dresses and the males in jackets or t-shirts. While it is positive that same-sex marriage is shown and that the book addresses childhood fears about abandonment and no longer being the favourite, it is distanced from reality since it is about guinea pigs.

Even if there are few married LGBTQ parents in picture books, I wondered if there might be more same-sex marriage in young adult novels. After all, as mentioned above in reference to emerging adults, young people may be growing up with more hopes and expectations because of changed political situations, in comparison to adults who may simply have accepted that they will get fewer rights as LGBTQ people. Alas, this does not seem to be true. Many YA novels with teenaged LGBTQ characters do not mention being committed to another person beyond boyfriend/girlfriend stage (Sanchez, 2001, Levithan, 2003, among others). Those that do consider the concept do so in a pessimistic way.

Robin Reardon, who has written several YA novels with gay male protagonists, has her main character, Jason, in *A Secret Edge* consider gay marriage. He thinks, "I've never given [marriage] much thought before. But now--I guess it's out of the question for me. I mean, you hear about two guys getting married, sort of, but it seems a little far-fetched to me. And suddenly a lot of things most people take for granted seem a little far-fetched for me. Living with someone you love. Having kids." (2007:56)

Jason's sad ponderings might make a reader pity gay people and their limited opportunities for a happy and fulfilling romantic relationship. Jason's uncle, who raised him, is sorely disappointed when he learns that his nephew is gay. He thinks, "No one should have to live like that. He'll be hated, ostracized. He won't be able to marry or have children." (2007:90) Like Jason's uncle, Liza's father in Nancy Garden's *Annie on My Mind* worries about what being gay will mean for his daughter. Although not as disgusted by her lesbianism as some of her teachers are, Liza's father says that he does not want this for her, because it will mean she can never marry or have children (1982:187-91). In the same novel, there is an older lesbian couple that Liza and Annie look up to, but these women are not married, do not have children, and eventually lose their jobs. In both these books, then, not only can LGBTQ people not marry, but they also apparently cannot have children, and may even have employment difficulties, so they are even more negative and gloomy than the picture books.

In most YA novels, the gay characters and their parents assume that marriage is, as Jason put it, "out of the question". One young character bucks the trend by realising that there are ceremonies for gay people. In Maureen Johnson's *The Bermudez Triangle*, Avery thinks about her girlfriend, "What if Mel wanted to get married and have a commitment ceremony and play Ani DiFranco and k.d. lang songs and have cats as bridesmaids? That would be great for Mel, but it just wasn't something Avery could picture. The thought scared her. A lot." (2004:204-5) While it is positive to see that there is some recognition that there are opportunities for gay couples to show their commitment to one another, this passage stereotypically mocks what lesbians are like (cat-mad avid Ani DiFranco listeners) and also suggests that the idea of a ceremony is not too appealing.

So in YA novels too, there are few indications that LGBTQ people might want or be able to have civil partnerships or marriages. Either their response is negative, as above, or the topic is never mentioned. What this analysis implies is that in American books with LGBTQ characters, it is acceptable to a certain extent to show same-sex couples, and particularly same-sex couples with children, but marriage is a step too far.

U.K. Books

As a very brief comparison, we can look at English-language books from the U.K. This comparison is brief because, as previously mentioned, it seems there are fewer books published in the U.K. with LGBTQ content. Rebecca Bailey-Harris's analysis of same-sex partnerships in the U.K. is now dated, because it is possible to have civil partnerships today and there will probably be civil marriage in the next few years. As she points out, however, it may be more complicated for same-sex couples to have children in the U.K. through adoption (2001:605-619), which perhaps is one explanation for why there are fewer children's books published in the U.K. that show LGBTQ parents with children.

One of the few picture books from the U.K. to feature gay marriage is Ken Setterington's *Mom and Mum Are Getting Married* (2004). The story here is about how Mom and Mum just want a small ceremony while their daughter Rosie wants to be the flower girl in the big event. It is a refreshing change to see a picture book normalise gay marriage and show a gay couple making a legal commitment, and this book is one of the few in English to depict this, along with Newman's latest book. The U.K. has civil partnership nationally, rather than in just a few states/jurisdictions, as is the situation in the U.S., so perhaps it makes sense that it would seem more acceptable in British children's books. On the other hand, another British book, Hedi Argent's *Josh and Jaz Have Three Mums* (2004), does not refer to marriage at all.

There are fewer YA books in the U.K. featuring LGBTQ characters and the arguably preeminent author of such books, Aidan Chambers, does not include marriage, although that could be because some of his works are from a decade or more ago. Philip Pullman's *The Broken Bridge* has a gay teenaged character, but he cohabitates with his partner, with no discussion of marriage (1990). Perhaps we need more contemporary LGBTQ books published and set in Britain, and civil partnership could therefore feature in them.

Northern European Books

Finally, we can turn to northern European books. As Yuval Merin points out, northern Europe has much more liberal, comprehensive, and non-discriminatory laws than many other parts of the world (2002:2), which means there are more options for same-sex couples (see "Partnerships in Europe" in Merin, 2002). For example, Merin writes that "the northern European registered partnership acts attempt to place same-sex couples on an equal footing with opposite-sex married couples. The United States, in contrast, is far from granting to same-sex unions legal recognition approximating that reserved for marriage, at either the national or the state level" (2002:2-3). As there have been options for partnership or marriage for same-sex couples in northern Europe longer than elsewhere, one would perhaps imagine that children's literature would reflect this.

We can look first at Sweden.[60] As Hans Ytterberg says, "Sweden is the country within the Nordic family which has gone the furthest down the road of introducing specific, civil law, family legislation on non-marital cohabitation." (2001:430) This might suggest that one would see more unmarried couples in Swedish work than in books from other countries, where cohabitation is less approved of or supported. Interestingly, however, same-sex marriage does appear with some regularity in Swedish books for children, which perhaps suggest that Swedish authors, editors, and/or publishers want to ensure readers that they are accepting of all relationship choices.

In Bodil Sjöström's *Trollen på Regnbågsbacken* [The Trolls of Rainbow Hill] (1999), two female characters are married to one another. Another character questions this and receives the response, "Alla som älskar varandra kan gifta sig...Därmed inte sagt att alla gör det. Man måste inte." (1999:n.p.) This translates to, "Everyone who loves each other can get married...That doesn't mean that everyone does it. You don't have to." (my translation)

Another Swedish text that portrays a same-sex marriage is called *Malins mamma gifter sig med Lisa* [Malin's Mama Marries Lisa] by Anette Lundborg and Mimmi Tollerup-Grkovic (1999). An afterword in the book by the authors captures their understanding about the situation:

> It is more and more common that homosexuals choose to become parents. In Sweden today, there are around

> 40,000 children that have at least one homosexual parent. Many homosexuals have children from previous heterosexual relationships, but evermore homosexuals choose to have children with their partners or as single parents. A life as a homosexual no longer stands in opposition to a life with children! (1999:n.p.; my translation)

From this afterword, one can suppose that if it is true that "more and more common that homosexuals choose to become parents" then those parents and their children would like to see themselves reflected in children's literature and also, as Susanne Bösche, author of *Jenny Lives with Eric and Martin*, pointed out such families "shouldn't come as a shock to anybody" (2000, n.p.).[61] So the goal with this kind of book seems to be two-fold. Also, as with Newman's English book, in Lundborg and Tollerup-Grkovic's, the focus is on the marriage and the child protagonist's feelings about it. Thus, the two Swedish picture books mentioned here both seem to take the normality of homosexuality for granted.

Merin puts the Netherlands together with the Nordic countries because he feels that northern Europe is distinctly different in its outlook regarding same-sex partnerships in comparison with other European countries or indeed countries in other parts of the world. As he points out, the "northern European model of registered partnership, to say nothing of same-sex marriage, in the Netherlands, is very different from the American domestic partnership model." (2002:250) Kees Waaldijk goes into more detail when he writes that "[t]he Netherlands appears to be the first country in the world where a legislative proposal to open up marriage to same-sex couples has become law and come into force." (2001:437) He proudly states:

> Although not always first, the Netherlands can certainly be ranked as one of the most gay/lesbian-friendly societies and jurisdictions in the world. Is there any other country where, since the early 1980s, the percentage of

> the population agreeing that homosexuals should be as free as possible to live their own lives, and should have the same rights as heterosexuals in such fields as housing, pensions and inheritance, has been 90 per cent or more? (2001:439)

Waaldijk gives reasons for why this is (2001:453), but what is important for my purposes here is that the Netherlands is a country that is supportive of same-sex marriage.

This is revealed in a picture book by Linda De Haan and Stern Nijland, *King and King* (2002). This was first written and published in Dutch, but has been translated to English, although no translator's name is given,[62] and it is the translation that is being discussed here. In this book, a prince is told by his mother, the queen, that it is time for him to get married (2002:n.p.). She parades a series of princesses in front of him, but none appeal to him. One princess is accompanied by her brother and the protagonist falls for him (ibid.). The two princes get married, and there is no confusion regarding this or any objection to their relationship; it is just accepted that the two male characters have fallen in love and should be married (ibid.). There is a sequel, *King and King and Family* (2004), where the two kings adopt a little girl.[63]

Such northern European children's books in my corpus seem to indicate a greater acceptance and more frequent occurrence of same-sex marriage than English-language children's books, and the secondary materials on these topics likewise support this idea.

Summary of Marriage

As Kathleen Hull states it: "Marriage: Personal commitment. Pillar of civilization. Spiritual covenant. Legal bond. Political football. Source of social status. Site of gender inequality. Tool of sexual regulation. Dying institution. Partnership for reproduction and childrearing. Path to material gain. Reflection of divine love. Legalized prostitution." (2006:1) Regardless of how one sees marriage, the fact is that it still is an existent and important institution, and that it is only open to same-sex couples in a small number of countries in the world. What I have attempted to do here is to look at children's books from those countries in order to explore whether and, if so, how same-sex marriage is portrayed, and to see how this relates to the laws in those countries.

Merin writes that "[m]any U.S. states protect gay and lesbian parenting without recognizing gay and lesbian couples, but we find an opposite trend in Europe, where some countries extensively regulate same-sex partnerships but provide very little recognition of gay and lesbian parenting." (2002:253) This means that the U.S. has more liberal, more child-centred laws about children and about same-sex couples adopting, creating, and raising them, but Europe, particularly northern Europe, is more liberal about marriage/partnership, and if one believes that literature reflects society, then it would make sense that northern European children's books feature more same-sex marriages or partnerships than American children's books. In Hull's research, one person referred to the lack of same-sex marriage as "state-sponsored prejudice" (2006:177), and perhaps here we could add that it seems to be literature-sponsored prejudice as well. What is essential to remember is that LGBTQ parents who raise children without the option of being in a marriage or partnership may suffer legal consequences (and, of course, parents and children alike may suffer psychological and/or emotional consequences), and this is scarcely mentioned in literature, though it is recognised by research.

It is essential to note, as I did above in the section on sex, that despite referring extensively to the LGBTQ community in this chapter, in reality I have only discussed the L and the G, i.e. lesbians and gays. I have not found any picture books with transgender or bisexual parents,[64] so I cannot comment on their marriage status. It is plausible that an author may have imagined a parent to be bisexual or transgender but for this not to have come up in the plot, but that means that readers (or the read-to) will not see same-sex marriage for bisexual or transgender characters (see the chapter on diversity for more on this).

Further research is needed here in general, especially into other countries. For example, due to the small selection of relevant texts, I have scarcely touched on the U.K., where there currently exists civil partnership but civil marriage might soon become a reality. Perhaps more authors will include it in the near future. And although I know the Scandinavian languages and have referred to some Swedish books here, more research can and should be carried out into other European countries and their literatures, and of course into non-EU countries. Perhaps further research would even find whether American publishers are more likely to publish children's books featuring same-sex parenting than European books, if the EU is indeed less child-centred than the U.S., as discussed above.

To conclude, then, LGBTQ children's books do seem to reflect the realities of the countries and cultures they are written, set, and published in. Same-sex marriage is not nationally accepted in the U.S., and thus it seldom appears in children's books there. Civil partnership is a fairly new option in the U.K., and therefore there are not yet many books that refer to it. On the other hand, northern Europe has longer-standing laws regarding domestic partnerships and same-sex marriages, and consequently it is not surprising that books from Sweden and the Netherlands might have more accepting, maybe even blasé, attitudes towards it. One rather sad note is that young adult books seem much less optimistic than picture books, which suggests that emerging LGBTQ adults are not yet looking ahead to marriage; this may, of course, reflect a decline in opinion regarding marriage in general rather than toward same-sex marriage in particular, but given that young heterosexual people seem to be looking forward to marriage, this seems less likely. In sum, based on this literature review, northern Europe seems to be more supportive of the nuclear gay family, as I am terming it, than English-speaking cultures, but this may change as new laws come into place.

Singletons

Although this chapter focuses on sexual relationships and marriage/partnerships, it is worth briefly mentioning single people. How single people are portrayed in literature varies greatly, and this depends to a large extent on gender. Christine A. Jenkins sums this situation up well:

> Notably, along with the ongoing and growing lack of lesbians noted earlier [in the article], is the near-absence of any single lesbians. There appears to be a continuing resistance on the part of authors and/or editors to view independent females as other than in a temporary state (if young) or other than unhappy (if adult). Males, on the other hand, appear to be capable of leading autonomous lives. (2011:154)

While her analysis is based on books only through 1992, in fact my findings have been the same. Young women who are not partnered in young adult literature tend to be unhappy about this and to want to find partners. If they have an argument with their partner and break up, they are reconciled by the end of the novel (as in Garden's *Annie on my Mind*). Male characters are less likely to feel a need to be in relationships and indeed they may even feel surprised if they find themselves in one (such as Ely in *Naomi and Ely's No Kiss List* by Rachel Cohn and David Levithan). One interesting exception is sex-obsessed Nelson, in Alex Sanchez's *Rainbow* trilogy, because he does long for the closeness of a relationship, and does actually find a boyfriend by the end of the series. In short, however, what Jenkins wrote still stands today, unfortunately, giving readers the impression that women cannot be on their own and perhaps even are nothing without a partner.

Conclusion

In this chapter, I have explored two aspects of relationships, namely sex and marriage. The findings are, perhaps, rather grim, and may reflect stereotyped ideas about LGBTQ people and the kinds of lives they can live. In regard to sex, young gay males blithely carry on adventurous, active, satisfying sex lives, while young gay females are shown to be tentative, nervous, emotional, and maybe even repressed when it comes to sex. What this means is presumably that authors (and editors, publishers, the audience, society at large, etc) view female sexuality in very frozen ways, perhaps finding it too threatening to be dealt with in any detailed fashion in YA literature. Meanwhile, other types of queers are apparently not having sex at all, but whether that is better than the "gentle", fear-tinged encounters the lesbians have is something I cannot judge. It is also worth noting the serious absence of protection, except in relation to gay men.

Marriage is markedly missing from American LGBTQ books, which may reflect the current political and cultural climate there, and this could change in the next decade or so, if the fight for same-sex marriage continues to make progress. Marriage appears to a certain extent in British books and even more frequently in northern European works, and again, this could very well be because these texts were written in more accepting cultures with more flexible marriage and relationship arrangements. Regardless of where books were written and published, however, it seems that young queers do not seem to consider marriage to be an option for their future lives, and this is a rather depressing fact, in my opinion. Perhaps the changing political situations in English-speaking countries will affect how both marriage and sex are portrayed in forthcoming LGBTQ books for young readers and also how young LGBTQ people themselves feel about their lives.

Conclusion

In this final chapter, I sum up what I have discussed in this book, and I end on an activist note, encouraging change. The overall message of my work, I believe, is that it is a positive step forward for literature, for queers, and for young people that there are books available that feature LGBTQ characters, but the problem is that some of these books have serious limitations. My concern is that some of the works discussed here could offer erroneous or even detrimental messages about what it means to be queer and to have a queer life; this can be harmful to both LGBTQ people and non-LGBTQ people. I would like publishers to begin publishing a broader array of LGBTQ texts for young readers, and this means that readers need to request such books from the publishers and that writers need to write and submit them. We need to que(e)ry the existing books and to try to queer the publishing industry more. So: where have we been and where can we go from here?

A Brief Summary

This book is in no way comprehensive. Due to the nature of research, I could only cover some of the LGBTQ books for children that have been published, and I could only write about some aspects of those books. Thus, I attempted to choose books that were contemporary, realistic, and easily available, and I chose to focus on some of the more prominent aspects of them, which in some cases were very worrying. In this section, I sum up the findings discussed in the foregoing chapters.

Michael Cart and Christine A. Jenkins suggest a three-part model for the stages of LGBTQ literature for teenagers: "homosexual visibility, gay assimilation, queer consciousness/community" (2006:xix). By this they mean that the publishing industry first features LGBTQ characters as a way of making them visible; in the second stage, the "stories include people who 'just happen to be gay' in the same way that someone 'just happens' to be left-handed or have red hair" (2006:xx); and in the final stage, queer consciousness stories "show GLBTQ characters in the context of their communities of GLBTQ people and their families of choice (and in recent years, often their families of origin as well)." (ibid.) Cart and Jenkins are somewhat more positive in their assessment than I am, as I would argue that we are still stuck to a great extent in the first stage, as I have shown in the foregoing chapters.

In the first main chapter of this book, Issue Books, I look at how many LGBTQ books for children seem to be written, published, read, and employed as though they are only for a niche market. They are, in short, viewed as problem books, texts about a particular issue that only speak to a specific audience. This happens in a couple of different ways. In part, these books seem aimed at confirming the "normality" of LGBTQ people. They offer storylines where the child of LGBTQ parents is comforted and reminded that queer parents are just as good and as loving and as acceptable as non-queer parents. Such texts are more often picture books. The other main type of issue book is usually one for slightly older readers, where queer issues – typically, this is specifically homosexuality, rather than other topics from within the LGBTQ spectrum – are problematised. Characters may learn about homosexuality by reading about it or hearing a lecture about it, and this allows readers to learn about it in the same way. These books seem to have an educational aim. In addition, where the books are kept in libraries and bookstores and which paratexts are bundled together with the texts emphasise their didactic, niche roles. My concern with issue books is that they set queer people and queer topics apart rather than treating being queer as simply one part of a full life. The latter would be equivalent to Cart and Jenkins's second and third stages, and beyond.

The next chapter of this book, Portrayal and Stereotypes, moves on to look at the ways in which LGBTQ characters are depicted in the texts. I find that there is a reliance on stereotyped tropes and that there is a rather disturbingly small range of character types and plots in many of the books. For example, it is suggested that being queer is a problem and that it is something that will create stress for the person concerned. Furthermore, it seems as though some authors believe that there are clear reasons why a person is LGBTQ, and it follows that if there is a cause for queerness, there may also be a solution; I would argue that we do not want to get into a situation where many young people believe that they can be "cured", or where they are pressured to attend programmes/camps where they might be "treated". Additional stereotypes discussed in this chapter include that there are particular ways of looking queer, acting queer, or being queer; this might mean that a gay female is described as humourless or that someone bisexual is said to be sexually voracious. Naturally, there are also some positive stereotypes, such as that a gay male is thought to be very stylish, but my argument is that it would be better to not rely so heavily on stereotypes and instead to use this sort of literature to challenge ideas about LGBTQ people and the LGBTQ community. This would show queers in all their variety and it would benefit everyone if we stopped thinking of them in terms of stereotypes and expecting them to be, look, and behave in certain ways.

Another aspect of stereotypes is explored in the third chapter, Diversity, which further expands the discussion in the previous chapter about the narrow ideas about LGBTQ people that form the basis for the characterisations in these texts. Here I look at how so many of these books seem to assume that LGBTQ people are white, middle-class, Christian, able-bodied, and otherwise "norm". This is to say that there are few books that recognise that all people have intersections of identities; this may be because authors or publishers think this is too complicated to show in literature, or in children's literature in particular, or it may be because they are unaware of how large and diverse the LGBTQ community actually is. Furthermore, what I have throughout this book called LGBTQ literature is in many ways mostly LG literature, because I believe that the BTQ segments are underrepresented. I would like to see more books that depict intersectionality (or intersextionality) and the LGBTQ community in its fullness.

The final main chapter is entitled Sex and Marriage. In it, I look in particular at romantic and sexual relationships in LGBTQ literature. Again, I note that BTQ people are generally absent and do not seem to be having much sex or thinking about marriage. As for gay men, they are very sexually active, and enjoy many types of sex – masturbation, oral sex, penetrative sex, phone sex – although STDs/AIDS are a worry for them, which again takes some of these books into issue book territory. Meanwhile, lesbians are often depicted as scared or hesitant about having sex. If they do have sex, it may not be satisfying, and they show no awareness of the need to use protection. In regard to marriage, how same-sex marriage is depicted seems to depend on the status of LGBTQ people and their relationships in a given country. It appears as an option much more in northern European books than in books from the U.K., and more in books from the U.K. than in books from the U.S., reflecting whether there is same-sex marriage or partnership in that country. On the other hand, the U.S. seems to be in some ways more child-centred than the other countries, as more books are published there that feature LGBTQ couples raising children.

In this book, then, I have not analysed every possible topic in connection to LGBTQ books for children and young people, but I have chosen several large, pertinent subjects to explore. I believe there is still a lot of work to be done and I hope future research will continue to discuss the topics mentioned here as well as all the other ones that space constraints kept me from analysing.

A Call to Arms (or Pens): Not a Conclusion, But a Proposal

In a sense, I see my analysis here as a sort of call to arms, or, rather, pens. What I think would be hugely beneficial is if we could look at all the LGBTQ books for children and young adults that have already been published, and be grateful to them for paving the way, and then write new books that go even further in their depiction of LGBTQ lives. In other words, I think the time is ripe for us to begin writing books that are more diverse, less stereotypical, and more liberal, and that treat being queer as a fact rather than as an issue. Think of the impact that such writing could have on today's young people, whether queer or not. As David Levithan writes:

> With books, courage comes on many levels. We authors have to find the courage to offer the words that will release the truth, in ways both small and large. We put our names on the cover of the book, offering those words out in the world with our lives attached. The publisher, too, offers its own reputation when it puts its name on the spine. Readers must take great courage in taking a book from a shelf, or being seen carrying it around. Librarians can—and often do—and *always must* find the courage to stand up to the fear that surrounds us. You are the gatekeepers of the representation. It's not just literature at stake; it's lives. (2004:n.p., italics original)

Authors, publishers, librarians, parents, teachers, and readers all need to "find the courage". There is still work to be done, and this work requires courage.

Cart and Jenkins write that "we clearly need more GLBTQ books featuring characters of color, more lesbian and bisexual characters, more transgender youth, and more characters with same-sex parents." (2006:165) They add that "[s]urely it is time for GLBTQ literature to abandon the traditional and too-easy equation of homosexuality with violent death." (2006:166) I would agree with them about all of that. And I would generally say that we just need more of everything: more books on all aspects of being LGBTQ. I would also say that we need that we need more research into the books that already exist, as I suggested in the previous section.

Andrew Solomon claims that "[n]eutrality, which appears to lie halfway between shame and rejoicing, is in fact the endgame, reached only when activism becomes unnecessary." (2012:19) We have not yet reached this stage; as the analysis in the previous chapters has suggested, many of these books are closer to shame than to rejoicing. For now, activism is still needed. There are huge power issues in relation both to literature for young readers and to gender and sexuality, and authors and readers alike must be aware of them. Children without experience of the world can easily receive negative messages from LGBTQ books, and such messages can cause them to feel shame and/or prejudice. An awareness of power may help us to eventually reach neutrality.

In closing, I want to reiterate that I strongly believe that it is important for LGBTQ young people and children of LGBTQ parents to see themselves and their families represented accurately and in all their diversity in literature, and also that young readers who are not LGBTQ and not from LGBTQ families should be able to learn about queer people and topics in an honest and open manner in books. Therefore it is essential that these books do not feature stereotyped depictions and that they are not limited and limiting in their perspectives. While it is wonderful that there are so many LGBTQ books for children and young people, there could be many more, and they could be better. I therefore urge all those who are willing and able to write better LGBTQ literature for young readers to do so. In addition, we could write to authors and publishers to complain about the constricted and not always correct portrayals we see in literature. We can also encourage publishers to publish and libraries and bookstores to offer or sell more such books by requesting them. This might help prove that LGBTQ literature is not just a niche subject about a particular "issue" but rather one that many readers are interested in. We can be activists; writing is activism. Whether it is a letter to complain to a publisher, a book review in a magazine, a thank-you note to an author, a short story, a novel, a critical essay or an academic book - we are helping to queer literature with every word we write. I hope we all pick up our pens and help literature to show that the queer kids indeed are all right.

Notes

1 I always use LGBTQ, as that is the common order of the letters in the U.K., plus I think it is important to make the female aspect visible by putting it first, but some of the sources I quote from employ the order more commonly used in the U.S., GLTBQ.

2 By "norm", I mean heterosexual and/or cisgender (i.e. identifying with one's biological sex) and/or monogamous. Non-norm would therefore include homosexual, bisexual, transgender, polyamorous, and much more. I am not making a value judgement.

3 Even if grammatically incorrect, in this book, I will use "they" as the singular, gender-neutral subject pronoun where others might use "he" or "he or she". I do this to acknowledge the limitations of "he" and "she" as pronouns; while some people identify as "he" or "she" and are happy to use those pronouns, others find them limiting and would prefer to identify as "he and she" or "they" or "ze" or something else altogether. "They" seems to me to cover a range of possibilities. I will therefore use "them" as the singular, gender-neutral object pronoun and "their" as the singular, gender-neutral possessive pronoun. I hope that at some point English will develop a term such as the Swedish "hen", which is a gender-neutral singular pronoun used instead of "han", or "he", and "hon", or "she".

4 Much of the discussion in this section was taken directly from my book, *Translating Expressive Language in Children's Literature* (2012), because it serves as a helpful and concise introduction to the topic.

5 Interestingly, in several articles on what adults think the best books for children are, many of the top picks are ones that were originally published for adults and are still available solely or mainly in the adult sections of bookstores or libraries, such as works by Charles Dickens or Jane Austen (see, for example, "Top ten books parents think children should read" in the Telegraph, 2012:n.p.).

6 Michael Cart and Christine A. Jenkins give a brief history of LGBTQ literature in their book (2006:3-17), and they explain that there were some LGBTQ texts for adults from the 1920s forward, but only mainstream ones from the 1940s forward, such as Truman Capote's *Other Voices, Other Rooms* and Gore Vidal's *The City and the Pillar* (2006:3). As they write about lesbian literature in particular, "Typical storylines featured naïve young women who are seduced by lesbians but finally won back to heterosexuality by men who could offer them marriage, a home, and children. If the lesbian character was actually a good person, she usually died before the end of the book. If she was evil, she might die or end up in a mental hospital, or she might head off to further conquests." (2006:4) As some of the discussions in this book show, in some ways, not much has changed from these early, stereotyped books.

7 Belkin writes that one out of five gay male couples in the U.S. has children and one out of three gay female couples does (2009:n.p.), and of course it is generally believed that one out of every ten people is LGBTQ, so when this is compared to the number of LGBTQ books for young people, it becomes even clearer that there really are not that many books for this population.

8 Despite looking at picture books here, I do not explore their illustrations in any great detail, as that is a different research project. I nonetheless mention them where appropriate.

9 There are certainly other LGBTQ books for children available besides the ones I discuss here; however, it is virtually impossible for any researcher to find and analyse every single text in a particular category. If I have missed any, I apologise in advance, and I would be grateful to learn of any other texts for future research.

10 There are a couple of collections of short stories aimed at young adult readers and of course there are many other published short stories with LGBTQ themes, but since the collections are not always solely LGBTQ and since the short story format is different from picture books and novels, I chose not to look at them in any great detail. In a few instances, I offer examples from them, such as from *Truth & Dare: Love, life and falling on your face*, edited by Liz Miles. The back cover of the anthology states that the stories are about "[g]irls and guys, straight or gay, striding or struggling" (2011:n.p.); the writing quality is hugely varying, just as the subject matter is.

11 I read the Scandinavian languages and have been working on a larger project comparing texts in them to English-language ones, but in general, I do not refer to that work here except where relevant.

12 These are approximate definitions; for a more thorough analysis of the types of books for young readers, see, for example, Travers and Travers, 2008. Books for children can be categorised based on the language used, the subject matter, and the intended audience, but it is not always a simple matter to say that a certain text clearly belongs to a particular genre and is for a certain age range.

13 Lois Tyson, for instance, interprets a short story with lesbian characters and looks at whether these characters are stereotyped. She analyses what positive qualities they show, how they interact with others, what attitudes they have towards men, what they look like, and how they are portrayed as sexual beings (2011:178-80). I carry out this type of analysis for many of the works discussed here.

14 Belkin also writes that children of LGBTQ families may even be more successful or may break down barriers. "There are data that show, for instance, that daughters of lesbian mothers are more likely to aspire to professions that are traditionally considered male, like doctors or lawyers — 52 percent in one study said that was their goal, compared with 21 percent of daughters of heterosexual mothers, who are still more likely to say they want to be nurses or teachers when they grow up." (2009:n.p.) It would be interesting to see similar research on LGBTQ young people themselves and their career options.

15 Both terms are employed in theoretical literature, but to be consistent, I will follow Genette, who considers paratexts to be more encompassing than peritexts. Peritexts, he argues, are on or within the primary text, while epitexts are outside the primary text, and paratext is the term to cover both (1997).

16 The American Library Association's website explains challenging and banning in this way: "A challenge is an attempt to remove or restrict materials, based upon the objections of a person or group. A banning is the removal of those materials. Challenges do not simply involve a person expressing a point of view; rather, they are an attempt to remove material from the curriculum or library, thereby restricting the access of others. As such, they are a threat to freedom of speech and choice." (ALA website, n.d.:n.p.)

17 It also happens to be the main public library in the city where I live and where the University of East Anglia, where I work, is located. The fact that it is in a university city also speaks to the likelihood that it will have a relatively diverse, wide-ranging collection.

18 By "norm", I mean two parents of opposite genders, for example a heterosexual couple and a child or several children. I must say here that I am not passing judgement on whether the so-called norm or nuclear family is the best set-up or not. But there is no denying that having opposite-gender parents is the most common arrangement in English-speaking countries.

19 Interestingly, Leanne Lieberman's *Gravity* also includes some paratextual material, but this is unrelated to queer issues; rather, her novel has a glossary of Jewish terms, with definitions of Hebrew and Yiddish words or phrases such as Abba, Baruch Hashem, Challah, Mishnah, and Zai Gazunt. Many of these words are also italicised in the text, setting them apart from English words. This suggests that Lieberman and/or her publisher assume that it is the Jewish aspect that will be an issue for the readers. I have used *Gravity* when teaching undergraduates and they regularly complain that the book is "confusing" because of the Jewish context, and that they find the italicised words distracting. They say they would rather read a book about non-religious Jews or about non-Jews; this, along with the paratextual items discussed above, implies that readers can be uncomfortable with differences, and that books that feature diversity may be viewed as being for niche audiences.

20 We could perhaps even call this the "conformation" of normality in that it both confirms normality and also encourages LGBTQ people to conform to certain ideas of the norm.

21 The spell-check feature in my word-processing programme does not approve of "my dads" or "my mums", as though the concept of plural fathers or mothers is completely alien and unthinkable.

22 Section 28 was a controversial amendment made in 1988 in the U.K., which stated that local authorities could not promote homosexuality or publish material that did so. This caused LGBTQ support and activist groups to shut down and publishers to self-censor, among many other effects, and generally promoted a non-LGBTQ-friendly atmosphere throughout the U.K. Section 28 was finally repealed in 2003.

23 It perhaps goes without saying that queer people primarily have access to texts about non-queer characters, and this does not turn them straight. Books simply are unable to change people's core identities, even though they can of course educate readers, and can be powerful.

24 This issue is not limited only to books for young readers, however. In a different research project, I have discovered that LGBTQ pulp fiction and its modern-day counterpart, LGBTQ paperback romances, tend to restrict couplings to butch-femme pairings and to emphasise the idea that queers must look and/or behave in very particular ways.

25 I use this as an example because it is one that I have experienced my entire life, so I feel able to refer to it. I explore LGBTQ stereotypes later in this chapter, and I would rather not repeat stereotypes about other groups.

26 According to Blaine, there is more hate crime in general against Jews, but more violence against LGBTQ people (2007:77).

27 Note that this is not the case for those who are overweight. As research in fat studies as shown, weight, like sexuality, tends to be seen as a moral issue and a choice.

28 See the section on Sex and Marriage in the chapter on Portrayal and Sterotypes and also note 50 for more on cheating.

29 While here I am focusing on English-language texts, it is worth pointing out that the same stress in regard to coming out appears in translated YA texts as well. For example, Perihan Magden's *2 Girls*, which was translated from Turkish by Brendan Freely, depicts "angry, overweight" Behiye (2005:back cover) as being crazy and obsessed with a female friend, Handan. The recognition of this obsession eventually leads to Behiye being rejected by her family and Handan's.

30 The only text I left out was Rosoff's *What I Was*, because it was never clear whether the character was dressing as a man in order to survive or was a transman.

31 In the Garfunkel and Oates song "Gay Boyfriend", the main character suspects that her boyfriend is gay, but says this does not matter because he is so in touch with his emotions, is a nice person, is fun to be with, and overcompensates by being especially attentive in bed, namely through giving cunnilingus. None of this is mentioned in these books, but having a gay boyfriend does seem to be a relatively common theme in society at large.

32 By "otherwise queer", as discussed in the introduction to this book, I refer to those who choose the queer label to represent their sexuality. This includes, among others, people involved in BDSM or so-called fetish practices, intersex people, those who are questioning their sexuality, asexuals, and pansexuals, but only if they choose the queer label themselves. Some do, while others

adamantly do not. I have not yet found, say, a young adult novel with a protagonist who is open about having a particular fetish, or a book for children where the parents are in a master-slave relationship. This is not the place to discuss whether such topics are appropriate or not for children, but I simply wish to point out that these people exist in reality but not yet in the realm of children's books, and my personal view is that children have a right to be exposed to the world around them, in all its permutations.

33 It is tempting to coin the term "intersextions", to highlight the fact that we are looking at intersections between sex, gender, and other aspects of identity.

34 In my research, I have found no overtly bisexual or transgender parents, even if some could potentially be read as such by a knowing audience. In fact, most of the parents seem to be lesbians, which suggests that authors and publishers think women are more likely to be parents. This leads one to consider whether gay males are not seen as potential parents or indeed are even feared as possible paedophiles and therefore not parenting material. Many of these books seem to reflect stereotyped ideas about gender and parenting, i.e. that men need women in order to parent, because women are viewed as being more natural parents, but that women do not necessarily require men. On the other hand, as Belkin points out, and as was mentioned in note 7 one out five gay male couples in the U.S. have children, while the number is higher for gay female couples at one out of three, so perhaps it makes sense that women are featured more often in these works (2009:n.p.).

35 Today, with a greater number of sexes/genders being recognised, due in part to the strength of the transgender movement, many would take issue with the idea that there are just men and women in the world. For the purposes of this book, however, I continue to use the older definition, because it is not as common for children

to identify as or be comfortable with terms such as "genderqueer" or "genderfuck".

36 One could add here that bisexual women are accused of bringing AIDS and other STIs into the lesbian community.

37 For example, actor Anna Paquin, who has said that despite being married to a man and pregnant with his child, she still identifies as bisexual and will not deny her sexuality or her attraction to women, has been praised for her commitment to the bisexual movement.

38 Solomon talks about the importance of using terms such as "declared" and "affirmed" over "male-to-female" and "female-to-male", as he considers the latter demeaning (2012:603).

39 Solomon adds that "[p]arents are right to fear for their transgender children. The level of prejudice against them is unimaginable for those who have not encountered the problem...Four out of five people surveyed had been harassed or physically or sexually attacked in school, almost half by teachers...More than half of trans youth have made a suicide attempt, as opposed to 2 per cent of the general population." (2012:650) While I do not doubt the statistics, and I agree we must do something about this situation, I do worry that focusing on the problems sends a negative message to readers about what it means to be transgender. It may even stop some young people from feeling able to come out as trans.

40 This work takes place some decades ago, when there were stricter gender roles, so when Hilary sees someone with short hair fishing, for example, he assumes that person is male.

41 It is intriguing to hear that Ewert has never received questions or confused responses from children, while my undergraduate students regularly say that they are certain children would find it confusing.

I think this is an example of how adults tend to underestimate children's abilities and understanding.

42 Sanchez frequently includes at least one Latino character in his work, perhaps in homage or reference to his own background. As his biography states, he was "born in Mexico to parents of German and Cuban heritage" (2006:back cover), so he may be writing from a semi-autobiographical position or out of a desire to speak to young people who might feel left out of literature the way he might have done. For example, the characters in his novel *Getting It* are of Mexican-American heritage and when Carlos is in a park with his father, he sees two white men with a young Asian girl. Carlos's father calls them "*maricones*", which is then defined in the text as "queers" (2006:16, italics original). So Sanchez creates a Latino queer space in his work.

43 I use this term with the acknowledgement that it is quite odd to say that someone is "half" anything. Which half?

44 Rather than get into the discussion of what the difference is between a religious group, a race, and an ethnic identity, I will simply say here that it is quite possible for one term to span two or even three of those areas. In other words, I would argue that one can be a cultural/ethnic Jew, but not a religious one. Likewise, someone can be a cultural Muslim or Christian or anything else, which means that person has been influenced by and raised within a particular ethnic group but may not subscribe to the religious beliefs, even if they do in fact celebrate some of the holidays, such as Christmas or Ramadan.

45 Another positive aspect of the book is that the rabbi is a woman. However, the book mostly shows boys in the pictures. The two girls depicted both wear pink and purple and Nate's sister Miri wears a skirt and high-heeled boots to the Purim party, and receives the

"most glamorous" award. It would have been even better if the book had also challenged ideas about gender.

46 It is difficult to know which term/s to employ here. As Dierdre Keenan discusses, some terms minimise problems, while others are too specific, and still others are too general and say very little at all; one example she offers is "differently abled", which she says is perhaps too inclusive (2004:124). Hence, until I find a better term, I will use "dis/abled", by which I refer to any mental or physical health problem or recurring illness.

47 This is not meant to be a complete list of possible health issues, but just a short sample.

48 The obvious exception is the trans characters, who wish for their bodies to conform to their gender. This is, however, a different matter than the one under discussion in this section.

49 Once, when giving a talk on this subject, I was heckled by a woman in the audience who said that I was "abusive" towards young people because they ought not hear about sex until they are eighteen or older. As I told her, they will certainly have had sexual thoughts and feelings before they are eighteen, and they will learn about sex from their friends, from TV, from films, and via the internet, so they might as well receive accurate, helpful information. She responded by calling me a "freak".

50 Note that I focus primarily on lesbians and gay males here because that is what my corpus of texts offers. Unfortunately, there are very few examples of bisexual, transgender, or otherwise queer characters engaging in sex or getting married. Indeed, when bisexual or possibly bisexual characters are seen in relationships, it is not unusual for them to cheat on their partners, which encourages the stereotype that bisexuals are sexually voracious and cannot or will

not limit themselves to one partner or one gender (see the chapter on stereotypes for more on this).

51 In an intriguing non-English-language example, a group of female friends regularly masturbates together in Mian Lodalen's Swedish novel *Tiger* (2010:128, 155, etc.). This may suggest that other countries are more comfortable with women pleasuring themselves.

52 This is the stereotyped idea that since women are supposedly not as sexual as men, lesbians will be even less sexual, and their sexual relationships will eventually peter out into nothing except perhaps a little cuddling.

53 As stated in note 18, I am not passing judgement on whether the so-called nuclear family is the best set-up or not. But there is no denying that it is the most common arrangement in English-speaking countries and therefore it is worth analysing.

54 There are more books from the U.S. than the U.K. that feature LGBTQ characters, hence the corpus from the U.S. is larger.

55 Following Yuval Merin, I am using "northern European" to refer to the Nordic countries, plus the Netherlands (see Merin, 2002:2-3, among other places). I am currently working on a project exploring Scandinavian LGBTQ books for young readers, because I can read these languages, and I think it is worth comparing cultures and texts.

56 I have analysed dozens of children's books with LGBTQ characters from the U.S., the U.K., Australia, and Sweden, but here I primarily discuss only those that refer to marriage, and this number amounts to a small percentage of the total.

57 Books such as by Hicks, 2011; Goldberg, 2010; Johnson and O'Connor, 2002; and Spilsbury, 2011 that refer to same-sex/LGBTQ parenting do not mention bisexual or transgender parents whatsoever, even if their relationships can fall into the category of same-sex.

58 I have subsequently learned but not been able to get a copy of a second, follow-up book by Willhoite entitled *Daddy's Wedding*. Reviews on amazon.com were not positive, because they felt the book was more political than literary, and it no longer seems to be in print. I cannot comment on it further though, unfortunately.

59 Although I focus on literature in this book, I can mention that some recent films have featured and even, to a certain extent, normalised LGBTQ people and issues, including LGBTQ parents with children. The American film *The Kids are All Right* was generally considered positive, because it featured a lesbian couple and their two children. However, I would argue that this film encouraged some of the stereotypes that I discuss in this book; for example, one of the women in the film cheats on her long-term partner with a man, which suggests that lesbian relationships are not sexually satisfying and also that they are not serious or real, so it is not that problematic for one partner to cheat on the other.

60 As previously referred to, I am currently undertaking another research project, comparing LGBTQ books in Scandinavia to those in English-speaking countries, and I have chosen Scandinavia not just for its more liberal laws, but because I know the Scandinavian languages. In some sections of this book, it is worth referring to the Scandinavian or northern European situation for comparative purposes, and this is one of those places. I hope people will carry out such research about other countries and their literatures.

61 This relates to some of the discussion in the chapter on issue books, in that some of the books seem meant to be employed as a way of educating readers about LGBTQ people, so it is not a "shock" when they meet queers.

62 As a translator myself, I object to translators being made invisible. I wrote to the publisher to complain and received a most unsatisfying response saying that they had no idea who the translator was and it was in any case not their problem.

63 One could point out that some of these storylines are normative in their attitudes to relationships in that they seem to suggest that relationships, regardless of the sexuality/ies involved, should be between two people, should be monogamous, should lead to marriage, and often should involve having children.

64 I wrote a picture book manuscript with a transgender parent, but the one publishing company I sent it to told me that "the world is not yet ready for this". This was a publisher with a history of strong LGBTQ and feminist work.

References

Aamodt, Sandra and Sam Wang (2011) *Welcome to your Child's Brain.* Oxford: Oneworld.

Abate, Michelle Ann and Kenneth Kidd (2011) "Introduction", in Abate, Michelle Ann and Kenneth Kidd, eds. *Over the Rainbow.* Ann Arbor: University of Michigan Press, pp. 1-11.

Abate, Michelle Ann and Kenneth Kidd, eds. (2011) *Over the Rainbow.* Ann Arbor: University of Michigan Press.

Abate, Michelle Ann and Kenneth Kidd (2011) "Queering the Canon", in Abate, Michelle Ann and Kenneth Kidd, eds. *Over the Rainbow.* Ann Arbor: University of Michigan Press, pp. 13-14.

Abraham, Laurie (2011) "Teaching Good Sex", in *The New York Times.* Available online at: http://www.nytimes.com/2011/11/20/magazine/teaching-good-sex.html?_r=1&ref=magazine&pagewanted=all.

American Library Association (n.d.) "Banned and Challenged Books". Available online at: http://www.ala.org/advocacy/banned.

American Library Association (n.d.) "Frequently Challenged Books Statistics".

Available online at: http://www.ala.org/advocacy/banned/frequentlychallenged/stats.

American Library Association (n.d.) "100 Most Frequently Challenged Books: 1990–1999".
Available online at: http://www.ala.org/advocacy/banned/frequentlychallenged/challengedbydecade/1990_1999.

Appleyard, J.A., S.J. (1991) *Becoming a Reader: The Experience of Fiction from Childhood to Adulthood.* Cambridge: Cambridge University Press.

Argent, Hedi (2007) *Josh and Jaz Have Three Mums.* London: BAAF.

Arnett, Jeffrey Jensen (2004) *Emerging Adulthood.* Oxford: Oxford University Press.

Ayto, John (1993) *Euphemisms.* London: Bloomsbury.

Bailey-Harris, Rebecca (2001) "Same-Sex Partnerships in English Family Law", in Wintermute, Robert and Mads Andenaes, eds. *Legal Recognition of Same-Sex Partners.* Oxford: Hart Publishing, pp. 605-619.

Bator, Robert, ed. (1983) *Signposts to Criticism of Children's Literature.* Chicago: American Library Association.

Beam, Cris (2011) *I Am J.* New York: Little Brown.

Beck, Evelyn Torton (1982) "Teaching about Jewish Lesbians in Literature: From Zeitl and Rickel to The Tree of Begats", in Cruikshank, Margaret, ed. *Lesbian Studies.* Old Westbury, N.Y.: Feminist Press, pp. 91-87.

Belkin, Lisa (2009) "What's Good for the Kids", in *The New York Times.*
Available online at: http://www.nytimes.com/2009/11/08/magazine/08fob-wwln-t.html?_r=1&ref=magazine.

Bennett, P. and Rosario, V.A., eds. (1995) *Solitary Pleasures: The Historical, Literary, and Artistic Discourses of Autoeroticism.* London: Routledge.

Blackburn, Maddie (2002) *Sexuality and Disability.* Oxford: Butterworth, Heieneman.

Blaine, Bruce E. (2007) *Understanding the Psychology of Diversity.* London: Sage.

Boock, Paula (1997) *Dare Truth or Promise.* Boston: Houghton Mifflin.

"Books for Kids in Gay Families." (n.d.)
Available online at: http://booksforkidsingayfamilies.blogspot.co.uk/.

Boys Don't Cry. (1999) DVD.

Brannen, Sarah S. (2008) *Uncle Bobby's Wedding.* New York: G.P. Putnam.

Brennan, Sarah Rees (2011) "The Young Stalker's Handbook", in Miles, Liz, ed. *Truth & Dare: Love, Life and Falling on your Face.* London: Constable and Robinson, pp. 17-33.

Brenot, Philippe (1997) *In Praise of Masturbation.* trans. P. Buck and C. Petit. London: Marion Boyars.

Brown, Helen Cosis and Christine Cocker (2011) *Social Work with Lesbians and Gay Men.* London: Sage.

Brown, Rupert (2010) *Prejudice: Its Social Psychology.* Malden, MA: John Wiley.

Brozyna, Martha A. (2005) *Gender and Sexuality in the Middle Ages.* Jefferson, N.C.: McFarland.

Bruhm, Steven, and Natasha Hurley, eds. (2004) *Curiouser: On the Queerness of Children.* Minneapolis: University of Minnesota Press.

Burchill, Julie (2004) *Sugar Rush.* London: Young Picador.

Butler, Judith (1990/2006) *Gender Trouble.* London: Routledge.

Bösche, Susanne (1983) *Jenny Lives with Eric and Martin.* trans. L. MacKay. London, England: Gay Men's Press.

Bösche, Susanne (2000) "Jenny, Eric, Martin…and Me", in *The Guardian.* Available online at: http://www.guardian.co.U.K./books/2000/jan/31/booksforchildrenandteenagers.features11.

Canning, Richard (2001) *Gay Fiction Speaks.* New York: Columbia University Press.

Cart, Michael and Christine A. Jenkins (2006) *The Heart Has Its Reasons.* London: Scarecrow Press.

Cash, Thomas F. and Thomas Pruzinsky, eds. (2002) *Body Image: A Handbook of Theory, Research, and Clinical Practice.* New York: Guildford.

Chambers, Aidan (1982) *Dance on My Grave.* London: Bodley Head.

Chambers, Aidan (1999) *Postcards from No Man's Land.* London: Bodley Head.

Chandler, Michael Alison (2008) "Two Guys and a Chick Set Off Tiff Over School Library Policy", in *Washington Post.*
Available online at: http://www.washingtonpost.com/wp-dyn/content/article/2008/02/16/AR2008021602213.html?referrer=emailarticle.

Chukovsky, Kornei (1963) *From Two to Five*. trans. Miriam Morton. Berkeley: University of California Press.

Clark, J. Michael (1994) "Men's Studies, Feminist Theology, and Gay Male Sexuality", in Nelson, James B. and Sandra P. Longfellow, eds. *Sexuality and the Sacred.* Louisville, KY: Westminster/John Knox, pp. 216-228.

Codell, Esmé Raji (2006) *Vive La Paris*. New York: Hyperion.

Cohn, Rachel and David Levithan (2008) *Naomi and Ely's No Kiss List*. New York: Alfred A. Knopf Books for Young Readers.

Cole, Babette (1995) *Mummy Laid an Egg*. London: Red Fox.

Coontz, Stephanie (2005) *Marriage: A History*. New York: Viking.

Cooper, Elaine and John Guillebaud (1999) *Sexuality and Disability: A Guide for Everyday Practice.* Abingdon: Radcliffe Medical Press.

Crisp, Thomas (2011) "The Trouble with *Rainbow Boys*", in Abate, Michelle Ann and Kenneth Kidd, eds. *Over the Rainbow*. Ann Arbor: University of Michigan Press, pp. 215-254.

Cruikshank, Margaret, ed. (1982) *Lesbian Studies*. Old Westbury, N.Y.: Feminist Press.

Cutler, Tom (2012) *Slap and Tickle*. London: Constable.

Czyzselska, Jane (2012) "The H-Word", in *Diva*, June 2012, p. 18.

Davenport, Doris (1982) "Black Lesbians in Academia: Visible Invisibility", in Cruikshank, Margaret, ed. *Lesbian Studies*. Old Westbury, N.Y.: Feminist Press, pp. 9-11.

de Beauvoir, Simone (1949/2009) *The Second Sex*. trans. Constance Borde and Sheila Malovany-Chevallier. London: Jonathan Cape.

de Haan, Linda and Stern Nijland (2002) *King and King*. No translator named. Berkeley, CA: Tricycle Press.

de Haan, Linda and Stern Nijland (2004) *King and King and Family*. No translator named. Berkeley, CA: Tricycle Press.

Diamond, Lisa M. (2008) *Sexual Fluidity*. Cambridge, MA: Harvard University Press.

Dollimore, Jonathan (1997) "Bisexuality", in Medhurst, Andy and Sally R. Munt, eds. *Lesbian and Gay Studies*. London: Cassell, pp. 250-260.

Donnellan, Craig, ed. (1998) *Homosexuality*. Cambridge: Independence.

Eagland, Jane (2009) *Wildthorn*. London: Young Picador.

Epstein, B.J. (2011) "Not as Queer as Folk: Issues of Representations in LGBTQ Young Adult Literature", in *Inis*, vol. 36, pp. 44-49.

Epstein, B.J. (2012) *Translating Expressive Language in Children's Literature.*

Epstein, B.J. (2012) "We're Here, We're (Not?) Queer: LGBTQ Characters in Children's Books", *Journal of GLBT Family Studies*, issue 8, pp. 287-300.

Eskridge, William N. (2001) "The Ideological Structure of the Same-Sex Marriage Debate (And Some Postmodern Arguments for Same-Sex Marriage)", in Wintermute, Robert and Mads Andenaes, eds. *Legal Recognition of Same-Sex Partners.* Oxford: Hart Publishing, pp. 113-132.

Eugenides, Jeffrey (2003) *Middlesex*. New York: Bloomsbury.

Ewert, Marcus (2008) *10,000 Dresses*. New York: Seven Stories Press.

Ewert, Marcus (2013) personal correspondence.

Faircloth, Christopher A., ed. (2003) *Aging Bodies*. Walnut Creek, CA: AltaMira.

Farley, Margaret (1994) "Sexuality and Ethics", in Nelson, James B. and Sandra P. Longfellow, eds. *Sexuality and the Sacred*. Louisville, KY: Westminster/John Knox, pp. 54-67.

Feinberg, Leslie (1994/2004) *Stone Butch Blues*. Los Angeles: Alyson Books.

Firestein, Beth A., ed. (1996) *Bisexuality*. London: SAGE.

Flanagan, Victoria (2008) *Into the Closet*. New York: Routledge.

Florsheim, Paul, ed. (2002) *Adolescent Romantic Relations and Sexual Behavior*. Mahwah, New Jersey: Lawrence Erlbaum.

Ford, Elizabeth A. (2011) "H/Z: Why Lesléa Newman Makes Heather into Zoe", in Abate, Michelle Ann and Kenneth Kidd, eds. *Over the Rainbow*. Ann Arbor: University of Michigan Press, pp. 201-214.

Fox, Geoff, Graham Hammond, Terry Jones, Frederic Smith, and Kenneth Sterck, eds. (1976) *Writers, Critics, and Children*. New York: Agathon Press.

Fox, Ronald C. (1996) "*Bisexual in Perspective: A Review of Theory and Research*", in Firestein, Beth A., ed. Bisexuality. London: SAGE, pp. 3-50.

Francis, Paul (1995) *The Seduction*. London: Marshall Pickering.

Freymann-Weyr, Garret (2002) *My Heartbeat*. London: Young Picador.

Furman, Wyndol and Laura Shaffer (2003) "The Role of Romantic Relationships in Adolescent Development", in Florsheim, Paul, ed. *Adolescent Romantic Relations and Sexual Behavior*. Mahwah, New Jersey: Lawrence Erlbaum, pp. 3-22.

Garber, Marjorie (1995) *Vice Versa*. London: Hamish Hamilton.

Garden, Nancy (1982) *Annie on My Mind*. New York: Farrar Straus Giroux.

Garden, Nancy (1999) *The Year They Burned the Books*. New York: Farrar Straus Giroux.

Garden, Nancy (2000) *Holly's Secret*. New York: Farrar Straus Giroux.

"Gay Men Have Higher Prevalence Of Eating Disorders" (2007), in *ScienceDaily*.
Available online at: http://www.sciencedaily.com/releases/2007/04/070413160923.htm.

Geen, Jessica (2011) "Gay author and Narnia producer Perry Moore dies at 39", in *PinkNews*.
Available online at: http://www.pinknews.co.uk/2011/02/22/gay-author-and-narnia-producer-perry-moore-dies-at-39/.

Geertz, Clifford (1973/2000) *The Interpretation of Cultures*. New York: Basic.

Genette, Gérard (1997) Paratexts: *Thresholds of Interpretation*. trans. Jane E. Lewin. Cambridge: Cambridge University Press.

Georgio, Solomon (2011) "Just Because You Belong to Another Minority Group Doesn't Mean You're Not Racist", in *The Stranger*.
Available online at: http://www.thestranger.com/seattle/racist-queers/Content?oid=8743212.

Giffney, Noreen and O'Rourke, Michael, eds. (2009) *The Ashgate Companion to Queer Theory.* Farnham: Ashgate.
Gilbert, Daniel (2006) *Stumbling on Happiness.* London: HarperCollins.

Gillette, Courtney (2011) "Never Have I Ever", in Miles, Liz, ed. *Truth & Dare: Love, Life and Falling on your Face.* London: Constable and Robinson, pp. 127-160.

Goldberg, Abbie E. (2010) *Lesbian and Gay Parents and Their Children.* Washington, DC: American Psychological Association.

González, Rigoberto (2005) *Antonio's Card.* New York: Children's Books Press.

Gopalakrishnan, Ambika (2011) *Multicultural Children's Literature: A Critical Issues Approach.* Thousand Oaks, CA: Sage Publications.

Gosling, Sam (2008) *Snoop.* London: Profile.

Gott, Merryn (2005) *Sexuality, Sexual Health and Ageing.* Maidenhead: Open University Press.

Grima, Tony, ed. (1994) *Not the Only One.* Boston: Alyson Publications.

Grogan, Sarah (1999) *Body Image.* London: Routledge.

Guttmacher Institute (2000) "Changing Emphases in Sexuality Education in U.S. Public Secondary Schools, 1988-1999", in *Family Planning Perspectives*, 32(6).

Harris, Paul (2006) "Flap Over a Tale of Gay Penguins", in *The Guardian.* Available online at: http://www.guardian.co.uk/world/2006/nov/19/gayrights.usa.

Harrison, Beverly Wildung and Carter Heyward (1994) "Pain and

Pleasure: Avoiding the Confusions of Christian Tradition in Feminist Theory", in Nelson, James B. and Sandra P. Longfellow, eds. *Sexuality and the Sacred.* Louisville, KY: Westminster/John Knox, pp. 131-148.

Hechter, Michael and Karl-Dieter Opp, eds. (2001) *Social Norms.* New York: Russell Sage Foundation.

Hegarty, P. (2009) "Queerying Lesbian and Gay Psychology's 'Coming of Age': Was the Past Just Kids' Stuff?", in Giffney, Noreen and Michael O'Rourke, eds. *The Ashgate Companion to Queer Theory.* Farnham: Ashgate, pp. 311-328.

Hicks, Stephen (2011) *Lesbian, Gay and Queer Parenting.* Houndmills: Palgrave Macmillan.

Horne, Christine (2001) "Sex and Sanctioning: Evaluating Two Theories of Norm Emergence", in Hechter, Michael and Karl-Dieter Opp, eds. *Social Norms.* New York: Russell Sage Foundation, pp. 305-324.

Hull, Kathleen (2006) *Same-Sex Marriage: The Cultural Politics of Love and Law.* Cambridge: Cambridge University Press.

Human Rights Campaign (n.d.)
Available online at: http://www.hrc.org/.

Hunt, Mary E. (1994) "Lovingly Lesbian: Toward a Feminist Theology of Friendship", in Nelson, James B. and Sandra P. Longfellow, eds. *Sexuality and the Sacred.* Louisville, KY: Westminster/John Knox, pp. 169-182.

Hunt, Peter (1994) *An Introduction to Children's Literature.* Oxford: Oxford University Press.

Hutchins, Loraine (1996) "Bisexuality: Politics and Community", in Firestein, Beth A., ed. *Bisexuality.* London: SAGE, pp. 240-259

James, Kathryn (2009) *Death, Gender and Sexuality in Contemporary Adolescent Literature*. New York: Routledge.

Jay, Meg (2012) "The unexpected downside of cohabiting before marriage", in *Today*.
Available online at: http://today.msnbc.msn.com/id/47077893/#.T5EmeKtul7c.

Jenkins, Christine A. (2011) "Young Adult Novels with Gay/Lesbian Characters and Themes, 1969-92", in Abate, Michelle Ann and Kenneth Kidd, eds. *Over the Rainbow*. Ann Arbor: University of Michigan Press, pp. 147-163.

Johnson, Suzanne M. and Elizabeth O'Connor (2002) T*he Gay Baby Boom*. New York: New York University Press.

Johnson, Maureen (2004) *The Bermudez Triangle*. London: Puffin.

Kanner, Melinda (n.d.) "Young Adult Literature", in *An Encylopedia of Gay, Lesbian, Bisexual, Transgender, and Queer Culture*.
Available online at: http://www.glbtq.com/literature/young_adult_lit.html.

Keenan, Dierdre (2004) "Race, Gender, and Other Differences in Feminist Theory", in Meade, Teresa A. and Merry E. Wiesner-Hanks, eds. *A Companion to Gender History*. Oxford: Blackwell, pp. 110-128.

Kelland, Kate (2007) "'Gay Fairytales' Anger British Religious Groups", in *Reuters*.
Available online at: http://www.reuters.com/article/2007/03/14/us-britain-gay-children-idUSL1363483820070314.

Keshet Ga'avah (World Congress of Gay, Lesbian, Bisexual, and Transgender Jews) (n.d.)
Available online at: http://www.glbtjews.org/.

Kilodavis, Cheryl (2011) *My Princess Boy.* New York: Simon and Schuster.

King, Ursula (2004) "Religion and Gender: Embedded Patterns, Interwoven Frameworks", in Meade, Teresa A. and Merry E. Wiesner-Hanks, eds. *A Companion to Gender History.* Oxford: Blackwell, pp. 70-85.

Kokkola, Lydia (2011) "Metamorphosis in Two Novels by Melvin Burgess: Denying and Disguising 'Deviant' Desire", in *Children's Literature in Education.* 42(1), 56-69.

Kramer, Lauren (2013) "Coming Out as Yourself: Elisabeth Kushner on her Purim Book for Kids", in *Jewish Independent.*
Available online at: http://jewishindependent.ca/Archives/feb13/archives13feb22-07.html.

Kushner, Elisabeth (2013) *The Purim Superhero.* Minneapolis: Kar-Ben Publishing.

Laqueur, Thomas W. (2003) *Solitary Sex: A Cultural History of Masturbation.* New York: Zone Books.

LaRochelle, David (2005) *Absolutely, Positively Not.* New York: Scholastic.

Lathey, Gillian, ed. (2006) *The Translation of Children's Literature.* Clevedon: Multilingual Matters.

Lee, Vanessa Wayne (2011) "'Unshelter Me': The Emerging Fictional Adolescent Lesbian", in Abate, Michelle Ann and Kenneth Kidd, eds. *Over the Rainbow.* Ann Arbor: University of Michigan Press, pp. 164-182.

Lepore, Jill (2010) "Too Much Information", in *The New Yorker.*
Available online at: http://www.newyorker.com/arts/critics/atlarge/2010/10/18/101018crat_atlarge_lepore.

Lerer, Seth (2008) Children's Literature: *A Reader's History from Aesop to Harry Potter*. Chicago: University of Chicago Press.

Lesbian and Gay Christian Movement (n.d.)
Available online at: http://www.lgcm.org.uk/.

Leslie, Julia and Mary McGee (2000) *Invented Identities: The Interplay of Gender, Religion, and Politics in India*. Oxford University Press.

Levithan, David (2003) *Boy Meets Boy*. New York: Alfred A. Knopf Books for Young Readers.

Levithan, David (2004) "An Advocate Speaks Out for Representation on Library Shelves", in *School Library Journal*.
Available online at: http://www.schoollibraryjournal.com/article/CA456885.html.

Levithan, David (2008) *Wide Awake*. New York: Alfred A. Knopf Books for Young Readers.

Levithan, David (n.d.) "About the Author".
Available online at: http://www.randomhouse.com/kids/catalog/author.pperl?authorid=54093&view=sml_sptlght.

Lieberman, Leanne (2008) *Gravity*. Custer, WA: Orca Book Publishers.

Lodalen, Mian (2010) *Tiger*. Stockholm: Månpocket.

Long, Hayley (2012) *What's Up With Jody Barton?* London: Macmillan.

Love, Heather (2010) "Transgender Fiction and Politics", in Stevens, Hugh, ed. *The Cambridge Companion to Gay and Lesbian Writing*. Cambridge: Cambridge University Press, pp. 148-163.

Lowenthal, Michael (2011) "Lost in Translation", in Miles, Liz, ed. *Truth & Dare: Love, Life and Falling on your Face.* London: Constable and Robinson, pp. 34-48.

Luecke, Julie C. (2012) "Reading Along the Gender Continuum", in *Horn Book.*
Available online at: http://www.hbook.com/2012/08/using-books/reading-along-the-gender-continuum/.

Lundborg, Anette and Tollerup-Grkovic, Mimmi (1999) *Malins mamma gifter sig med Lisa* [Malin's Mama Marries Lisa]. Stockholm: Eriksson & Lindgren.

Mackie, Diane M., David L. Hamilton, Joshua Susskind and Francine Rosselli (1996) "Social Psychological Foundation of Stereotype Formation", in Macrae, Neil C, Charles Stangor and Miles Hewstone, eds. *Stereotypes and Stereotyping.* New York: Guildford Press, pp. 41-78.

Macrae, Neil C, Charles Stangor and Miles Hewstone, eds. (1996) *Stereotypes and Stereotyping.* New York: Guildford Press.

Magden, Perihan (2005) *2 Girls.* trans. Brendan Freely. London: Serpent's Tail.

Manning, Sarra (2005) *Pretty Things.* London: Hodder.

Maybin, Janet and Nicola J. Watson, eds. (2009) *Children's Literature: Approaches and Territories.* Hampshire: Palgrave Macmillan.

McDowell, Myles (1976) "Fiction for Children and Adults: Some Essential Differences", in Geoff Fox, Graham Hammond, Terry Jones, Frederic Smith, and Kenneth Sterck, eds. *Writers, Critics, and Children.* New York: Agathon Press, pp. 140-156.

McRuer, Robert (2011) "Reading and Writing "Immunity": Children and the Anti-Body", in Abate, Michelle Ann and Kenneth Kidd, eds. *Over the Rainbow*. Ann Arbor: University of Michigan Press, pp. 183-200.

Meade, Teresa A. and Merry E. Wiesner-Hanks, eds. (2004) *A Companion to Gender History*. Oxford: Blackwell .

Medhurst, Andy and Sally R. Munt, eds. (1997) *Lesbian and Gay Studies*. London: Cassell.

Merchant, Ed (2010) *Dad David, Baba Chris and Me*. London: British Association for Adoption and Fostering.

Merin, Yuval (2002) *Equality for Same-Sex Couples*. Chicago: University of Chicago Press.

Miles, Liz, ed. (2011) *Truth & Dare: Love, Life and Falling on your Face*. London: Constable and Robinson.

Millington, Karen (2012) "Ex-gay survivor's tales of exorcism in middle England".
Available online at: http://www.bbc.co.uk/religion/0/19475393.

Moore, Perry (2007) *Hero*. London: Random House.

Moore, Susan and Doreen Rosenthal (2006) *Sexuality in Adolescence: Current Trends*. London: Routledge.

Moraga, Cherríe and Barbara Smith (1982) "Lesbian Literature: A Third World Feminist Perspective", in Cruikshank, Margaret, ed. *Lesbian Studies*. Old Westbury, N.Y.: Feminist Press, pp. 55-65.

Morgan, Patricia (2002) *Children as Trophies?: Examining the Evidence on Same-Sex Parenting*. Christian Institute.

Nagel, Joane (2003) *Race, Ethnicity, and Sexuality*. Oxford: Oxford University Press.

Nelson, James B. and Sandra P. Longfellow, eds. (1994) *Sexuality and the Sacred*. Louisville, KY: Westminster/John Knox.

Newman, Lesléa (1989) *Heather Has Two Mommies*. New York: Alyson Books.

Newman, Lesléa (2009) *Mommy, Mama, and ME*. Berkeley , CA: Tricycle Press.

Newman, Lesléa (2009) *Daddy, Papa, and ME*. Berkeley, CA: Tricycle Press.

Newman, Lesléa (2012) *Donovan's Big Day*. Berkeley, CA: Tricycle Press.

Newman, Lesléa (2012) personal correspondence.

No to Age Banding (n.d.)
Available online at: http://www.notoagebanding.org/.

Norfolk County Council (n.d.)
Available online at: http://www.norfolk.gov.uk/leisure_and_culture/libraries/branch_libraries/ncc012447.

Norton, Jody (2011) "Transchildren and the Discipline of Children's Literature", in Abate, Michelle Ann and Kenneth Kidd, eds. *Over the Rainbow*. Ann Arbor: University of Michigan Press, pp. 293-313.

Nye, Robert E. (2004) "Sexuality", in Meade, Teresa A. and Merry E. Wiesner-Hanks, eds. *A Companion to Gender History*. Oxford: Blackwell, pp. 11-25.

Ochs, Robyn (1996) "Biphobia: It Goes More than Two Ways", in Firestein, Beth A., ed. *Bisexuality*. London: SAGE, pp. 217-239.

Oittinen, Riitta (2000) *Translating for Children.* New York: Garland, Inc.

Orbach, Susie (1988) *Fat is a Feminist Issue and its Sequel.* London: Arrow.

O'Sullivan, Emer (2005) *Comparative Children's Literature,* trans. Anthea Bell. London: Routledge.

Parr, Todd (2008) *We Belong Together: A Book about Adoption and Families.* New York: Little Brown.

Paul, Lissa (2009) "Multicultural Agendas", in Maybin, Janet and Nicola J. Watson, eds. *Children's Literature: Approaches and Territories.* Hampshire: Palgrave Macmillan, pp. 84-99.

Peters, Julie Ann (2004) *Luna*. New York: Little, Brown Books for Young Readers.

Peters, Julie Ann (2006) *Between Mom and Jo*. New York: Little Brown.

Peters, Julie Ann (2007) *Far from Xanadu*. New York: Sphere.

Petrow, Steven (2013) "When James Becomes Janice: What Not to Ask a Transgender Friend," in *The New York Times*.
Available online at: http://www.nytimes.com/2013/03/05/booming/when-james-becomes-janice-what-not-to-ask-a-transgender-friend.html?ref=civilbehavior&_r=0.

Pinello, Daniel R. (2006) *America's Struggle for Same-Sex Marriage.* Cambridge: Cambridge University Press.

Pinsent, Pat (2005) "Language, Genre and Issues: the Socially Committed Novel", in Reynolds, Kimberly, ed. *Modern Children's Literature.* Houndsmills: Palgrave, pp. 191-208.

Pizurie, D. J. (1994) "The End of the Rainbow", in T*he Lesbian Review of Books*. 1(1), 19.

Plum-Ucci, Carol (2002) *What Happened to Lani Garver*. San Diego: Harcourt.

Polikoff, Nancy D. (2001) "Lesbian and Gay Couples Raising Children: The Law in the United States", in Wintermute, Robert and Mads Andenaes, eds. *Legal Recognition of Same-Sex Partners.* Oxford: Hart Publishing, pp. 153-67.

Poor, Matile (1982) "Older Lesbians", in Cruikshank, Margaret, ed. *Lesbian Studies*. Old Westbury, N.Y.: Feminist Press, pp. 309-325.

Prosser, Jay (1997) "Transgender", in Medhurst, Andy and Sally R. Munt, eds. *Lesbian and Gay Studies*. London: Cassell, pp. 250-260.

Pullman, Philip (1990) *The Broken Bridge*. London: Macmillan.

Pullman, Philip (1996) "Carnegie Medal Acceptance Speech". Available online at: <http://www.randomhouse.com/features/pullman/author/carnegie.html>.

Reardon, Robin (2007) *A Secret Edge*. New York: Kensington.

Reardon, Robin (2008) *Thinking Straight*. New York: Kensington.

Reardon, Robin (n.d.) "The Case for Acceptance". Available online at http://robinreardon.com/author/documents/THECASEFORACCEPTANCE_RobinReardon_004.pdf.

Reynolds, Kimberly, ed. (2005) *Modern Children's Literature.* Houndsmills: Palgrave.

Reynolds, Kimberley (1998) "Publishing Practices and the Practicalities of Publishing", in Reynolds, Kimberley and Nicholas Tucker, eds. *Children's Book Publishing in Britain Since 1945*, pp. 20-41.

Reynolds, Kimberley and Nicholas Tucker, eds. (1998) *Children's Book Publishing in Britain Since 1945*, Aldershot: Scolar Press.

Richardson, Justin and Peter Parnell (2006) *And Tango Makes Three.* New York: Simon & Schuster Children's Books.

Robinson, Kerry H. (2002) "Making the Invisible Visible: Gay and Lesbian Issues in Early Childhood Education", in *Contemporary Issues in Early Childhood.* vol. 3, no. 3, pp. 415-434.

Rose, Jacqueline (1993) *The Case of Peter Pan: Or the Impossibility of Children's Fiction.* Philadelphia: University of Pennsylvania Press.

Rosen, Michael (2011) "Introduction", in *Writers' and Artists' Yearbook.* London: A & C Black.

Rosenfeld, Dana (2003) "The Homosexual Body in Lesbian and Gay Elders' Narratives", in Faircloth, Christopher A., ed. *Aging Bodies.* Walnut Creek, CA: AltaMira, pp. 171-203.

Rosoff, Meg (2007) *What I Was.* London: Penguin.

Rothblum, Esther D. (2002) "Gay and Lesbian Body Images", in Cash, Thomas F. and Thomas Pruzinsky, eds. *Body Image: A Handbook of Theory, Research, and Clinical Practice.* New York: Guildford, pp. 257-265.

Saguy, Abigail (2011) "Why Fat is a Feminist Issue", in *Sex Roles*, 68, no. 9, pp. 600-607.

Sanchez, Alex (2001) *Rainbow Boys*. New York: Simon & Schuster.

Sanchez, Alex (2003) *Rainbow High*. New York: Simon & Schuster.

Sanchez, Alex (2005) *Rainbow Road*. New York: Simon & Schuster.

Sanchez, Alex (2006) *Getting It*. New York: Simon & Schuster.

Savage, Dan (2011) "You Need to Come Out to Your Friends and Spouses—Now", in *The Stranger*.
Available online at: http://www.thestranger.com/seattle/bisexuals/Content?oid=8743322.

Schneider, David J. (1996) "Modern Stereotype Research: Unfinished Business", in Macrae, Neil C, Charles Stangor and Miles Hewstone, eds. *Stereotypes and Stereotyping*. New York: Guildford Press, pp. 419-453.

Schools Out (n.d.).
Available online at http://www.schools-out.org.uk/.

Segrest, Mab (1982) "I Lead Two Lives: Confessions of a Closet Baptist", in Cruikshank, Margaret, ed. *Lesbian Studies*. Old Westbury, N.Y.: Feminist Press, pp. 16-19.

Selvadurai, Shyam (2007) *Swimming in the Monsoon Sea*. Toronto, Canada: Tundra Books.

Setterington, Ken (2004) *Mom and Mum Are Getting Married*. Toronto: Second Story.

Sjöström, Bodil (1999) *Trollen på Regnbågsbacken* [The Trolls of Rainbow Hill]. Stockholm: Atlas.

Skutch, Robert (1995) *Who's in a Family?* Berkeley: Tricycle Press.

Smith, Richard (2008) "Behind the Story – Section 28", in *Gay Times*. Available online at: http://www.gaytimes.co.uk/Magazine/InThisIssue-articleid-3489-sectionid-650.html.

Solomon, Andrew (2012) *Far From the Tree*. London: Chatto and Windus.

Spilsbury, Louise (2011) *Same-sex Marriage*. London: Wayland.

Stein, Joel (2012) "I Had a Gay Old Time", in *Time*. 14 May, Available online at: http://www.time.com/time/magazine/article/0,9171,2113812,00.html#ixzz1xUoDUBqc.

Stevens, Hugh, ed. (2010) *The Cambridge Companion to Gay and Lesbian Writing*. Cambridge: Cambridge University Press.

Stuart, Elizabeth (1992) *Daring to Speak Love's Name: A Gay and Lesbian Prayer Book*. London: Hamish Hamilton.

Sullivan, Nikki (2011) *A Critical Introduction to Queer Theory*. Edinburgh: Edinburgh University Press.

Sunderland, Jane (2010) *Literature, Gender and Children's Fiction*. London: Continuum.

Talbot, Margaret (2013) "About a Boy", in *The New Yorker*. 18 March, pp. 56-65.

Tanner, Lindsey (2012) "Sex-changing Treatment For Kids: It's On The Rise", in *The Huffington Post.*
Available online at: http://www.huffingtonpost.com/2012/02/20/sexchanging-treatment-for_n_1288871.html.

Taxel, Joel (2002) "Children's Literature at the Turn of the Century: Toward a Political Economy of the Publishing Industry", in *Research in the Teaching of English*, 37, pp. 145-197.

"Top library complaint: Story About Same-sex Penguin Couple" (2011). Available online at: http://news.blogs.cnn.com/2011/04/11/top-library-complaint-story-about-same-sex-penguin-couple/.

"Top Ten Books Parents Think Children Should Read" (2012), in *The Telegraph.*
Available online at: http://www.telegraph.co.uk/culture/books/booknews/9485677/Top-ten-books-parents-think-children-should-read.html.

Townsend, John R. (1990) *Written for Children*. London, England: The Bodley Head Children's Books.

Travers, Barbara and Travers, John (2008) *Children's Literature: A Developmental Perspective*. New York: Wiley.

Trembling Before G-d (2001)
Available online at: http://www.snagfilms.com/films/title/trembling_before_g_d/.

Tucker, Nicholas (1998) "Setting the Scene", in Reynolds, Kimberley and Nicholas Tucker, eds. *Children's Book Publishing in Britain Since 1945*, pp. 1-19.

Tyson, Lois (2011) *Using Critical Theory*. London: Routledge.

Van Meter, William (2010) "Bold Crossings of the Gender Line", in *The New York Times.*
Available online at: http://www.nytimes.com/2010/12/09/fashion/09TRANS.html?_r=1&ref=fashion&pagewanted=all.

Waaldijk, Kees (2001) "Small Change: How the Road to Same-Sex Marriage Got Paved in the Netherlands", in Wintermute, Robert and Mads Andenaes, eds. *Legal Recognition of Same-Sex Partners.* Oxford: Hart Publishing, pp. 437-464.

Watts, Julia (2001) *Finding H.F.* Los Angeles: Alyson Books.

Webster, Alison (1995) *Found Wanting.* London: Continuum.

Weinreich, Torben (2000) *Children's Literature: Art or Pedagogy?* Roskilde, Denmark: Roskilde University Press.

Weisbard, Phyllis Holman (2001) "Review of Frances Ann Day's Lesbian and Gay Voices: An Annotated Bibliography and Guide to Literature for Children and Young Adults", in *Feminist Collections.* 22(3-4), 42.

Wickens, Elaine (1994) *Anna Day and the O-Ring.* Boston: Alyson.

Wilkinson, Lili (2009) *Pink.* Crows Nest, Australia: Allen & Unwin.

Willhoite, Michael (1990) *Daddy's Roommate.* Los Angeles: Alyson Publications.

Wilson, Jacqueline (2007) *Kiss.* London: Random House.

Winter, Kathleen (2011) *Annabel.* London: Jonathan Cape.

Wintermute, Robert and Mads Andenaes, eds. (2001) *Legal Recognition of Same-Sex Partners.* Oxford: Hart Publishing.

Wittlinger, Ellen (1999) *Hard Love*. New York: Simon and Schuster.

Wittlinger, Ellen (2007) *Parrotfish*. New York: Simon and Schuster.

Woodson, Jacqueline (2003) *The House You Pass on the Way*. New York: Speak.

Writers' and Artists' Yearbook. (2011) London: A & C Black.

Wyndham, Lee, revised by Arnold Madison (1968/1988) *Writing for Children & Teenagers*. Cincinnati: Ohio.

XXY. (2007) DVD.

Yonge, Gary (2012) "Marriage Equality and the Civil Rights Inheritance", in *The Guardian*.
Available online at: http://www.guardian.co.uk/commentisfree/cifamerica/2012/feb/24/marriage-equality-civil-rights-inheritance.

Ytterberg, Hans (2001) "'From Society's Point of View, Cohabitation Between Two Persons of the Same Sex is a Perfectly Acceptable Form of Family Life': A Swedish Story of Love and Legislation", in Wintermute, Robert and Mads Andenaes, eds. *Legal Recognition of Same-Sex Partners*. Oxford: Hart Publishing, pp. 427-436.

Zimmerman, Bonnie and Toni A. H. McNaron, eds. (1996) *The New Lesbian Studies*. New York: Feminist Press at the City University of New York.

Annotated Bibliography

PB = picture book
MG = middle-grade book
YA = young adult novel
AS = anthology of short stories

Note that although some novels for adult readers, non-fiction works, and DVDs are also mentioned in the book, they are not listed here. Nor are primary texts that are not available in English.

Argent, Hedi (2007) *Josh and Jaz Have Three Mums*. London: BAAF.
PB
In this book for young readers, two children are unsure what to write in the family trees that their class is producing. The children's mothers confirm that their family is just as acceptable as other set-ups.

Beam, Cris (2011) *I Am J*. New York: Little Brown.
YA
J is a trans man who has to handle his parents' lack of understanding in order to be able to live fully as himself. This novel is more diverse than many others since J has one Puerto Rican Catholic parent and one Jewish one. While J faces difficulties and ends up switching schools and running away from home, everything does work out for him in the end.

Boock, Paula (1997) *Dare Truth or Promise*. Boston: Houghton Mifflin.
YA
Willa and Louie are teenage girls in New Zealand who start a romantic relationship. The setting makes this young adult novel somewhat different, but otherwise the story is similar to many others, and the characters can seem rather wooden.

Bösche, Susanne (1983) *Jenny lives with Eric and Martin*, translated by L. MacKay from the Danish *Mette bor hos Morten og Erik*. London, England: Gay Men's Press.
PB
This translated picture book apparently helped spark Section 28 in the UK. It is a confirmation of normality story, where Jenny hears negative comments about her two fathers and has to learn that her family is just as acceptable as any other.

Brannen, Sarah S. (2008) *Uncle Bobby's Wedding*. New York: G.P. Putnam.
PB
This picture book is about a family of guinea pigs. Uncle Bobby announces that he is marrying his male partner and the protagonist is jealous because she likes getting all of Bobby's attention. But soon she realises that she is not losing an uncle; she is gaining one.

Burchill, Julie (2004) *Sugar Rush*. London: Young Picador.
YA
Kim's mother leaves and she has to switch schools. However, in the new school, she meets and falls for Sugar, and they start a briefly passionate relationship. In some ways, the culture shock caused by Kim moving between classes is more in focus than the relationship. The book was made into a TV series that was more sexual and made Kim seem much more sure of her lesbian sexuality.

Chambers, Aidan (1982) *Dance on my Grave*. London: Bodley Head.
YA

Chambers' novel is stylistically experimental as it tells the story of Hal, who has a relationship with Barry. When Barry dies, Hal withdraws from the world, and also forms an unlikely pact with Kari, with whom Barry also had an affair.

Chambers, Aidan (1999) *Postcards from No Man's Land.* London: Bodley Head.
YA
Two stories in Amsterdam take place fifty years apart. In the contemporary one, Jacob meets one of the people from the earlier one, and this, along with his experiences in Amsterdam, leads him to reconsider who and what he is. Some of the Dutch characters are more fluid about their sexuality.

Codell, Esmé Raji (2006) *Vive La Paris.* New York: Hyperion.
MG
The story is about Paris, who is trying to find a space to be herself. There is an implied gay character, but this is not a major or explicit part of the book.

Cohn, Rachel and David Levithan (2008) *Naomi and Ely's No Kiss List.* New York: Alfred A. Knopf Books for Young Readers.
YA
Straight Naomi is in love with her best friend, gay Ely, and seems to believe that he will eventually love her romantically too. Ely kisses Naomi's boyfriend, causing an argument between the friends.

de Haan, Linda and Stern Nijland (2002) *King and King,* no translator named. Berkeley, CA: Tricycle Press.
PB
A prince's mother tells him it is time to get married, but he does not like any of the princesses she parades in front of him. He does, however, like one of the princesses' brothers. This story is a refreshing change from all the picture books that focus on how homosexuality is acceptable since it just takes for granted that being gay is fine.

de Haan, Linda and Stern Nijland (2004) *King and King and Family,* no translator named. Berkeley, CA: Tricycle Press.
PB
This book continues on from the first one, wherein the two princes, who are now kings, adopt a little girl.

Eagland, Jane (2009) *Wildthorn.* London: Young Picador.
YA
This is a historical novel set in the Victorian era. Louisa wants to study but this is unacceptable to her family, as is her love of women, so she is put into an insane asylum. It is very reminiscent of Sarah Waters's *Fingersmith.*

Ewert, Marcus (2008) *10,000 Dresses.* New York: Seven Stories Press.
PB
Bailey dreams of dresses, but her family does not accept her for who she is. They insist that she is a boy who should avoid girlish things. The only support Bailey gets is from a friend.

Freymann-Weyr, Garret (2002) *My Heartbeat.* London: Young Picador.
MG
Ellen is in love with her brother's best friend. It turns out that her brother and his friend may actually be a couple, and Ellen has to deal with this.

Garden, Nancy (1982) *Annie on My Mind.* New York: Farrar Straus Giroux.
YA
Liza falls in love with her friend Annie. They are from different worlds, different schools, and different backgrounds. Their relationship is found out and Liza gets in a lot of trouble at school. The two girls then go to university on opposite coasts, but the question is whether their relationship can survive.

Garden, Nancy (1999) *The Year They Burned the Books.* New York: Farrar Straus Giroux.
MG

Jamie and Terry call themselves "maybe"s, because they are not certain about their sexuality yet. Meanwhile, an organisation called Families for Traditional Values burns books they think are inappropriate.

Garden, Nancy (2000) *Holly's Secret*. New York: Farrar Straus Giroux.
MG
Holly and her younger brother and two mothers move to a new town, and Holly decides to change her name to Yvette and not tell people about her two mothers. Naturally, she gets tangled in lies.

González, Rigoberto (2005) *Antonio's Card*. New York: Children's Books Press.
PB
Antonio wants to make a card for Mother's Day for his mother and her partner, Leslie, but his classmates make fun of Leslie. Antonio is unsure of whether or how to make Mother's Day into Mothers' Day. This book is bilingual, which makes it unusual among English-language LGBTQ texts.

Grima, Tony, ed. (1994) *Not the Only One*. Boston: Alyson Publications.
AS
As many anthologies do, this one varies a lot in regard to subject matter and writing quality. The stories can feel quite dated now.

Johnson, Maureen (2004) *The Bermudez Triangle*. London: Puffin.
YA
Nina, Mel, and Avery are the so-called Bermudez Triangle, three young women who are best friends. When Nina leaves town for a summer school programme, Mel and Avery begin dating. How their new romance affects the three-way friendship is the main subject.

Kilodavis, Cheryl (2011) *My Princess Boy*. New York: Simon and Schuster.
PB
A young boy wants to wear princess clothes and his family loves and accepts him for who he is.

Kushner, Elisabeth (2013) *The Purim Superhero.* Minneapolis: Kar-Ben Publishing.
PB
Nate wants to be an alien in the Purim costume parade, but all the other boys are dressing as superheroes. Does Nate dare be different? His two fathers and sister encourage him to be himself, but he worries he will be lonely if he does.

LaRochelle, David (2005) *Absolutely, Positively Not.* New York: Scholastic.
YA
Steven is a nice guy who goes square-dancing with his mother and is working on getting his driver's license. He collects pictures of girls in bikinis and tries to go out on dates with girls. But of course it turns out he is gay.

Levithan, David (2003) *Boy Meets Boy.* New York: Alfred A. Knopf Books for Young Readers.
YA
This is a somewhat over-the-top book where everyone is more or less accepted, even the cross-dressing football player. It is a light, fun read that skims over any possible prejudice, which makes it both refreshing and unbelievable.

Levithan, David (2008) *Wide Awake.* New York: Alfred A. Knopf Books for Young Readers.
YA
This is set in some years in the future, when most Americans are mixed-ethnicity and LGBTQ people are more accepted. But is the U.S. population willing to vote for a gay Jew for president? And will the young gay couple Duncan and Jimmy stay together?

Lieberman, Leanne (2008) *Gravity.* Custer, WA: Orca Book Publishers.
YA
Ellie is an orthodox Jew who is attracted to other girls and who starts a

relationship with Lindsey. Ellie struggles with whether she can be both religiously Jewish and a lesbian.

Long, Hayley (2012) *What's Up With Jody Barton?* London: Macmillan.
YA
Jody and his twin sister Jolene both have a crush on Liam. When Jody makes a move on the boy, he is rejected by both Liam and his sister, and he worries that he will face more rejection and ostracisation at home and school.

Magden, Perihan (2005) *2 Girls*. translated by Brendan Freely from the Turkish. London: Serpent's Tail.
YA
In Istanbul, Behiye is an overweight, angry feminist who desires her friend Handan and obsesses over her. Handan dates men; Behiye is jealous and they end up fighting, with Behiye going somewhat mad.

Manning, Sarra (2005) *Pretty Things*. London: Hodder.
YA
A group of young people explore their sexuality. Brie is in love with her gay best friend, Charlie, and refuses to accept that he cannot love her romantically. Meanwhile, Daisy is a lesbian who starts a relationship with a man.

Merchant, Ed (2010) *Dad David, Baba Chris and Me*. London: British Association for Adoption and Fostering.
PB
Ben's birth parents could not take proper care of him, so he is raised by a gay male couple. Some of his classmates tease him about having two fathers but a teacher supports him through this.

Miles, Liz, ed. (2011) *Truth & Dare: Love, Life and Falling on Your Face*. London: Constable and Robinson.
AS
The quality of these short stories varies wildly, with some clichéd and

obvious and others interesting. Not all feature LGBTQ characters.

Moore, Perry (2007) *Hero.* London: Random House.
YA
Thom's father was a famous superhero. Now Thom, too, has a chance at becoming a superhero, but can there be a gay superhero? And can Thom and the ragtag group of wannabes actually do anything heroic?

Newman, Lesléa (1989) *Heather Has Two Mommies.* New York: Alyson Books.
PB
This book was an early one to feature LGBTQ parents and though it is important historically, it can seem very dated now, with its stereotypical and simplistic pictures and storyline. It confirms the normality of Heather's mothers' relationship.

Newman, Lesléa (2009) *Mommy, Mama, and ME.* Berkeley, CA: Tricycle Press.
PB
In this board book, a gender-neutral child does activities with their two mothers.

Newman, Lesléa (2009) *Daddy, Papa, and ME.* Berkeley, CA: Tricycle Press.
PB
In this board book, a gender-neutral child does activities with their two fathers.

Newman, Lesléa (2012) *Donovan's Big Day.* Berkeley, CA: Tricycle Press.
PB
Donovan has an important role to play in his mothers' wedding. This book works well because it is mainly about Donovan and his experiences on this big day, rather than trying to convince readers that it is normal or acceptable that two women should get married.

Parr, Todd (2008) *We Belong Together: A Book about Adoption and Families.* New York: Little Brown.
PB
The families depicted here have varying set-ups, and the premise is simply that different sorts of families can work. The pictures are bright and cheerful.

Peters, Julie Ann (2004) *Luna.* New York: Little, Brown Books for Young Readers.
YA
Luna is a transgender teen and this book is told from her younger sister's point of view and because of that Luna can seem rather self-centred. Luna wants to be fully recognised as herself rather than as Liam – the name she was given at birth – but this may mean having to leave home.

Peters, Julie Ann (2006) *Between Mom and Jo.* New York: Little Brown.
MG
Nick is raised by his birth mother and her partner Jo, who he feels is more like his real mother. When Jo and his mom split up, his mother seems to think he should not have a relationship with Jo any more, but Nick feels differently about it.

Peters, Julie Ann (2007) *Far from Xanadu.* New York: Sphere.
YA
Mike is a high school student and a star softball player and she runs her father's plumbing company after he commits suicide. Xanadu is a beautiful, straight girl sent to live with her aunt and uncle after she sells the drugs that kill a classmate. Mike falls for her.

Plum-Ucci, Carol (2002) *What Happened to Lani Garver.* San Diego: Harcourt.
YA
Claire was ill for part of middle school because she had cancer and she

feels she missed out on a lot, but she is nonetheless popular in high school. Lani Garver is a new student who confuses the people on the island where they live. Lani's gender is unclear, and Lani gets bullied. Claire befriends Lani, but soon there is a tragedy on the island.

Pullman, Philip (1990) *The Broken Bridge*. London: Macmillan.
MG
Mixed-race Ginny is raised in Wales by her white father. She has a crush on her gay male friend Andy and also tries to find her mother. Meanwhile, her half-brother moves in with her and her father, which Ginny is not thrilled about.

Reardon, Robin (2007) *A Secret Edge*. New York: Kensington.
YA
Jason is a runner who is being raised by his aunt and uncle. Despite some bullying and his uncle's unhappiness about him being gay, Jason dates Raj, an Indian immigrant. They discover that being gay gives them a "secret edge".

Reardon, Robin (2008) *Thinking Straight*. New York: Kensington.
YA
Taylor feels God made him gay, but when his religious parents find out, they send him to a Christian programme to cure him. The programme offers a very disturbing "cure", and Taylor tries to hold on to who he is in the face of this cure.

Richardson, Justin and Peter Parnell (2006) *And Tango Makes Three*. New York: Simon & Schuster Children's Books.
PB
The true story of two male penguins who seem to develop a relationship and are given an egg of their own to raise.

Rosoff, Meg (2007) *What I Was*. London: Penguin.
YA
In the 1960s, the main character, Hilary, runs away from his boarding

school and shares a hut with a character called Finn. It is only some time later that Hilary is told that Finn is actually female, although Finn was ostensibly living, dressing, and behaving as a male.

Sanchez, Alex (2001) *Rainbow Boys*. New York: Simon & Schuster.
YA
The Rainbow trilogy follows Jason, Kyle, and Nelson through their high school years, up until the summer before they start university. They are three distinct types of gay men and in the series, they have a range of experiences, including coming out, having relationships, getting tested for AIDS, making choices about their futures, and working through familial difficulties.

Sanchez, Alex (2003) *Rainbow High*. New York: Simon & Schuster.
YA
See above.

Sanchez, Alex (2005) *Rainbow Road*. New York: Simon & Schuster.
YA
See above.

Sanchez, Alex (2006) *Getting It*. New York: Simon & Schuster.
YA
Straight Carlos goes to gay Sal to get advice because he wants to be stylish and to learn how to attract women. But Sal wants something in return – for Carlos to help start a gay-straight alliance at school.

Selvadurai, Shyam (2007) *Swimming in the Monsoon Sea*. Toronto, Canada: Tundra Books.
YA
In Sri Lanka, Amrith has no interest in girls, but knows he is expected to marry one day. Then he meets his cousin, Niresh, who is visiting from Canada. Niresh is very different since he has been raised in another country, and Amrith falls in love with this fascinating boy.

Setterington, Ken (2004) *Mom and Mum Are Getting Married.* Toronto: Second Story.
PB
Rosie's mothers are marrying and she really wants to be part of the ceremony, though they just want a small event. Will she get what she wants?

Skutch, Robert (1995) *Who's in a Family?* Berkeley: Tricycle Press.
PB
This book explores some of the different family set-ups that exist.

Watts, Julia (2001) *Finding H.F.* Los Angeles: Alyson Books.
YA
H.F. is raised by her religious grandma in the south of the U.S. She and her best friend Bo are both gay and they wonder whether there is a place for them to be themselves in the conservative town where they live. They decide to go find H.F.'s mother and to have an adventure.

Wickens, Elaine (1994) *Anna Day and the O-Ring.* Boston: Alyson.
PB
Evan and his two mothers try to put together a tent, but their dog, Anna Day, seems to have hidden a key component.

Wilkinson, Lili (2009) *Pink.* Crows Nest, Australia: Allen & Unwin.
YA
Ava is a lesbian who has been completely accepted by her family and has a girlfriend. However, Ava decides to switch to a different school, to try to be different and more feminine, and to date a guy. Throughout the book, she struggles with her sexuality, which she had initially seemed so sure of.

Willhoite, Michael (1991) *Daddy's Roommate.* Los Angeles: Alyson Publications.
PB

The protagonist's parents got divorced the previous year and now his father has a male "roommate".

Wilson, Jacqueline (2007) *Kiss.* London: Random House.
MG
Straight Sylvie is in love with her gay male best friend, Carl, but does not realise that he might not be heterosexual. The novel explores Carl's coming out as well as Sylvie's feelings about it.

Wittlinger, Ellen (1999) *Hard Love.* New York: Simon and Schuster.
YA
John is unsure about his sexuality but he thinks he is developing a crush on his lesbian friend Marisol.

Wittlinger, Ellen (2007) Parrotfish. New York: Simon and Schuster.
YA
Angela came out before high school as a lesbian but now has come out as transman. He changes his name to Grady and has to deal with bullying in school. Grady develops a new friendship, gets support from a teacher at school, and eventually finds acceptance at home, all while his family works on their annual Christmas play.

Woodson, Jacqueline (2003) *The House You Pass on the Way.* New York: Speak.
MG
Staggerlee is a mixed-race young woman who develops feelings for a female friend of hers. A cousin helps her understand what she is going through.

Index

Ability (see Disability)
Age 183-4
America and American Literature 227-232, 244
Appearance (also see Body Shape/Size) 98-105, 187-8
Argent, Hedi 42, 233
Asexuality 80, 157

Beam, Cris 38, 52, 81-2, 95, 145, 146-8, 165, 173, 217
Behaviour 105-118
Biphobia (see Bullying, Violence, and Phobia)
Bisexuality 91, 124, 134-42
Body Shape/Size 102, 114, 187-8
Body Image (see Body Shape/Size and also Appearance)
Boock, Paula 36, 210
Brannen, Sarah S. 33, 230-1
Brennan, Sarah Rees 102
Britain and British Literature 21, 232-3
Bullying, Violence, and Phobia 78, 81, 85, 86, 87,88, 90, 92, 95, 111
Burchill, Julie 77-9, 94, 102, 119, 155-6, 213-5
Bösche, Susanne 57-8

Censorship (see Challenges to Books)
Challenges to Books 30, 56, 58-9
Chambers, Aidan 79, 141, 173, 233

Cheating 78, 79, 113, 119-20
Christianity (also see Religion and Spirituality) 84, 88, 167-9, 175-9
Class 184-6
Codell, Esmé Raji 109
Cohn, Rachel 109, 111, 122, 196, 197-8, 205, 239
Coming Out 74-93, 134-5, 141-2
Controversy (also see Challenges to Books) 56-60

Disability 181-2
Diversity 132-90, 243-4
Dutch Literature (see Northern Europe)

Eagland, Jane 88, 116, 209, 210
Ethnicity (see Race and Ethnicity)
Ewert, Marcus 59, 150-2

Freymann-Weyr, Garrett 50-1, 86, 119, 122

Garden, Nancy 38, 59, 82-3, 86, 89, 138, 185, 209, 216, 231-2, 239
Gay Males 45-9, 71, 72, 79, 83-8, 90, 91-2, 94, 95-6, 99-102, 105-115, 118, 120-3, 126, 196-7, 201-3, 205-9
Gender (also see Transgender) 3-6, 125-6
Gillette, Courtney, 103, 119
González, Rigoberto 164, 229

Haan, Linda De 58, 236
HIV/AIDS 37, 39, 45-9, 71, 199-204
Homophobia (see Bullying, Violence, and Phobia)

Illustrations, 98, 175
Intersex 141
Islam (also see Religion and Spirituality) 180

Johnson, Maureen 76-7, 96-7, 103-5, 115-6, 117, 139-40, 213, 232

Judaism (also see Religion and Spirituality) 89, 170-5

Kilodavis, Cheryl 43, 150
Kushner, Elisabeth 173-5

LaRochelle, David 92
Lesbians 76-80, 82-3, 88-9, 90-1, 94-5, 96-7, 102-5, 107, 115-7, 123-4, 198, 209-17
Levithan, David 28, 35, 62, 91-2, 109, 111, 122, 137-8, 163, 173, 196, 197-8, 205, 218, 231, 239, 245
Lieberman, Leanne 51, 89, 116, 170-2, 198
Long, Hayley 51-2, 83-4, 99
Lowenthal, Michael 197
Lundborg, Anette 234-5

Magden, Perihan 75, 116, 166, 180
Manning, Sara 83, 100, 102-3, 209, 116, 122-3, 124, 126, 139
Marriage 118-20, 223-38, 244
Masturbation 194-9
Merchant, Ed 33, 43, 96
Moore, Perry 86-7, 197

Newman, Lesléa 61, 98, 229-30, 233
Netherlands (see Northern Europe)
Nijland, Stern 58, 236
Northern Europe 233-6, 244

Parents and parenting 89, 221-3
Parnell, Peter 58
Parr, Todd 33, 41-2
Paratexts 32-39, 43, 49, 242
Peters, Julie Ann 82, 89, 115, 145-6, 149, 217
Plum-Ucci, Carol 55, 87
Polyamory 114, 155-7, 217

Prejudice 64-74
Problems (also see Stereotypes) 74-124
Protection (also see HIV/AIDS) 199-204
Publishing 9, 12, 29-31, 61, 241-7
Pullman, Philip 12, 121, 164, 233

Race and Ethnicity 161-7
Reardon, Robin 36, 46, 49, 52, 84-6, 93, 95-6, 99, 110, 112, 130, 165, 180, 196-7, 201-2, 206-9, 218, 231
Religion and Spirituality 167-81
Richardson, Justin 58
Rosoff, Meg 148

Sanchez, Alex 37, 38, 46-9, 52, 54-5, 59, 60, 90, 94, 99-100, 101-2, 108, 110, 112-5, 119, 148-9, 156, 163, 173, 186, 188, 202, 205-6, 215, 217, 218, 231, 239
Scandinavia and Scandinavian Literature (see Northern Europe)
Sex 118-20, 191-220, 240, 244
Sex Education 15-9, 112, 191-2, 200
Selvadurai, Shyam 165
Setterington, Ken 33, 98, 233
Shape (see Body Shape/Size)
Single People 239
Size (see Body Shape/Size)
Sjöström, Bodil 234
Skutch, Robert 41
Spirituality (see Religion and Spirituality)
STDs/STIs (see HIV/AIDS and also Protection)
Stereotypes 63-131, 200-1, 243
Sweden and Swedish Literature (see Northern Europe)

Tollerup-Grkovic, M. 234-5
Transgender 80-2, 125-6, 142-55, 217, 237-8
Transphobia (see Bullying, Violence, and Phobia)

U.K. (see Britain and British Literature)
U.S. (see America and American Literature)

Violence (see Bullying, Violence, and Phobia)

Watts, Julia 88-9, 93-4, 94-5, 108-9, 115, 178-9, 186, 211-2
Wickens, Elaine 229
Wilkinson, Lili 35-6, 90-1,100-1, 103, 109, 116, 124, 138-9, 177, 199, 203, 212, 214
Willhoite, Michael 43, 58, 136, 229
Wilson, Jacqueline 35, 109, 121, 125
Wittlinger, Ellen 38, 52-4, 78-81, 123, 125-6, 130, 145, 146, 149, 157, 175, 217
Woodson, Jacqueline 164

Lightning Source UK Ltd.
Milton Keynes UK
UKOW02f2054250814

237557UK00002B/29/P